By James Grippando

Blood Money *+
Need You Now
Afraid of the Dark+
Money to Burn+
Intent to Kill
*Born to Run**+
*Last Call**+
Lying With Strangers
*When Darkness Falls**+
*Got the Look**+
*Hear No Evil**
*Last to Die**
*Beyond Suspicion**
A King's Ransom
Under Cover of Darkness+
Found Money
The Abduction
The Informant
*The Pardon**

And for Young Adults
Leapholes

* A Jack Swyteck Novel
+ Also featuring FBI agent Andie Henning

JAMES GRIPPANDO

BLOOD MONEY

HARPER

An Imprint of HarperCollinsPublishers

This is a work of fiction. The characters, incidents, and dialogue are products of the author's imagination and are not to be construed as real. Any resemblance to actual persons, living or dead, is entirely coincidental.

HARPER

An Imprint of HarperCollins*Publishers*
10 East 53rd Street
New York, New York 10022-5299

First Harper premium printing: December 2013
First Harper hardcover printing: January 2013

10 9 8 7 6 5 4 3 2

To Tiffany, with love. Always.

BLOOD MONEY

1

·

"Mr. Swyteck, I'm calling from Judge Matthews' chambers."

Jack gripped his smartphone a little tighter. The judge's assistant was on the line. Jack was on verdict watch at his Coconut Grove law office, eating lunch with his best friend, Theo Knight.

"Is there a verdict?"

"Yes, sir. There is a verdict."

The words hit him like a 5-iron. *This is it.*

Criminal Case No. 2010-48-CF, *State of Florida v. Sydney Louise Bennett*, had spanned twenty-nine court days, plus two weeks of jury selection. Fifty-nine witnesses over eighteen days for the prosecution. Another forty-seven witnesses for the defense. The jury had been drawn from a pool in the Vero Beach area, a hundred miles away from the Miami Justice Building, after three years of intense pretrial publicity. The twelve selected to serve had been sequestered since day one, the week before Memorial Day. Deliberations had started on the Fourth of July, despite the holiday. The jury had been out for ten hours. Six hours longer than the jury in the O. J. Simpson trial—the trial of the other century.

"The verdict will be announced at two fifteen P.M.," the assistant said.

Jack thanked her and hung up. He wanted to speak to his client, but she was in the detention center across the street—lucky Thirteenth Street, as it was known—from the courtroom where Jack had last seen her, where Judge Matthews had released the jury at nine A.M. to begin day two of deliberations. Jack wondered if Sydney had been biting her nails again. It was a nervous habit she'd started before the trial, sometime after her twenty-fourth birthday, the third she'd spent behind bars without bail. Her chestnut hair was two feet longer than when they'd first met, her prison pallor a few shades whiter.

"Showtime?" asked Theo.

Jack didn't have to say anything; the news was all over his face. He speed dialed his cocounsel, but she'd already seen the "breaking development" on Twitter. Jack had assiduously avoided the social media during trial, but like everyone else under the age of thirty, Hannah Goldsmith was addicted to all electronic forms of information overload. Fortunately, she was as facile on her feet in a courtroom as she was with her thumbs on a keypad. They agreed to meet at the courthouse.

The moment Jack's call ended, Theo asked the proverbial $64,000 question—one that only the jurors could answer.

"Is ten hours a good sign or a bad sign?"

Jack paused. Conventional wisdom among prosecutors and many defense lawyers is that quick verdicts mean a conviction. But most homicide cases in which the state seeks the death penalty aren't based entirely on circumstantial evidence. And there was that well-known outlier—the Simpson case. Sydney was no celebrity, but comparisons in the media between the two high-profile murder trials were relentless. "Juani Cochran" they called her lawyer, the Latino version of Johnnie Cochran, even though Jack was only half Hispanic and had been raised a complete gringo, his Cuban American mother having died in childbirth. It was intended as an insult, triggered by a broken-English interview his *abuela* had given on talk radio in defense of a grandson who, even in her view, was on the wrong side of the case.

"I think it's a good sign," Jack said.

Theo glanced up from his iPhone, where the news was streaming in real time. "Talking heads are all saying guilty."

As if that mattered. More than six hundred press passes had been issued for media coverage, and every major broadcast network had at least one reporter at the trial. HLN and MSNBC had built two-story air-conditioned structures across from the courthouse for reporters and crews. *People* had daily in-court coverage, splashing the case on its magazine cover in the midst of trial. Legal analysis on Breaking News Network extended from early morning through prime time. BNN's regular nightly segments competed with network specials like "Inside the Trial of Sydney Bennett" on *Dateline NBC* and "Only Sydney Knows" on *48 Hours Mystery* at CBS. Courtroom 3 had become another Miami tourist destination, like South Beach and the Seaquarium, with spectators coming from as far away as Japan to vie for the fifty seats available to the public. Verbal altercations were common, at least one having escalated to an all-out fistfight that required police intervention. Critics said it was the defense who courted the media. They neglected to mention that, unlike the prosecution, Jack had avoided all interviews and had issued not a single press release. Never in his fifteen years as a lawyer had he done television ads, billboards, or anything of the sort. Sydney Bennett was definitely not someone he had gone out looking to represent.

The case had found him.

Jack glanced at the flat-screen television on the wall. The anchor at BNN studios in New York—the ringmaster of "Sydney Watch Central"—was on the air. The excitement in her eyes made the banner at the bottom of the screen superfluous: JURY HAS REACHED A VERDICT.

Jack left his uneaten lunch on his desk, grabbed his briefcase, and hurried out to the car. Picketers had been marching outside his law office since the start of jury deliberations, but they were too busy scrambling to their vehicles, posters tucked under their arms, to pester Jack any longer. They'd already gotten word of the BNN news flash and knew the wait was over. Theo drove, so gravel flew when they pulled out of the parking lot. The picketers followed.

"You never asked me if Sydney did it," Jack said.

Theo's gaze remained fixed on the road. Theo Knight was Jack's best friend, bartender, therapist, confidant, and sometime investigator. He was also a former client, a one-time gangbanger who easily could have ended up dead on the streets of Overtown or Liberty City. Today he was Jack's self-appointed bodyguard, having insisted on driving Jack back to his office after closing arguments—after Jack's second anonymous death threat, one that seemed a bit too credible.

"None of my business, dude," said Theo.

That struck Jack as funny.

"Why you laugh?" asked Theo.

Sydney's guilt or innocence had become the entire country's business. Everyone professed to "know" she was the worst kind of killer.

"No reason," said Jack.

They rode in silence, the afternoon sun glaring on the windshield. Jack thought of Emma. Almost three years old at the time of her death. Two years, nine months, and twenty-four days, if you believed the defense and placed the date of death on April 28. If you sided with the prosecution, there was no way to know how long Emma had lived. She was two years and . . . something. The state had never proved a time of death. Or a cause of death. Even the alleged manner of death—homicide—was a matter of opinion. So many things, unproven. There was no disputing, however, that the badly decomposed remains of Sydney's daughter had been found in a plastic garbage bag near the Florida Everglades. Emma would be almost six years old now, a beautiful little girl fresh out of kindergarten, full of personality, ready to crack the books, meet Junie B. Jones, and conquer the first grade. Jack wondered what she might be doing on this hot summer day with her mother or grandmother if things had not gone so wrong, if this nightmare had never happened. But it had happened. Nothing could change that. Across the nation, people who had never met Emma or Sydney, many who had never felt compelled to follow a courtroom trial in their life, were demanding justice.

"Justice for Emma."

Throngs of spectators waited outside the Richard E. Gerstein Justice Building. Choppers from local television news stations circled overhead. Traffic around the courthouse was shut down. News of the impending two P.M. announcement had spread across the country. Jack's gaze drifted up to the top floor of an unremarkable building that betrayed the glamorized shots of Miami on television and resembled the architecture of the former Soviet Union. Behind those walls, the jury would render its verdict, insulated from the onlookers who jostled with the media for a place to stand on the sidewalk and steps outside the courthouse. The growing buzz of activity was surreal, like armies of angry fire ants making quick work of fallen mangos, which were everywhere this time of year. Theo pulled up as close to the courthouse as the police perimeter would allow. Jack got out at the curb.

"Good luck," said Theo.

"Thanks," said Jack.

July in Miami is a veritable sauna, especially west of the interstate, away from the breezes off Biscayne Bay. In a sea of sweaty bodies clad in short pants and sleeveless shirts, a criminal defense lawyer dressed in pinstripes was an easy mark. No single voice in the crowd was discernible, so what Jack heard was more like a collective "There he is!"

Some spectators suddenly rushed toward the courthouse, others toward Jack. Cameramen flanked him on the sidewalk. Television reporters got right in his face, elbowing out their competition, firing off questions that presumed the outcome and that all ran together.

"How worried is your client?"

"Was it a mistake for Sydney not to testify?"

"Who will defend her on appeal?"

Jack answered none of them. Most onlookers were women, many of them red with sunburn, anger, or both. A line of police officers kept the crowd at bay as Jack climbed the courthouse steps. The jeers were nothing he hadn't heard before, but they seemed louder and angrier than usual.

"Baby killer!"

"Today's the day, Jack ass!" That and "Jack off" had become the preferred terms of endearment, at least when they weren't calling him Juani Cochran.

Jack pushed through the crowd, funneled through the revolving door, and headed to the security checkpoint, where armed guards with metal-detecting wands shuffled visitors along. The standard security check took only a minute, but with a mob on the courthouse steps, some with faces pressed to the windows, the process seemed much longer. Jack gathered his belongings, crossed the rotunda, and squeezed into an open elevator. The unwritten rule of crowded elevator etiquette—silence—was broken by one especially persistent reporter, but Jack didn't respond. No one got off until the elevator reached the sixth floor, an effective express ride, as if nothing else happening in the courthouse mattered. As Jack started toward the courtroom doors, the sound of another elevator chime stopped him.

The metal doors parted. It was the team of prosecutors.

Melinda Crawford and her entourage looked decidedly confident as they approached, just as they had since the first day of trial. Admittedly, Crawford's three-hour closing argument had been nothing short of brilliant. Jack held the courtroom door for her. She opened the other door for herself, leaving Jack holding his for no one. The team followed her inside.

"You're welcome," said Jack.

The prosecutors went to the right, toward the long rectangular table nearer the empty jury box. Jack started toward the defense table, where his co-counsel was already seated.

For Jack, just seeing Hannah Goldsmith triggered memories of his first trial—with Hannah's father. Neil Goderich had founded the Freedom Institute to handle the overload of "death cases" generated at the hand of Jack's father, Harry Swyteck, the law-and-order governor who had signed more death warrants than any governor in Florida history. Four years of defending the guilty would prove to be enough for Jack. His resignation didn't end the friendship, however, so Jack naturally said yes when Neil had come down sick and asked Jack to cover "just one lousy hearing" in a new case. "Not since Theo Knight have I believed so strongly in a client's innocence," he'd told Jack. Two years later—a month before trial—Neil was dead. By then, *State v. Bennett* had become a pop-culture juggernaut. Postponing trial to find new defense counsel wasn't an option the judge would consider. Jack hadn't so much as thought about Sydney Bennett since that favor for Neil, but that single hearing two years earlier made him the only living "attorney of record." Jack wasn't the first lawyer to get stuck in a criminal trial after making a pretrial appearance—that's why criminal defense lawyers insist on being paid upfront—but it was the first time it had happened *to him*. Jack could defend Sydney or go to jail. "No good deed goes unpunished," Judge Matthews had told him, the perfect TV sound bite to punctuate the court's denial of Jack's motion to withdraw. Hannah called Jack that evening and agreed to second-chair the trial.

Somewhere, high above the fracas, Neil undoubtedly found peace in knowing that his last case had turned Jack and Hannah into national pariahs.

"Is Sydney on her way up?" Jack asked.

As if on cue, the side door near their table opened. A pair of deputies escorted the guest of dishonor into the courtroom.

Criminal defendants were not required to be shackled or clothed in prison garb in front of a jury. Sydney was wearing a conservative pink ruffled blouse and beige slacks, her long chestnut hair up in a bun. Of course the lawyers had chosen the outfit for her, as they had for each day of trial. The media had excoriated the defense for that, too, as if Jack were expected to tell his client to show up for court like Michael Jackson, dressed in pajamas and sun-glasses.

Sydney appeared tentative at first, a normal re-action to the obvious tension in the courtroom. Her step quickened as she approached her lawyers. Hannah embraced her, but Jack didn't. "No public display of affection" was a holdover from his days at the Freedom Institute, days of defending the worst that death row had to offer. Jack's adherence to that rule, however, had done nothing to stem the Freud-ian babble of pop psychiatrists, so-called expert commentators who spent hour after televised hour dissecting Sydney's "seductive glances," "naughty pouts," and "Bambi-like blinks" at her handsome attorney. The dichotomy of her prior life—loving single mother by day, slutty cocktail waitress by night—was part of the public fascination.

"I can't stand this waiting," Sydney whispered.

"Not much longer," said Jack.

"Do we have anything to appeal if . . . you know?"

She was no dummy, managing her defense right up to the moment of truth. "We can talk about that later."

Sydney took a seat and immediately started to bite her nails. Hannah gently took her hand and whispered to her about the television cameras. The talking heads on the air were surely taking note of her nerves. Sydney lowered her hands into her lap. Jack took a seat beside her, and before he could feel the full weight of all eyes upon them, the door to Judge Matthews' chambers swung open, and the bailiff called the courtroom to order.

"All rise!"

The packed courtroom fell silent, everyone standing as Judge Matthews ascended to the bench. He instructed all to have a seat and immediately issued a few admonitions—"no in-court reactions to the reading of the verdict" and so forth. Jack was only half listening. The second-guessing had begun.

Should I have worked harder for a plea?

The charges against Sydney included first degree murder. Death by lethal injection was still on the table, so to speak. If Sydney was convicted, the sentencing phase of the trial would begin. The jury would hear additional evidence and recommend death or life imprisonment. Sequestration had immunized the jury from the constant drumbeat of hatred in the media so far, but there was no guarantee that the jury would remain sequestered for the sentencing hearing. Ultimately, the punishment would be in the hands of Judge Belvin Matthews—a former prosecutor whose impressive list of convictions on behalf of the state attorney's office included the first woman ever to be executed in Florida. Matthews had personally witnessed her death. Since his election to the circuit bench, not a single one of Judge Matthews' death sentences had been overturned on appeal. A verdict of guilty could well mean that Sydney would be the fourth woman sent to Florida's death row since January—the most of any given year in the state's history.

"Bailiff, please bring in the jury," said the judge.

"All rise!"

Behind Jack, in the packed gallery, the bumps and thuds of the rising crowd sounded like a ragtag army on the march. Jurors in Florida courtrooms were never shown on television, so even as the jury entered, the cameras remained fixed on Jack and his client. Jack had become almost immune to the constant coverage. Sydney had never gotten used to it, having complained to Jack throughout the trial that when she looked calm, the media attacked her as coldhearted; if she cried, they said she was faking; when she flashed even the slightest smile, they declared her a sociopath.

The jury took their seats, and everyone else in the room did the same.

"They're not looking at me," Sydney whispered.

Somewhere—probably TV—Sydney must have heard a lawyer say that if the jurors didn't make eye contact with the defendant as they filed into the courtroom, it signaled a guilty verdict. For Jack, a far better indicator was the number of courtroom deputies hovering around the defense table, ready to grab his guilty clients before they could make a mad dash for the door. Somehow, the deputies always seemed to know.

The judge broke the silence. "Good afternoon, ladies and gentlemen of the jury, have you reached a verdict?"

"Yes, sir," the twelve answered in unison.

Jack glanced over his shoulder and spotted Sydney's parents in the back row. Geoffrey Bennett, hands clasped and praying, was seated beside his wife. Behind them stood the police investigators who had found Emma's body.

"Would the foreman hand the verdict form to the court deputy, please."

A woman in the dark blue uniform of courtroom

deputies approached the jury box and received the verdict form. She handed it up to Judge Matthews. He inspected it, making sure that all was in order, showing no expression as he turned page after page. Finally, he looked directly at Jack and his client.

"Will the defendant rise along with counsel."

I know it's going to be okay. That was what he wanted to tell his client. But how could anyone say such a thing? How could anyone *know*?

Jack's gaze swept the jury box. Each juror had taken the same oath to "render a true verdict according to the law and the evidence," and the evidence against Sydney was entirely circumstantial. Cause of death, unknown. Manner of death, a matter of inference upon inference and expert opinion. No eyewitnesses. No confession from the accused. Yes, the jury had been told that in a court of law circumstantial evidence is as probative as direct evidence—a point that the prosecution hammers home in every trial. Beyond their own awareness of what they had decided, however, the jurors didn't *know* anything more than the rest of the players in this courtroom drama. For all their forceful argument, the prosecutors didn't know what had happened. Neither did Judge Matthews, the investigators on the case, or the experts who had testified at trial. The pundits on television sure as hell didn't know.

"Madam clerk," said the judge, "you may publish the verdicts."

Not even *Jack* knew.

"In the circuit court of the eleventh judicial circuit in and for Miami-Dade County, Florida, State of Florida versus Sydney Louise Bennett . . ."

None of them knew, because they hadn't been there for Emma's final moments.

"As to the charge of first degree murder . . ."

What they knew was in actuality nothing more than what they believed. And what Jack believed as he stood at Sydney's side and heard those words— "We the jury, find the defendant"—is what he would believe to his dying day: There was more than one person in that courtroom who *knew* what had happened to Emma. And Jack could have proved it.

If only Sydney had wanted him to.

2
.

"Not guilty!"

The shout from atop the courthouse steps carried across the street and all the way to the jurors' parking lot, loud enough for most of the sunbaked crowd to hear. Silent and filled with anticipation, many of the onlookers were following a slightly delayed Internet live stream on smartphones and electronic devices, which just a moment later confirmed the verdict. Those not stunned into speechlessness erupted in anger.

"What?"

"How?"

"That jury must be nuts!"

By default—not a seat to be had in the courtroom—Theo had made himself part of the outdoor vigil, conspicuously taller and darker than the predominantly white, female crowd around him. The shade of an oak cut the glare on his iPhone. BNN was covering the trial live, and their on-screen graphic summarized the verdict. First degree murder: not guilty. Manslaughter: not guilty. Criminal child neglect: not guilty. Sydney was convicted on one count of providing false information to police investigators. Essentially, the jury believed what the defense lawyers had said about their own client: She was a liar, not a murderer. Television cameras captured her fighting back tears of relief, propped up by Hannah Goldsmith. The camera cut to Jack as the court polled the jurors, and Theo was glad to see that Jack wasn't flashing some cocky lawyer's grin and slapping high fives with everyone around him. One by one, each juror verbally confirmed that this was his or her verdict.

"Unbelievable," was the running commentary from BNN's anchor. Through his earbuds, Theo heard the judge thank the jurors and dismiss them. Then the BNN anchor said it again, this time with attitude: "Simply *un—be—lievable*."

Theo glanced around him. The crowd was becoming more vocal, their expressions of anger and despair making it hard for him to hear the TV coverage. Theo increased the volume, then lowered it. Faith Corso was on a rant that needed no amplification.

Corso, a tough former prosecutor turned TV personality, had spotlighted the Sydney Bennett case from the beginning. It had started with a desperate, monthlong search for a missing two-year-old girl—but without the usual sympathy for the mother. Police quickly pegged Sydney as a liar about everything, from her place of employment to her whereabouts on the day of Emma's death. She'd led her parents to believe that she was holding a steady day job as a bookkeeper at a Key Biscayne resort. In fact, she was a "shot girl" at a popular South Beach nightclub—one of the scantily clad young women who roamed through the crowd with a bottle of tequila in one hand and a tray of shot glasses in the other, cajoling drunk young men into spending ten bucks for a shot and quick squeeze of the shot girl.

Sydney's biggest deception, however, was in what she *hadn't* said.

"What mother fails to report the disappearance of her own child if she isn't covering up a homicide?" asked Corso, her voice laden with disgust. "And what kind of mother goes out partying the night her daughter goes missing, parties again the next night, and the night after that?"

Corso had been asking those questions for three years. The prosecutor had put them up in bold letters on a projection screen during closing argument. Corso, the prosecution, the crowd outside the courthouse, the millions of viewers on television— all had expected the jury to answer with a verdict of guilty.

Theo's iPhone flickered, but the Internet connection remained strong enough for him to hear something about the scheduling of a sentencing hearing on the "false information" conviction. The judge announced that Sydney would remain incarcerated until then. Corso quickly explained to her viewers that the maximum sentence for the conviction on the lesser count was one year. Because Sydney had already spent three years behind bars awaiting trial, she would likely serve no additional time.

"Shot Mom will be free and back to her wicked ways in a week," said Corso. Dubbing her "Shot

Mom"—a play on "shot girl" and "hot mom"—was one of the signature devices that Corso had used throughout the trial to express her contempt for Sydney Bennett.

Corso checked with one of the BNN reporters on the scene: "Heather, what's the reaction outside the courthouse?"

"Faith, it is way beyond disappointment. People here are genuinely heartbroken. I've spoken to a group of mothers who traveled all the way from Arizona, college students from New Orleans, retirees from New York. All of them filled with a sickening sense that there has been no justice for Emma."

Theo suddenly sensed an echo. He looked up from his iPhone and realized that he wasn't just hearing the roving reporter's voice on television through his earbuds. Heather Brown and the BNN cameraman were standing just fifteen feet away from him. She was suddenly coming his way, speaking into her microphone.

"Faith, let me see if I can get a word with the man who brought defense lawyer Jack Swyteck to the courthouse today. Sir!"

Theo froze. "Me?"

"Yes, can I have a quick word with you, please?"

Being six feet six and black in this crowd had definitely proved to be a liability. "You must have me confused with someone else."

"Wait a second, I know that man," said Corso, and Theo could hear her in his earbuds. "Viewers may recall that, a few years back, I did a BNN special investigative report on capital punishment, and one case we featured told the story of how Jack Swyteck used his family name to pull strings and get Theo Knight off Florida's death row."

If by "pull strings" you mean DNA evidence . . .

"Heather, ask Mr. Knight if he—"

"Gotta go," said Theo as he broke away.

"Mr. Knight!"

Theo was off like a running back. It had taken Jack four years to prove Theo's innocence. Twice he'd come so close to the electric chair that they'd served him a last meal, sent him to the prison barber, and shaved his head and ankles for placement of the electrodes. Theo had nothing to prove to anyone— ever again.

"Mr. Knight, please!"

The reporter tried to follow, but the crowd closed around her and the cameraman. Theo pushed all the way to the street in front of the courthouse, past clusters of angry onlookers, around several other reporters who were delivering up-to-the-minute reports. His cell rang, and he made the mistake of answering. It was Faith Corso.

"Mr. Knight, where will Shot Mom go from here?"

Theo did a double take. "Are we on the air? And how did you get my number?"

"There's an app for that. Would you answer my question, please?"

"I have no idea where Sydney is going."

"You're the defense team's driver, are you not?"

"No."

"Apparently you're about as truthful as Shot Mom. We caught you on camera driving Jack Swyteck to the courthouse today."

"That doesn't make me his driver, Miss Daisy." The film reference was probably lost on her, but Morgan Freeman was one of Theo's favorites. "Are we on the air or not?" he asked.

She wouldn't answer. "When Shot Mom is released, will you be the one driving her wherever she plans to go?"

"I got nothin' to say about that."

"Nothing at all?"

"Nope."

"Correct me if I'm wrong, but wasn't that the same thing you told police when they found a convenience-store clerk dead on the floor and your hands in the cash register?"

Theo held his tongue. "I'm hanging up now."

"No, wait! People have a right to know. Where will you be taking Shot Mom? Hollywood for a movie? New York for a book deal?"

"You need to ask Sydney that."

"What about your buddy, Jack Swyteck? What's his cut of the blood money?"

"I got no idea what you're talking about."

"I'm talking about turning the tragic death of an innocent little girl into profit. Isn't that the next move for Shot Mom and her lawyers?"

Theo almost hung up, but Corso's hold on him wouldn't allow it.

"Mr. Knight, people have a right to know the truth."

"All right," said Theo, "I'll give it to you straight. But only if we're on the air."

"Of course we're on the air," she said, her voice rising with excitement. "And for my friends in the viewing audience, you're watching another BNN exclusive. I am speaking on the telephone with one-time death row inmate Theo Knight, a close personal friend and former client of Shot Mom's lawyer, Jack Swyteck. Go ahead, sir. Tell us what business deals are in the works now that this astounding verdict has left Shot Mom completely unaccountable for Emma's tragic death."

Theo wasn't a news junkie, but Jack had told him how the Sydney Bennett circus had pushed BNN's ratings into the stratosphere—and how, in particular, Faith Corso's stature as a TV personality skyrocketed every time she uttered the words *Shot Mom*.

"I can only speak for myself," said Theo.

"Yourself?" said Corso. "So even the driver for Shot Mom's lawyer has his eye on a deal of some sort? This ought to be good."

"Oh, this deal is beyond good. As soon as we hang up, I'm going straight to your Web site and I'm buying two of those 'Rot in Hell, Sydney' snuggies for just nineteen ninety-five, plus shipping and handling. And if I order in the next three minutes, I get a free 'I heart the death penalty' bumper sticker."

Theo could hear the hiss of anger in her next breath. "That is so typical of the way the defense team has treated this entire tragedy," said Corso. "A joke, a complete mockery of our system of jus—"

Theo hung up, reeling in his anger. He continued away from the courthouse, stepping outside the ring of frenetic reporters with way too much hair and makeup for the ninety-five-degree heat, beyond the reach of microphone-toting assassins who seemed eager to interview anyone who was willing to say something outrageous on camera. He stopped at the street corner and wiped the sweat from his brow.

Lashing out at Corso on national television wasn't the smartest thing he'd ever done. Of course she wasn't actually selling snuggies or giving away bumper stickers, but she'd pushed him, and it was Theo's nature to push back. The exchange was sure to be replayed many times over, and the last thing Jack needed was to be coldcocked by the BNN broadcast. He knew Jack didn't have a cell phone inside the courthouse, so Theo shot him a text for later.

Heads up. Thx 2 yer driver, they wanna kill us both.

Theo's gaze turned back to the crowd outside the courthouse. No one was leaving. If anything, folks were only getting more worked up.

After they kill Sydney.

3

Thursday's sentencing hearing went as the pundits had predicted. Sydney Bennett was sentenced to time served for her conviction on one count of providing false information to police. Her release from the women's detention center was set for some time after midnight the following Saturday, probably very early Sunday.

On Friday morning, Jack met with his client to talk logistics. It was just the two of them, as Hannah Goldsmith was delivering an opening statement in one of the other 143 murder cases pending in Miami-Dade County.

"How scared should I be?" asked Sydney.

She was seated on the opposite side of a small table, attorney and client surrounded by windowless walls of yellow-painted cinder block. Bright fluorescent lighting lent their meeting room all the warmth of a workshop. Sydney was a grown woman, but dressed in pajama-like prison garb, with no makeup, she seemed more like a teenager to Jack. It was hard for him to fathom that Sydney and Hannah were just three years apart in age. Light-years apart in maturity.

"I'm not telling you to be scared," said Jack. "I'm just saying we have to be careful."

"They want to kill me, don't they?"

"If 'they' killed everyone 'they' wanted to kill, death row would be the most overcrowded place on Earth."

"Don't sugarcoat it. I'm not clueless. I can watch television in here now."

That was new. Until her acquittal on murder charges, Sydney had been housed under the category of Protective Custody Level One in the high-security section of the detention center. One hour a day to take a shower, sit in the dayroom, and make collect calls from the jail phone. She could access books from a library cart to take back to her cell, but Level One inmates had no television or computer privileges.

"Okay," said Jack. "Some people may want to kill you. Some want to marry you. Some want the trial to start all over again so they have something to do while they knock off two bottles of chardonnay before lunchtime. You can drive yourself crazy thinking about what 'they' want."

"You're right. From now on, the only thing that matters is what *I* want."

That wasn't exactly what Jack was saying, but he moved on. "Let's talk procedure. And safety."

"Safety's a good thing."

"The correctional facility is walking a fine line," said Jack. "Until you get outside the gate, you're their responsibility. The last thing they want is for something bad to happen to you on their turf. On the other hand, they don't want to be accused of giving you special treatment. They want this to go according to standard procedure, as much as possible."

"Seems weird that turning a woman out on the street after midnight would be standard procedure."

Jack had once filed a lawsuit on behalf of a twenty-year-old woman who was raped by a carload of gangbangers on the night of her release. The case was dismissed, since putting women on the street alone after midnight actually *was* standard procedure.

"You won't have to fend for yourself," said Jack. "I'm walking out with you, and we're going straight to an SUV."

"SUV, huh? Faith Corso said I was getting a limo with a hot tub."

Jack didn't doubt it. "It's a Chevy Suburban with a hundred and thirty-two thousand miles on it. I use it to trailer my boat."

"Cool. We're escaping by boat?"

It was a rare attempt at humor. Acquittal suited her well. "No. Theo is under strict orders to leave the boat behind."

"Theo," she said, smiling thinly. "So I actually get to meet your friend Theo?"

"Yes. Theo's driving."

"Loved his interview with Faith Corso. That crack about the rot-in-hell snuggies was hilarious."

"Yeah, he's a real stitch."

"He seems totally my type."

"Theo is nobody's type."

"That's exactly my type."

Jack drew a breath, then let it out. "Sydney, let me give you some fatherly advice."

"You're not old enough to be my father."

"*Yeee* . . . almost. Let's call it friendly advice. You need to keep a low profile when you get out."

"You think I don't know that?"

"I don't mean just for a week, or even a month. It's going to take a long time for this craziness to subside. The first photograph of you in a club having a good time is going to be worth a hundred thousand dollars."

"So that's no B.S. from Faith Corso? Someone is actually willing to pay me a hundred thousand dollars for my picture?"

"No, they won't pay *you* a thing. They'll pay the photographer who snaps the picture."

She pursed her lips, then an idea came. "I know. Your buddy Theo's a bartender, right? We go to his bar, you snap the picture, and we split the hundred grand."

"No."

"Why not?"

"First of all, I'm not interested. Second, as things stand right now, I would say that I'm concerned about your safety, but we can manage it. The moment this trial puts ten cents in your pocket, it's a different story."

"How do you mean?"

"Let me be clear. No magazine can pay you enough for a photo, no publisher can pay you enough for a book, no movie studio can pay you enough for the film rights to cover the costs of the security you will need if Faith Corso tells her viewers that you've turned the murder of your daughter into personal profit."

Sydney gripped the table's edge. "I didn't kill my daughter."

"We didn't prove that."

"I'm not supposed to have to prove it."

"That's true. That's why you're about to be a free woman."

"Free enough to work for free? Is that it?"

"I didn't say you can't work for a living."

"Who's going to hire me? Other than a porn king?"

Those calls had already come to Jack's office. "Don't go that route."

"I may have no choice. In two days I have to pay rent, eat, just like everyone else."

"This will pass with time."

"When?"

"That's up to you. It could be never, if you become the poster child for taking blood money."

The words made her cringe. "I don't get that term, 'blood money.' On *The Sopranos* that was what a hit man got for a contract killing."

"It's one of those terms that has gotten away from its original meaning. Technically, blood money is what a murderer pays to compensate the victim's family."

"Perfect. TV murdered my daughter. Over and over, day after day. They can pay me for the rights to the made-for-TV movie. All nice and legal. Blood money. You can cut the deal."

"I'm not cutting any deals."

He said it with finality, no room for negotiation—

which elicited a cold glare from Sydney. She suddenly didn't look like a teenager in pajamas anymore. Reporters who had watched their interaction in the courtroom and described similar expressions as "pouty" had no idea what the real Sydney was like.

"Then I'll find someone who will," she fired back.

Jack let her simmer, but she wasn't cooling down. Sydney rose. "Are we done, Jack?"

"We haven't really covered the whole plan for Saturday night."

She walked to the green metal door and knocked for the guard. "I don't care about the fucking plan," she said, not even trying to get her temper under control. "Just do your job and get me out of here."

The door opened. Sydney stepped out, and one of the corrections officers led her back to the housing unit. Jack gathered his briefcase and exchanged glances with the other officer at the door. The guards had seen many meetings between Jack and his client end this way—Sydney gnawing at her lip, fists clenched, red-faced with anger.

"What's she so mad about now?" the guard asked.

"I handed her my bill," said Jack.

The guard laughed. It was public knowledge that Sydney was indigent. "Good luck with that, partner."

"It takes luck," said Jack, continuing to the visitors' exit.

4
.

South Beach called to him. Theo was speeding east on the Dolphin Expressway, well aware that if he kept going for another twenty minutes, past I-95 and across the causeway, he would run smack into Ocean Drive, where hundreds of bad girls were ready to party. Ironically, a quick exit at Twelfth Avenue put him on a collision course with hundreds of others who were more than ready, but who weren't going anywhere tonight.

Except for one Sydney Bennett.

Theo parked the SUV in a dark lot beside a tall chain-link fence, followed the cracked sidewalk beneath the interstate overpass, and walked across the street to the Miami-Dade County Women's Detention Center.

The multistory center north of downtown Miami housed 375 female inmates. Some were awaiting trial. Others were serving time. Theo remembered the days of contact visits from his childhood, when his mother—in and out of jail on drug-possession charges—could hug him. Contact was no longer allowed, which was one of the many tidbits of information that Theo had picked up while listening to Faith Corso and her panel of experts on BNN fill hour after hour in the final chapter of Shot Mom coverage. The thought of Sydney Bennett's return to the comfort and pleasure of human contact after killing her daughter had so many loyal viewers upset. Many were downright furious. Some—"an army of thousands," according to Corso—were fed up with the system and ready to take justice into their own hands. The exact temperature of the crowd was hard to determine, but it was undeniable that few, if any, corrections facilities had scheduled a more anticipated release than Sydney's.

Most of the detention center's windows had been dark since nightfall, but lights were still shining in the ground-floor lobby, the release point for inmates in the system. A pair of corrections officers stood guard, and all appeared quiet on the other side of the glass doors. It was completely unlike the spectacle on Seventh Avenue and the park directly across the street.

"Ho-lee shit," Theo muttered.

The night air was thick with humidity, the mercury still in the high eighties, and all those bare arms and legs were a veritable feast for hungry mosquitoes. People were milling about, walking with no particular destination in mind, just wanting to be there for "the moment." It was as if the beaches had closed, happy hour was over, and an armada of sunburned tourists had wandered over to the jail for free entertainment. Parents with their young children. High-school kids on their bicycles.

College students with rum-filled go-cups in hand. Vendors selling boiled peanuts and bottled water. Drivers on the elevated stretch of expressway above it all honked their horns as they passed the detention center, as if it were New Year's Eve or the Super Bowl. One young man stood outside the center with a homemade sign that was sure to get him on television: MARRY ME, SYDNEY.

"Snuggies," a vendor called out, "get your hand-stitched snuggies."

Theo did a double take. ROT IN HELL, SYDNEY was the stitched message. Theo had been joking on the *Faith Corso Show*, but this entrepreneur had stolen his idea and run with it.

The bright lights of a camera crew caught his attention. A BNN reporter had staked out a position on the sidewalk just a few feet behind him. She was interviewing the young man with the handheld marriage proposal, earnestly trying to find out what would make him want to spend the rest of his life with Sydney Bennett.

"Well, uhm, she's really hot," he said, reaching up inside the John Deere cap to scratch his head. "Obviously she, uh, likes to party. And did I say she's hot?"

Theo's phone vibrated. He stepped away from the small gathering around the television crew and checked the text message. It was from Jack.

"*Hang,*" it read.

They had worked out a system back at the hotel. The release could happen any time between midnight and two A.M. Such a broad window of time made it impractical for Theo to sit in the SUV with the motor running. The agreement was that Jack would update Theo by text every fifteen minutes. "Hang" meant nothing was happening. When it was time to bring the SUV around, the message would read "Greenlight."

Theo slid his phone into his pocket. He had at least another fifteen minutes to kill, probably more. He continued down the sidewalk, beyond the detention center's main entrance, toward the more secure wing that butted up against the elevated expressway. Razor ribbon topped a high chain-link fence that extended beneath the overpass, and the streetlamps cast the yellowish glow of high-security vapor lights. Theo was sweating, but he suddenly felt goose bumps. The dark prison walls, the guard towers and ribbon wire, the vigil keepers outside the chain-link fence—it was eerily reminiscent of the darkest time of his life, those hours before the execution he had narrowly avoided at Florida State Prison. This time, however, there was no competing right and left ideology, no clash of capital punishment proponents versus death penalty opponents, no "eye for an eye" versus "Kumbaya." This crowd was unified in its vitriol, especially at this end of the parking lot. This was where the hard-core Shot Mom haters had set up camp.

"No blood money!"

A middle-aged woman, hoarse from hours of shouting, was screaming at Theo. Theo kept walking, but she stayed with him, shaking a poster that delivered the same message in bloodred letters:

NO BLOOD MONEY FOR SHOT MOM!

"And for her lawyer, neither!" another woman shouted.

Theo stopped and fired back a response that these women undoubtedly thought was still part of the black-speak lexicon. "Right on, sistuh."

The women continued their chant, and a group behind them picked it up: "No blood money, no blood money, no blood money!"

The mantra had started a week earlier on the *Faith Corso Show*, when a guest commentator had reported incorrectly that Jack was in New York City shopping a million-dollar book deal for Sydney. Corso had seized the moment to rally her troops: "We *cannot* let this happen," she'd told her viewers. "The injustice of Shot Mom's acquittal will forever stain the hands of those twelve jurors who ignored the clear evidence of guilt. But if we stand aside and let Shot Mom sign her million-dollar deal with publishers in New York or filmmakers in Hollywood . . . well, then shame on all of us. There truly will be no justice for Emma. So stand up, friends. Stand up with me and say it:

"No blood money!"

The glare of the television lights caught Theo's eye, and again he found himself just a few yards away from the BNN reporter with her camera crew. The live interview of the moment was with an elderly woman from Lake City who had followed Faith Corso's coverage of the case from the beginning. She was describing the poster that she and her eleven-year-old granddaughter had created to protest Sydney Bennett's release. It was a collage of headlines and photographs spanning three years of newspaper coverage. Her voice quaked with emotion as she told the reporter about the photograph in the middle of the poster, a five-by-seven headshot of Sydney's daughter, Emma.

"We glued on all these pictures this morning with plain old white glue," the woman said, "and we used the exact same glue on Emma's picture. But Emma's is the only one where the glue soaked through the paper and left these red marks. Not a single one of these other pictures have that. You see what I'm talking about?" she asked, pointing.

"Yes, I do see," said the reporter. "Let's get the camera in closer for our viewers."

"It looks like tiny red tears on her little cheeks, don't it?"

"Remarkable," the reporter said. "Viewers can draw their own conclusions, but, seeing it with my own eyes, I can only say that this is truly remarkable."

"I believe that's the Lord's way of telling us that we're doing the right thing here tonight, and I believe—"

A shout from across the parking lot halted the interview: "There she is!"

Theo's gaze locked onto the commotion in the middle distance, and the BNN reporter signaled her cameraman to zoom onto the building.

"Hold on, Faith," said the reporter. "We may have a Shot Mom sighting."

Heads turned as random voices carried the news of one sighting after another.

"It's her!"

"There's Shot Mom!"

Onlookers jumped up from their lawn chairs and picnic blankets. Demonstrators grabbed their posters and sprinted across the street toward the high-security end of the building. A crowd that, minutes earlier, had been milling around and waiting was suddenly a cohesive ball of energy, catapulted by the Sydney sighting.

Theo ran, too, not sure what had happened to Jack's plan, wondering if he had missed the "Greenlight" message. He checked his iPhone, but the display showed NO SERVICE. The Sydney sighting had overloaded the system, but word of mouth was spreading all around him.

"I see her!"

"Yeah, that's her!"

Theo tried to get closer, but it was human gridlock ahead of him. Demonstrators blocked the sidewalk and the exit to the parking lot, but he was tall enough to see over most of the people in front of him. The most vocal and aggressive in the crowd, the tip of the human spear, had surrounded a young woman whose white blouse made her an easy mark in the darkness. People shook their fists and brandished their posters, shouting at her. She shouted back, but that only seemed to unify the mob.

"No blood money, no blood money!"

She darted in one direction, then in the other, desperately seeking a way out. The human circle around her drew tighter, and the angry crowd moved closer.

"No blood money!"

The BNN reporter and crew tried to push forward, but there was nowhere for them to go. Theo was trapped beside them and could hear the on-the-scene reporter shouting into her microphone with an update for the studio.

"Faith, you are absolutely correct. It does appear that this is the moment, the dreaded moment of Sydney Bennett's release from prison."

A big guy from BNN's lighting crew gave one more shove. Suddenly, the logjam broke, there was a collective surge forward, and Theo nearly fell over the woman in front of him. He helped her up, and then peered across the sea of heads that stretched all the way to the chain-link fence. The buffer zone—a few feet of separation—between the mob and its prey had disappeared. The woman in the white blouse had been swallowed up in the crowd, her body somewhere beneath the hysteria.

"No blood money!"

Theo checked his cell again, but he was still without service. He wasn't sure what to do, but things were turning ugly. He gripped the phone, useless as it was, frustrated enough to shout at the top of his lungs, but he kept it inside.

What the hell is going on, Jack?

5

Jack stared at the television in disbelief. He was seated at a table in the detention center lounge with a corrections officer whose walkie-talkie was crackling with updates from the dispatcher: "Backup needed, zone five. Backup, zone five."

The *Faith Corso Show* was coming in loud and clear on an old fifteen-inch television that rested on the counter next to the coffeemaker. BNN's coverage had switched to an aerial shot from the helicopter, the studio having temporarily lost contact with the camera crew in the field. Jack increased the volume as Corso described the carnage to her national audience from her studio desk.

"Once again, friends, you are watching BNN's exclusive coverage of the live action outside the Miami-Dade County Women's Detention Center. We are trying to reestablish contact with our reporter on the scene, Heather Brown, but this much we know. At approximately twelve nineteen A.M., Shot Mom was spotted on the north side of the building. As incomprehensible as this sounds, her defense team apparently thought she could slip through the crowd unnoticed. Things have gone terribly wrong, riot police are trying to establish order, and we can only hope that no innocent people have been caught up in this maelstrom."

A camera from a media helicopter tracked an ambulance as it sped down Seventh Avenue, orange and yellow lights flashing as it pulled into the parking lot.

"Emergency vehicles are now on the scene," said Corso, "and I'm told we have reconnected with Heather Brown. Heather, what is the situation on the ground now?"

"Utter and complete chaos," said Brown. There was audio contact, but no video.

"Do we have official confirmation that Shot Mom was, in fact, in the parking lot?"

Brown said something to her cameraman, and the on-screen image switched from the helicopter view to ground level. Brown was standing on the sidewalk, just outside the perimeter of panic and confusion.

"Faith, there is no official word yet from the Department of Corrections, but we have accounts from eyewitnesses who have stated in no uncertain terms that Sydney Bennett is somewhere in the middle of all this. We are trying to bring one of those eyewitnesses over here now to talk with us on camera." Brown adjusted her earpiece, listening to her producer, then spoke with greater urgency. "Faith, I am told we do have someone with us now," she said.

"Mic her up so I can talk to her," said Corso.

"She's right here. I can ask her directly."

"Heather, this will work so much better for everyone if you just hand over your earpiece and microphone and let me speak to her."

The "my show" attitude was what Corso's fans loved about her. Even Jack was starting to find her schtick engrossing in its own way. As the reporter on the scene complied, Corso set the dramatic stage for her own breaking-news moment.

"Once again, friends, you are watching Breaking News Network, live from the women's detention center, where we are just moments away from bringing you an exclusive eyewitness account of this very dangerous situation that Shot Mom and her lawyers have created."

"That her *lawyers* created?" said Jack. It was involuntary, and the corrections officer next to him ignored the fact that Jack was talking to a TV.

"Hello, this is Jenna Smith."

The voice from the television was weak and shaky. Alone and on camera was a frightened young woman clutching a BNN microphone. The crowd in the background flashed from red to orange to yellow, as a full complement of swirling lights from emergency vehicles bathed the parking lot.

"Jenna, this is Faith Corso with Breaking News Network. Thank you for joining me. I understand that you were right in the thick of this terrible, terrible mess. Can you tell us what happened?"

The young woman gnawed her lip, timid in her response. "Uhm, we were, like, it was Celeste and me, and we were just . . . oh, I don't think I can do this."

"Take a deep breath," said Corso, using the voice

of a skilled prosecutor who had comforted countless victims in court. "Who is Celeste?"

"Celeste. My BFF. We're roommates at the U. We wanted to go to Club Vertigo. They had this party."

"Where is this Club Vertigo?"

"South Beach. Tonight it was, like, you drink free if you come dressed up. Celeste was so perfect."

"Wait a second," said Corso, her tone no longer so soothing. "You're saying that a South Beach bar was giving away drinks if you got dressed up?"

"Right."

"Dressed up *how*?"

"They had this Sydney Bennett look-alike contest, and—"

"A *look-alike* contest?"

"Mmm-hmm. Celeste should have won first prize, but it was like so rigged, the bouncers wouldn't even let us in. So we, uhm, decided to come here. We thought it would be funny, you know? And like, all of a sudden, people were screaming, 'There she is, there's Sydney!' It was like people went crazy or something. I got knocked down by some jerk, and then . . . I don't know. A group of women were screaming about bloody money, and when I tried to get up, somebody bashed me in the arm with a pipe. Maybe a baseball bat—I don't know what it was. My elbow feels like it might be broken."

"Where is your friend Celeste now?" asked Corso.

"I don't know," Smith said, her voice quaking. "I got whacked in the arm, and then I saw Celeste go down."

"She got hit?"

"I'm not sure, I—"

"Coming through!" a paramedic shouted. A member of BNN's sound crew pulled the girl aside, and the camera captured a team of paramedics racing past with a woman on a gurney.

"Celeste!" the woman shouted. "Oh, my God, that's Celeste!"

The BNN reporter grabbed the microphone and earpiece, and the young woman chased after the gurney. The reporter didn't miss a beat, her voice racing with excitement.

"Faith, that would appear to be the friend identified by our eyewitness as Celeste. I did manage to get a good look as paramedics raced past us with the gurney. An oxygen mask covered the young woman's nose and mouth, and while I can't say whether she was breathing or not, she did not appear to be conscious. I hate to speculate, but the paramedic at her side had a defibrillator at the ready, and the entire team looked gravely concerned to me."

Corso lowered her head, took a deep breath, and expressed her "heartfelt concern" for the injured young woman, the young woman's family, and young women everywhere in the world who suffered at the hands of evil, the kind of evil that was personified by people like Shot Mom and her lawyers.

It was amazing to Jack, the way Corso could turn even a touching expression of compassion into one more shot at her enemy.

"Mr. Swyteck?"

Jack turned at the sound of the guard's voice. "Yes?"

"Our plan was to bring inmate Bennett down now, but I wanted to advise you that the warden has put your client's release on hold until further notice."

"That's a bad move," said Jack.

"It's for your client's safety as much as anyone's."

Jack's gaze returned to the television. BNN's coverage had reverted to the aerial view from the helicopter, tracking the ambulance as it left the parking lot.

"This is already beyond your control. An innocent young woman in the hospital isn't going to make people calm down."

"We'll just have to wait and see."

"Wait for *what*? An hour from now the bars will start closing. A hundred thousand drunks will be looking for something to do, someplace to be. And how much longer before the insanity out there spreads to your overcrowded population in here? These walls aren't soundproof. This craziness is contagious, even if you've never heard of Sydney Bennett."

The guard didn't answer, but he was seasoned enough to know that prison uprisings weren't just for men.

Jack said, "I've had enough of the Sydney Bennett circus. I'm betting you have, too. Tell the warden I need to see her. My client and I are leaving. Tonight."

6

.

Behind the detention center, bathed in the yellow glow of high-security sodium lights, a Miami-Dade ambulance backed all the way up to an entrance for Authorized Personnel Only. There was barely enough room for the door to swing open. Two corrections officers practically launched Sydney over the bumper and onto the gurney. Jack followed, and the double doors slammed shut. With no siren, emergency lights off, the ambulance pulled away from the building, through the employee parking lot, beneath the expressway, and eventually onto Seventh Avenue.

"Stay down," the paramedic said. It was just three of them in the rear. Sydney lay motionless on the gurney. Jack kept low, seated on the floor next to the paramedic in the jump seat.

The risk of being spotted by anyone on the street was minimal. The small rectangular windows on the rear doors were tinted to near blackout. Every few seconds, with each streetlamp they passed, a weak flash of light pierced the darkness inside the vehicle.

"How did this get so screwed up?" Sydney muttered.

Jack had already explained. He took her question as rhetorical, or perhaps she was soul-searching about her life in general.

The ambulance would take them directly to Opa-locka Executive Airport. That was the deal Jack had struck with the warden—who, as it had turned out, was more than eager to get "the Shot Mom problem" off her watch, pronto. There had been no need for Jack to tip his hand and explain that the need to get Sydney released on schedule wasn't just about public safety and prison riots. The flight plans were in place, and special arrangements had been made for a two A.M. takeoff. Sydney's parents stood to lose thousands of dollars if the chartered plane didn't leave on schedule.

Sydney sighed in the darkness. "I thought you knew what you were doing, counselor."

"Hard to foresee a mob attack on a Sydney Bennett look-alike," Jack said.

"I bet it's all a publicity stunt. Five hours from now she'll be on the *Today Show* with her lawyer grabbing her fifteen minutes of fame. Taking my time slot, no less. Little bitch."

The paramedic grumbled in the darkness. "For your information, that young woman will be lucky to be alive in the morning."

The prognosis cut through Jack like razor wire.

"Oh," said Sydney, "and I suppose that's my fault, right?"

"Sydney, please stop talking," said Jack.

"Why should I? You know I'm right. The prosecutor will write a book and blame me. The investigators and psychiatrists will do the talk shows and blame me. Faith Corso will do a two-hour special during prime time and blame me. They'll all blame me, and they'll all get rich. Why shouldn't I get rich?"

Jack was officially over her. "Sydney, shut up."

The ambulance stopped. The driver got out, walked around the back of the vehicle, and yanked open the doors. Jack climbed out and helped Sydney step down. Before Jack could even thank them, the paramedics jumped into the front seat, and the ambulance pulled away.

Opa-locka Executive is a three-runway facility that serves as a designated reliever for nearby and much busier Miami International Airport. Jack had flown into Opa-locka only once in his life, years before on a private plane with his father. Upon their descent, then Governor Swyteck had commandeered the microphone and subjected all twelve passengers to a narrated, bird's-eye tour of Hialeah, a largely Hispanic community south of the airport, a city with numerous points of interest but which also ranked as the most densely populated U.S. city without a skyscraper. Harry Swyteck was a veritable walking encyclopedia of Florida history, and he'd recounted with particular interest that Opa-locka Executive was just north of former Miami Municipal Airport, where in 1937 Amelia Earhart had begun her ill-fated journey around the world, never to be heard from again.

Jack thought his client could have taken a cue or two from Amelia.

"This way," said Jack, leading her toward the gate.

At two A.M. the 1,800-acre facility was mostly dark and quiet. The major exception was the U.S. Coast Guard Station, one of the busiest in the country, which was abuzz with activity of some sort that required a helicopter. It had nothing to do with Sydney, though it was not beyond the realm of possibility that it involved a future client of Jack's. The only other sign of life was the Piper aircraft on Runway 1, lights on and twin engines running.

"Thank God they're here," said Sydney.

Jack and his client were still outside the security gate, about twenty yards away from the plane. A man stepped out from behind the tail. Jack had been expecting to meet Geoffrey Bennett, but this man was much younger.

"That's not your father," said Jack.

"Nope."

"Who is it?"

Sydney turned and looked him in the eye. "Are you jealous?"

"That's a really stupid thing to say. Who are you flying with?"

She paused, as if savoring the fact that her lawyer wasn't in on the family secret. "I know you don't approve, Jack. It probably even makes you feel a little better about yourself to think that tonight's screwup killed any chance I had at a movie deal or book. For sure, the TV shows tomorrow were supposed to be all about where am I, what am I doing, when will I talk. Now it'll be nonstop from the hospital about some stupid girl and her costume party. But it's just a hiccup. She's either going to get better . . . or not. Whichever way it cuts, the spotlight will swing back to me. Whether you like it or not, this is going to make me a rich woman."

"Don't kid yourself. That young woman is in the hospital tonight because people thought she was you. Doesn't that tell you something?"

"Yeah. Avoid angry mobs. Got it covered."

"No, you don't. The world of public opinion is not a courtroom. There are no rules. You, Sydney, are the hunk of bloody meat in the shark tank."

"You underestimate me."

"You underestimate fame."

"Fame," she said, a wry smile of satisfaction cutting across her lips. "I really am famous, aren't I?"

Jack's gaze shifted again to the man waiting by the plane. "Is that guy with an entertainment agency?"

"You could say that," said Sydney.

"Well, that's just beautiful."

"You got a problem?" she said.

"Sydney, the trial's over, the cameras are off, and if you're smart, you'll thank God you've been given a second chance and live your life. Going out of your way to stay in the limelight is a huge mistake."

She extended her hand, and Jack shook it. "Thanks for everything," she said. "And thanks in advance for not writing a book of your own about this case."

"You definitely don't have to worry about that."

"I know. Because if you do, you'll be all over the X-rated chapters of mine."

"Are you actually threatening me?"

She flashed one of those pouty, bad-girl looks that had generated so much ink in the tabloids. "And people thought you were representing poor, indigent me for free."

Jack just shook his head. "Honestly, Sydney, I wish I had a REPLAY button so you could hear how ridiculous you sound. You act like someone who thinks she's living in a reality-TV show. Stop trying to be someone you're not."

She leaned closer, her eyes narrowing. "I really don't like threatening you, Jack. But I am deadly serious. It's *my* story. Not yours. Not the judge's. Not the prosecutor's. *Mine*."

"All true," said Jack. "But here's the thing: You're the only one who wants it."

"We'll see about that."

Jack wanted to drill some sense into her, tell her to wake up. But there was only so much he could do. "There's probably not another person on the planet who would admit this, but a part of me actually feels sorry for you."

"Whatever. Good-bye, Jack."

She turned and headed for the plane, gaining speed with each footfall on the asphalt, and finally breaking into a run. She threw herself into the arms of the man who was waiting. Jack watched for a minute, until the embrace broke and they climbed into the plane together. He had no idea where Sydney was headed. No idea who had come to get her.

The engine revved, and the plane started down the runway.

Jack wondered if he would ever see her again. He thought about Emma, thought about the Sydney

look-alike in the hospital, thought about the devastated parents who had just gotten the dreaded
phone call and learned that their beautiful daughter
would be "lucky to be alive in the morning" . . . and
he wondered if Sydney even cared.

He glanced over his shoulder for one last look as
the plane left the runway, the taillights disappearing
into the night.

Not a chance.

7

It was nine P.M., and Theo was working both sides of the big U-shaped bar. Even on a Sunday evening, Cy's Place oozed that certain vibe of a jazz-loving crowd. Creaky wood floors, redbrick walls, and high ceilings were the perfect bones for Theo's club in the heart of Miami's Coconut Grove. Art nouveau chandeliers cast just the right mood lighting. Crowded café tables fronted a small stage for live music.

Cy's Place was special in Jack's book. It was the club Theo had always dreamed of owning, and on these very barstools, at the grand opening, sparks had begun to fly for Jack and FBI agent Andie Henning. They'd talked and laughed till two A.M., listening to Theo's uncle Cy give them a taste of Miami's old Overtown Village through his saxophone. A few months later, on the second anniversary of Jack's thirty-ninth birthday, Jack had put a ring on her finger. More than a few pages had flipped on the calendar since then, and still no date for the wedding.

But that was another story.

"Nacho?" asked Theo as he set a heaping plateful on the bar in front of Jack.

"Thanks, man."

Jack was starving. Since "not guilty," he'd been paying the sole practitioner's price for a monthlong trial and countless missed deadlines. He'd caught a few hours of sleep after dropping Sydney at the airport and then headed to the office. Not until he smelled the nachos under his nose did he realize that he'd forgotten to eat since breakfast. He was snagging a fourth chip before Theo could get one.

"Dude, you took the *Bacon* nacho," said Theo.

"There's no bacon on these nachos."

"Not bacon, *Bacon*. It's the nacho that can't be touched without stealing the cheese from all the other nachos, the nacho that—in a weird, culinary, six-degrees-of-separation way—connects to every other nacho on the plate. The Kevin Bacon nacho."

"Sor-*ree*," Jack said as he put it back.

"You can't put it back!"

"What do you want me to do?" Jack asked, strands of gooey cheese hanging over the edges of his chip.

A thirsty customer at the other end of the bar signaled for two beers. Theo stepped away to serve him, carrying on loud enough for Jack to hear him say, "Can you believe that skinny piglet over there took my Bacon nacho?"

Jack's phone chimed with a text message. It was from the other half of the Sydney Bennett defense team. *Name of Sydney look-alike is Celeste Laramore*, Hannah's text read.

The victim's identity had been withheld since the attack. Jack texted back: *How do you know?*

Turn on F Corso. Dunno how she always gets it first.

The thought of more Shot Mom was enough to bring up his Bacon nacho, but he reached over the bar, grabbed the remote, and tuned to BNN. It was a split screen, with Faith Corso in the studio talking to a BNN reporter who was standing outside the lighted entrance to Jackson Memorial Hospital in Miami. Cy's Place was too noisy for Jack to hear, but the closed captioning sufficed. In fact, seeing the printed white letters scrawl against the black banner gave the word even greater impact.

COMA.

It felt like a punch in the chest. Suddenly, the closed captioning was garbling every other word. Jack reclaimed the remote and raised the volume. The TV was annoying to the couple seated next to him at the bar, but the TV was competing with crowd noise and music, and the report was wrapping up, so he begged their pardon and cranked it up.

Corso asked, "Is the young woman showing any signs of alertness?"

"Not to my knowledge," the reporter said. "As I said at the top of the report, this is late-breaking news. We are told that Celeste Laramore's parents arrived from out of town early this morning, but virtually no information had been released about the young woman's condition until just a few moments ago."

"What a horrible, horrible thing for those parents," said Corso. "Tell me this: Do we have any further information on who might have done this?"

"Faith, that is an equally startling part of this development. After BNN broke the news that she is, in fact, in a coma, I immediately followed up with contacts at Miami-Dade Police. While no one in the department is speaking on or off the record about a possible suspect in this attack, sources who would talk to BNN only on the condition of anonymity did provide a shocking insight into how Celeste Laramore ended up outside the women's detention center last night dressed like Sydney Bennett."

"Let me stop you there," said Corso, "and remind viewers that I spoke *exclusively* with Celeste's roommate on the air last night; she told me they had been at a Sydney Bennett look-alike contest on Miami Beach."

"Well, that story may be unraveling," said the reporter.

"What do you mean?"

The gleam in the journalist's eye gave Jack cause for concern. The reporter continued:

"BNN has learned that the defense team for Sydney Bennett may have actually *hired* Celeste as a decoy to distract the crowd. The plan, sources tell us, was for Sydney Bennett to slip away unnoticed while the media and the crowd focused their attention on the look-alike."

On screen, Faith Corso's mouth was agape. Jack nearly fell off his barstool.

Corso continued in a tone dripping with contempt: "That is the most cowardly and despicable ploy I have ever heard. The very idea of putting a college student in a situation like that just so Shot Mom could slip away off-camera and hop on an airplane to Fiji or Cancun or wherever she's hiding and sipping piña coladas while her lawyer hawks her book—well, that is just criminal in my mind."

"Yes, I would say that Sydney Bennett's lawyers will be facing some very tough questions in the coming day or two."

Corso broke for a commercial. Jack lowered the volume and apologized again to the couple seated next to him for the news intrusion. Seconds later his phone vibrated with an incoming call. He checked the number. It was the FBI—in a manner of speaking. It was Andie. The BNN reporter had been absolutely right: Sydney's lawyer *would* be facing some tough questions.

Jack stepped away from the bar and took his fiancée's call in the relative quiet of the back hallway that led to the restrooms.

"Hey, love. What's up?"

"I just got off the phone with Ben Laramore. He called here at the house."

"Laramore? I presume that would be . . ."

"Celeste Laramore's father. His daughter is at Jackson in a coma."

Jack collected himself, feeling for the family. "What does he want?"

"To talk to you. Man to man."

"When?"

"Tonight. He wants you to come to the hospital."

Jack sighed. "I guess I owe him that much."

"You're *not* going. This case is out of control. For all you know, the poor man is so distraught that he wants to shoot you dead."

"If that's what he wants, he'll find me sooner or

later. It's important to meet with him and tell him face-to-face that this story about hiring his daughter to be a decoy is nonsense."

"How do you know it's nonsense?"

"Because I didn't do it."

"How do you know someone else didn't? Like her parents, her brother, some old boyfriend?"

That guy who met Sydney at the airport.

Jack let a woman pass on her way to the restroom, then continued. "I need to tell Ben Laramore that *I* didn't do it. And I want to assure him that if somebody on my team was involved, I'll get to the bottom of it. That's the right thing to do."

"Fine. Then I'm coming with you."

"What?"

"Trust me. He'll respect you more if you show up with an FBI agent. Especially if she's your fiancée. And armed."

Jack could have pointed out that he'd done just fine as a lawyer for fifteen years without FBI protection, but he didn't argue.

"I'll pick you up in ten minutes," she said, then ended the call.

8

"Y ou should never have gotten involved in this case," said Andie.

They had made it all the way to the parking lot before she said it. Jack figured it was all the media trucks outside the hospital entrance that had finally triggered the told-you-so comment. It wasn't typical Andie.

Andie Henning was unlike any woman Jack had ever known, and not just because she worked undercover for the FBI. Jack loved that she wasn't afraid to cave dive in Florida's aquifer, that in her training at the FBI Academy she'd nailed a perfect score on one of the toughest shooting ranges in the world, that as a teenager she'd been a Junior Olympic mogul skier—something Jack hadn't even known about her until she'd rolled him out of bed one hot August morning and said, "Let's go skiing in Argentina." He loved the green eyes she got from her Anglo father and the raven-black hair from her Native American mother, a mix that made for such exotic beauty.

He hated when she tried to manage his career. "You're violating our agreement."

The "agreement" was for the sake of their relationship: Jack didn't question her undercover assignments; Andie didn't judge his clients.

"Sue me," she said.

The crowd outside the University of Miami Jackson Memorial Hospital was a fraction of the turnout for Shot Mom's release from jail, but it was still sizable. Hard-core Shot Mom haters had gathered in circles of support outside Jackson, keeping vigil and occasionally joining hands to pray for the full recovery of Celeste Laramore. It was just minutes before the eleven o'clock news broadcasts, and at least a dozen reporting teams were jockeying for position and preparing for live updates from the hospital.

"Better find another way in," said Jack.

Andie steered past the crowd at the main entrance and drove to the ER on the other side of the building. A pair of squad cars were positioned in the driveway, beacons flashing. Jack presumed they were there to redirect the vigil keepers and the media toward the main entrance so that the ER could actually deal with tonight's share of nearly a quarter-million visits annually. Andie found a parking spot, and they walked inside.

Jackson was Miami's premier public hospital, which meant that in addition to its stellar reputation for groundbreaking research in everything from cancer to spinal injury, it was also a workhorse for the world of Medicaid and no health insurance. The ER waiting room was a virtual cross-section of lower-income Miami. An old Haitian woman hung her head into a big plastic bucket that reeked of vomit. A homeless man with no legs slept in the wheelchair beside her. A single mother comforted a crying baby as her four other children played leap-frog on the floor, shouting at one another in Spanish. A drug addict in withdrawal paced back and forth across the waiting room, talking to himself. Anything less than a bullet to the head meant hour upon hour of waiting. Free treatment from some of the best doctors in the world was their consolation.

Jack started toward the admission desk to ask how to get to the intensive care unit, but Andie stopped him.

"I seriously doubt that Mr. Laramore wants you up there," she said. "Let me call and see if he wants to come down to meet us."

Andie moved to the other side of the waiting room, near the window, for better reception on her cell phone. Jack found an open chair facing the television, right beside a man with an ice pack on his knee who was cursing at the Marlins for blowing a three-run lead in the bottom of the ninth. The guy seemed eager to engage anyone who would listen to him, but Jack didn't bite. Jack was thinking about what, if anything, he could say to comfort the father of a young woman in a coma. Nothing came to him, but it wasn't for lack of effort. He was so deep in thought that he didn't hear Andie approach.

"I was wrong," said Andie.

Jack looked up. "Wrong?"

"Mr. Laramore *does* want you come up. In fact, he insists."

Jack considered that word—*insists*. That sounded

like someone who wanted Jack to see the damage
he'd inflicted. A strange feeling came over him, no
doubt akin to what his death row clients had felt
when the guard swung by to say, "It's time."

"Okay. Then I'll go up."

"You don't have to do this," said Andie.

"Yeah, I do," said Jack.

They got visitor badges from the registration
desk, and after a painfully slow elevator ride, the
doors finally parted at the fifth floor. Polished tile
floors glistened beneath bright fluorescent lighting,
and the after-hours quiet seemed only to enhance
an assault on the eyes that rivaled snow blindness.
The hallway led to a set of locked doors marked IN-
TENSIVE CARE UNIT. Jack identified himself over the
intercom, and a nurse's response crackled over the
speaker.

"Room six," she said, "but only one more visitor
can come in now. Maximum of three at a time."

Jack took that to mean that both parents were at
their daughter's bedside, which heightened his anxi-
ety. He'd been preparing to meet only Mr. Laramore. An angry father was one thing; a devastated
mother took it to an entirely different level.

Andie appeared to be on the verge of invoking
her law enforcement status to clear an exception to
the three-visitor limit, but Jack cut her off. "One at
a time is fine," he said into the intercom, but Andie
shot him a look that said it was not fine.

"The *mother's* in there," said Andie, her clear
implication being that an FBI agent who also happened to be a woman could only help the situation.
But this wasn't Andie's problem.

"Rules are rules," said Jack. "I got it from here."

He gave her a kiss and entered alone.

The door closed behind him, and the click of the lock gave him a little rush of adrenaline. The lighting inside the unit was much softer than in the hallway, and only the steady beep of patient monitors pierced the silence. In the center of the ICU was the nurses' station, an open island of charts and records surrounded on all sides by a wide corridor. Lining the outer perimeter were the glass-walled rooms for patients. Most patients were in open view, and the unit appeared to be full, but in some rooms the privacy curtains were drawn, so it was hard to know. Jack spotted several busy nurses making the medication rounds. As he rounded the corner to room six, there was no doubt in his mind that the man walking toward him was Celeste Laramore's father.

"Thank you for coming," the man said.

The warm and appreciative handshake surprised Jack, and he even wanted Jack to call him by his first name—Ben. Jack had braced himself for everything from bitter coldness to outright confrontation.

"It was the least I could do," said Jack.

Laramore was younger than Jack had expected, probably late forties. The stress was all over his face, however, and if this coma persisted, it required no crystal ball to see how quickly it would age him. Laramore glanced over his shoulder toward room six. The privacy curtain was drawn, so Jack was unable to see inside. It made his chest tighten to think of Mrs. Laramore in there with a comatose daughter.

Laramore said, "Let's go down to the lounge a minute, if you don't mind."

Jack followed him around to the other side of the unit, where there was a small room for visitors to catch a moment alone when needed. Laramore got them each a bottle of water from the vending machine, and they sat across from each other at a small table.

Laramore checked his watch. "Tomorrow already."

Jack noted the time on the microwave oven. It was three minutes past midnight.

"Exactly two weeks from today is Celeste's twenty-first birthday."

It was a painful place to start, but there was no easy route. Jack wasn't sure what to say, so he let him keep talking.

"They tell me someone in the crowd grabbed Celeste by the throat," he said. "She had no pulse by the time paramedics got to her. They were able to restart the heart with a defibrillator. But . . . uhm . . ."

"I heard," said Jack. "She's in a coma. You don't have to go into details."

Ben was face-to-face with Jack but looking past him, numbness and disbelief guiding his line of sight to the middle distance. "I spoke with three different neurologists this morning. Cardiologist came in after that. A pulmonologist is keeping an eye on her to see if she needs any assistance in breathing. Just before you got here, we met a gastro specialist about inserting a feeding tube, if it comes to that. Physical therapist is scheduled to come by twice a day to move her limbs." He paused, then took a deep breath.

Jack said, "They do have excellent doctors here."

"Yes, they do. But not a single one of them can tell us if Celeste will ever regain consciousness. If she does . . . well, it's just not clear if she'll be the same."

"I'm very sorry to hear that," said Jack.

Laramore drank from his water bottle, then shifted gears. "Do you know how much it costs per day for Celeste to stay here?"

"I can only imagine."

"No, you probably can't. No one can, until you land in the ICU with no health insurance."

"Celeste is uninsured?"

"She had student coverage through the university."

"Why wouldn't that pay for hospitalization?"

"It would, normally. But see, I got laid off last November. I worked for a plumbing subcontractor, mostly new construction. When the housing market tanked, Celeste took a part-time job to cover her tuition. What I didn't realize is that she cut her course load when she started working. She became a part-time student."

Jack could see where this was headed. "A part-time student isn't eligible for student health insurance."

"Nope. Like most twenty-year-old kids, I guess my daughter didn't really see a need. So she never told us she'd had to drop her student coverage. I found out this morning when I spoke with the insurance company."

Jack didn't know how to respond. "Are you sure there's no way around it?"

"The policy was canceled seven months ago. How do you get around that?"

Jack had no answer.

Laramore said, "But that's not what this is about."

Jack waited for him to explain what it *was* about, but silence hung between them. Jack suddenly was aware of the hum of fluorescent lights above them. It was getting awkward, so he spoke.

"When my fiancée told me that you called, I wasn't sure why you were reaching out to me. But I'm glad you did. One of the reasons I came here is to assure you that I didn't use your daughter as a decoy to get my client out of jail. Anything you may have heard in the news to the contrary is completely untrue."

"Jack, let me tell you something about myself: I don't believe *anything* I hear on BNN."

"That's helpful to know. But . . . I'm guessing that you didn't ask me here just to tell me that."

"No. I wanted you to know how much I love Celeste. And to tell you that her mother and I want to do everything possible for her."

"I understand."

"And we want your help."

"What can I do?"

He leaned into the table, leveling his gaze. "My wife and I want to sue the jail. Failure to provide adequate security and crowd control."

"That's what this is about? You want a lawyer?"

"Not that I went out looking for one. But today at lunch, a couple of attorneys tracked me down in the hospital cafeteria and said I should sue the Miami-Dade Department of Corrections."

Nothing like a twenty-year-old woman in a coma to bring out the ambulance chasers. "Real class acts," said Jack.

"Tell me about it. They want forty percent of whatever I recover. Plus fifty grand or more in costs."

"I hate the way they tracked you down, but that fee arrangement isn't just for sleazebags. It's fairly typical."

"That's what I understand. Which is why I called you. My wife and I were hoping that . . ."

"I would do it for less?"

"For free, actually."

"Free?"

"Look, we're hoping and praying for the best, but the doctors aren't exactly bursting with optimism. The hospital bill aside, what are we going to do if Celeste has long-term issues? We need every penny for Celeste's recovery."

"I'm sure."

"I mean, it's not like I'm trying to get rich off of this."

The allusion to blood money wasn't lost on Jack. "I don't question your motives. But a lawsuit is not a quick answer to anything."

"You got a better idea for a guy who's been out of work for eight months?"

"I know you're not a fan of BNN, but Faith Corso could actually be a force for good here."

"Did I just hear you correctly?"

"I know she abused me pretty badly, but I honestly think that a lot of her mean side on television is for effect. My bet is that she would be genuinely moved by the fact that you have no way to pay your daughter's medical bills. Her fans are in the millions—literally. I could see her making a plea for contributions."

Laramore shook his head, scoffing. "Funny. My brother-in-law had the same idea. He actually got through to one of the producers on the phone. A nice young woman who seemed willing to help. Pete ended up hanging up on her."

"Why?"

"Quid pro quo. BNN wanted the first photograph of Celeste in a coma."

Jack could barely fathom it, even for BNN.

Laramore said, "Truth is, even if Faith Corso stepped up to help, how long would that last? A week? We need a long-term solution. And we need a lawyer who isn't going to grab forty percent of it."

Jack read between the lines. Maybe the Laramores didn't believe the BNN reports about Jack having hired their daughter as a decoy, but implicit in the request that Jack work for free was the notion that Jack bore some responsibility for Celeste's injuries. Jack couldn't help but feel accused. Even Andie had made him at least consider the possibility that someone close to the defense team had put Celeste in danger.

How do you know someone else didn't do it? Her parents, her brother, some old boyfriend?

A nurse entered. "Mr. Laramore, your wife asked me to check on you."

He rose, alarmed. "Is something wrong with Celeste?"

"No, there's been no change there. Mrs. Laramore just seems to be having a moment. I think she needs you."

He glanced at Jack, who could only wonder how many of those "moments" were in the pipeline. "I should be going," said Jack.

"No, come with me. Please. There's someone I'd like you to meet."

"It sounds like your wife is upset. Maybe now isn't a good time."

"I meant my daughter. I want you to meet Celeste."

Jack hesitated, a bit embarrassed that the very idea of "meeting" someone in a coma had caught him so off guard. The man was so sincere, however, that Jack quickly got over it. "I'd be honored to meet her," said Jack.

Jack followed him out of the lounge and back into the ICU. As they walked in silence to room six, Jack could almost hear the growing weight of concern in a father's footfalls. The door was open, but they stopped before entering.

"Wait here for a sec," he told Jack.

Jack did so. Laramore entered alone, and although Jack couldn't make out the words, he could hear him speaking to his wife. A moment later he emerged and said, "Just so you know, Celeste's mother and I firmly believe that Celeste can hear us. So if you say anything, be positive."

Jack nodded and went inside.

Celeste's bed was slightly elevated, allowing her to rest comfortably in less than the full upright position. The soft lighting was soothing, though her eyes were closed. Fluids fed into her veins from

three different tubes that connected to a cluster of
clear sacks hanging from the IV pole. The blood
pressure cuff on her left bicep connected to a cardiac
monitor, which beeped to the rhythm of her heart.
An oxygen mask covered her nose and mouth. She
was not yet on a ventilator, but Jack quickly recalled
Mr. Laramore's mention that a pulmonologist had
come by to make that assessment.

Celeste's mother was seated in a chair at the bedside. Her skin tone was off, a clear indication of too
much stress and too little sleep, and her eyes were
puffy, undoubtedly from crying. She leaned closer
to her daughter and spoke in a gentle voice. "Celeste, there's a man here to see you. His name is
Jack."

Then she signaled him closer and added, "Jack is
going to help us. He's going to help us get the care
you need to get all better, baby."

It felt like a dagger to Jack, one that sliced through
his professional skin and laid bare his reluctance to
get involved.

He came forward, his gaze fixed on Celeste.
The blanket was chest high, and a few inches of
the striped hospital gown showed above it. At first
Jack didn't notice the bruising, but only because the
marks were so high up on her neck, right beneath
the jawbone, and the shadows obscured them. Jack
tried not to stare, but it pained him to see such telltale signs of the senseless attack.

Celeste's mother reached over and removed the
oxygen mask, and Jack felt his own breath slip away.

Her nose, the mouth, the beautiful young features framed by the chestnut hair—Jack didn't say a

word in front of her parents, but he was certain that it was written all over his face: The resemblance to Sydney was uncanny.

Jack glanced at Celeste's mother, and he sensed that it was time to leave. Ben Laramore was of like mind, and he guided Jack out into the hallway.

"Please give serious thought to what we talked about," he told Jack.

The nurse was right outside the room, and Jack was feeling the weighted stare from two pairs of eyes. There was no question that the nurse had recognized him as Sydney Bennett's lawyer. Jack had seen that look of contempt before.

"I will," said Jack. "I'll definitely think about it."

9

Jack thought about it—nearly all night long.

Of course he felt sorry for the Laramores, felt their pain for Celeste. A personal profit in the form of legal fees, even on contingency, would have made Jack public enemy number one in Faith Corso's war against blood money. The pro bono route would silence the critics, but taking on another case for no pay was no small commitment. Legal fees aside, the out-of-pocket cost of bringing a case like this to trial—experts, court reporters, investigators, and more—could easily push fifty grand. Probably more.

At six o'clock the bedroom began to brighten, hinting at a new day. Jack had a severe case of the Monday-morning blues. He was staring at the ceiling, having drifted in and out of sleep since retiring around one A.M. Andie was sound asleep, her head and torso on Jack's side of the bed, her legs and feet on hers. Andie's idea of sharing a mattress was a bit like their golden retriever's notion of sharing the couch. At least Andie didn't drool when she kissed him.

"Quiet, Max," he whispered.

Max was the most talkative dog Jack had ever known. Mornings especially. It was a throaty rumble that preceded the insertion of a big wet nose into Jack's ear and seemed to say, *I just love Andie's shoes—they're delicious!*

Jack snatched a slipper from Max's mouth and rolled out of bed quietly, careful not to wake Andie. Max happily followed him to the bathroom, the kitchen, the backyard for a pee—the dog, not Jack—and then back to the bedroom and into the walk-in closet. Weeks had passed since Jack and Max had started the week with a Monday-morning run to the beach and back. As Jack pulled on his cycling pants and shoes, Max was obviously fooled into thinking that today was the day when life returned to situation normal: Dogs rule. Jack hated to disappoint him, but he was cycling into work—a one-way trip, no dogs allowed.

"Sorry, pal," he said. "Andie will have to take you."

Max didn't understand a word of it, but he looked sad, and part of Jack imagined that it was because Andie could actually outrun Max.

Jack filled his water bottle, sneaked into the garage without Max, and hopped onto his eighteen-speed with the titanium frame. The touring bike had been a fortieth birthday present from a group of friends who swore they were just trying to save his knees from running. Jack wondered if they were trying to get him killed. Key Biscayne had bike trails—some of the most scenic in the world. But cycling just about anywhere else in Miami was the great battle of man versus automobile, where most drivers were of the mind-set that anyone with the audacity to enter the roadway on two wheels deserved swift and severe punishment. After several brushes with instant death, Jack attached an extra water-bottle carrier to the frame to hold an air horn. It was useless against true homicidal maniacs, but it would at least save him from the growing number of idiots who thought they could text and drive at the same time. Jack gave it a test blast before leaving the driveway. The ringing in his ears confirmed that it was still in working order.

By six thirty Jack was on his way. He didn't need to be in the office until after eight A.M., which meant that he had time to pedal over the bridge, onto the mainland, and into Coconut Grove for breakfast. He was a regular at Greenstreet's, a corner café on Main Street where an hour or so at an outdoor table beneath a shade umbrella could feel like a visit to the Left Bank. Jack made the mistake of checking his e-mails over coffee, and his quick breakfast turned into an hour of thumb exercises. It was after nine o'clock by the time he got back on the bicycle and reached his office. Central Grove had the canopy of a rain forest, and tucked behind a stand of oaks and royal poinciana trees that lined Main Highway was an eighty-year-old house with yellow siding and bright blue shutters. It didn't look like a law office, and that was what Jack liked about it. He carried the bike inside, along with his helmet and trusty air horn. His assistant was already at her desk and on the phone.

"Morning, Bonnie."

She hung up the telephone and glared in his direction. From the tense expression on her face, Jack might have guessed she'd been negotiating a hostage release.

"What's wrong?" he asked.

"What's wrong? You want to know what's *wrong*?"

The phone rang. Bonnie didn't flinch.

"Aren't you going to answer that?" he asked.

"No. You answer it."

Jack didn't know what was up, but he'd worked with Bonnie long enough to know that tone. He got it himself: "Swyteck and Associates."

"And associates?" the caller said. "Who in their right mind would *associate* with you, scumbag? *Scumbag, scumbag, you are a scum—*"

Jack hung up. Immediately, the phone rang again. He glanced at Bonnie, who breathed out through her nose with the force of a charging bull.

"Go right ahead," she said. "Answer it again."

He did. "Swyteck and—"

"How do you live with yourself, you disgusting piece of—"

Jack slammed down the phone.

Bonnie shot him a look of desperation. "This has been going on all morning," she said. "It's even worse than when the verdict was announced."

A third call. Jack answered and braced himself.

"This is blood money of the worst kind, you repulsive—"

Jack held the phone away, put the air horn to the mouthpiece, and gave it a five-second blast. Then he checked the line. The caller was gone.

"Here," he said, handing Bonnie the horn. "This ought to take care of it."

Bonnie took it and smiled. Jack wheeled his bicycle down the hall toward the back bedroom, then stopped when he heard Bonnie's phone ring in the other room—followed by a blast from the stadium air horn.

"It works!" she shouted.

She was actually using it, which made him chuckle. He checked the closet to make sure he had a business suit—charcoal gray would do—and then headed to the bathroom for a shower. Bonnie headed him off in the hallway, telephone in hand.

"It's Andie," she said, wincing apologetically. "She might be a little perturbed. I blasted her by accident."

"Oh, boy," said Jack. He stepped away and took the call in his office.

"Has Bonnie lost her mind?" said Andie. "She nearly busted my eardrum."

"Sorry," said Jack. "I really gotta get her to lay off the breakfast burritos."

"What?"

"Nothing. What's up?"

"Just—please tell me it's not true," said Andie.

Jack wadded up a stray Post-it and pitched it into the trash can. "Tell you what's not true?"

"I've heard this from a half dozen people already. Faith Corso was on one of the morning talk shows. Her latest 'exclusive' is that you went to Jackson last night and tried to talk the Laramore family into filing a lawsuit with you as the lead attorney."

"That's crazy."

"Is it? On our car ride home, you were awfully vague about what you and Mr. Laramore talked about."

"That's because an attorney's conversation with a prospective client is no less confidential than a conversation with an existing client."

"So it *is* true? You're going to be their lawyer?"

"No. I don't know. All I can tell you is that it didn't go down the way Corso is reporting it."

"Oh, my God. Jack, you can't be serious. You are actually trying to convince these poor people that they should sue BNN?"

"What?"

"That's what Corso's sources are saying—that you are cooking up a lawsuit against BNN for getting the crowd so whipped up that someone attacked a Sydney Bennett look-alike."

"Wait a second," said Jack. "First of all, I'm smart enough to know that no one has ever succeeded in suing the media for inciting some nut-job TV junkie to commit a violent act. Second, I could get disbarred for going to a hospital and trying to talk the victim's family into filing a lawsuit. I'm not an idiot."

"Faith Corso says you *are* an idiot and that you *will* be disbarred."

Jack gripped the phone, amazed that just ten hours earlier he had been trying to convince Ben Laramore that Corso had a good heart. "Very odd to me that Corso is the first journalist in the country to find out that I went to the hospital last night. And even more interesting that she presumes to know what Ben Laramore and I talked about."

"Are you saying the invitation from Mr. Laramore was a setup?"

"I'd hate to think so."

There was a blast of the horn from the other room. Bonnie was fighting off another attack on line two.

"But stranger things have happened," he said, as he got up to close the door.

10

·

Jack wanted to blow his brains out, which, generally speaking, is a predictable reaction to defending a client for seven hours in a deposition taken by the newest member of the Florida Bar.

At five o'clock he grabbed a cab back to the office to catch up on other work, hopefully something that would remind him why he had become a lawyer in the first place. Monday-evening traffic was even worse than usual, and it could have pushed him over the edge, had he let it get to him. Instead, he savored a random "Miami moment," finding amusement in the company name on the stalled landscaping truck that was blocking the road: *Jesus & Sons*. Jack wondered if the proprietor had ever read *The Da Vinci Code*.

Bonnie was still at the reception desk when Jack stepped through the door.

"Phone calls stopped yet?" Jack asked.

"What does this tell you?" she asked, then pressed the button on the air horn. It peeped, as spent and exhausted as she was.

"Maybe we should just stop answering the phone for the next day or so."

Bonnie reached all the way down to her New Jersey roots and shot him some attitude. "Brilliant, Jack. And if that doesn't work, we can put up the hurricane shutters, fly out to Vegas, and see if we win enough money to pay next month's rent. You can't run a law office that way. And if I ignore the landline, they'll call your cell."

Jack removed his tie and laid it aside. "That's already started. It was vibrating all day in the deposition from hell. Not sure how these people got my cell number."

"From the Web site."

"The BNN Web site?" asked Jack.

"Not directly," she said, "but it's kind of linked to it—'no-blood-money.com.'"

"You're kidding."

"Nope. Take a look."

Jack watched over her shoulder as Bonnie brought up the site on her screen. He was of course aware that blogging and other online chatter about the Sydney Bennett trial had been rampant. It was news to him, however, that in a matter of days the no-blood-money campaign had organized to the point of developing an official Web site.

Bonnie dragged her cursor to the About Us button. "The site manager is the same woman who started the Justice-for-Emma Web site when trial started."

The home page was a three-paneled display. On the left was the infamous photograph that the prosecutor had shown on a projection screen during her closing argument, a candid shot of Sydney dressed in a tight halter top and belting back a shot of tequila on the night of Emma's disappearance. On the right was a photo of Jack with links to daily coverage of the trial. The middle panel was for Latest Developments. The feature du jour was a prominent link to the BNN headline about Jack's alleged solicitation of the Laramore family, together with "a personal message" from "special guest blogger" Faith Corso: TELL JACK SWYTECK WHAT YOU THINK ABOUT HIM. CALL TODAY! NO BLOOD MONEY! Jack's office and cell phone numbers were in bold red letters.

A pop-up suddenly took over the screen. It looked like an advertisement for red wine.

"What the heck is that?" asked Jack.

"Monataque," said Bonnie.

"Mona-what?"

"*Mona-taque*. It's a juice they make from some exotic tropical berry. Sells for about forty dollars a bottle. It's supposed to be good for you. Cures acne. Hemorrhoids. Cancer. You name it."

"*That's* who's sponsoring the Web site?"

"Not directly. Monataque is one of those multi-level marketing programs."

"You mean a pyramid scheme?"

"Not all MLMs are pyramids. I sold cosmetics for two years and actually made some money. But to your point: From what I hear, Monataque is a classic pyramid. It's all about recruiting members at five hundred dollars a head, and ninety-nine percent of them never sell enough juice to earn it back. The husband and wife who run this Web site also happen to be one of Monataque's top recruiting teams."

"So the no-blood-money Web site is also a recruiting tool for snake-oil salesmen?"

"It takes all kinds, Jack. This is a grassroots movement."

"Yeah, and grass is green. Like money. I wonder how much the kickback to Faith Corso is."

Bonnie logged off, switched off the computer, and grabbed her purse. "I'm beat. I'll see you in the morning, chief."

Jack thanked her for slogging through a rough day, locked the door after her, and went back to his office. He kept more clean clothes at the office than at home, and as he changed out of his suit, the phone rang with eleven separate calls, each going to voice mail. On the twelfth, he pulled the cord from the jack.

The best therapy would have been to dive into his work and forget it, but the distractions had gotten to him, and after an hour of wasted time, he gave up. He'd managed to get through the Sydney Bennett trial without too much second-guessing, but now that the case was over, regrets were flooding in, some from the distant past. More than a decade had passed since his defense of Eddie Goss, a confessed sexual predator who stood accused of savaging a teenage girl. After the verdict, protesters had pelted him with exploding bags of animal blood on the courthouse steps—no subtlety in the blood-is-on-you symbolism. Bonnie had been there for him, pleaded with him not to resign from the Freedom Institute. But *State v. Goss* was the trial that had pushed Jack out of the world of defending the guilty, the most gut-wrenching, controversial case of his career.

Until this one.

Jack switched off the lights and locked up the office. It was just a few minutes past sunset, but the leafy canopy that provided shade by day made dusk seem like the dead of night. Riding his bicycle all the way back to Key Biscayne wasn't an option, the spent air horn being the least of his concerns. It was a recurring transportation problem that Jack solved once or twice a week by walking six blocks into the Grove for a beer at Cy's Place and catching a ride home from Theo. He shot Theo a text to let him know:

Need a ride tonight. Walking over now.

To his surprise, Theo actually responded: *Watch out for the boogeyman.*

It was funny, but it wasn't.

The asphalt trail was a familiar path, and in the darkness, he was able to avoid the biggest potholes and tree roots almost from memory. This was one of the safest stretches in Coconut Grove, where churches and synagogues butted up against some of the oldest and most prestigious private schools in Florida. Hundreds of schoolchildren made this walk every day, no problem. Preschoolers, hand in hand with a parent. Teenage girls dressed in the traditional plaid uniforms of Sacred Heart Academy. Ivy League hopefuls in their new Range Rover or BMW convertible. Some even arrived by boat on the waterfront side of the lush campuses. Five days a week, a mixed parade of innocence, wealth, and privilege—all without incident.

And every last one of them was on Cape Cod or in the Hamptons during the dead of Miami's summer, the Grove a virtual ghost town.

Stop it.

Jack kept walking, and he was about a quarter mile from Cy's Place when he noticed the sound of footsteps behind him. They had the rhythm of his own footfalls, seeming to match his pace and direction. He stopped, looked back, and said the first thing that came to mind—something a little less paranoid than *Is anyone out there?*

"Theo, are you messing with me?"

Nothing.

"Theo?"

A car passed, then more silence. Uncomfortable silence. Then another car passed, and in the glow of the headlights Jack spotted the orange reflective tape on the heels of a jogger across the street. She obviously had no problem being alone on Main Highway. It gave him a sense of relief, which quickly turned into anger at himself. *Main* Highway. Which fed into *Main* Street. This wasn't a side street or a back alley. He could almost hear Theo laughing at him as that text message replayed in his mind's eye:

Watch out for the boogeyman.

It was essentially the same thing Neil Goderich had told him right out of law school, when Jack had joined the Freedom Institute: Threats came with the turf. Over the years, Jack had gotten plenty of them from cops, clients, witnesses, and even the creepy anonymous source. Any criminal defense lawyer who couldn't handle a dose of intimidation needed to find a new career.

Still, as Jack reached the darkest part of the trail, he found himself walking faster. Streetlamps were of little help, their glow smothered by sprawling banyan trees on either side of the highway, the highest and longest limbs reaching across both lanes, as if to join hands. It was the lush, tropical version of a tunnel—one without lights. Jack had just passed the gated entrance to Ransom Everglades Upper School when, out of nowhere, it felt as if he'd been broadsided by an all-pro linebacker. The force sent him tumbling over the waist-high wall of coral rock that extended the full length of the trail. He landed facedown in the grass on the other side of the wall. The attacker was on him immediately.

"What the—"

Before Jack could finish his sentence, much less react, his hands were behind his back, a nylon loop closed around his wrists, and another loop joined his ankles. He was hog-tied, unable to move. The man rolled him over and grabbed Jack by the throat.

"Don't move, just listen," the man said.

The man's grip was atomic, the fingers of a mountain climber, and the pressure around Jack's neck made it difficult to focus on what he was saying. The thick, slurred speech didn't make things any clearer.

"Where is Sydney Bennett?"

Where ish Shyndy. It wasn't that he was drunk. He had something in his mouth—a wad of cotton or some spy toy to make his voice unrecognizable.

Jack could barely breathe, let alone talk. "I don't know where she—"

"Don't lie. If you lie, you die."

Jack was having trouble following even that simple line of logic. The pressure around his neck had his head pounding and lungs burning as he struggled to breathe. Jack couldn't see the man's face, couldn't see much of anything. His attacker, like everything else, was a blur.

"If you don't know where she is, then it's your job to find her for me."

"I don't—"

"Shut up!"

The grip tightened. The burning sensation in Jack's lungs was unbearable. A hint of blood flavored his mouth, the pressure somehow having triggered it. Jack fought for air, but his attacker was in complete control.

"You *are* going to lead me to Sydney," the man said, his hand like a vise around Jack's neck, the words slurring through the wads of cotton in his mouth. "If you don't, I promise you this: Someone you love will get what Sydney deserves."

The hand around Jack's throat rose higher on his neck and closed even tighter. Jack had one final burst of resistance left in his body, and then nothing more. The pounding in his head seemed to explode into his ears, and then the night went from black to blacker—to nothing.

11

·

It was Jack's second visit to a hospital in as many days. This time, he was the patient—in the emergency room.

"How do you feel?" asked Andie.

It was just the two of them in the small patient bay. A privacy curtain separated them from the buzz of activity that was the nerve center of Mercy Hospital's ER. The adjustable bed was in the upright position, forcing Jack to sit up.

"I'm totally fine," he said. "Can we get out of here, please?"

With all the tests they were running, Jack knew he wasn't leaving anytime soon. His visit to the ER was going on four hours, and Andie had been at his side almost that long. A security guard at the high school had found Jack in the bushes and called an ambulance. By the time paramedics arrived, Jack had regained consciousness, somewhat disoriented but lucid enough to realize that his attacker had removed the bindings before fleeing. His wrists and ankles were raw, however, red bracelets that confirmed his recollection. He'd already recounted the entire attack twice, once to the ER physician and again to Andie. He was tired of talking about it, tired of saying the name Sydney Bennett. He was especially tired of the neck brace.

"This thing has got to go," he said as he tugged at the Velcro.

"Leave it," said Andie.

Frustrated and exhausted, Jack let his head settle back into the pillow. The privacy curtain parted, and in walked a man who could have been straight out of an episode of *Law & Order.*

"Jorge Rivera," he said in a voice that was just right for a police station, a little loud for a patient with a throbbing head. "City of Miami Police."

The neck brace prevented Jack from turning his head, but he cut his eyes in Rivera's direction, then toward Andie, who explained what the detective was doing there.

"I called him," she said.

For a moment, Jack was speechless. "Andie, what if I didn't want to involve the police?"

Andie paused, her turn to be speechless. It was one of those patented disconnects in their relationship, as if Jack had asked, What if I wanted to paint myself blue and run naked through the ER?

She rose and shook Rivera's hand. "Thanks for coming."

"No problem." He said "no" like a cow, a long moo with an "n." From Jack's vantage point, the bovine analogy seemed to fit in more ways than one. He was a large man, undoubtedly muscle-bound in his younger years, simply thick in middle age. He

wore a necktie with the top button of his shirt unbuttoned, not to be casual but because the jowls
made it impossible to button it. Folds of skin on the
back of his neck led like steps to his crew-cut head.
He had a set of matching stairs on his forehead.

"I know you're hurtin'," said Rivera, "but I'll be
quick. I got most of what I need from Agent Henning's report."

Jack shot another look in Andie's direction—
more than just eye movement this time, despite the
neck brace. "You did a report?" he said, incredulous.

"Yes, I had to."

"No, you didn't *have* to. This isn't an FBI matter."

"You're wrong there, Jack. Your attacker threatened an FBI agent."

Someone you love will get what Sydney deserves.
Andie had probably filled in the blank correctly, but
other alarming possibilities came to mind.

"What about *Abuela*?" Jack said. "And my father?"

"Theo is spending the night at your grandmother's. I spoke to your father. It was three A.M. his time,
and he didn't seem particularly concerned."

Jack blinked, confused.

Andie said, "Your father and stepmother are va-
cationing in London. They're five hours ahead of
us. Six hours ago, your head was clear enough to
remember that."

Jack had completely forgotten, which told him
that he wasn't recovering from the attack as quickly
as he had thought. "I'll call them in the morning."

"Anyone else you want to call?" asked Rivera.

"Let me think a minute," said Jack. "My head's
a little cloudy, and I don't want to forget if there's

anyone else I should—oh, hell yes. Sydney's parents."

Rivera looked confused. "You put Sydney's parents in the category of 'someone you love'?"

"No, no," said Jack. "The threat wasn't just against me and my loved ones. This guy is out to do harm to the Bennetts' daughter—that's his ultimate objective. They need to be made aware of that."

Andie said, "I spoke to them. Neither one of them claims to have a clue where Sydney is."

"Do you believe them?" asked Jack.

"Actually, I do," said Andie. "Lord knows that if they were in touch with Sydney, we would have heard about it on BNN by now."

Jack sensed a hint of sarcasm. "Maybe I should follow up with them."

"No," said Andie. "They really don't want to hear from you."

"I'm not surprised," said Jack. The defense hadn't explicitly played the "abuse excuse" at trial, but they hadn't portrayed the Bennetts as model parents, either.

"I'll work that angle," said Andie. "For now, I made it clear that they need to call me if they hear from Sydney. My message to them was that Sydney didn't do anything illegal by going into hiding, but she could be doing something really stupid if she decides to come out of hiding."

"Oooo-kay," said Rivera, another moo. "My turn. Just a few questions for you, Mr. Swyteck." He removed a pen and notepad from his pocket, then started down his checklist.

"First, Agent Henning said you've been getting

threatening phone calls. Did any of those callers sound like the guy who attacked you?"

"No. First of all, the guy had some kind of voice distorter, like he had cotton or something in his mouth. But aside from that, every call I got was from a woman. You could ask my secretary if any of the calls she took were from men."

"Already did that," said Andie. "All women."

Rivera put a check mark on his list, then stumbled through a few generic questions that could have fit everything from a dog bite to a terrorist attack. He was rambling, almost as if stalling, which was annoying. Finally, a police photographer arrived, and Rivera got to the heart of the matter.

"Mind if I take a look at your neck?"

"Sorry, Dr. Henning here says I have to leave this contraption on."

Andie rolled her eyes and said, "I'll check with the doctor."

Rivera and the photographer discussed the shots they needed while Andie was away. Her quick return told Jack that she had definitely flashed her badge out there in the ER jungle. A doctor accompanied her. Jack had one of those feeling-old moments, struck by the way doctors seemed to get younger every time he needed one. This one looked like a teenager.

"I'm Dr. Cohen," she said as she removed the brace. "This won't hurt a bit."

"Ouch!" said Jack.

"As long as you don't turn your head," the doctor added.

The photographer moved in quickly for the shots they needed—straight on, side angles, close-ups.

"Keep your head just like that," Rivera told him.

Jack's chin was raised slightly, but with a little effort he was able to see what was going on at shoulder level. Rivera held an eight-by-ten photograph below Jack's chin for comparison. The tone of the discussion changed, as if Jack was no longer in the room, Rivera and Andie talking cop to cop.

Rivera said, "You see the bruising pattern that is emerging here, right along his carotid artery?"

"Definitely," said Andie.

"Now look at the photograph."

Andie paused, seeming to study it. "Bruising is virtually in the same spot," she said.

"Same spot as *who*?" asked Jack.

Andie touched his hand, as if to reassure. "Celeste Laramore."

Jack took a minute to absorb the comparison, but his skepticism bore out. "This is junk science, folks. Wouldn't anyone who gets choked have a bruise like mine?"

"No," said Rivera. "That's the interesting thing. I asked our medical examiner to take a look at Celeste Laramore's photos. He says the bruising pattern on her neck is more like a hanging, where the rope jerks up higher on the neck. It's the simple force of gravity, the weight of the body pulling the victim down. Choking someone with your bare hands tends to produce a bruising pattern much lower than this. Unless you were lifting them up by the neck."

"He didn't lift me up. I was on the ground."

"That's my point. No one saw Celeste Laramore's feet leave the ground, either."

"You're suggesting we had the same attacker?"

"It's an assumption based on the M.O."

"Strangulation?"

"More than that. It's *the way* he strangles his victim. He seems to be trying to simulate the effects of a hanging with his bare hands."

Jack gave it some thought. "Well, I don't necessarily agree that you can ascribe an M.O. to someone in a mob who reached out and grabbed Celeste Laramore by the throat. But for the sake of discussion, let's say you're on to something. Why would anyone try to simulate a hanging?"

The doctor spoke up. "Possibly to involve the carotid sinus."

"The what?" asked Jack.

"The carotid sinus is a dilatation of the lower end of the internal carotid artery," Dr. Cohen said, gently putting her hand to Jack's neck. "It functions as a baroreceptor, which is complicated, but basically it plays a key role in short-term blood pressure control."

The doctor no longer seemed like a teenager to Jack. "So . . . you're saying what? The carotid sinus comes into play in hanging but not in other forms of strangulation?"

"Not exactly. But there have been studies on this, partly out of morbid fascination with what actually causes death in a hanging, which isn't fully understood. It's safe to say that a hanging would more likely involve pressure above the carotid sinus—

like your injury. Other forms of manual strangulation might involve pressure on or below the carotid sinus."

"Above or below—what's the difference?" asked Jack.

"Pressure above the carotid sinus can interrupt parasympathetic pathways between the brain and heart, which can result in anything from fainting to instantaneous death."

"To coma," said Jack, thinking of Celeste Laramore.

"Yes. Coma is possible. Depending in part on the duration and force of the compression. Don't get me wrong. You can get the same end result with pressure on or below the carotid sinus. But there are researchers who posit that pressure above it—as in a hanging—is more, shall we say, efficient. Or maybe 'expedient' is the right word."

The doctor refastened Jack's neck brace, but Jack was watching Andie, almost able to feel her next question coming.

"Doctor," said Andie, "how difficult is it for someone to know how much force and compression are needed to achieve a specific result along the continuum you described?"

"Are you asking me if someone could learn how to squeeze a person's neck just long enough to make him pass out, how to apply enough pressure to make sure he's dead, how to stop just short of death and induce a coma?"

"Yeah, that's what I'm asking."

"Virtually impossible."

"Well, you're the doctor," said Jack. "But isn't

controlled deprivation of oxygen the whole idea behind erotic asphyxiation?"

Andie's mouth opened, but the words were on a few-second delay. "Not that he learned that from *me*."

The detective snickered. "Henning, I knew you had a wild side."

"No, no," Jack said nervously. "I wasn't implying . . . Actually, this was another woman I dated who used to like to—"

Jack stopped, frozen by a glare from his fiancée that said, *Way too much information.*

An awkward silence hung between them. Finally, the doctor bailed Jack out.

"Mr. Swyteck raises a good point," said Dr. Cohen. "The notion that oxygen deprivation is something you can manipulate with precision is a myth. Even when the participants know each other intimately, and the strangulation is intended only to enhance sexual gratification, mistakes happen. So you can only imagine what a guessing game it is when the victim is a stranger. There's absolutely no way to know how far you can push it without fatal results. Too many different variables come into play. One person's fainting episode is another person's cardiac arrest."

Jack was reluctant to say more on the subject, but it was worth pursuing. "There's always someone who *thinks* he's smart enough, who thinks he can play God and get whatever result he wants."

Andie picked up on Jack's point, apparently having forgiven his faux pas. "I see this in my criminal profiling. Predators with enough experience to fancy themselves experts on such matters."

The doctor considered it. "That would be one very sick human being."

Andie took Jack's hand, her eyes clouding with concern. "I've known a few of them."

Jack would have nodded, if not for the neck brace. "You and me both," he said.

12

.

Jack left the ER just after midnight. He could have walked out on his own power, but the nurse insisted that "hospital policy" required him to remain in a wheelchair until they were through the doors and were completely outside the building. It was standard procedure for patients who have experienced any loss of consciousness.

"And for lawyers," the nurse told him.

Jack did a double take.

"Kidding," she said, only half smiling.

Andie held his hand a little tighter than usual as they started toward the stairs, making sure he was stable. From the top step Jack could see all the way across the parking lot to the bay. Not many hospitals shared a breathtaking stretch of shoreline with some of the most expensive waterfront homes in Miami, and the sparkle of the moon on Biscayne Bay reminded him why, year after year, the *New Times* survey of south Florida attractions rated Mercy Hospital as "best view from a death bed." Jack stopped at the base of the stairs. A certain aspect of their conversation in the ER was weighing on his mind.

"Andie, when Dr. Cohen and I started talking about erotic asphyxiation—"

"Jack, let's not go there."

"Please. I want you to know—"

"I don't need to know anything about it. Really."

"But I don't want you to think that—"

"Jack, just stop."

"It's not that we were into strangling each other. She would just hang her head off the edge of the mattress when we—"

"La-la-la-la-la-la-la-la," she said with her hands over her ears. "I can't hear you."

A camera flashed. Jack turned so quickly that not even the neck brace could stop him from hurting himself. Another flash blinded him. His vision returned in time for him to see the photographer leap over a small hedge and jump into the passenger side of a car that was waiting at the curb with the motor running. The tires squealed as it sped away.

The color had drained from Andie's face. "Did we just get paparazzied?"

"Is that a word?"

"I don't care if it's a word or not," she said, then quickly lowered her voice so only Jack could hear. "Jack, I work undercover. The absolute last thing I need is for a magazine photograph of me to go viral over the Internet."

She'd just flagged the proverbial white elephant in their relationship. "Andie, it's not like I started working on this case yesterday. You knew how much media coverage it's gotten."

"I *knew* that my fiancé was attacked and ended up in the emergency room. I came to help you."

"And I love you for that. But this is why I didn't want to involve the police. No police report, no news coverage."

"Oh, so you're saying it's *my* fault because I called Detective Rivera?"

"No, that's not what I'm saying at all. Just, let's not overreact."

"Don't tell me I'm *overreacting*," she said, again realizing that she was too loud. She took it down a few decibels. "I'm not even allowed to have a Facebook page. How do you think the bureau is going to react when they see this?"

"See what? Some random guy snapped a picture. You're acting like he works for Associated Press."

"Sydney Bennett's lawyer is walking out of the emergency room at midnight wearing a neck brace. It doesn't take Pulitzer Prize credentials to sell that shot to Faith Corso. The woman will have an orgasm—with or without erotic asphyxiation."

Jack had no rebuttal, but he needed to do something about the negative energy between them. He took a feeble stab at humor. "Don't worry. Knowing BNN, they'll Photoshop you out of the picture and insert Sydney Bennett."

"That's not funny."

"You're right. It's not."

Andie breathed in and out, saying nothing.

Jack moved closer. "I'm sorry."

"I know you are."

"This will work out," he said. "We'll be fine."

Andie didn't answer.

"Let's go home," he said, taking her hand.

She didn't move.

"Andie?"

Her gaze was fixed on the sidewalk, no eye contact with Jack.

"Andie, say something."

Finally, their eyes met.

"I think I should stay at my place tonight," she said.

That put Jack back on his heels. They hadn't officially moved in together, but only because Andie's lease had yet to expire. Even Max had come to expect her on a daily basis and whimpered when she was away.

"That's not necessary," he said.

"It's the smart thing. You were exactly right: It's not like you started working on this case yesterday. I should have taken this precaution a long time ago. As it stands now it's just for a few days, until Sydney Bennett is completely behind you and the media coverage goes away."

"And what happens the next time I handle a high-profile trial?"

"I don't know."

"Really? You *don't know*? I thought we had talked about this."

"We did, but on a whole different level. A little bit of local media coverage is one thing. This case is in the news nationwide, twenty-four/seven. The problems are on a different scale for me. I need to step back and think."

"Step back? You mean from us?"

"No," she said, struggling. "Just, step back from . . . things."

Jack was having trouble seeing a difference, but her proposal didn't seem negotiable. "Okay then. We'll step back."

Andie dug her car keys from her purse. "I'll drive you home. I'm glad you're okay with this."

I'm glad you think I am.

"Sure," said Jack. "Perfectly okay."

13

Tennis anyone?" said Jack, grumbling. He was still in bed, too tired to fight off the fuzzy yellow ball that Max was trying to insert into his master's left eye socket.

"Max, down!"

In golden-speak, Jack's words translated to something along the lines of *Please hop your eighty-pound carcass right up here on the mattress and maul me until I take you outside.* Jack rolled out of bed before Max landed his battered body back in the emergency room.

Damn, I miss Andie.

He'd managed to be awake for all of thirty seconds before the thought crossed his mind. Not bad.

Jack stepped in front of the mirror and checked out the bruise on his neck. It was indeed high, like a hanging, just as Detective Rivera had pointed out. Whether it matched the bruising pattern on Celeste Laramore's neck was a question beyond Jack's pay grade. He'd be interested in the opinion of the forensic experts, which was simple enough to find out. All he had to do was call Andie and—

No. Give her space. Call Rivera.

A banging on the front door interrupted his thoughts. Jack knew only one person rude enough to come knocking so early in the morning, but then he checked the time and discovered how late it actually was: 11:09 A.M. The painkiller he'd taken before going to bed had knocked him out for ten hours. He pulled on a pair of jogging shorts and answered the door. His suspicion had been on the money; it was Theo.

"Dude, I been calling your cell for an hour. You all right?"

"Yeah, fine. I was just out of it."

Theo smiled. "Good drugs?"

"Mi vida," said Abuela. Jack's grandmother was a few steps behind Theo, shuffling through the open doorway as quickly as she could. *"Mi vida"*—literally "my life"—was what she always called Jack, what he meant to her. They embraced, and Jack tried to say something reassuring in her native tongue, which, as usual, he mangled. She winced and covered her ears.

"Ay. English, *por favor."*

Jack's Spanish was notoriously bad. The death of his Cuban American mother in childbirth left him "culturally challenged," a half-Cuban boy in a completely Anglo home with no link to his Hispanic heritage. Decades later, when Jack was in his thirties, Abuela had finally fled Cuba. For a time, her mission in life had been to give her gringo grandson a crash course in everything Cuban. He'd worked his way up to a C-minus before she'd virtually given up on making him fluent.

"Your neck!" said Abuela.

"It looks worse than it feels," Jack said.

"When you last eat?" Her English was only slightly better than Jack's Spanish.

"I don't remember."

Abuela shook her head and went to the kitchen. Keeping him fed was the one aspect of his cultural education that had not failed. Jack closed the door, and he and Theo sat in the living room while Abuela searched the cupboard for something that in her book even remotely qualified as "food."

"Thanks for staying with Abuela last night," said Jack.

"No problem. What's the plan going forward?"

"I don't know. We can't leave her exposed. The threat was against 'someone you love.'"

"And you assume that means Abuela, not me?" Theo said with a cheesy grin.

Jack ignored it. "I don't assume it's Abuela. We're just being cautious. Andie thinks the threat is directed at her."

Theo glanced around the place. "Where *is* Andie?"

"Work."

"Everything good between you two?"

"Yeah, fine."

Theo chuckled. "Liar, liar, pants on fire."

Jack was taken aback. "Did you talk to her?"

"Nah, I read the blog."

"The blog?"

"BNN: no-blood-money.com."

"Bonnie showed that to me. What are you reading that trash for?"

Theo shrugged. "I take my bodyguard role seriously. Gotta suck up all the information I can."

"That's even less reliable than Faith Corso."

"What are you talking about? It *is* Faith Corso."

"No, it's not. Bonnie showed me the site. Corso was just a guest blogger, and there was a link to BNN."

"Not anymore. Faith Corso's picture is all over it," Theo said as he retrieved it on his iPhone. "Look at the address: www.BNN/FaithCorso/no-blood-money.com."

"Corso must have liked it so much, she took it over."

"Anyway, this morning's front page is all about your ass-kicking."

"I didn't get my ass—"

"Dude, I saw the picture. Nice neck brace."

"Damn, I knew I should have taken that thing off."

"Wouldn't have mattered. Looks like the picture was taken inside the ER. Kind of grainy, like maybe a nurse or another patient snapped it with a cell phone from far away and then had to blow it up. Anyway, it's the other picture that's the money shot. You and Andie arguing outside the hospital. The caption says your fiancée dumped you."

Jack groaned.

"Clever headline, actually: 'Broken Neck, Broken Heart for Shot Mom's Lawyer.'"

"Oh, my God."

"Is it true?" asked Theo. "You and Andie, kaput?"

"No. Not exactly."

"What does 'not exactly' mean?"

"Andie isn't happy about the publicity this case is getting. She's afraid the bureau might rethink her role as an undercover agent. When some jackass jumped out of the bushes and snapped our picture last night, it sent her over the edge. We decided to separate for a few days until the hoopla blows over."

"Cool. So you're single?"

"No, I'm not single. This is temporary."

"Really? Do you mean 'temporary,' as in temporary custody of the children awarded to the mother, pending finalization of the divorce, which always means permanent? Or do you mean 'temporary,' as in temporarily laid off, which means permanent only ninety-nine percent of the time?"

"Why are you such a smart-ass?"

Jack heard his cell vibrating on the kitchen counter. He got up and checked it. The incoming number was unfamiliar at first, but something in the back of his mind made him realize that he'd seen it before. The text message confirmed his hunch. The sender was definitely no stranger.

"Something wrong?" asked Theo.

Jack cleared the look of surprise from his face. "It's from Rene," he said.

"Wha-a-at?" said Theo, chuckling. "See, dude, you *are* single. Man, word sure travels fast."

Rene had been Jack's most serious steady after his divorce—until Andie had come along. Jack had sometimes wondered "what might have been" between them if she hadn't been so geographically undesirable. The last time they'd talked, Rene was committed to Children First in West Africa.

"She works at Jackson now," said Jack.

"Yeah, so?"

"That's where Celeste Laramore is hospitalized."

"Interesting."

"Says she needs to talk to me about the Laramores." Jack glanced again at the message, then read aloud the last two words that Rene had typed in all caps. *"VERY IMPORTANT."*

14
.

Jack drove across town to meet Rene for coffee.
They were in agreement that the hospital was not the place to have a talk about the Laramores, but selecting an alternative had been surprisingly difficult, each trying to suggest a spot that was familiar enough to be findable, while at the same time avoiding a place with too many memories. They'd settled on San Lazaro's Café in Little Havana, close enough to Jackson for Rene to get away on her break, but far enough to ensure that none of the reporters on "coma watch" would happen by.

Jack found her at a booth in the back, near a sixty-year-old map of pre-Castro Cuba. She rose to greet him, and they exchanged an awkward air kiss that made them both smile.

"How you been?" he asked as they settled into the booth.

"Good, you?"

Rene signaled the waitress to bring another *café con leche* for Jack. Small talk abounded as they waited for the coffee to arrive. Memories flowed, too.

The first time Jack had laid eyes on Rene she had been covered with dust, like everything else in the grasslands of the Côte d'Ivoire when the Harmattan winds blew each autumn. She had been running a children's clinic in Korhogo, and over a light lunch that involved some kind of unidentifiable meat, Jack found himself captivated by a woman who fully understood why he had turned down the big bucks of private practice to work long hours for little pay at a place like the Freedom Institute. The next day, a stunning strawberry blonde sans dust showed up in a dilapidated Land Rover for a trip to the cocoa region, and Jack's tumble was complete. From then on, virtually every spare dime went to round-trip airfare between Abidjan and Miami.

Inevitably, geography took its toll.

The coffee arrived. As Jack stirred in a packet of raw sugar, Rene leaned closer, almost halfway across the table. A man less committed to his fiancée would have simply grabbed an eyeful of cleavage. Jack squirmed.

"You like my necklace?" she asked.

"Oh, your necklace." He took a closer look. It appeared to be made of copper, with a colorful bead. "Pretty. Looks like an African work of art."

"The Senufo people hold on to their traditional beliefs very strongly. When I left Korhogo, the juju priest blessed the necklace and presented it to me at a ceremony. Probably two hundred people showed up, lots of them former patients at the clinic."

"Nice."

"The glass bead is actually a gris-gris," said Rene. "Some people in this country associate that with voodoo, so the juju priest made mine teeny-tiny enough to wear on a necklace. Less conspicuous."

"Very thoughtful."

"In Côte d'Ivoire they say it brings good luck. Some even believe it's a form of birth control, but I'm not putting that one to the test."

"Good call," said Jack.

"So no jewelry for you?" she said, glancing at his naked ring finger. "I thought you'd be remarried by now."

The segue seemed rather calculated, and Jack wondered if she was playing dumb—if her out-of-the-blue text message had been prompted by the inaccurate reports that his engagement was off. *Broken neck, broken heart* . . .

"I'm engaged."

"Oh, I had no idea. Congratulations. Who's the lucky woman?"

He told her about Andie, though without so much as a hint at her undercover work. Even in the broadest of terms, however, the very concept of a criminal defense lawyer with plans to marry an FBI agent was sufficient to trigger the usual skepticism.

"Sounds like . . . a perfect match."

"Yeah. If there is such a thing."

She smiled, catching his drift. "Touché."

Rene had a great smile. All they needed now was for Andie to walk by like Adele, singing "Someone Like You."

Never mind, I'll find . . . It was time to shift gears—fast.

"You still in pediatrics?" he asked, knowing it was a dumb question.

"Of course. That's what brought me in touch with the Laramore family. Celeste's primary physician back in Tennessee is still her pediatrician."

Jack felt another twinge of pain for the family. The fact that she was still young enough for a pediatrician underscored the tragedy.

"Are you one of her treating physicians?"

"No. But one of my colleagues is on the team."

"So you two share information?"

She averted her eyes, and Jack still knew her well enough to read her apprehension. "Look, Rene. I appreciate your reaching out to me. But I don't want you to breach any confidences."

"No, this is totally on the up and up."

"You look uncomfortable."

"It's a little complicated. His name is Dr. Ross. Stefan Ross. We've been seeing each other for about two months now."

"Got the picture. Two pediatricians at the same hospital date each other. Naturally, you share information."

"We talk. If I look uncomfortable, it's because Stefan probably didn't expect me to pass this bit of information along to the Laramore family."

"Like I said, if you're breaking a patient confidence—"

"No," she said, interrupting. "Just the opposite. Trust me, there's already a buzz about this at the hospital. This is something that Celeste's family should know. Something their lawyer *needs* to know."

"I'm not their lawyer yet. I'm considering it."

"After you hear what I have to say, you'll want to be their lawyer."

"If you put it that way, I'm all ears."

"Just, please don't ever attribute this to me."

"Understood."

She shifted in her seat, as if building up her nerve. Then she let it fly: "Celeste Laramore should not be in a coma."

Jack allowed her words to hang for a moment, the impact growing. "Exactly what are you trying to tell me?"

"Let me put a finer point on it," she said. "If it weren't for BNN, she wouldn't be in a coma."

Jack measured his response, trying to be polite. "Rene, I appreciate your concern for the family. But I have no intention of filing yet another frivolous lawsuit against a media giant whose television program allegedly provoked some loser to commit a violent act. Those claims just don't cut it."

"I hear you," she said. "And clearly, Faith Corso was talking about a claim along those lines when she broke the news that the Laramore family was considering a lawsuit against BNN."

"I'm aware of that report," he said, stating the obvious. "But I can't talk to you about what the family is considering."

"I understand. I didn't come here to find out what's under consideration. I'm here to tell you what you *should* consider."

"Fair enough."

"I don't think it was a coincidence that BNN was the first to report that the Laramore family is planning to sue them. They know what they did wrong. Faith Corso just got out in front of the story, trying to obscure the fact that the cause and effect is much tighter than anyone would ever suspect. Much clearer than BNN would like anyone to believe."

"Meaning what, exactly?"

Rene leaned closer, folding her hands atop the table, locking eyes with Jack. "Meaning that in both a medical and legal sense, BNN is directly responsible for what happened to Celeste Laramore."

"That's easy to say. But proving in a courtroom that BNN was the legal cause of Celeste's coma is the Achilles' heel in the case."

"I didn't say it would be a breeze. But I can help you prove it."

"How?"

Her eyes narrowed, her stare tightening. "Do you think a television network could have a problem if its news-gathering tactics interfere with a hospital's ability to treat an injured patient?"

"Possibly," said Jack. "It might depend on what those tactics are."

"Fair point," she said. "But listen to what I'm saying, Jack. Because this time, BNN went *way* too far."

15

.

Jack reached Cy's Place in time to catch the 7:10 P.M. start of the Marlins' game on TV. Theo wanted to hear all about his meeting with Rene. Jack gave him next to nothing, sharing instead nearly everything else he'd done since. An hour wasted at the courthouse on a calendar call. Another hour driving Abuela to a friend's house for the night so she wouldn't be alone. A useless follow-up with Detective Rivera, who was still without leads on Jack's attacker. A phone call to Andie.

"Andie who?" said Theo.

"Very funny," said Jack.

The conversation seemed to stick on Andie, mostly Jack's doing, which prompted Theo to render more pithy advice on "temporary" versus "permanent"—pop psychology on the order of Charlie Brown, Lucy, and "THE DOCTOR IS IN." A lonely customer a couple of stools away overheard and joined in.

"I know the feeling," he said as he loosened his tie. He had out-of-towner written all over him, a businessman who had wandered over from one of the Grove hotels. "Just got divorced myself."

Jack nodded but said nothing, wanting no part of that conversation. Theo overrode him.

"Okay, I'll bite," said Theo. "What's your story, pal?"

He leaned closer, resting one elbow on the bar, as if he were about to divulge the secret formula for Coca-Cola. "My wife called me a wimp."

Jack blinked, not quite comprehending. "You divorced your wife for *that*?"

"No. She divorced *me*. And you know why?"

Jack had an inkling, but it was Theo who said what they were both thinking.

"Because you *are* a wimp?"

"No," he said, smiling awkwardly, not sure it was a joke. "I had knee surgery. Torn ACL. Hurt like you wouldn't believe. Did I get even one minute of sympathy from my wife? Hell, no. All I ever heard from her was that I don't know what pain is because I've never had a baby."

"She has a point," said Jack.

"No, you're both wrong. Just because I've never felt that kind of pain doesn't mean I'm not in pain. That's like saying I've never had the pleasure of sex because I've never had sex with a porn star."

"You told her that?"

"Damn right."

"So, lemme get this straight: You made a point about pain that disrespects women by drawing an analogy to sex that totally disrespects women. Is that basically the picture?"

The man fell silent, searching for a response. Finding none, he slapped a ten-dollar bill on the bar and walked away, muttering something to the effect of, "Everybody takes that bitch's side."

Theo cleared away the empty beer glass. "I was wrong."

"About what?"

"What I said at your house this morning. About you being single. You're sounding more married all the time."

"You agree with that guy?"

"I'm just saying."

Theo brought him a fresh bowl of mixed nuts. Jack cherry-picked the cashews and the almonds while watching the Marlins load the bases but fail to score in the bottom of the first inning. His cell rang during the commercial break, and he practically fell off his stool as he reached for it, hoping it was Andie. It wasn't.

"Guess who."

He recognized Sydney's voice in an instant. Jack closed out the bar noise with a finger to his ear. "Where are you?"

"None of your business."

The threat from his attacker was still fresh in Jack's brain: *Tell me where Sydney is or . . .*

"Actually, it is my business."

"Jack, I need help, and I can't talk long, so please just listen to me."

The reception was poor, and the bar noise didn't help. Jack hurried to the exit and found a quiet spot on the sidewalk beside a five-foot-tall fiberglass peacock. The extra few seconds was time enough for him to think better of responding to her jab in kind. "All right, I'm listening," he said.

"I need to know if you really are the lawyer for the Laramore family."

"They asked me to represent them. I haven't made a decision yet."

"Faith Corso said you're planning to sue BNN. Is that true?"

"If I agree to be their lawyer, that decision will be between the Laramore family and me."

"You *are* going to sue BNN, aren't you?"

"Sydney, even if I end up not taking their case, my conversations with the Laramores are still privileged. I can't talk about this."

There was a brief silence, but Jack suspected that Mount Sydney was on the verge of eruption. Her response was at least an octave above shrill: "How could you do this to me?"

"It's not about *you*, Sydney."

"Yes, it is! It's me who people turn on their TVs to watch, not you. I'm the one people talk about. I even had an agent pick me up in his airplane."

"Right. And how did that work out for you?"

"It's been hell, okay? Complete hell. I'm done with him."

"What a shock."

"Stop treating me like I'm some kind of joke. The fact is, we were *this close* to a seven-figure deal with Cornerstone Publishers."

"Sydney, every agent in America is on the verge of a million-dollar deal."

"This is real, damn it. But you are making it

almost impossible for me to hold this thing together."

"Me?" he said, scoffing.

"Connect the dots, Jack. Cornerstone is owned by *BNN*. Without an agent, what do you think my chances are of salvaging this deal if my lawyer hauls off and *sues* BNN? It will blow up everything. You are going to kill my deal!"

"That's really not my concern."

"I deserve this, Jack. Don't take this away from me!"

Jack's personal experience with spoiled brats in general was limited, and the fact that some attacker had nearly choked him to death demanding to know Sydney's whereabouts didn't make it any easier to handle this one. "Is this really why you called, Sydney? To whine about your million-dollar book deal?"

"This is important!"

"It's more important for me to know where you are."

"I can't tell you that."

"Then we have nothing more to talk about."

"No, please!"

"When you're willing to tell me where you are, we can talk."

"You're not listening to me!"

"Good luck with your book."

"Good luck?" she said. "I don't even have an agent. What am I supposed to do now, huh? What am I supposed to do, Jack?"

"Grow up," he said, ending the call.

There was a pit in Jack's stomach. Part of it was the possibility, however remote, that some publisher actually would pay a million dollars to keep the Shot

Mom express rolling along. More troubling, however, was the realization that he probably needed Sydney's cooperation if the police were going to find the sick puppy whose idea of a proper introduction was to grab people by the throat and send them to the ER.

Jack started back into Cy's Place, then stopped. The meeting with Rene was just a few hours old, and Jack hadn't made a decision one way or the other about the Laramores; in fact, he had promised himself that he would sleep on it. But if what Rene had told him was true, if the meddling of an overzealous BNN reporter had kept Celeste from getting the immediate medical treatment she'd needed, the case might actually be winnable.

Every Goliath had its David.

The feeling inside him continued to grow. "Winnable" might be pushing it. But the case could have serious settlement value. And the overly altruistic notion that he was the world's pro bono clinic needed to stop. He was a sole practitioner, not Mother Teresa, and he was engaged to marry a woman who was even more underpaid than Jack Swyteck, P.A. He would just have to work out a modified fee arrangement that was fair to him and the Laramores. It might actually make up for the financial hit he took defending Sydney Bennett.

To say that Sydney's call had pushed him off the fence might have been overstatement. But there was definitely something to be said for helping people who wanted to be helped, who didn't go out of their way to prove that they were beyond help. It was one of those moments when he wished his old friend

Neil were still alive, when he would have liked to pick up the phone say, "Neil, we got a job to do." His daughter Hannah wasn't a bad second choice. Jack still had her number on speed dial from Sydney's trial. She answered with a cheery "hello" on the second ring.

"Hannah, hey. Can you meet me at the institute in an hour?"

"Sure. What's cookin', good lookin'?"

That was one of the corny expressions she'd inherited from her father, which brought a little smile to Jack's face.

"Partner, you and I got a complaint to draft."

16

Jack and Hannah spent most of the night drafting the complaint against BNN. A phone call to Ben Laramore had triggered the green light. Jack had been more than reasonable in his proposed contingency fee. The suit against the Department of Corrections would have to proceed on a separate track, since suing a state agency in Florida had special prefiling procedures and notice requirements. Jack also needed time to investigate and determine if the detention center had done anything wrong. The plan was to file and serve BNN on Thursday. A quick settlement was a long shot, but BNN's lawyers agreed to a prefiling conference at the company headquarters on Wednesday at four o'clock.

"Hotter in New York than Miami," said Jack.

He wasn't kidding. Jack could see the heat rising from the sidewalk as they stepped out of the cab on Sixth Avenue. Miami had its humidity, but temperatures never even got close to the afternoon highs of a mid-July heat wave in Midtown Manhattan. Three gold letters on a black marble facade—BNN—told them they were outside the right building. An air-conditioned lobby beckoned, and Hannah nearly had to trot to keep up with Jack as they crossed the busy sidewalk and approached the revolving door.

"What are the odds we walk out of here with a check?" she asked.

"Somewhere between Sydney Bennett getting nominated to the Supreme Court and Faith Corso giving up on calling me Sly-teck." It had been Corso's name for him ever since learning that his surname rhymed with "Sky-tech."

The lobby wasn't as cool as Jack had expected, and he dabbed away the sweat on his forehead as they signed the visitors' register. A security guard led them past the bank of common elevators that served floors two through forty-nine. The ride to the penthouse was an express. The chrome doors parted, and a receptionist who could have made the cover of *Vogue* greeted them by name.

"This way, please," she said.

They followed her across the two-story lobby, the receptionist's five-inch heels clicking on the parquet floor of maple and mahogany. The view of Central Park was one of the most impressive Jack had ever seen, and he imagined that Hannah was doing her level best not to act like a bumpkin and snap a photo with her iPhone. The view quickly got worse, as they were led down a hallway lined with photographs of BNN's top news personalities. Faith Corso was the most prominent, staring straight at them from the focal point of the "T" in the intersection of hallways.

"Here we are," the receptionist said, but she

tripped as she reached for the door handle, nearly falling off her five-inch heels.

Subtly, so only Jack could see, Hannah rolled her eyes. Hannah was four feet eleven, always wore flats, and loved the look on people's faces when they discovered that the shortest person in the room was also the most tenacious.

"My bad," said the receptionist. She gathered herself and opened the heavy door to the main conference room.

A team of lawyers—three men and three women—was already seated at a long, polished table made of burled walnut. As if on cue, all six checked their watches as Jack and Hannah entered the room. Jack was familiar with the big-firm power play of making the plaintiff's lawyer wait around for half an hour or more before defense counsel deigned to show up. This was the flip side: making the opposition feel as though they've kept everyone waiting, forcing them to start the meeting with an apology for being late—a position of weakness—even though they were right on time.

"Sorry y'all were early," said Jack, refusing to play into their strategy.

The lawyer with the most gray in his hair rose and shook Jack's hand. Stanley Mills was BNN's general counsel and vice president of legal affairs. A round of introductions revealed that the most junior lawyer at the table was one of nineteen attorneys who worked in-house under Mills. The remaining lawyers on BNN's side of the table were outside counsel from the Wall Street law firm of Marston & Qualls. Jack recognized one of them: Ted Gaines, routinely rated

as one of the top trial lawyers in the country by
American Lawyer magazine, famous for closing arguments that resonated with the rhythm of a Baptist
revival. Mills thanked Jack and Hannah for coming
and showed his guests a seat on the opposite side of
the long, rectangular table. But it quickly became
clear that Gaines was running the show.

"Got your love letter," said Gaines as he tossed a
copy of the ten-page complaint on the table. It didn't
land flat, and it lay there exactly the way Gaines had
intended: like a dirty napkin.

Jack looked at it, then at Gaines. "It's not a love
letter," he said dryly.

"Right, right. Even love letters are more grounded
in reality than this piece of work." Gaines glanced at
the junior lawyer at the end of the table. "Shannon,
lights, please."

The room darkened. A projection screen lowered
from a slot in the ceiling, and a beam of light from a
projector shot from the opposite wall. Gaines pulled
a remote control from his pocket and brought up
the first slide of his presentation: *Laramore v. Breaking News Network*.

Gaines paused. "Pardon me if this comes across
as condescending, Mr. Swyteck. But I think it's important that we put this in terms you can understand."

The lawyers in his peanut gallery smirked.
Gaines continued.

"Let's start with the allegations of your complaint
that we can agree on," he said as slide number two
flashed on the screen. It summarized several para-
graphs from the complaint.

"'On July eleven at approximately two A.M., a nine-one-one operator dispatched an ambulance to Miami-Dade County Women's Detention Center in response to a report that a young woman had been injured in the parking lot. At approximately two thirteen A.M., paramedics from Jackson Memorial Hospital arrived on the scene and immediately began treatment of the young woman, later identified as Celeste Laramore. At approximately two twenty A.M., the patient was placed in an ambulance and taken to Jackson Memorial Hospital.'" Gaines paused and said, "So far, so good. Unfortunately, that's about all we agree on."

Gaines moved to the next slide. "In the interest of brevity I'm going to move quickly through my main points of contention, so try to follow along.

"Paragraph twelve: 'At approximately two twenty-two A.M.—just two minutes after Celeste Laramore was placed in the ambulance—BNN reported that the patient was unconscious and in V-fib.' Slight disagreement there," said Gaines. "It was actually two twenty-one A.M. One minute after loading her in the ambulance. Nobody denies that BNN gets it fast."

The peanut gallery smirked again. Gaines moved to the next slide. "Our remaining points of disagreement are not so benign. Paragraph thirteen: 'Upon information and belief, plaintiff alleges that BNN co-opted information about Ms. Laramore's medical condition through surreptitious and illegal means. Specifically, BNN (or someone acting on BNN's behalf) intercepted critical and confidential patient data as it was transmitted by paramedics from the moving ambulance to doctors at Jackson Memorial Hospital.' Hogwash. Next.

"Paragraph fourteen: 'BNN's illegal interception of Ms. Laramore's patient data interfered with the paramedics' transmission of real-time information to emergency room physicians. As a result, the ER physicians never received the intercepted transmission, and they were unable to prescribe real-time measures to the paramedics that would have addressed the patient's life-threatening condition.' More hogwash. Next.

"Paragraph fifteen: 'Plaintiff further alleges . . .'" Gaines stopped. "You know what? I'm already tired of this. Lights, please."

The junior attorney jumped from her chair and switched on the lights. Gaines returned to his seat and cast his most intimidating glare across the table, directly at Jack.

"In plain English, this is a bullshit lawsuit, Mr. Swyteck. I don't know where you came up with your '*information* and *belief*,' but pulling allegations out of your ass won't cut it in a court of law. The only kernel of truth here is that ninety seconds after the ambulance pulled away from the scene, BNN was the first news organization to report that Celeste Laramore was unconscious and in cardiac arrest. BNN gathered those details the way it always gets its information: nose-to-the-grindstone, feet-on-the-ground, tireless reporting.

"Now, I fully understand that Faith Corso said some harsh things about you during the trial of Sydney Bennett, and I'm sure you'd love to nail Faith and her network. But—"

"This isn't personal," said Jack.

"Noooo," Gaines said, his voice dripping with sarcasm, "of course it isn't."

Jack leaned into the table, returning the stare. "This meeting wasn't my idea. My clients asked me to arrange it. They're reasonable people. Their hope was that you would be reasonable, too. It's clear they were wrong."

"What did you expect us to do? Roll over?"

"I would have expected you to tell me not to come if this was the way you intended to treat us. Let's go, Hannah." They rose and started for the door.

"Swyteck," said Gaines.

Jack stopped and turned.

"I've done all the talking for the team today," said Gaines. "But with me at this table are some of the best lawyers in the country. Trust me. On so many levels, this is a fight you don't want to pick."

"Too late," said Jack. "Hannah really wants to kick your ass."

Hannah did a quick double take, then for some reason felt the need to speak. "Yeah, I'm gonna kick your—"

Jack silenced her with a sideways glance. He opened the door, and they started down the hall to the elevator.

Hannah spoke through her teeth. "Did I just sound like a sixteen-year-old girl in there?"

"Fifteen," said Jack.

"Oy vey."

Jack pushed the call button for the elevator. "We're cool," he said.

17

Jackson Memorial Hospital is virtually around
the corner from Miami International Airport,
right on the way home for Jack. His flight from La-
Guardia was a few minutes late, but the Laramores
were at their daughter's side around the clock. Jack
made a quick stop to give Ben Laramore a flavor of
how the meeting with BNN's lawyers had gone.

"We've got a battle on our hands," said Jack.

They were at a table in the ground-floor cafeteria, which had stopped serving for the night and was
a few minutes from closing. Most of the chairs were
upturned and resting on the dining tables, out of
the way for a floor mopping. Only one other table
was occupied, an intern on her cell phone.

"Is there any hope of a quick settlement?" asked
Laramore.

"It's going to take more than filing a complaint
to bring them to the bargaining table. We need to
push the case forward, take some depositions. Even
then, this could be one of those cases that doesn't
settle until the eve of trial, if it settles at all."

"Then we need to push the case to trial. Fast."

"We'll push, but civil suits don't typically move quickly. Realistically, the soonest we can expect that judge to set the case for trial would be six to eight months from now, and we can pretty much bank on at least one continuance. Probably a year or more, when all is said and done."

"A *year*?" Ben said, running his hand through his hair. The worry lines in his face seemed carved in wax, each day taking a toll. Laramore dug an envelope from his pocket and handed it to Jack. "I can't wait a year."

Jack checked inside. It was a hospital expense report. "Ninety-two hundred dollars," said Jack, reading the bottom line aloud.

"That's just for *today*. No insurance. Virginia doesn't work. I'm a laid-off plumber. Whoever strangled my daughter is still out there, and I can't even afford to post a security guard outside the door. I asked for daily printouts, just so I can keep a handle on expenses, but what's the point? How are we supposed to pay for *this*?"

"First off, I wouldn't worry about a guard. This happened only because her attacker thought she was Sydney, and even if for some reason he comes after Celeste now, he has to get past the cameras, security guards, locked doors, and all the other restrictions on access to the ICU. But the bills . . ." Jack paused, searching his mind for some way to help. "I'm no expert in this field, but I believe that if we can get Social Security to determine that Celeste qualifies for disability income, Medicaid will cover her hospitalization."

Laramore shook his head. "I've already had that

conversation with the hospital. This place deals with brain injury every day. They know the ins and outs of these programs. To be eligible for Social Security, you have to be totally disabled for a full year."

"There has to be an exception for a patient in a coma."

"There's not. The problem is that no doctor can tell the Social Security Administration when Celeste will recover or what her recovery will look like. She could be in a coma a year or more and end up totally disabled. Or, God willing, she could snap out of it tomorrow and be just fine."

Jack could hear it in Ben's voice—the fear that each passing day made the chances of "just fine" all the more remote.

"I'll do some research. If not disability, maybe there's another way to qualify Celeste without bankrupting you and your wife."

"I spent over two hours with a hospital administrator today. She truly wanted to help, but we simply fall through the cracks in the system. Even if Virginia and I could qualify our family for Medicaid, we couldn't get Celeste covered as our child because she's over the age of nineteen. And Celeste can't apply for Medicaid on her own because she has no kids and is under age sixty-five."

Jack took another moment to think. "When my grandfather was in a nursing home, I read about something called the medically needy program. It's for people who don't strictly qualify for Medicaid. It may be worth looking into."

"Let's be real, Jack. Most Medicaid programs in this country are on life support themselves. How long do you think the state of Florida is going to pay for us to keep Celeste on life support?"

"We have to be prepared to fight day to day."

"I appreciate your intentions. But each day Celeste spends in a coma, the pressure to pull the plug is going to build. I want to give my daughter a fighting chance. I don't want a bunch of bean counters telling me it's time to give up hope. BNN caused this mess. They should at least pay the hospital bills to fix it."

"That's part of our claim."

"But we can't wait for trial. Our only real hope is for you to find the magic bullet that brings those bastards to their knees."

No pressure.

"I'll do my best," said Jack. "Step one is to file the complaint as soon as the court opens tomorrow."

"What about suing the Department of Corrections, like I asked about in the first place? Maybe they'd be quicker to settle."

"That's actually more complicated. You can't just sue a state agency in Florida. We have to give the department written notice of our claim. We're working on that now. The department has six months to respond before we can even file suit."

"*Six months?* I can't believe this." Laramore's cell rang. Jack heard one side of the conversation, which lasted only a few seconds, ending with Laramore telling the caller that he was in the cafeteria.

"UPS," Laramore told Jack. "Got a delivery for me."

"At eleven o'clock at night?"

A man approached, interrupting. "Mr. Laramore?"

"Yes."

The man wasn't wearing a UPS uniform and

wasn't even dressed in brown. "This is for you," he said as he handed him a packet. He left quickly, without asking for a signature.

Jack said, "That was a process server if I ever saw one."

"Am I being sued?" Laramore asked, opening the packet. He handed it to Jack, who read it quickly.

"It's a temporary restraining order," said Jack.

"What does that mean?"

"It means that while I was in New York meeting with BNN's lawyers, another team of lawyers for BNN went before a judge in Miami and got him to enter an order against you, your wife, and me."

"Don't we get to present our side of the story?"

"It's called an ex parte order. It's not an easy thing to get, but sometimes judges will enter orders without notice to the other side."

"An order to do what?"

Jack found the operative language in the order. "It requires us to file our complaint against BNN under seal, meaning that it won't be part of the public record. And it forbids us from discussing the allegations publicly. Essentially, it's a gag order."

"They convinced a judge to issue a gag order *before* we even filed our lawsuit? What kind of system is this?"

Jack considered the question, which strangely echoed public sentiment since the Sydney Bennett verdict.

"This can work to our advantage," said Jack.

"How?"

"Right out of the blocks, BNN's lawyers have overplayed their hand. And I intend to make them pay."

Laramore's cell rang a second time. Again, Jack got a one-sided perspective on the conversation, but this time he could tell who was on the line: Celeste's mother.

Laramore ended the call and put his phone away. "I need to go back upstairs," he told Jack. "Virginia could use some company."

"I understand. I'll call you in the morning," said Jack.

They shook hands. Laramore went to the elevators, and Jack stopped in the men's room. He was actually hungry enough to eat hospital food, had the cafeteria been open. On the way out, he stopped at the vending machines for a granola bar.

"Hey, stranger."

Jack turned at the familiar voice. Rene had popped into the vending room after him.

"Hi," said Jack. "You working tonight?"

She dropped a few coins into the soda machine. "Yup. You?"

"No. Well, I was. Working. Not for the hospital. Law stuff. You know."

She grabbed her diet soda and smiled. "You're cute when you're tongue-tied. I'm off at midnight."

"Rene, I told you, I'm enga—"

She laughed. "Got ya. You are such an easy target. Stefan is picking me up in an hour. I'd ask you to join us, but you look really tired. Plus, Stefan's not really into that stuff."

Jack was a half beat behind her.

"Got ya again, Swyteck. This is way too easy." She popped open her soda and gave him a wink. "I'll see you around."

As she headed out, a folded yellow Post-it fell from her pocket to the floor. Jack was about to say something, but he quickly realized that the drop had been intentional. He opened it and read.

Can't talk here. There's more. 2 P.M. tomorrow. Same place.

"More" obviously meant about Celeste Laramore. "Same place" was the coffee shop in Little Havana. Jack tucked the note away and headed for the exit.

Things had been quiet outside the hospital when he'd arrived, but the eleven o'clock news had since started, and "coma watch" had returned for the obligatory live update. The media presence was nothing compared to what it had been earlier in the week. Tonight it was down to a handful of news vans. Tomorrow was sure to bring an uptick in coverage with the filing of the lawsuit against BNN—or not, with a gag order in place. Jack hurried out the door and down the sidewalk before anyone could recognize him. He chose the long route through the parking lot, trying not to walk so fast that he might draw attention to himself. He took a modicum of satisfaction in getting all the way to his car without having a single microphone thrust in his face. He found his key and was aiming in the dark at the ignition when his phone rang. It was an unknown number, but he answered anyway.

"I heard your conversation with Sydney," the caller said.

It was that thick, disguised voice again—Jack's attacker, the man with cotton in his mouth. "You're eavesdropping on my cell?"

"Does that really surprise you? How else would

I have known that I could find you walking down Main Highway to Cy's Place Monday night? Remember that text to your buddy Theo?"

Need a ride tonight. Walking over now.

"Nothing surprises me anymore," said Jack. "What do you want?"

"There's been a change in our arrangement."

Jack massaged between the eyes, staving off a massive headache. "There is no arrangement."

"Relax and listen. This is all good. See, now that I heard you and the party slut talk, I believe you. You really don't know where she is."

"That's what I told you from the beginning."

"No worries. Just a little glitch. We can work around this."

"I'm not interested in working anything out."

"Sydney won't just walk away from a book and movie deal. She'll call you again. Especially after that lawsuit is filed tomorrow against BNN."

"How do you know about—"

"I know these things, Jack. When she calls, I want you to insist on meeting her face-to-face."

"No."

"Don't tell me *no*. You know what happens if you don't do your part."

Jack said nothing, but he remembered the threat well: *Someone you love will get what Sydney deserves.*

"We're a team, Jack. We'll find her."

The call ended, and the light from Jack's keypad faded, leaving him alone in the dark.

18

Jack met Andie the following morning in Miami Gardens, a short ride away from the FBI's Miami field office. Andie didn't want a meeting at the office. Over the years, Jack had done legal work for the St. Thomas University Center for Justice and Peace, and he'd spent enough time on campus to remember that the coffee at the book center was drinkable. They each grabbed a cup and a bagel and walked across the parking lot to the baseball diamond, where a travel team was practicing. Alone in the bleachers behind home plate, they could talk freely.

Jack had left a message for Andie immediately after the call from his attacker. It had taken another phone call and two text messages to get a callback, which told him either that she was really mad at him, or that something big was in the works.

"I'm going undercover again," she said.

Something big—which explained her hypersensitivity about the publicity over the Sydney Bennett case. But it didn't rule out the possibility that she was also mad.

"When?" he asked.

"You know I can't tell you that. But soon."

The *ping* of an aluminum bat sounded on the other side of the batting cage. The baseball team was fielding ground balls. Jack watched, working on a chewy bagel. He was reluctant to ask, but he needed to know.

"Is this in response to the threat?"

Andie seemed put off by the insinuation. "Are you asking if I'm going undercover to run away from the man who attacked you?"

Hearing Andie rephrase it made the question sound insulting. "Sorry," said Jack. "I asked only because you were the one who immediately thought that the threat against 'someone you love' meant you."

"It has nothing to do with that. This assignment has been in the works for months."

Jack's attention turned briefly to the infielders, then back to Andie. "So . . . where does this leave us?"

"We'll be fine," she said.

He smiled a little. "Does that mean I'm off the FBI's ten most *unwanted* list?"

She returned the smile, more with her eyes. "You're such a goofball. Yes, you're off the list. Or at least out of the top ten."

"So you still love me?"

She gave him a little kiss. "Yes, I love you. Even though I was right."

Jack knew it wouldn't be simple. "Right about what?"

"That photograph of us walking out of the emergency room. It took less than eight hours for it to show up on the Internet."

"True. But you're barely recognizable. Obviously, the bureau doesn't think it's an issue if they're sending you back undercover."

"We got lucky. This time."

Jack drank his coffee, watched the infielders turn a double play. There was more to sort out. "Who will be my contact at the FBI when you go undercover? It's clear I haven't heard the last from this guy."

"Until I'm reassigned, the contact is still me. Then it will be up to the assistant special agent in charge. Depending on how this plays out in the short term, it's possible that the bureau will defer to local police. In that case, you would follow up with Detective Rivera."

"Rivera?" Jack said, uneasy. "I'm not so keen on that guy."

"He has an excellent reputation."

"Do you agree with him? Celeste and I were victims of the same attacker?"

"Yes. Our forensic experts were already leaning that way based on the comparison of your photos to her bruises. Last night's call removes all doubt. He attacked Celeste thinking she was Sydney. Now he's after you to get to Sydney."

"What's the plan when he calls me again?"

"I wish you would listen to me and let us tap your phone."

"I'm not going down that road. Mr. Shake-Hands-with-My-Throat has already hacked into my old phone."

"What do you mean your 'old' phone?"

"I'm picking up a new one in an hour. I'll text you the new number."

"And exactly what is your plan to stop this guy from hacking into your new phone?"

"I'm meeting with a spyware expert to sort that out."

"You're going to pay a private spyware expert instead of trusting me?"

"It's not a matter of trusting you. Just on general principle, a criminal defense lawyer doesn't need the FBI checking out his address book and examining his call history, let alone tapping his phone conversations."

"Well, you've already had one trip to the emergency room. Maybe you should reconsider."

"I might if you were the only one involved. But I'm not going to share my line with any old agent in the FBI. And I'm definitely not sharing it with Detective Rivera."

"I told you, Rivera's a good guy."

"Call it defense lawyer's intuition. He's got an ax to grind. He doesn't even return my phone calls."

Andie dug her cell from her purse. "I'll take care of that right now," she said, dialing.

"Don't," said Jack, but it was too late. Andie already had the detective on the line. Jack heard one side of the conversation as she gave Rivera the FBI lecture on the importance of communication with victims. A minute later, she put the phone on speaker and laid it on the bleacher seat between them. "Rivera has an update," she told Jack. "Go ahead, Detective."

"I had a very interesting heart-to-heart with Celeste's friend this morning," said Rivera, his voice a bit tinny on the speaker.

"You mean Celeste's roommate?" asked Andie.

"Yeah. The girl who went to the detention center with her on the night of Sydney Bennett's release. Her story has completely unraveled."

"How so?"

"She told Faith Corso on the air that she and Celeste had just come from a Sydney Bennett lookalike contest at Club Vertigo on South Beach. We called the club manager. It turns out that the contest was canceled. Never happened."

Jack and Andie exchanged glances. Andie followed up with the detective: "Why would she lie about that?"

"She was covering for her friend," said Rivera.

"Covering up what?" asked Andie.

"It took me a while to get it out of her, but she finally admitted it this morning. Despite all the accusations that BNN reporters were making things up, it turns out that somebody did, in fact, hire Celeste Laramore to go to the women's detention center that night."

"Hire her—why?" asked Andie.

"Celeste's friend doesn't know why," said Rivera, "but it's at least plausible that it's just like BNN reported it. Celeste got paid a thousand bucks to show up and make people think she was Sydney Bennett. She was a diversion to stir things up and draw the crowd's attention so that Sydney could slip away."

"That's just not true," said Jack.

Andie gestured, telling Jack to stay out of it. Then

she put another question to Rivera: "Did Celeste's friend tell you who put up the money?"

"She doesn't know, and we're still trying to find out. Mr. Swyteck, you got any ideas?"

"I told you it's not true," said Jack.

"Don't get defensive," said Rivera. "I didn't accuse you. I asked if you had any idea who might have done it."

Again, Jack's first thought was the man who had met Sydney at Opa-locka Executive Airport. But he still didn't trust Rivera. "No, I don't have any leads," said Jack.

"Well, if any names come to mind, you be sure to let us know."

"Will do," Jack said.

Rivera had to take another call, so Andie thanked him and hung up. Jack was thinking about his case against BNN, but even his best poker face couldn't stop Andie from reading his mind.

"You already told the Laramores that you would take their case, didn't you?" Her question sounded more like a statement.

"Yes, I did."

"You seriously plan to sue BNN?"

"Yup."

Andie tucked her phone into her purse, then gave him a troubled look. "You *like* the publicity, don't you?"

"What do you mean?"

She glanced toward the playing field, as if measuring her words, then looked right at Jack. "When we got engaged, you weren't such a publicity hound. Tell me what's going on?"

"Andie, this isn't about the publicity."

"Don't kid yourself. If it weren't about the publicity, you would have done the legwork, just like Rivera did. You would have talked to Celeste Laramore's friend and realized that this is not a good case."

"Hannah did call her. She wouldn't talk to us."

"Didn't that tell you something?"

"Yeah, it tells me I need to file a lawsuit so I can get a subpoena issued and take her deposition. That truth is, it doesn't matter if Celeste was hired to be a Sydney Bennett look-alike. The fact that she voluntarily put herself into an angry crowd might be an issue if we sue the correctional facility for providing inadequate security, but it doesn't excuse what BNN did to her after she got hurt."

"Exactly what did BNN do?"

"I can't get into details. The judge issued a gag order before we could even file the complaint—which should only prove to you that I'm not doing this case for the publicity."

"Fine. It's not about publicity. The real issue—like *always*—is the clients you choose to represent."

"Are you comparing Celeste Laramore to accused criminals now?"

"No. But Celeste obviously has something to hide. Don't you think you should know her secrets before you haul off and file a lawsuit against one of the biggest media companies in the world?"

"You're not hearing me, Andie. For purposes of our claim against BNN, it wouldn't matter if Celeste Laramore had gone to that parking lot to set the building on fire and steal a getaway car. Once she got hurt, BNN had no right to interfere with her getting the medical treatment she needed."

"Well, you're the lawyer. But this can't help your case."

"There's no such thing as a perfect client. Unless you're a probate lawyer."

"I just don't want you to end up looking foolish."

"If I tried to unravel every surprise before filing a lawsuit, I'd never file a lawsuit."

"I'm not talking about *every* surprise. Damn it, Jack. Do you think it's fun for me to turn on the television and watch the commentators make fun of you? I've never told you this, but every time Faith Corso blasts you, I get e-mails from other agents. The last one came from the head of our public-corruption unit and said something like 'Looks like "MISTER Andie Henning" stepped in it again.'"

"Cop humor," said Jack. "Lovely."

"Fine. Dismiss it. But I don't see why you can't at least check this out before you file."

Jack was already committed to the case, but there was no need to be a cowboy, even when trying to help a twenty-year-old college student in a coma. This was going to be a very public fight, and a little more sensitivity to the impact on the people in his life wasn't too much for Andie to ask. "All right. It can't hurt to make one more run at Celeste's roommate before the complaint is filed," he said as he dialed Hannah's number.

"You're suing BNN *today*?"

"And Faith Corso."

"Oh, my God," Andie said, groaning.

Hannah was on the line. She was riding in an open convertible, yelling into her cell above the wind noise, which forced Jack to hold the phone a comfortable distance from his ear, even if it did mean that Andie could overhear. "I was just about to call you with an update," Hannah shouted.

"Has the complaint been filed yet?" asked Jack.

"Yessiree. Filed under seal this morning at nine-oh-five. BNN was served at nine thirty."

Jack was silent.

"Jack?" said Hannah. "Are you there?"

"Yeah, I'm here."

"Is everything okay?"

Jack looked at Andie. The glare she shot back at him could have melted steel. Professionally speaking, he was perfectly fine with letting the lawsuit go forward. The question was how to deal with the personal reality that his fiancée clearly wasn't.

"Yeah," Jack said into the phone. "Everything is just dandy."

19
.

Jack took an afternoon ride into Little Havana.

Every available minute after his meeting with Andie had been devoted to legal work for paying clients, but at two P.M. he had a follow-up with Rene, who had promised there was more to the case against BNN. He needed all the ammunition he could get. He took Theo with him, knowing that if he was to stay off the FBI's "unwanted" list, there should be no more one-on-one meetings with old girlfriends.

Theo drove with his usual disregard for speed limits. They reached San Lazaro's Café fifteen minutes ahead of schedule and grabbed the same table that Jack and Rene had shared, the old map of Cuba right behind Jack's head. Theo ordered a double espresso. Jack's adrenaline was already pumping, no need for any more caffeine.

"Where's Bejucal?" asked Theo, studying the map on the wall.

Bejucal was the birthplace of Jack's mother. He turned and pointed. "Right outside Havana. I'm impressed you remembered it."

"Got a history lesson from Abuela the night you were in the emergency room."

"Really. How did that come up?"

"Mostly her carrying on about how the threat against 'someone you love' couldn't possibly mean her." Theo put on a sad face, speaking in Abuela's broken English. "Jack no call me. He no visit. *Mi vida* no love me no more."

"Oh, for Pete's sake. I call her every day."

Theo chuckled as he stirred a pack of sugar into his cup. Jack loosened his tie, reached inside his collar, and massaged his neck. The bruises were fading, but it still hurt at times.

"You packin' a Glock these days?" said Theo.

"No."

"I am. Just give me the word, dude. I'll find that guy and give him a lot more than a pain in the neck."

"You're kidding, right?"

"Sort of."

"I'm leaving things to the FBI. For the time being, anyway. But now that you mention it, there is someone I need to track down."

"Who?"

"This morning I found out that someone actually *did* hire Celeste Laramore to show up at the detention center looking like Sydney."

"No shit?"

"Totally serious. I spoke to Ben Laramore on the phone over the lunch hour, and he fully believes that it wasn't me who hired her. But we agreed that we need to find out who did. I was thinking you could maybe help with that."

"You want me to interview a girl in a coma?"

"No, moron."

"Cuz I can do it, you know. Had many a conversation with your ex-wife."

"Low blow, Theo. There was a guy who flew out of Opa-locka with Sydney. You got any contacts over there?"

"Opa-locka," Theo said, searching. "A buddy of mine got arrested flying in there from the Bahamas with about two kilos of—"

"That's not the kind of contact I'm talking about."

"Actually, it is, dude. Lobo—that's what we call him. It means 'wolf.'"

"I know what it means. I speak some Spanish."

"Not according to your grandmother."

"Will you back off, please?"

"Anyway, Lobo took the rap himself, refused to cut a deal and testify against a half dozen dudes who worked in baggage. They love him. Even better, they owe him."

"Could be promising," said Jack. "See what you can find out."

"No problem."

Jack checked his watch. Ten minutes past two. "Hope I'm not being stood up."

Theo was actually quiet for a minute or two, which Jack savored. Until his cell rang. It was his new iPhone—he'd cut himself loose from the old one and its spyware over the lunch hour—so he almost didn't recognize the ring tone. But he did immediately recognize the incoming number. It wasn't entirely rational, but the mere sight of it made Jack feel like a cheater.

"It's Andie," he said.

Theo snorted so hard he nearly coughed up his espresso.

"Quiet," Jack said, and he answered. "Hey, sweetheart. How are you?"

"Thank God you answered," she said, her voice filled with urgency. "Where are you?"

"Little Havana. Having coffee. Just me and Theo." Literally true, but the obvious omission made him feel even more like a cheater.

"Get in the car and meet me at the medical examiner's office."

"What's wrong?"

"Listen to me. Don't stop anywhere or for anyone on the way."

"Did something happen to Celeste?"

"Don't even stop at traffic lights if you can avoid them."

"Damn it! I didn't think she needed a guard so long as she was in the ICU."

"Jack, I don't care if this is your new phone, that's all I can say on your line."

Of course it was. Nothing short of surrendering his privacy to the FBI would make an FBI agent trust the security of his phone lines.

"Just go!" said Andie.

"Right," he said. "I'm on my way."

20
.

The medical examiner's office is in the Joseph H. Davis Center for Forensic Pathology, a three-building complex on the perimeter of the University of Miami Medical Center campus and Jackson Memorial Hospital. Typical for midafternoon, the campus was bustling with activity, people headed to the spine institute, the eye institute, and other world-class specialists. Theo nearly flattened a line of them as his car sped through the crosswalk and into the parking lot, only to lose a race with an SUV for what seemed like the last remaining parking spot in Miami-Dade County. Theo jumped out of his car and threatened to pick up and physically remove the two-thousand-pound intruder that had taken the parking space that was rightfully his. Jack didn't have time to mediate the argument. He jumped out and ran to the main entrance. The guard buzzed him in, and Jack hurried across the lobby to reception.

"I'm here to meet Agent Andie Henning," he said, winded from the run. "Jack Swyteck's my name."

"Wait here, please. I'll let the doctor know."

Jack was tempted to burst through the locked door to find Andie himself, but he didn't need B&E charges added to his list of troubles. There was a couch in the waiting room, but he was too wired to sit. He dug his cell phone from his pocket. He'd been trying to reach Ben Laramore since leaving the coffee shop. He dialed again. Same result. No answer. It probably didn't help that the phone number flashing on Laramore's display screen was Jack's new number, as yet unknown to Ben. Jack had told him not to answer any calls from strange numbers, as it might be the media—or worse.

Jack took a seat and caught his breath. A trip to the medical examiner's office wasn't exactly a daily occurrence for a criminal defense lawyer, not even for one who defended death row inmates. It had nonetheless been only a matter of weeks since Jack's most recent visit; it was on the eve of Sydney Bennett's trial.

Jack had vehemently opposed the disinterment of Emma Bennett's remains, but the prosecution had convinced the judge to overrule his objection. It was "regrettable but necessary," the judge had stated in his ruling. As of that pretrial stage of the case, the defense had offered nothing in the way of scientific evidence to counter the prosecution's theory: that Emma Bennett's late-night crying was simply too much for a party-minded mother who didn't get home from the clubs until after one A.M.; that Emma's grandmother had refused to babysit past two A.M.; and that in a drunken fit of rage, Sydney Bennett had snapped sometime before dawn, yanked her crying two-year-old child out of bed, and slapped or suffocated her into a state of unconsciousness, only to wake the next morning and find Emma not breathing. In the judge's view, the state had demonstrated a "compelling need" to reexamine the body in order to counter the defendant's eleventh-hour change of position—Sydney's newly minted claim as to the "real" cause and manner of Emma's death.

Jack's ensuing visit to the medical examiner's office was one that he would never forget.

Torrents of icy air gushed from the air-conditioning vents in the ceiling, making the autopsy room so cold that Jack almost had to remind himself that he was still in Florida. Bright lights glistened off the white sterile walls and buffed tile floors. Jack watched through the discerning eyes of a criminal defense lawyer as an assistant medical examiner led him to the small mound beneath a white sheet on a stainless steel table. Dr. Hugo Flynn, a pathologist, was waiting beside the table. Flynn was the expert witness for the defense.

"I think you'll find this very interesting," said Dr. Flynn.

The assistant stepped aside to observe from a distance, far enough away so that Jack and Dr. Flynn could talk without being overheard by a government employee. Flynn adjusted the spotlight and took hold of the corner of the sheet.

"Now, be forewarned," he told Jack. "As you know, the body was hidden in the Everglades before it was discovered and given a proper burial. According to the autopsy report, there were no internal organs, very little of the shell of the torso remaining. Much of that was lost to predators. We are now adding to that the natural effects of almost three years of decomposition in the grave."

"So . . . what remains?"

"Bones. Hair. Teeth."

He pulled back the lower corner of the sheet. Dr. Flynn's powers of concentration were such that his bushy gray eyebrows had pinched together and formed one continuous caterpillar that stretched across his brow. Whatever he was examining did not even resemble a human body part to Jack, which made him uneasy. The fact that these remains were those of a child made it that much worse.

"What do you see?" asked Jack.

The doctor took a step back and sighed deeply. "The first thing you have to understand," said Dr. Flynn, "is that even when the corpse is fresh, drowning cannot be proven by autopsy. It is a diagnosis of exclusion, based on the circumstances of death."

"Emma Bennett's death has some pretty vague circumstances."

"Yes, it does. And her remains are indeed minimal."

"So in your process of diagnosis by exclusion, what does that tell you, Doctor?"

"Not much. There is really not enough for me to rule out every other possible cause of death. But we do have something to hang our hat on."

The doctor laid his iPad on the table and motioned Jack toward him. The image on the screen was right next to the actual remains—to what appeared to be the bones of a small foot.

"This photograph is from the autopsy report," said Flynn. "It's the right foot, the remains of which you see here on the table. Do you see this?" asked Flynn, adjusting the size of the image on the screen.

"I see it, but I don't really know what I'm looking at."

"As I mentioned, the lungs and internal organs decomposed or were eaten by scavengers while the body lay in the weeds. But as of the time of this photograph, the bottom of one foot was relatively well preserved. The extremities are away from the internal organs, slower decomposition."

"I still don't know what I'm supposed to see."

"This photograph shows a rough patch of skin on the bottom of her right foot. And I believe that those striations," Flynn said as he zoomed the image, "are abrasions."

"Caused by what?"

"That's where my professional opinion comes in. To me, that's a sign of drowning."

"I'm not following you," said Jack.

"Abrasions of this sort can be a critically important fact if you think about what happens when you drown. Your normal reaction when the head goes underwater is to hold your breath. Eventually, you can't do it any longer, and your body is forced to gasp for air. That presents a major problem if you can't reach the surface."

"Or if you panic."

"Exactly. The victim starts gulping water into the mouth and throat, literally inhaling water into the lungs. This, of course, sends the victim into an even more frenzied panic, and the struggle becomes more desperate. If she doesn't break the surface, her lungs continue to fill, struggling and gasping in a vicious cycle that can last several minutes, until breathing stops."

"And these abrasions tell you what?"

"Again, the final moments of a drowning are utter terror and panic. The victim may sink and propel herself up from the bottom in the struggle. Her legs may be churning. The feet come in contact with whatever surface is below. If the surface is rough, her feet will show abrasions."

"But Sydney's version of events is that Emma drowned in the family swimming pool. That's a smooth surface."

"No, it's not. You're thinking of the standard white or colored plaster surfacing, which is smooth, almost slippery. The Bennett family pool has a textured, nonslip surface. My neighbors have the same thing. My kids come home with raw feet every time they swim over there. Multiply that by a factor of a thousand when a child is struggling for her life, not merely playing around in the pool."

Jack focused his gaze on the remains, then on the photograph.

Dr. Flynn asked, "Are you okay?"

"Yeah," said Jack. "I'm fine."

What he wanted to say was that he was embarrassed for a moment, put off by the way his job made him stand beside the remains of a child, put all emotion aside, and slap on a label like "death by drowning."

"That's where your examination leads? Death by drowning?"

The doctor nodded once, but firmly. "It would be nice if we had lungs or some other body tissue to examine for traces of chlorine from the pool water, but we don't. The medical examiner didn't even have that three years ago, when the body was recovered. So, yes: Based on what remains, it is my expert opinion that the abrasions on the bottom of her feet as shown in the autopsy photos are consistent with death by drowning. Nothing I see in these remains contradicts that opinion."

"Abrasions. That's really all you got?"

"That's more than you got now."

The doctor had him there. "How soon can you get a written report for us?" asked Jack.

"A week. The cost of that is included in my retainer. But you should know that I charge four hundred dollars an hour if I have to testify at trial."

"You realize that my client is indigent, right? The law allows me to submit a formal request to the Justice Administrative Commission to pay more than the guidelines specify, but even in a capital case, realistically we're looking at about half that amount. I may end up asking you to cut your fee."

"I don't cut anything. My rate is four hundred dollars an hour. Period."

Jack considered it. The battle of experts had always seemed like a game, but as his gaze drifted back to the sheet that was draped over Emma's remains, the game seemed hardly worth playing.

"You know," said Jack, "based on the way the state attorney has prosecuted this case, I might actually get you four hundred bucks an hour. On a net-net basis, it seems only fair."

"How do you mean?"

"I'm beyond confident that the state of Florida will hire *two* whores to call my *one* whore a quack."

"Jack, come on back."

He looked up and saw Andie standing in the open doorway.

"Have you spoken to Celeste's parents?" he asked, rising from the couch.

"It's not Celeste," said Andie.

Jack felt a wave of relief . . . then trepidation. "Who is it?"

"We don't know. We were hoping you could tell us."

Chills ran the length of his spine. Jack followed her down the hallway. She walked quickly, as if eager to be done with this, and he had to hurry to keep up.

"You think it's . . . somebody I know?"

"Possibly," said Andie. "About my age. Female. Blond. Pretty."

Jack continued to follow, his heart in his throat, fearing the worst.

"She had no identification," said Andie. "A landscaper found her body, naked, next to the canal along Tamiami Trail."

Rene would have crossed the Tamiami Trail to get from the hospital to the coffee shop in Little Havana. It took all his effort, but finally Jack managed to get a few words out. "How did it happen?"

Andie opened the door to the morgue. "Strangled," she said.

Jack followed her inside. A wall of stainless steel drawers was before him. One to the right, three drawers from the bottom, was open. Andie led him to it. An assistant medical examiner pulled the drawer farther from the wall, drawing the sheet-covered body into the room. Jack held his breath. With a nod from Andie, the examiner lifted the white sheet.

Jack's knees nearly buckled. Her hair was mussed, her color was flat and lifeless, but there was no mistaking that classically beautiful face.

"Her name is Rene," said Jack.

"Then you do know her?"

"Yes. Rene Fenning. She's a doctor at Jackson." He paused, then added, "We used to date."

The assistant draped the white sheet back over her face.

Jack was suddenly puzzled. "If she had no identification, no clothes, how did you know to call me to make the ID?"

On Andie's cue, the assistant lifted the sheet again, this time from the middle, exposing Rene's torso.

Jack froze. Below the navel, about two inches above her pubic hair, was a handwritten message in black marker:

SOMEONE YOU LOVE.

It chilled Jack, and he could almost hear the voice of his attacker as he read those three words to himself.

"That's the reason I called you," said Andie.

The examiner replaced the sheet. Jack was still trying to comprehend that Rene was dead, and it hit him that much harder to think that it could have been Andie under that sheet. He looked at her, speechless.

Andie seemed to be staring right through him. "When is the last time you saw her, Jack?"

"Last night," he said, and he immediately felt Andie do a double take. "At the hospital," he added. "Andie, this is not what you think it—"

She raised a hand, which silenced him.

"Let's go outside, Jack. Sounds like you and I need to talk."

21

He called himself Merselus. It was the surname of his best friend in high school back in Paterson, New Jersey. Ironically, it was his math teacher—recognizing his tenacity, pegging him as a rare Eastside High success story—who had dubbed the two of them Merselus and Merciless. If she only knew.

Three weeks before the start of the Sydney Bennett trial, he'd used another name entirely to lease a one-bedroom apartment on the Miami River, just minutes away from the courthouse. William Teague was a week-to-week tenant in his third month of occupancy, which practically made him the mayor of a decaying village of drug addicts and prostitutes who came and went from the riverfront like water rats.

Merselus entered with a turn of the key and locked the door—lower deadbolt, upper deadbolt, and then the chain. The venetian blinds were drawn, though it was superfluous; the lone window in the apartment was boarded over from the inside, iron bars on the outside. The only light in the room was the glow from a laptop computer, which he'd left open and running on the desk. The Google satellite image was still on the screen, displaying the result of his last search: Little Havana/Tamiami Trail. His eyes narrowed as he studied it again. The slope from the highway to the brown canal. The knee-high brush along the shoreline. The perfect place to drop a warm body that Merselus wanted the police to find quickly, before his handwritten message fell to decomposition. All of it, as captured in the satellite image, was virtually identical to the actual place he'd visited a little later in the day. He gave a thin smile of appreciation to the technocrats in Silicon Valley who had made it so easy to plan.

He wondered if any of them even remembered him, ever wondered what he was up to these days.

Merselus sat on the edge of the bed, dropped his backpack between his feet on the floor, and opened it. First, he removed the essential tools of his mission—latex gloves, which left no fingerprints; a nylon cord, in case he met with resistance; the serrated diving knife, in case he met with even greater resistance. He laid each of them neatly on the bed, side by side. Deeper inside the pack, in a separate pouch, was his latest acquisition. He unzipped the pouch and carefully, almost lovingly, collected his prize. A "trophy" was what one of those self-proclaimed geniuses in criminal profiling would have called it, like the panties, jewelry, and other keepsakes that serial killers took from their victims in order to relive their fantasy, over and over. Collecting such objects was part of the sociopath's compulsive personality. So said the experts, whom

Merselus had watched repeatedly on BNN and the *Faith Corso Show*, all of whom uniformly overlooked one crucial fact: Their profiles were based on the assholes who got caught. Merselus didn't consider himself a serial killer, though his work could be measured in more than one victim. He didn't think of himself as a sociopath, either, though that term was thrown around pretty loosely these days. And he was definitely no trophy hunter.

He just thought Rene Fenning's necklace was cool.

It was made of polished copper, the kind of necklace that kept its shape and didn't collapse like a chain when taken off. He put his hand through the necklace, which made the opening seem small. Like Rene's gentle neck. It almost fit his wrist like a bracelet, a testimony to the size and strength of his hands. He reached over and switched on the lamp to get a better look.

The glass bead on the front of the necklace was most intriguing. It opened with a tiny latch. Inside were three pebbles, each about the size of a BB. It was unlike anything Merselus had ever seen. He laid it on the white bedsheet and took a photograph. He took several more until he got the right lighting, a pristine image. Then he went to his computer and uploaded the image. He wasn't certain that his image-recognition software would find a match on the Internet, and it wasn't at all crucial. But he was curious—not just to check out the trinket, but more to test the limits of the software. This kind of search tool wasn't something the average person on the street could have walked into the Apple Store and purchased. In the private sector, only the most elite security firms could get their hands on it. It was a trade secret still in development. A stolen trade secret.

Merselus hit SEARCH.

It took a couple of minutes to populate the results, another minute for him to eliminate the extraneous hits. Then he found a match, though the one pictured on the computer screen appeared to be larger than the one fastened to Rene's necklace.

"A gris-gris," he read aloud. "An amulet originating in Africa which is believed to protect the wearer from evil or brings luck."

That brought a smirk to his face. *Not very lucky for the good doctor.*

He closed the software program, impressed by its performance—and pleased, as always, to be one step ahead of the good guys on the technology curve.

With great care, Merselus carried the necklace across the room and opened the closet. Taped to the back of the door, right below a coat hook, was an eight-by-ten photograph. It was the image of Sydney Bennett that the prosecution had shown the jury at trial—the one of Sydney laughing off the effects of tequila, the hands of at least three different men pawing her tight body, her clingy white halter unable to hide her protruding nipples.

Of all his Sydney photographs, this one was Merselus' favorite.

"For luck," he said as he hung the necklace on the coat hook above the photograph. "See what good care I take of you?"

He closed the closet door and lay on the bed. Not

nearly enough rest last night, with all the preparation. He could have nodded off in a moment and
slept through till the next morning, but he forced
himself to set an alarm: six thirty P.M. Barely time
for a catnap.

There was more work to do. Tonight.

22
.

Rene's death changed everything. Almost everything.

"This won't change us," said Jack. He had wanted to sound sure of it, but it probably hadn't come across that way. "We can't let it," he added.

They were in Andie's car, driving to Jack's house on Key Biscayne. For five minutes and without a single interruption, Andie had listened to Jack's full explanation—how Rene had contacted him after Celeste was admitted to Jackson, how she'd been his source for the Laramores' lawsuit against BNN, how their coffees in Little Havana had had nothing to do with rekindling a romance. Jack was certain that Andie had heard it and understood, but whenever there was work to be done, Andie's ability to put personal moments on hold was unmatched. At her behest, a couple of FBI agents were already on the way to Jack's house—a tech guy, a surveillance expert. She was in full-fledged FBI mode, focused on stopping a killer.

"Jack, I don't have it in my head that you were

chasing an old girlfriend two minutes after I said we should take a step back, if that's what you're worried about." She reached across the console and brushed the back of her hand against his face, a proxy for not looking him in the eye while driving. "I know you better than that."

"Thank you."

Her attention was on the road, and Jack's gaze locked onto her profile. It was little more than a silhouette in the dark car, but against the sparkling Miami skyline in the distance, it was like a work of art. The views of downtown Miami and the financial district were killer from the causeway to Key Biscayne, especially at night—the south Florida version of Manhattan as seen from the Brooklyn Bridge.

"I also know the mind-set of Rene's killer," said Andie. "He didn't leave that message because he thought Rene was 'someone you love.' He's like a shark. He draws closer and closer to his prey, tighter and tighter circles. Each one of those circles allows him to live out the perfect fantasy he has created in his head. Eventually, he'll move in for the ultimate kill, the fulfillment of the fantasy."

"Someone I love?"

"Not exactly."

"I'm not sure I follow you."

"My take is that he probably believes all the BS on BNN that you and Sydney couldn't wait to rip off each other's clothes the minute she got out of prison. Yeah, he threatened to hurt someone you love, which could be anyone from me to an old girlfriend. But if you ask my professional opinion, he isn't taunting you just because he thinks you know where Sydney is hiding. He could threaten her parents, if that's all he wanted out of this. His anger—his *hatred* for you—is driven by his belief that you've actually had your way with Sydney."

"Someone he loves."

"Someone he's obsessed with. Got nothing to do with love."

That all made sense to Jack. Andie always made sense. "I love you," he said.

"Of course you do," she said.

That drew a little smile as they pulled into his driveway behind the "bucar"—FBI lingo for the bureau's standard-issue sedans. The agents Andie had summoned were already there. Jack invited them inside, and Max greeted them at the door, wagging his tail and jumping up and down as if it had been five hundred years since he'd last seen Andie. Jack let him loose in the backyard, and the humankind gathered in the Florida room to take care of an entirely different kind of business.

Jack took a seat beside Andie on the couch. Special Agents Burns and Waters sat across from them. They were "tech agents," which meant that Jack was the proverbial old man in the room. As a general rule, not many techies hung around till retirement age. A good one with a few years of law enforcement experience on his résumé could make a fortune in the private sector, and Jack guessed that the bureau would have the services of these two crackerjacks for maybe another six months.

"Truth is, I should have listened to Andie sooner," said Jack. "I resisted the idea of having the FBI monitoring my phones. Obviously, this changes things."

Burns spoke for the tech team. "There are ways to make this work and still protect the privacy of your clients."

"You may be right from a technical standpoint," said Jack. "But good luck trying to convince my clients of that."

Burns opened his bag of electronic toys and showed Jack his new cell phone. "Wireless is never the most secure option, but if you have to use a cell phone, this one is encrypted. Use it when you are not in the office and absolutely have to speak to one of your clients. Agent Waters and I will set up encrypted landlines for the calls you make from home and the office, which is of course the most secure option."

"What about e-mail?"

"Best thing is to tell your clients no e-mail."

"Can my clients call me on the encrypted lines?"

"If you give them the number, yes. But don't do that. The basic rule you should live by is, 'Don't call me, I'll call you.' "

"That's impossible. What if they need to reach me?"

"They should call your existing cell or landline. They should say nothing but 'call me,' and then you return the call on the encrypted line. I know that seems cumbersome, but the minute you give the phone number to anyone, you run the risk of compromising the security on the encrypted line."

"Won't they see the number when I call them?"

"Your encrypted phone is impervious to caller ID. That's pretty basic, Mr. Swyteck."

"It may be basic to you," said Andie, "but you're talking to a guy who started practicing law when Post-its were still a technological marvel."

"Not quite, honey. But almost."

Burns continued, "The overall objective here is for Rene Fenning's killer to remain under the impression that your existing cell phone, landlines, and e-mail addresses are still in use, still fully operational. So long as he has that impression, we can intercept, trace, and react to any message he sends you."

"How do I know the FBI won't be monitoring the encrypted line?"

"That won't happen," said Andie. "I'll make sure of it."

Jack wanted to believe her, and he knew it was greater assurance than most people got. He was still skeptical, but again, Rene's death had changed everything.

"Okay. Let's go with it."

"Great. We'll start here in the house. Where do you want the line?"

"My home office, I guess. Down the hall, right next to the bedroom."

"You got it."

The techies got up and went to work. Jack's gaze drifted toward the window. Max was in the yard, digging the Key Biscayne version of the Grand Canyon.

"I guess I'll need to send Max away," said Jack.

"He's still a puppy," said Andie. "Digging is what they do."

"I mean send him away for his own protection. It may be a bit of stereotype to think that all sociopaths like to hurt animals, but I already lost one dog to a pissed-off client."

"Sometimes stereotypes are true," said Andie. "Jeffrey Dahmer used to love up the neighborhood dogs, lure them into his kitchen—and then send them yelping home with their testicles sliced open. Just for grins."

It made Jack cringe. "My neighbors spend their summers in Charleston. Their son RJ loves Max. I'm sure they'd take him." Jack took another gander out the window. Max was covered in dirt, still digging. "Maybe Max can hook up with the Army Corps of Engineers and widen the harbor while he's up there."

"What are you going to do with *Abuela*?"

"She has a brother in Tampa. She'll feel safe there. Then there's my dad and stepmother. I guess they should just extend their vacation, stay in Europe."

Andie looked at him with concern. "These are all just precautions, you understand. Like I said before, I don't think the targets would be Max, *Abuela*, your father, your stepmother. With Rene, he was acting out a sexual fantasy that will lead him to the big moment with Sydney Bennett."

"I can't believe this happened to Rene," Jack said, but the regrets quickly turned into concern. "What about you?" he said. "Aren't you at risk?"

"I would say yes. But you don't need to worry about that."

"What do you mean I don't need to worry? You're my fiancée."

"Your fiancée is an FBI agent. You don't have to worry about protecting me."

It was intended to put him at ease, but it didn't sit entirely well with Jack. He didn't fully understand why, though deep down he realized that there was still enough of the caveman gene in every male to make it unpleasant to hear that he didn't need to protect his woman.

Jack's cell rang. He didn't recognize the incoming number.

"Is this a test, or should I answer it?" he asked Andie.

Agent Burns shouted from the next room, "Go ahead and answer it."

Jack took the call.

"Swyteck, this is Ted Gaines."

It was the first time Jack had heard from opposing counsel since their meeting in New York, and the last thing Jack felt like talking about at the moment was the lawsuit against BNN. "Not really a good time, Ted."

"This is not a discussion. We've seen the postings on Celeste Laramore's Facebook page. Remove them immediately."

"What?"

"I fully expected you to claim ignorance."

There was a beep on the line, and suddenly there was a third voice. "Good evening, gentlemen. Judge Burrows here."

Judge? Jack didn't know the voice, but he certainly knew the name: Burrows was the judge in *Celeste Laramore v. Breaking News Network*.

Gaines took control. "Thank you for agreeing to conduct this emergency hearing telephonically, Your Honor."

"Mr. Swyteck, it would appear that there has been a violation of my order to keep the allegations of the complaint in this action confidential and under seal."

"Honestly, I have no idea what this is about," said Jack.

Gaines said, "It's about the posting of confidential information on Celeste Laramore's Facebook page. Judge, if you're at your computer, I can get you to the proper Web page."

Jack followed along on his iPhone and pulled up Celeste's Facebook page.

The judge said, "I'm looking at the page now. What postings are you talking about?"

"Right there on her wall. It's the only information posted since Celeste Laramore went into a coma."

Jack scrolled down, knowing that the judge was doing the same. Sure enough, there were a series of status updates from that afternoon, bubbles of information stacked one on top of the other. Jack read the first, the second, the third—then skimmed the rest. Each status update was a few sentences in length. Collectively, the updates—sixty-seven in all—repeated, verbatim, the substantive allegations of the complaint in *Celeste Laramore v. Breaking News Network*.

"This is very troubling," said the judge.

Gaines jumped on the sentiment. "Your Honor, this is a blatant violation of a court order to file the complaint under seal and keep the allegations confidential. We demand that Mr. Swyteck remove the posts immediately."

"Mr. Swyteck, how soon can you make that happen?"

"I'll look into it as soon as this call is over."

"Look into it?" said the judge in a reproving tone. "Counsel, you need to *remove* it."

"Yes, Your Honor. But I want to be clear that I don't know how this information even got here. It's never been my practice to monitor the Facebook pages of my clients, and that's especially true in this case. Obviously, Celeste didn't do this."

"Obviously," said Gaines. "But it doesn't take a computer genius to know that these postings could have been made only by someone with account-manager status for Celeste's Facebook page. Ruling out Celeste doesn't rule out a single other person in her camp who had access to her username and password."

"That's a ridiculous accusation," said Jack.

The judge intervened. "You'd better hope so, Mr. Swyteck. Because if this violation was willful and done at your direction, the sanctions against you and your client will be severe."

"Judge, we would like a hearing on the issue of sanctions as quickly as possible," said Gaines.

"We'll deal with that in due course," said the judge. "For now, I'm ordering Mr. Swyteck to remove these postings by midnight tonight. Further, I want a written certification delivered to my chambers no later than nine A.M. stating that the plaintiffs and their counsel are in full compliance with the confidentiality order. Is that understood?"

"Yes," said Jack.

"That's all for this evening, gentlemen," the judge said. A beep confirmed that he had dropped from the conference call.

"I'm checking that page at twelve-oh-one A.M.," said Gaines. "It had better be clean."

Gaines hung up. Jack took a deep breath and tucked his phone away. Andie came to him and massaged his neck.

"That didn't sound good," she said.

It would have been easy to unload on the spot and tell Andie what he would have liked to have told the judge—that the five horrendous days between Sydney's release on Sunday and Rene's murder on Thursday had been the personal and professional equivalent of a tsunami, and that the last thing any human being in his position should be held accountable for was the Facebook page of a client in a coma.

"Nothing I can't handle," said Jack.

"Really? Isn't there anything I can help with?"

Jack appreciated the sentiment, then actually considered it. "Well, maybe there is."

"Tell me."

"What do your tech agents know about Facebook?"

23

It was league night at Bird Bowling Lanes, and all twenty-two lanes were filled. While each team bore the name and logo of a different sponsor, collectively they had to be the largest display of baby-blue shirts south of Chapel Hill, North Carolina. Merselus found a small table near the shoe rental counter, sat down with his cheese pizza and beer, and waited. If he'd been at a pizzeria, he would have sent the pie back to the kitchen as too greasy. Funny how being at a bowling alley made it tasty. To a point. He finished one slice and pushed the rest aside.

Merselus checked his phone. Ten minutes before seven. Ten minutes until showtime. He kept an eye on the main entrance as he drank from his longneck. Technically, he was working, but one beer wasn't against the rules. Especially since he made the rules.

"Could I squeeze by you and get to those balls, please?" a woman asked.

She was dressed in one of those baby-blue shirts,

and Merselus was sitting in front of a rack of nine-pound pink bowling balls, so he knew exactly what she was after, but he turned it into something else.

"Lady, your only hope of squeezing by anybody is a ten-week gig on *The Biggest Loser*."

She looked more hurt than angry, but she just stood there.

"Take a hike, fatso," said Merselus.

She hurried away. Merselus watched her ass shake as she made a beeline to another rack on the other side of the alley. He was about to check his phone again for the time, then stopped himself. Patience was normally one of his virtues, but on a night like this, after all the planning, even Merselus had to remind himself to be cool.

His gaze swept the alley. A guy on lane fifteen was in the seventh frame of a perfect game, and a crowd was beginning to gather. Merselus ignored the excitement, his focus shifting back and forth from the main entrance to the men's locker room.

It took about a week to get approved for a locker at Bird Bowl, and Merselus had reserved one with a stolen ID and fifty bucks in cash. The bait was inside the locker. It was just a matter of minutes before the dumbest fish in the sea came along to take it. Merselus recognized him the minute he walked through the main entrance doors.

The dossier Merselus had compiled on Brian Hewitt was pretty simple. Twenty-seven years old. Unmarried. Unemployed. Two years of community college. He'd lived the fast life during Miami's real estate boom, once upon a time having owned a town house in Coral Gables, a duplex in Hollywood, and six waterfront condos from Fort Lauderdale to Miami Beach. His typical Friday night had involved two lucky friends and a table full of women who were thrilled to take turns going down on a guy who could shove enough fraudulent mortgage applications through the system to afford a thousand-dollar bottle of Cristal at a South Beach nightclub. The burst of the subprime bubble had left him sharing a shitty two-bedroom apartment with three other losers who had been on a downward spiral since their glory days of high school football. Bankruptcy had seemed like the only answer to seventy thousand dollars in credit card debt. Until Merselus had come along. Not that Mr. Hewitt would ever hear the name Merselus, or have even the slightest idea who he was dealing with.

Merselus allowed himself one more check of the time: seven P.M. Hewitt probably wasn't as stupid as he looked, but he was prompt. And desperate. Not to mention way out of his league.

Merselus watched Hewitt weave through the crowd, past the game room, past the billiard tables, past the ladies' lounge. He walked briskly, a man on a mission, a complete newbie who had never been on the receiving end of a drop in his life. The clincher was the telltale glance over the shoulder before stopping at the water fountain. He knelt down and pretended to tie his shoe—*ah, very smooth*—and found the key exactly where Merselus had promised it would be: in the gap between the loose rubber baseboard and the wall beside the fountain. Hewitt tucked the key into his pants pocket, gave another nervous glance over his shoulder, and disappeared into the men's locker room.

Merselus drank his beer and waited. He had no fear that Hewitt or anyone else would recognize him. The eyeglasses, the flat-billed baseball cap, and the three-day stubble were disguise enough for this simple task. Across the bowling alley, he could see the agents in plainclothes moving into position, which gave him a rush of excitement and satisfaction. His call to the FBI had been anonymous, and he was pretty sure that he'd shared enough details to make his tip credible. But there had been no guarantee that the bureau would act on it. Thankfully, they'd not only acted on it, but they'd been smart enough to figure out for themselves that flooding the bowling alley with uniformed police officers would have scared off Hewitt and blown the setup.

A minute later, Hewitt emerged from the lounge with a bowling-ball bag tucked under his arm—the same bag Merselus had left inside the locker. The excitement on his face quickly turned to fear. Two men stopped him right outside the men's lounge. One flashed a badge. The other took the bag, zipped it open, and looked inside.

There was no bowling ball in there, of course.

A split second later, Hewitt was up against the wall, feet spread, hands cuffed behind his waist as the FBI read him his rights. The bowler who was working on the perfect game in lane fifteen had suddenly lost his audience. The curious crowd was gravitating toward the men's lounge. The manager stepped out from behind the counter and pushed toward the center of the commotion.

Merselus finished his beer and headed for the exit. The heat and humidity of another summer night hit him as the doors opened. He was in the parking lot, halfway to his car, when he noticed that someone had followed him out.

"Hey, asshole," the guy called out.

Merselus kept walking.

The heckler kept coming, now just a few steps behind him. "Hey, you owe my wife an apology."

Great, the thin-skinned fat chick sent her husband.

Merselus wanted to ignore him, but the footsteps were closing in from behind. Merselus stopped, turned sharply, and cast a laserlike glare that very few people had seen and lived to remember.

The guy nearly screeched to a halt.

"Back off," said Merselus.

Two simple words and the expression on Merselus' face were enough to make the guy's voice shake in response.

"You are, uh, gonna go back in that bowling alley and you're gonna, uhm, apologize to my wife."

The fear was audible. Merselus approached slowly, looking him straight in the eye, not stopping until they were nearly nose to nose.

"No. I'm not." His tone wasn't agitated or even argumentative—just a simple statement of fact, which made it all the more effective.

The guy was built solid, obviously no stranger to the gym, and there was no question in Merselus' mind that he'd successfully defended his wife's honor in the past. This time, however, the knight in shining armor nearly dissolved on the spot, smart enough to sense that he wasn't dealing with just another bully at a bowling alley. Not even close.

The man took a step back, then turned and started away, walking at first, but nearly at a trot by the time he reached the doors and retreated into the safety of the bowling alley.

Good call, thought Merselus. *Really good call.*

He reached deep into his pocket and dug out his keys—sans the locker key—and headed toward his car.

24
.

Jack drove himself to Jackson Memorial Hospital that Thursday night. Rene's murder made a thing like a civil lawsuit seem trivial, but the Facebook posting was a bona fide legal emergency, and to Jack's knowledge no judge had ever excused a direct violation of a court order based on the there-are-other-things-in-life-that-are-more-important defense. A frank conversation with his clients was in order.

Jack stopped for the red light at the main entrance to the medical campus. A homeless man working the left-turn lane flashed a cardboard sign that said NO FUCKING JOB OR FAMILY, NEED MONEY TO GET DRUNK. WHAT'S YOUR EXCUSE? Jack could relate. He rolled down the window and gave him a couple bucks for being honest.

"Bless you," the guy said.

Jack's "You're welcome" caught in his throat. He'd suddenly noticed the green directional sign posted on the other side of the intersection: MEDICAL EXAMINER'S OFFICE, it read. The crushing reality had set in hours earlier, and Jack wasn't headed back to the ME's office. But the mere sight of the sign took the pain to another level, and the words just came out.

"Rene, I am so sorry."

"Who you callin' Rene?" said the homeless guy.

A horn blasted from behind. The light had turned green, and someone was in a hurry. Jack put the car in gear, followed the street to the parking garage, and walked across the courtyard to the hospital entrance. He met Ben Laramore in the ground-floor cafeteria, seated at the same table where, less than twenty-four hours before—it seemed so much longer—a process server had served them with the judge's order to file the complaint under seal and keep the allegations confidential.

"I'm sorry about your friend," said Laramore.

"Thank you for that," said Jack.

"I feel even worse now that I realize you were trying to call me while all this was going on. I didn't realize the number I was ignoring was your new phone."

"Changing my number was the only way to stop the crazy calls I was getting. But don't worry about it. I was the one who told you not to answer calls from numbers you don't recognize."

Laramore sighed deeply. "Is this story on the news yet?"

"So far it's just local reports about a body found along Tamiami Trail. Once the next of kin is notified, something will need to be said about the fact that she worked here at Jackson. It's not clear when the media will make the connection between Rene and me, but it doesn't seem to take BNN long to connect anything to me. That's not something you need to worry about, though."

"I am worried. You said Rene was your source. She was the whole reason we knew about BNN's interference and how it prevented the paramedics from transmitting information from the ambulance to the ER physicians. Don't we lose that evidence now that she's dead?"

"No. Rene was our source, not our witness. Everything she told me was hearsay. Even if she were alive, I'd need to subpoena the ER doctors, the paramedics—all the people who were actually involved in treating your daughter. Don't worry. We'll get all that. Nothing is lost."

Laramore did a quick check around the cafeteria, as if to underscore the confidentiality of what he was about to say. "Do you think that's why she got killed? Because she was the source?"

"No."

Laramore paused, as if expecting Jack to say more. "That's it, that's your answer: 'No'?"

"BNN is not exactly a model corporate citizen. But I don't think they kill people to win civil lawsuits."

"I suppose you're right," said Laramore. "They probably draw the line at putting young women in comas."

Jack fully understood the bitterness.

"Sorry," said Laramore. "Don't mean to be so sarcastic. This whole thing is just getting . . . it's getting to be too much."

"I know. It's okay."

Laramore sat back in his chair, breathing out.

"So, of all things, we now have a social media problem."

"I had a tech agent from the FBI check out Celeste's Facebook page. There is no sign of hacking into her account. Which means that whoever posted the allegations of our complaint on Celeste's Facebook page used her username and password."

"Well, that puts that person one step ahead of Celeste's mother and me. We have no idea how to access Celeste's account. In fact, I don't know the first damn thing about Facebook."

Jack spoke while pulling up Celeste's page on his iPhone. "It has about eight hundred and fifty million users worldwide. It's especially popular with people your daughter's age. They constantly update their status, telling their friends that they're going out for pizza, dumping a boyfriend, getting a zit."

"Getting a zit?"

"I'm not exaggerating. Most of the stuff is utterly useless, food for online information addicts whose sphere of knowledge is forever shrinking until someday they wake up and realize that they know absolutely nothing about anything except for whatever it is that happens to be going on at the moment." Jack laid his phone on the table, the screen facing Laramore. It was Celeste's Facebook page with the sixty-seven status updates that recounted verbatim the allegations of the complaint.

"But then, of course, there are things like this."

Laramore looked at it. Jack could tell from the look on his face that he wasn't reading anything. He was staring at Celeste's profile photograph—the way she'd looked just a week earlier.

"Beautiful, wasn't she?" he said.

"Yes," said Jack. "She is beautiful."

Ben looked up, smiled sadly, as if appreciating Jack's respect for the rule Virginia had laid down about using the present tense.

"I don't really want to read this," said Laramore. "If you say it's all there, I'll take your word for it."

"It's all there," said Jack.

"But just so I understand: Anyone with a Facebook account can read a status update?"

"This one was designated 'public,' so, yeah, anyone with an account can see it. Anyone on the Internet, for that matter."

"Still, I find it hard to believe that BNN's lawyers are scrolling through Facebook updates. This just went up on Facebook this afternoon. How did they find it so fast?"

Jack considered it. "That's a good question. But keep in mind that these status updates didn't just appear on Celeste's Facebook page. They went out to every single one of her friends. It's possible one of them forwarded it to BNN's lawyers."

"Celeste's friends wouldn't do that."

"Well, a Facebook 'friend' might." Jack took back his phone and checked the page. "I see here that Celeste has almost four thousand Facebook friends."

"So that means any one of four thousand people could have told BNN that the complaint was posted on Celeste's Facebook page?"

"That's about the size of it," said Jack. "There's another possibility, of course."

"What's that?"

"Whoever stole her username and password to

access her account and send out the status update also told BNN that the information was all over Facebook."

"What would be the point of that?"

"What's the point of any of this? Someone is either trying to piss off BNN or get us in trouble with the judge. It's one of the two."

"Or both."

"Or both, right. The immediate problem we have to address is getting this information down as quickly as possible. It's not that easy if you and your wife don't know Celeste's username and password."

"I could take a few educated guesses, but—"

Laramore stopped, seeing a doctor approaching.

"Mr. Swyteck?" the doctor asked. He had an urgent expression on his face, alarming enough to make Jack rise to respond.

"Yes, I'm Jack Swy—"

A crushing blow to Jack's jaw not only cut off his words, it knocked him to the floor. Both Jack and Laramore were too stunned to retaliate, and the doctor himself seemed content to have landed just one good punch. He didn't come at Jack. Jack rose up on one knee, looked up, and saw equal parts rage and grief in the doctor's eyes. Then Jack noticed the hospital ID badge: STEFAN ROSS, MD. Rene's boyfriend.

"That's from Rene, you son of a bitch."

Jack massaged his jaw back into place and said, "I'm sorry for—"

"*Sorry?*" said Ross. "No, you're not. You used her, and you put her in a dangerous situation that she should've never been in."

"Actually, she called me."

"Don't justify it. And don't you dare show your face at the funeral. Spare us the phony sympathy. Please."

Ross turned and walked away, so much anger in his step that his rubber soles squeaked on the tile floor. Jack climbed back into his chair.

"Are you all right?" asked Laramore.

Jack thought about it, thought about Rene, thought about the joy all this suffering must have been bringing to the sick bastard who had taken Rene's life.

"I will be," he said. "I suppose."

25

It had been Andie's intention to be home for Jack when he returned from the hospital, but when the assistant special agent in charge of the Miami Field Office called and said, "Get over here now," she didn't even ask why.

"I'm on my way," she told Schwartz.

Andie shot Jack a quick text to let him know that her tech agents had "successfully guessed" Celeste's username and password. The FBI couldn't lawfully remove anything from her Facebook page, but at least Jack had everything he needed to comply with Judge Burrows' midnight deadline. Andie added a second text to tell him that something had come up, and that she didn't know when she'd be back.

Speed limits be damned, she flew all the way up I-95 and reached the field office around eight thirty. She found Schwartz in the observation room. With him was an assistant U.S. attorney who was junior enough to be stuck with after-hours "confession duty." The lawyer shook Andie's hand, then quickly turned her attention back to the other side of the one-way mirror, where a two-agent team was in the make-nice phase of the interrogation of a handsome young man who looked scared to death.

"His name is Brian Hewitt," said Schwartz.

Andie, Schwartz, and the federal prosecutor were facing the glass, watching. The audio was on, which allowed them to hear everything that transpired in the interrogation room, but nothing was being said at the moment. Hewitt was seated at a small table in the windowless room. One agent was leaning against the wall behind Hewitt. Another was seated across from Hewitt, who was eating a hamburger and french fries, compliments of the FBI. Andie could only surmise that the interrogators had already gotten what they wanted from him—or that they had simply transitioned into the good-cop phase of the age-old routine.

"Hewitt," said Andie, searching her memory. "That name sounds familiar for some reason."

"He was the foreman of the twelve-person jury that acquitted Sydney Bennett," said Schwartz.

Mere mention of the Bennett trial was enough to make her heart skip a beat. Jack's connection to it—more precisely, Andie's connection to Jack—was an ongoing headache. "We arrested the jury foreman?"

Schwartz nodded. "Our agents followed him to a bowling alley. The subject walked into the men's lounge empty-handed and came out carrying a bowling bag. When the agents stopped him and asked to see inside the bag, he complied. There was a hundred thousand dollars in cash inside."

"A drop and pickup?"

"No doubt about it."

"Somebody tipped us off, I presume?"

"Anonymous call came in this afternoon around three thirty. Said that the foreman of the Sydney Bennett jury was going to Bird Bowl at nine P.M. to pick up a hundred grand in cash. According to the tipster, it was payment for delivering a not-guilty verdict."

It was suddenly hard not to be scared for Jack, even harder not to show it. "Can we prove that?"

Schwartz glanced at the interrogation team, then back at Andie. "There's no denying that Hewitt was the foreman of the jury. There's no denying that he went into the bowling alley with nothing and came out with a hundred thousand bucks. And according to his confession, he got paid to deliver the verdict."

"He already confessed?"

"Yes," said Schwartz.

"In his own handwriting," the assistant U.S. attorney added.

Schwartz pulled a copy of the one-page confession from his sport-coat pocket and laid it on the table. With his finger, he skimmed past that preliminary language about the free and voluntary nature of Hewitt's confession, all provided by the assistant U.S. attorney. Then he found his eyeglasses and read the operative language aloud for Andie's benefit: "'The offer to me was fifty thousand dollars in cash for a hung jury and one hundred thousand dollars for a verdict of not guilty.' Those are Hewitt's initials right there," he said, indicating.

"The offer *from whom*?" asked Andie.

Schwartz turned his attention back to the work

in progress on the other side of the one-way mirror. "That's phase two of the interrogation," he said.

Andie sensed that she was there only to watch, but she felt the need to speak up. "Look, I appreciate your calling me in, but I can tell you right now that Jack Swyteck did not make that offer."

Schwartz didn't respond. Nor did the assistant U.S. attorney.

"Jack would never do that," said Andie.

Schwartz raised a hand, silencing her. At the table on the other side of the glass, Hewitt was finishing his hamburger, and the interrogation team appeared ready to get back to work. Schwartz adjusted the volume and listened.

The special agent at the table checked his yellow notepad in front of him, then looked at Hewitt. "Let me get this straight. This guy who offered to pay you a hundred thousand dollars for 'not guilty.' You say you never met him?"

Hewitt pushed aside what was left of his hamburger. "No, I didn't say that."

"I have it right here in my notes," said the agent. "Your answer was that you talked to him only by phone. No e-mails, no texts, no handwritten messages?"

"Right. Two phone conversations. Then we met. Face-to-face."

"So now you're telling me there was a face-to-face meeting. You changing your story?"

"I'm not changing it. I forgot."

"Forgot about a face-to-face meeting, huh? Where did you meet?"

"Downtown. By the Metromover station at Government Center."

"How many times?"

"Just the once."

"What did he look like?"

"White guy, dark hair. A lot taller than me. Maybe your age."

"Now, how did you get out and meet him if you were on a sequestered jury and locked up in a hotel?"

"I told you before," Hewitt said, groaning. "We weren't sequestered until the lawyers gave their opening statements and the trial started."

"So the two phone calls and the meeting were during jury selection?"

"Right. I was the second juror to be accepted by both sides. They had to pick a total of twelve plus two alternates. Jury selection went on for at least another week after I got picked."

"All right," the agent said. "So walk me all the way through this. The first phone call came when?"

"Let's see. I got picked on that first day, Monday. So the first call was Tuesday night. Around eight o'clock."

"And what did the guy say to—"

The lead interrogator stopped, interrupted by a firm knock on the door. The other agent answered it and stepped outside. A minute later, that same agent entered the observation room and delivered the news to Schwartz and the assistant U.S. attorney:

"Mommy and Daddy hired Justin Bieber here a lawyer. He's outside banging on the door right now."

"Shit," said Schwartz.

The assistant U.S. attorney hit the intercom button so that her announcement could be heard in both rooms: "Shut it down."

The agent shrugged and started toward the door. Schwartz stopped him and said, "You guys did great. Really good stuff."

The assistant U.S. attorney echoed the sentiment. "Hewitt's looking at five years for obstruction of justice. We'll put something on the table to get him to give up whoever paid him the money."

The agent nodded and left the observation room. The assistant U.S. attorney went right behind him, off to speak to Hewitt's lawyer. On the other side of the glass, the lead interrogator took Hewitt out the door, and the interrogation room went dark.

Andie and Schwartz were alone in the observation room. She had a dozen questions for him, but he spoke first.

"I'm putting Cynthia Jenkins on Operation Big Dredge."

Operation Big Dredge was to be Andie's next undercover assignment. It was a top-priority investigation into organized crime and corrupt politicians from south Florida to Shanghai, where deals were being cut to exploit the increase in smuggling that would flow through a newly widened Panama Canal and into an expanded Port of Miami.

"That makes no sense," said Andie. "I've been training for this."

"I don't have any choice."

"Is that why you called me up here? You think my fiancé bought off a juror, so you're pulling my undercover role?"

"I don't know who Mr. Hewitt will implicate, but this decision was made when Dr. Rene Fenning was murdered."

"The 'someone you love' threat," said Andie. "That's what you're talking about?"

"Exactly. Your fiancé's old girlfriend is dead, and the standing threat—'someone you love'—makes you a potential target. We can't give you the added protection you need while you're working undercover."

"I won't need protection while I'm undercover. I'm no longer Andie Henning."

"That may be true, to a point. But I can't send you undercover knowing that someone may be trying to track you down. That could blow the whole operation."

"He won't find me."

"You can't guarantee that. And he doesn't have to find you to blow the operation. If he figures out you're working undercover, that's enough."

Andie knew he was right, and the only solution to the problem was one that she didn't like. But she was desperate. "What if I was willing to go all-in for the duration of the assignment—no rights to contact anyone, including Jack."

"Andie, Operation Big Dredge is budgeted and approved up to five months. I'm not saying it will go that long, but it could."

"I understand."

"You really want to do that? No phone calls, no nothing for five months?"

"It's not my preference," she said. "But if you pull me because I'm a threat to the integrity of the operation, you and I both know that headquarters will not view this as an isolated incident."

"I won't let you be blackballed."

"That's a really nice sentiment, but getting pulled from an assignment like this is huge. I'll be damaged goods. So, please: Get on the phone with whoever it is at headquarters who's pushing your buttons, and tell them I'm willing to go all-in."

Schwartz studied her expression, and Andie stared right back at him, conveying nothing but her resolve.

"All right," said Schwartz. "I'll let you know what headquarters says. But before I make that call and put your offer on the table, do you want to talk with your fiancé about it?"

Andie thought for a moment. Perception was everything in the bureau, and having to check with your fiancé on a decision that could define the rest of your career as an FBI agent was the wrong perception to create. Yes, five months was a long time—but not with someone you planned to spend the rest of your life with.

"No need," said Andie. "Jack will understand."

I hope.

26

BNN had "the exclusive" in time for Faith Corso's nine P.M. show.

It began with Corso's rapid-fire summary of the day's events, followed by a live update from an on-the-scene reporter in Little Havana's Tamiami Trail, "where the nude body of Rene Fenning, a beloved pediatrician at Miami's Jackson Memorial Hospital, was discovered late this afternoon." Jack was relieved to see that law enforcement had been careful not to divulge details that might compromise the investigation: Even BNN had yet to uncover the killer's signature—"someone you love." Still, Corso worked in Rene's past relationship with Jack, coupled with a healthy dose of innuendo as to a current "romantic link."

Then it was back live and in-studio for Corso's big story of the night: the hundred-thousand-dollar payoff to the jury foreman in the Sydney Bennett trial. The graphic behind Corso said it all, yet another slutty photograph of Sydney with a catchy tagline:

NOT GUILTY: THE PRICE OF INJUSTICE.

Jack had known the personal attacks were coming five minutes before airtime. Corso's producer had called him for a comment, which he'd declined to give—which Corso proceeded to use against him on the air.

"Of course Jack Sly-teck isn't talking," Corso told her television audience. "He refused to say a word when we asked him to explain how something like this could happen on his watch. Keeping his mouth shut is probably the smart thing to do in a situation like this. Maybe Shot Mom's lawyer isn't quite as dumb as we thought he was."

Jack found her easy to stomach compared to the ensuing parade of expert speculators—expeculators, he called them, a play on expectorant that in Jack's mind put their venom-spitting rhetoric on the level of hacking up a lungful of phlegm. None had the least bit of expertise on the charge of jury tampering, and, from the outset, they disagreed on the most basic question put to them by Corso:

"Does this mean that Sydney Bennett will stand trial again?" she asked her panel. "Or does double jeopardy preclude a retrial even if a juror was paid off?"

"Good question," said Theo. He was on the other end of Jack's couch, having shown up uninvited about ten minutes after Andie had sent the text saying she was headed to the field office.

Jack scratched Max's head. "I know golden retrievers who could answer it more intelligently than these bozos."

Theo wasn't listening. His full attention was on

the TV, on Faith Corso's response to her own question. She did that a lot.

"Clearly the government is free to bring charges of jury tampering against Mr. Hewitt and whoever bribed him," said Corso. "But I could easily see Shot Mom hiring a new lawyer who will deny that she had anything to do with the bribe, and who will argue that once a verdict is entered it's too late for the court to declare a mistrial. Shot Mom was acquitted, period, end of story."

Jack snatched the remote from Max's jaws. "End of story," he said, scoffing. "Mark your calendar, Theo. You and I will have grandchildren before Faith Corso utters those words again in connection with Sydney Bennett."

Theo made a face. "I like you, Swyteck, but I don't want to have grandchildren with you."

Jack rolled his eyes, then checked the time on the TV info banner. With Andie's help on Celeste's username and password, Jack had solved the Facebook problem more than two hours before the midnight deadline. There was no telling when Andie would be back, however, which was probably a good thing. She might have tried to talk him out of heading over to the Bennett house and confronting Sydney's parents about the bribe. Theo not only loved the idea, but he would be Jack's hedge against a my-word-versus-their-word situation if ever their conversation became an issue.

"I'll drive," said Theo.

They were in Miami Shores before ten. Jack had visited the Bennett home only once before, and he almost didn't recognize the place without the battalion of media vans and onlookers in front. The telltale tire ruts in the yard, visible in the glow of a streetlamp, confirmed that they were in the right place. Theo parked in the driveway, and they started up the sidewalk.

"You want me to do the talking?" asked Theo.

"You want me to be disbarred?"

One ring of the bell brought Mr. Bennett to the screen door. Jack wasn't expecting a warm welcome, and he didn't get one.

"What the hell do you want?"

Geoffrey Bennett was a retired salon owner who, in Jack's mind, could have been a 1970s TV game-show host—hair too perfect, skin too tan, teeth too white, almost too good-looking. The only photographs Jack had seen of him without his shirt unbuttoned and chest hair showing were from the trial, where both he and his wife had made a point of dressing as if they were on their way to church. "The look" had only fed the rumors, and while Jack had not explicitly mounted the "abuse excuse," Bennett still held it against him for having done too little to squelch the talk of sexual abuse that had spread from the hallways outside the courtroom to the farthest corners of the Internet. For Jack, Sydney's murder trial simply wasn't the place to deal with her father's battered public image. Bennett, however, had flat-out accused Jack of feeding the rumors in order to build sympathy for Sydney.

"We need to talk about a certain juror," said Jack.

Bennett stared back through the screen door, then glanced at Theo. "Who's he?"

"Faith Corso," said Theo. "My morning-after look. No makeup."

"I don't like smart-asses."

"I don't like chumps who pretend not to know who I am."

"Never seen you before, pal."

"Me and 'rot-in-hell' snuggies was the highlight of the *Faith Corso Show* on verdict day. How many six-foot-six African American friends you think Jack's got?"

Jack gave his friend a sideways glance, telling him to tone it down.

"This is Theo Knight, my investigator," said Jack. "Please, may we come in? It's important."

Bennett hesitated another moment, then opened the door. He led them to the family room, offered them a seat on the couch. "Is your wife home?" asked Jack. "I'd like her to be part of this."

"This is all very upsetting to her," said Bennett.

"I'm sensitive to that," said Jack.

Bennett stared back at him for a moment. "I'll see if she's up to it," he said. He headed down the hall toward the bedroom.

"Faith Corso's morning-after look?" Jack muttered beneath his breath.

"He deserved it. Like he doesn't *know* who I am."

"If we tick him off, he'll just tell us to get lost."

"If we don't call him out at the first sign of bullshit, we'll get nothing but bullshit. You watch. He's a scumbag liar who doesn't know who I am, doesn't know where his daughter is, doesn't know what happened to his granddaughter, doesn't know nothing about nobody."

"Can I offer you fellas something to drink?" Mrs. Bennett asked as she entered the room.

Jack rose and prompted Theo to do the same. "No, thanks," said Jack.

The Bennetts sat in the matching armchairs on the other side of the coffee table, facing Jack. Jack noted the collection of framed photographs, all of Emma, on the wall behind them. He tried not to be obvious, but as he lowered himself back to the couch, Jack's gaze swept the room. Not a single photograph of Sydney anywhere, as far as he could tell.

"Geoffrey and I watched the *Faith Corso Show*," she said. "Other than the times we saw him in the courtroom, we have no idea who this Brian Hewitt is."

"To put a finer point on it, we didn't buy off a juror," said Mr. Bennett. "Anybody who thinks I have an extra hundred thousand dollars in cash lying around is out of his mind."

"Not that we would do it even if we had the money, of course," said Ellen Bennett.

Her husband shook his head, frustrated. "Ellen, why would you even add that? It goes without saying. Those are the kind of stupid things that need to stop coming out of your mouth."

"You're right. I'm sorry."

Theo sat forward, placed his hands on his thighs in a way that gave him the shoulders of a defensive tackle. "I didn't think it was stupid," he said, his glare practically burning a hole through Bennett's skull.

"I don't care what you think," said Bennett.

Jack reached across the couch, guiding Theo back into a less threatening position. "Let's keep this cordial, if we can. Does that sound good to everyone?"

"Sounds good to me," said Ellen. The men didn't answer.

"Good," said Jack.

Bennett asked, "Did you buy him off?"

"Geoffrey," said his wife, bristling.

"Quiet, Ellen."

Jack checked Theo back into place with a hand gesture. "It's a fair question," said Jack. "The answer is no."

"But we would've, if we had the money," said Theo, speaking in a tone that said, *Fuckhead*.

"Let's all chill for a second," said Jack, "and assume everyone in this room is telling the truth. You didn't do it. I didn't do it. Who did?"

"Obviously not Sydney," said Ellen.

"Well, *is* it that obvious?" said Jack.

"To me it is," said Ellen.

"Let me tell you why it's not to me," said Jack. "Let's start with this simple question: Where is Sydney?"

"We don't know," said Bennett. "That was true when your FBI girlfriend came here last week asking questions, and it's true now."

"Okay, let's assume that's the case," said Jack. "Nobody in this room knows where Sydney is. But here's what we *do* know. Somebody paid Celeste a thousand dollars to show up the night of Sydney's release dressed up and looking like Sydney. Somebody paid for a private airplane to fly Sydney out of Miami. Since then, somebody has been paying a lot of money to keep Sydney out of sight—that doesn't just happen for free. And tonight, somebody plunked down a hundred thousand dollars to pay off a juror. Altogether, we're talking well into six figures. Maybe north of a quarter million, depending on where she's hiding, whether she's moving from one place to the next in order to stay one step ahead of the media, what kind of lifestyle she's leading."

"Which makes my point," said Bennett. "It's not us, and it's not Sydney. We don't have that kind of dough."

Bennett's answers were a match for the low expectations Jack had brought to the meeting, but he still needed to ask the question that was at the heart of the matter. "Who's the young man who met her on the runway at Opa-locka Airport?"

"No idea," said Bennett.

"Here's my trouble with that answer," said Jack. "When you and I talked about Sydney's release, it was my impression that you were paying for the airplane."

"I never said that. I told you what Sydney told me—that there would be a plane waiting for her, and there was no refund if you didn't get her there before two A.M."

"I took that to mean you were footing the bill."

"You took it wrong," said Bennett.

"Then who did pay for it?" asked Jack.

"I have no idea," said Bennett.

Jack and Theo exchanged glances, and Jack could almost hear the refrain: scumbag liar.

Theo said, "You might as well tell us. I got contacts at the airport. I'm gonna get a name."

"Good," said Bennett. "When you get it, you call me. Because like I said: I have no idea."

"Let me make sure I understand," said Jack. "Your daughter gets out of jail, it's a national media circus, and some people are even threatening her life. She gets on a private plane in the middle of the night, you don't know who paid for it, don't know who met her at the airport, don't know where he took her— and you still have no idea where she is. That's what you're telling me?"

"That's what I'm telling you," said Bennett.

Jack glanced at Mrs. Bennett. "Is that what *you're* telling me?"

"Yes, she is," said Bennett, answering for her.

"Jack was askin' your wife," said Theo.

She glanced at her husband, then at Jack. "Well, you know, we have—"

"Ellen," said Bennett.

She pursed her lips, the words coming like a reflex: "We don't know," she said.

Jack let her response hang in the air, watching her, seeing her discomfort. "It's a funny thing," said Jack. "Going all the way back to day one as Sydney's lawyer, I've never had a one-on-one conversation with Ellen. It's always been me, Ellen, and you."

"With good reason," said Bennett.

Jack's gaze remained fixed on Mrs. Bennett. He knew it would lead nowhere, but he wanted to plant the seed. "Do you think that would be possible—a conversation, just the two of us?"

"No," said Mr. Bennett.

Theo was again on the verge of eruption. "Jack was talking to—"

"I don't care who he's talking to," said Bennett. "Look, you two come into my house, acting like we have all the answers, like this is easy for us. Do you have any idea how many medications Ellen has taken over the last three years, Mr. Swyteck? Do you know what it's like to be afraid to step outside your house, to have to run back to your car and get away from reporters every time you go to the grocery story?"

"It has to be tough, I know."

"No, you don't know. This has been more than Ellen can bear. So you can think whatever you want about why I do the talking. But you, Faith Corso, and everyone else in this screwed-up world who wants time alone with Ellen can just shove it. I am not going to let you take my wife into some back room, tear her down, and push her back into depression, all to serve your own agenda. At some point a man has to step in and protect what's left of his family."

"I just want to have a conversation," said Jack.

"No, you don't," said Bennett. "Everyone in this room knows that this Brian Hewitt is going to point his finger at someone. Maybe your interests will align with ours, Mr. Swyteck. Or maybe they won't. Tomorrow morning I'm calling an attorney to represent Ellen and me, and I'm sure the first thing he'll tell us is don't talk to anyone. I've been far more accommodating to you than necessary. This has gone on long enough, gentlemen."

Bennett rose. Jack and Theo stayed in their seats.

"The conversation is over," said Bennett, his tone firmer.

Slowly, Jack and Theo rose. Jack thanked Mrs. Bennett, and then he and Theo followed her husband to the foyer. They stopped before opening the screen door.

"Be sure to pass along to your girlfriend what I just told you," said Bennett. "If the FBI wants to question us again, she should call our lawyer."

"That's your right," said Jack.

Bennett opened the door, showing them out. The screen door closed behind them. "Might not be a bad idea for you to get yourself a lawyer, too," Bennett said through the screen. "You just never know who Mr. Hewitt might implicate."

It didn't sound like a threat, but it didn't sound like an idle observation, either. It was somewhere in between.

"Very true," said Jack. "You never know."

He started down the front steps, Theo at his side. The porch light went black before they reached the driveway.

"Scumbag liar," said Theo as they got into the car. "Protect his family. Right."

"Ellen Bennett is a mess. You can look at her and see it."

"And we're supposed to believe it's all about fear of the media? Come on. Fear of sumptin', but it ain't the media. Those walls he put up around her ain't for her benefit."

"I know that."

"Then why'd you just sit there like you're buying into it. I told you, man. You gotta call a scumbag a scumbag. You can't let him win."

"He didn't win."

"He did by the count on my scorecard."

"Theo, I came here with one objective: to throw a

lifeline to Ellen Bennett, to make her want to reach out to me and talk, one-on-one. Trading insults with Geoffrey Bennett is a waste of energy."

Theo dug his keys from his pocket. "Okay, if that's your strategy, you may be right."

"I know I'm right."

"But you're no damn fun."

Theo started the engine, the headlights shining across the lawn as they backed out of the driveway. Alongside the house, behind a chain-link fence, Jack spotted the Bennett family's swimming pool that had figured so prominently in the defense of Sydney Bennett.

"Lots of lies," said Jack. "Lots and lots of lies."

27

Sean Keating watched the *Faith Corso Show* from BNN headquarters in Manhattan. The CEO of BNN couldn't watch every show on his network, but Keating never missed Corso. Her show had all the markings of his next mega-success.

"Damn, she's good," said Keating as the show ended.

His bodyguard nodded in agreement. Roland Sharp had no official title at BNN, but he was known by most as the "Shadow." Keating rarely set foot outside the building without the Shadow or some other trusted member of the security team at his side, or at least lurking in the background, ready to draw a concealed weapon in defense of one of the most hated CEOs in corporate America. It wasn't purely paranoia. Hate e-mail arrived by the virtual truckload on a daily basis, and even some death threats had come since Al Jazeera's profile of Keating and his network's anti-Islamic bent.

"She's the best," said Sharp. They were alone in "the brain room," a subterranean office that no one at BNN could enter without special clearance.

"Tell Faith I want to see her."

The Shadow hesitated. The *Faith Corso Show* had been born in the brain room, but Corso herself had never been invited inside. Her set, however, was not far away, one of several in the windowless expanse below street level. The "BNN bunker," as people called it, was the gloomy corporate expression of the CEO's siege mentality, born of Keating's oft-expressed fears that everyone from Islamic extremists to the Jewish Defense League was out to get him.

"Go," said Keating. "Bring her."

His bodyguard left the room, which involved bypassing an alarm and deactivating two electronic locks. Keating rose from his old leather chair to refresh his drink.

Keating loved scotch, and pouring his own glass or two every night was a ritual, his personal reward for another job well done. On the wall behind the bar, right above the bottles of Blue Label, were his two favorite portraits in the entire building. One of Don Corleone. The other, Don Rickles. An old *Vanity Fair* article about Keating's creation of the BNN empire had called him a combination of the two. It wasn't intended as a compliment, but like everything else at BNN, the insult was stripped of all original meaning and spun into something it was never intended to be, something that served the network's purpose and agenda. In truth, Sean Keating was neither mafioso nor comedian. He was a frustrated political strategist whose on-air remarks in the first and only campaign he had ever managed were so racist that he was fired before the election, and no serious candidate from either party would ever hire him again. Four decades later, the more mature and refined ideology that oozed without apology from each and every one of BNN's programs was his outlet for those frustrations.

There was a polite knock on the door. Keating checked the security screen and saw Faith Corso outside the door. He buzzed her in, and the door relocked automatically as it closed behind her.

"Faith, come on in," he said. "Have a seat."

The pit bull of television news entered like a kitten, aware that she was officially part of the privileged few who had visited Keating's inner sanctum.

"Not much to look at, is it?" he said.

It was a simple room, no fancy furnishings. The conference table was Formica. The chairs around it were covered in dull vinyl. The carpeting showed signs of wear. Only the electronics were state of the art, no expense spared on the monitors and display screens of all sizes, each broadcasting a different show, some from sister companies of BNN, some from competitors.

"I guess I don't know what I was expecting to see."

He smiled the only way he knew how, which wasn't much of anything, just a crease across his mouth that rose almost imperceptibly on the right side. He offered her a drink, but she declined.

"Good show tonight, Faith," he said as they moved toward a small sitting area, away from the conference table. Corso took a seat on the couch and Keating in his leather chair.

"Thank you."

"You've been riding the Sydney Bennett train a long time. How much more steam is left?"

"Honestly, I thought it would be over already. But this story could be bigger than the trial. Sort of the way the Watergate cover-up became bigger than the break-in."

"Interesting way to look at it," Keating said. "But not what I want to hear from you."

"I'm sorry. Did I say something wrong?"

"I just had a marketing meeting yesterday. When I started BNN, the median age of our viewers was fifty-five. Now, it's sixty-five. Basically our bread-and-butter commercials cater to the fallen-and-can't-get-up age group—folks for whom the good, the bad, and the ugly are now the immobile, the infirm, and the incontinent. If we stay on this track, the only things our sponsors will be able to sell are burial plots and quickie cremations. The audience that got us where we are today isn't going to be here tomorrow. You're my new girl, my chance to change that demographic and tap into the more lucrative thirty-five-to-fifty-year-old audience. So stop making references to things like Watergate."

"I understand."

He tasted his scotch, then continued. "I don't think you do, fully. Here's a little pop quiz on BNN history. Do you know how many viewers BNN had on the very first day it went on the air?"

"I don't know. Half a million?"

"Twenty-five million."

"I don't see how that's possible."

"No one did. That's because in the normal course of the television business, cable companies paid content providers like MTV or ESPN for the right to air their programs. I turned that whole paradigm on its head. I didn't just give BNN away. Before we aired a single program, we paid the cable companies to sign an agreement to put us on the air. As much as twenty bucks a subscriber. A half billion dollars later, before we even went on the air, we had our mass audience, bought and paid for."

"That's not why they keep tuning in, day after day, year after year."

"True. But our audience is shrinking, and advertising revenues aren't what they used to be. It's not enough for my shows to be a success. We need mega-success."

Mega was one of his favorite words. He sat up, leaned closer, looking Corso in the eye. "*You* are my next mega-success."

She could barely contain her glow. "Thank you."

"But there are some things to clean up first. Starting with coma girl."

Not even Corso had stooped to calling her coma girl. "Celeste Laramore," she said.

"Yes. Celeste. I've authorized my lawyers to put up to a million-dollar offer on the table to make it go away."

That raised her eyebrows. "Excuse my disagreement, but I am a lawyer myself. I have serious qualms about paying that kind of money when we have done nothing wrong."

"Well, Faith, consider this your official welcome to the brain room: We *did* do something wrong."

She chuckled, then realized that he wasn't joking. "What do you mean by 'we'?"

"One of our boys in the field," he said, shooting a sideways glance at the door. He knew that the Shadow was standing guard on the other side of it.

"Okay, I got it. And exactly what did 'we' do?"

"We got a little too aggressive and cracked into the LIFENET system that allows the EMS crew to transmit vital signs wirelessly. Again, it's wireless, so intercepting that data to be the first news station to know if she was dead or alive would have been no big deal, except that somehow our techie crashed the whole damn system. The EMS crew was essentially flying solo all the way to the hospital, no input from cardiologists back at the hospital on how to treat the patient."

It took a moment to digest what she was being told. "So . . . we did cause her coma?"

"No, no, no," said Keating. "We crashed the wireless system. The thug in the crowd who grabbed her by the neck caused her coma. But that's a nice distinction that I don't care to press in a public forum. It happened on your show, and I can't take the risk of tarnishing the image of my newest superstar."

Corso took a breath. "This is . . . disturbing."

"Yes. But the fact that we've earmarked a million dollars to solve the problem is the good news."

"So what's the bad news?"

"The million dollars is coming out of your salary."

Her mouth fell open. "That's not fair."

"You're right. It's not. But like I said: Welcome to the brain room."

"I just don't see why you're punishing me. I didn't

know anything about this. Why should it come out of my salary?"

"Are you suggesting that it should come out of mine?"

"No, but—"

"If you don't like it, Faith, there are other networks."

He could almost feel her shiver.

"Sean, I didn't say, you know, that I was walking out the door. I just said a million dollars out of my salary isn't fair. But I'm . . . happy. Overall. Just, uh, not about this."

It wasn't easy to make Faith Corso stammer, but Keating had made tougher cookies crumble. "Then help me find another solution."

"Okay. How can I help?"

"My lawyers tell me that the only way to make the Laramore case go away quickly is to settle it. Find me another way to make it go away."

"I'd have to give that some thought."

"That's what we do best right here," he said, opening his arms wide, reminding her that they were in the brain room. He walked to the bar, added another finger of scotch to his glass, and then sat on the edge of the table, facing her. "Let me tell you how I see it. One option is to settle the case and get a confidentiality agreement. That would cost us— excuse me, cost *you*—a million. Which brings us to option number two: Make Swyteck dismiss the suit, for nothing."

"How do you make a lawyer even think about dismissing a personal-injury lawsuit when his client is a twenty-year-old woman in a coma?"

"We've already got Swyteck on the run. Ted Gaines tells me that the judge is furious about the Facebook postings in violation of the court order. Gaines said that cases do get dismissed for willful violations of court orders."

"It's rare," said Corso.

"Exactly. Which is why I prefer a more direct approach."

"Meaning what?"

"We need to exploit this jury-tampering story."

"I agree that we need to exploit the story," said Corso. "But I don't see how jury tampering in the Sydney Bennett trial leads directly to the dismissal of the civil suit by Celeste Laramore."

"Let me be clear. Somebody lurking behind the scenes paid a juror a hundred thousand dollars for a not-guilty verdict. We don't know who paid it, but the guy who took the money is now on the hot seat. You're a former prosecutor. You *know* that Mr. Hewitt is getting hammered right now to cough up a name. They're probably offering him probation and a parade in his honor if he turns state's evidence."

"I don't know about the parade, but I see your point. A deal is in the works, no doubt."

"Right. You know it. I know it. And Jack Swyteck knows it. So, if I'm Jack Swyteck, I'm getting very nervous about which way the finger may point."

"I would be nervous if I were the defense counsel of record."

"Yes," said Keating. "You'd be concerned not only about how it might play out in the courtroom, but also how it plays in the media. So, just to make my point, let's suppose Mr. Swyteck gets a phone call."

"A phone call?"

"Yeah," he said, putting his thumb and finger to mimic the call. "'Hello, Sly-teck?'—love that name you gave him—'Faith Corso here. Let me tell you how it is. We have a reliable source linking you to the payment of a hundred-thousand-dollar bribe to a juror. Now, we can either run with this story, or we can shelve it. Which would you like us to do?'"

Corso read between the lines—not that his approach had left much in the way of hidden meaning to begin with. "You want Jack Swyteck to convince the Laramores that they have no case against BNN and should dismiss their lawsuit. And to make him do that, you want me to threaten him with a bogus story about jury tampering?"

"Who said the story is bogus?"

"You have a source?"

"Not yet. But we'll find one."

Corso took a deep breath. "That would be one hell of a story. But I can't make that phone call."

"Maybe you prefer to be a bit more subtle. It's all a matter of style."

"Let me push back a little harder: *I'm* not making that phone call to Jack Swyteck."

He noticed the placement of her emphasis. "So what you're saying is that you're willing to run with the story, but it's really not necessary that the phone call come from you."

She tightened her gaze, eyes narrowing, so completely repeating herself in both words and tone that it was as if Keating had never asked for clarification. "*I'm* not making that phone call to Jack Swyteck."

She was demanding deniability, he realized, a

little distance between the talk-show host and the threat. It was a reasonable middle ground. A commitment to the story was all he'd really wanted from her anyway. Other players on his team were much better at making threats.

"I think we understand each other perfectly," he said.

"Good."

He raised his glass and gave her that one-sided smile again. "*You* are my newest superstar."

"I'm glad you didn't say 'a star is born.'"

It took him half a second, then he got the allusion to the wrong demographic. "You're good, Corso. You are *so* good."

28

Game face. Jack put on his as he crossed the street and approached the crowd outside the Criminal Justice Building.

News reports of a bought-off juror had reignited the army of Shot Mom haters. A busload of them had come from somewhere, and Jack didn't think it too cynical to wonder if BNN had actually rounded them up from some retirement home, promised them a free lunch, and brought them in for the sake of good television. One thing was clear: None of their anger was for the juror who had taken the bribe. Sydney Bennett, whereabouts unknown, left Jack as the only visible target. Game face was the only way to deal with reporters who pushed one another out of the way and thrust microphones in Jack's face, prodding him for a comment as they climbed the courthouse steps. Game face was his only response to the barrage of insults hurled from the crowd.

"*Tramposo!*"

"Cheater!"

Much uglier things were shouted, but that one in

Spanish stung the most—because it was from an old Cuban woman who looked like his grandmother. Jack wasn't trying to torture himself, but he nonetheless allowed himself to consider the remote possibility that this little old woman with the big voice could be someone who knew *Abuela*, someone his grandmother would have to avoid in shame the next time she showed her face at church. For some lawyers, the out-of-court fallout was "collateral damage." For Jack, there was nothing collateral about it.

"Welcome back, counselor," said the security officer. She was anything but sincere, and even though it wasn't overly sarcastic, her snide tone of voice was one that Jack had never heard from courthouse staff. It was a heavy reminder that for anyone who worked in the system, buying a jury was about as low as you can go.

It was déjà vu as Jack cleared security, rode the elevator to the ninth floor, and started down the crowded hallway to Judge Matthews' courtroom. Jack passed the same reporters and many of the same spectators who had followed the murder trial. He knew his way through the obstacle course, and the heavy doors closed with a thud as he entered the courtroom. The gallery was packed, though most would soon be disappointed to hear that Shot Mom would not be making an appearance in this encore performance of the Sydney Bennett show.

"This is for you," said the prosecutor as she handed him a legal memorandum.

It was the first Jack had seen of Melinda Crawford since her postverdict press conference. Jack gave her memo a quick look. It was on double jeopardy—the prosecution's legal argument as to why the U.S. Constitution didn't preclude the retrial of Sydney Bennett.

"Read it and weep," she said.

Crawford walked to her table with the same confidence she'd displayed before the verdict—maybe more. The prosecution always sat near the jury box, and Jack wondered if it was any coincidence that Crawford had positioned her chair so that it was directly in front of seat five—the seat Brian Hewitt had occupied for nearly a month before he was chosen foreman.

Jack was still getting ready when he heard the knock on the side door to the judge's chambers. The bailiff's announcement—"All rise!"—brought an abrupt end to the buzz of conversation from the gallery. Judge Matthews entered the courtroom and climbed to the bench. It felt like a dream—a nightmare—as the bailiff called the case.

"State of Florida versus Sydney Bennett . . ."

It's freakin' Groundhog Day, thought Jack.

"Good morning," said the judge. "The court has before it the prosecution's motion to set aside the verdict of not guilty entered in this case on grounds of jury tampering. Ms. Crawford, let me hear from you first."

"Thank you," she said as she stepped to the podium. "Your Honor, I have mixed feelings this morning. Of course I felt that the verdict of not guilty in this case was a miscarriage of justice. Even though I accepted that verdict, in my heart I wished that there was some way to undo it. I'm here to tell the court that it should indeed be undone—that the law requires this court to set aside this verdict and order Sydney Bennett retried on the charges set forth in the original indictment. But I wish to state from the get-go that the grounds for this motion— the affront to the entire judicial system that is jury tampering—is nothing for anyone to celebrate."

"Let me stop your speech there," said the judge. "I agree that it's nothing to celebrate. But it's not something that this court can rush to judgment about, either. As I understand it, a juror in this case has been accused of accepting a bribe. Last time I checked, he is presumed innocent until proven guilty."

"Mr. Hewitt will be in federal court this afternoon to enter a plea of guilty," said Crawford.

The judge glanced at Jack, as if curious to know if the defense was as surprised as everyone else in the courtroom. "Is that so?" said the judge.

"Yes. Mr. Hewitt's attorney is here this morning to answer any questions the court may have." Her gaze drifted toward the gallery, where a man rose— and Jack's jaw nearly dropped.

"May it please the court, I'm Ted Gaines, counsel for Brian Hewitt."

The judge invited him forward. Gaines walked to the end of the row of bench seating, stepped through the swinging gate, and joined the prosecutor at the podium. He shot a quick glance in Jack's direction, which Jack could only interpret to mean, *You're fucked.*

"Is this true, Mr. Gaines?"

"It is, Your Honor. We have a signed plea agreement with the U.S. attorney, under which my client will enter a plea of guilty this afternoon."

"This seems like an unorthodox way to present it," said the judge.

"Unusual circumstances, yes," said Gaines. "But an important part of the plea arrangement is Mr. Hewitt's agreement to testify in connection with the state of Florida's motion to set aside the verdict entered in this case."

"Interesting," said the judge. "I must say, that's an impressive display of expedited coordination between state and federal prosecutors."

Crawford said, "It was a late night, Your Honor."

Jack rose. "And I guess I must have left the phone off the hook, because this is the first I've heard any of this."

The judge raised a hand, stopping him. "The defense will have its opportunity to respond. Ms. Crawford, I presume you would like to present this testimony."

"Yes, I would."

"Objection," said Jack.

"On what grounds?" asked the judge.

"No notice was given that this would be an evidentiary hearing with testimony from witnesses. My client isn't even here. The Sixth Amendment guarantees her the right to be present and confront witnesses against her."

It was lame, but it was the best Jack could do. The judge seized on it, offering up his BNN sound bite for the day. "Consider this your notice: Men in black robes sometimes hear evidence. Ms. Crawford, proceed with your witness."

"The state calls Mr. Brian Hewitt."

The double doors in the back of the courtroom

opened, and the deputy brought Hewitt down the center aisle. Jack watched him all the way, but Hewitt never made eye contact. The witness cast his gaze at the floor as he swore the oath, and when he finally took a seat and looked at the prosecutor, whereupon everyone could see his face, it was obvious to Jack—as it must have been to all—that Hewitt hadn't slept a wink last night.

"Please state your name," said the prosecutor.

The preliminaries were familiar to Jack. It was his practice to commit to memory the basic personal information for every juror, and the recent flood of news coverage about Hewitt had more than refreshed his recollection. Jack was less interested in the litany of background information and more interested in Hewitt's demeanor. The guy had the fidgets—as Jack's late friend and mentor at the Freedom Institute would have said, "nervous as a long-tailed cat in a room full of rocking chairs." The deeper the prosecutor led him into the proverbial room, the longer his tail grew.

"Mr. Hewitt," said the prosecutor, "please describe for the court the first communication you had about the payment of money to you in exchange for a not-guilty verdict."

Jack listened and took notes as the prosecutor walked Hewitt through two different phone calls and finally a face-to-face meeting. Five minutes, ten minutes, almost twenty minutes of testimony. Jack expected at each turn for the prosecutor to pause for dramatic effect and ask the witness if the man who had offered to pay him six figures for a verdict of not guilty was in the courtroom, at which time all eyes would follow the accusatory finger that was pointing straight at Jack. But that moment didn't come.

And the judge seemed bothered by it.

"Ms. Crawford, as powerful and disturbing as this testimony is," the judge said, "I'm concerned by what I'm not hearing. The prosecution is asking the court to set aside a verdict of not guilty and order Sydney Bennett to stand trial again on the same charges. I'm willing to hear your evidence, but let me say this unequivocally. There is *no way* I'm going to order another trial if you can't show me that it was the defendant or her counsel, or someone acting under their direction, who bribed this juror. In other words, if you can't show me that the *defendant* tainted this verdict, it's my view that a retrial would constitute double jeopardy."

Jack rose. "That's our view as well, Your Honor."

Crawford glanced across the courtroom at Ted Gaines, then back at the judge. "No worries, Your Honor. We can link the bribe to the defendant."

With the court's permission, a projection screen lowered from the ceiling, Crawford's assistant went to the computer and brought an image onto it. Jack couldn't tell what it was, but his finger was on the OBJECT button, figuratively speaking. Crawford walked over to Jack, gave him a copy of an affidavit, and then handed up the original to the judge.

"Your Honor, this is an affidavit from Petty Officer Charles Cook, United States Coast Guard," said Crawford. "Officer Cook is stationed at Opa-locka Executive Airport in Hialeah, Florida."

The image on the screen suddenly became clearer to Jack.

Crawford continued, "Officer Cook was on duty the night of July eleven. As set forth in the affidavit, Officer Cook shot two minutes of video on his iPhone from two forty A.M. until two forty-two A.M. For the record—and this is not a matter of dispute—Sydney Bennett was released from the Miami-Dade Women's Detention Center at two twelve A.M."

Jack was on his feet. "Your Honor, if the prosecution intends to offer this video into evidence, I object on numerous grounds, not the least of which is that this affidavit is no assurance of the authenticity of this recording."

"Fine," said Crawford, "if that's the way Mr. Swyteck wants it. Judge, as I mentioned, Officer Cook is on active duty in the Coast Guard. We'd be happy to bring him in live when he's not in a helicopter flying over the Gulf Stream."

"That seems fair to me," the judge said. "This isn't a jury trial. We're all here. Let's see the video, and if the defense still has authenticity concerns, we can bring in Officer Cook for cross-examination. Roll it."

The lights dimmed, and on Crawford's cue, the grainy, still image on the screen came to life. It was a man and a woman standing by a chain-link fence.

"Stop it right there," said Crawford. "Judge, I should add that since it was dark, our tech expert has enhanced this video to make the people in it more visible."

"Your Honor, that's yet another reason to exclude this video," said Jack.

"I understand the defense's position. In addition to the Coast Guard officer who shot this video, the prosecution will make their tech expert available for cross-examination. But right now we are going to see this video. Ms. Crawford, proceed."

"Thank you," said the prosecutor, and then she turned to the witness. "Mr. Hewitt, do you recognize the two people in this frame?"

"Yeah, the man looks like—"

"Objection," said Jack. "The witness is clearly speculating."

"Really?" said the judge. "It looks like *you*, Mr. Swyteck, which is what I believe the witness was going to say. Are you telling me that it's *not* you?"

"With all due respect, I'm not on the witness stand."

"We can put you there," the judge snapped.

A chorus of chuckles washed over the courtroom.

"That objection is withdrawn," said Jack.

"Good decision," said the judge. "The witness may answer the question."

Hewitt leaned forward, speaking into the microphone. "That appears to be Mr. Swyteck."

"And the woman who he is with," said Crawford, "do you recognize her?"

Hewitt nodded once, firmly. "I spent a month in this courtroom looking at Sydney Bennett. I'd swear that's her."

"Thank you," said Crawford. She cued her assistant, and the video resumed.

Jack watched, riveted. It was an actual recording of the image that had replayed in his mind many times since that night. Sydney turning away from him. Sydney walking across the runway, slowly at first, gaining speed. Finally, Sydney running into the arms of a man who was waiting for her outside the small aircraft. After three years in prison, Sydney Bennett was in the full embrace of an unidentified man.

"Stop," said Crawford.

The image froze on the screen—Sydney locked in the man's arms.

Crawford faced her witness. "Mr. Hewitt, do you recognize the man in this frame?"

Jack froze. It was the question he'd been asking since the night of Sydney's release.

"Yes, I do," said Hewitt.

"Who is it?" asked Crawford.

Hewitt said, "That's the man who I met at the Metromover station at Government Center."

"The man who offered you the bribe?"

"Yes," said Hewitt. "That man."

Crawford paused, allowing the answer to linger. Her assistant turned off the video, and the lights came up. "I have no further questions."

Jack did a double take. He was expecting to hear a name, but obviously the government didn't know it. Or they didn't want Jack to know it.

"Mr. Swyteck, you may cross-examine, if you wish."

Jack rose slowly. That second possibility—that the government knew the man's name but simply didn't want Jack to know it—was burning in his mind. Instinct told him that he would be playing into Crawford's hands if he rushed through this witness, no preparation.

"Judge, the defense would like a recess before cross-examining this witness. In my mind, this case has been over since the not-guilty verdict, Mr.

Hewitt was just arrested last night, until ten minutes ago I had no idea no idea this video existed, and I—"

"You can stop there, counselor," the judge said. "I have another jury trial that I'm trying to finish today anyway. I'll give you the weekend to prepare. Let's reconvene here at nine A.M. Monday morning."

"Thank you," said Jack.

"Don't thank me, counselor. Based on what I've seen, the government has done a convincing job of linking your client to the man who bribed Mr. Hewitt. I'm not going to tell you how to do your job, but it may require nothing short of Sydney Bennett herself coming into this courtroom to rebut this showing. Now, she may want to invoke the Fifth Amendment, and that's her decision. But without her testimony, I don't see how you can even begin to explain the fact that on the night of her release from jail, she was throwing herself at the man who bribed a juror."

"I understand," said Jack.

"Make sure you do. I'll see you all Monday morning."

The judge stepped down from the bench, and the packed courtroom rose on the bailiff's command. Jack had one eye on the judge as he headed to his chambers, but his gaze slowly shifted to the other side of the courtroom. Finally, when the judge was gone and people started talking and heading to the exit, Jack caught sight of Ted Gaines in the crowd. He was behind the prosecutor's table, standing at the rail with his client, when he glanced in Jack's direction. Gaines mouthed the words, and Jack could plainly read his lips.

Call me.

29

Jack's car was waiting at the curb with the motor running. The group of demonstrators outside the courthouse was mostly people who wanted to get on television, and the BNN cameraman was happy to oblige. The gathering would look much larger and much more passionate on the evening edition of the *Faith Corso Show*; there was nothing like well-edited crowd-scene video to obscure the fact that no one inside the courtroom had actually presented any evidence to link Jack "Sly-teck" to jury tampering. One protester managed to thrust a sign in Jack's face as he raced down the granite steps, but before the reporter could catch him and demand a comment, Jack jumped into the passenger seat and slammed the door shut. Theo hit the gas, and the car pulled away.

"Thanks, man," said Jack.

Judge Matthews had deferred ruling until at least Monday, but Jack could count on one hand the people on the planet who believed that someone other than Jack and his client were behind the jury tampering. Two of them were in the car—Theo and *Abuela*.

Theo glanced in the rearview mirror and said, "She ain't happy."

Abuela was in the backseat behind Theo, with her packed suitcase on the seat beside her. If Rene's murder had proved anything, the threat against "someone you love" was pretty broad. It was time to follow through on getting *Abuela* out of town.

"Jack, *el* ticket," said *Abuela*. "Is one way."

Jack glanced over the passenger's-side headrest. His grandmother was studying her itinerary.

"We'll buy a return when it's time to come home," he said.

"How long I go?"

"I don't know," said Jack.

"You send me away for you don't know how long?"

"It's all about keeping you safe," said Jack.

"An old woman alone in a strange land—this is safe?"

Jack tried not to roll his eyes. "You're going to Tampa to stay with your brother."

"Forty years I fight to get out of Cuba to see my grandson. He sends me away on one-way ticket. *Ay, Dios mío.*"

"*Abuela*, please—"

Theo reached across the console, stopping him. "Dude, you're not gonna win this one."

Jack's phone rang. It was Ted Gaines.

"Swyteck, I asked you to call me."

Jack recalled the gesture at the end of the hearing. "I was getting around to it."

"We have a hearing at two P.M.," said Gaines.

"No, Judge Matthews said Monday morning."

"I'm talking about *Laramore versus BNN*. You know, the frivolous lawsuit you filed against my client?"

Jack ignored the swipe. "I didn't get notice of any hearing."

"I'm sure his assistant will be calling you any minute now. It was just scheduled at BNN's request."

"I'm getting tired of the sniper tactics, Ted. What's this about?"

"More postings on Celeste Laramore's Facebook page. Everything you took down is back up. Plus more."

Jack caught his breath, not sure he had enough fingers to plug another hole in the dam. "When did this happen?"

"While we were in court at this morning's hearing."

"That can't be. We reset the username and password to freeze Celeste's Facebook account."

"I assure you, the account is up and running, telling the world all about your lawsuit against BNN in flagrant violation of Judge Burrows' order."

"I'll take care of it."

"At this point, Swyteck, I don't care if you do or you don't. BNN's position is that this is the second willful violation of a court order, and I'm going to ask the court to dismiss your case."

"Fine," said Jack. "Do what you gotta do."

Gaines ended the call. Jack immediately accessed Facebook on his iPhone. Sure enough, Celeste's page had been reactivated. The only way to remove the postings was to log in as the administrator, but when Jack typed in the username and password, he got an error message: username and password invalid.

"Somebody hijacked Celeste's Facebook page," said Jack.

"Hijack?" said Abuela. "Someone hijack plane?"

"No," said Jack. "Not the plane."

Theo glanced over from behind the wheel. "Say what?"

Jack didn't have time to explain, and this wasn't something that Theo could fix anyway. "Just keep driving," he said.

Jack put an emergency call in to a tech expert who owed him a favor or two. The call went to voice mail, and Jack left the essential details in an urgent message.

"You calling who I think you're calling?" asked Theo.

"Chuck Mays," said Jack.

"Ah, good ol' Chuck-my-name-rhymes-with—"

"Stop," said Jack, saving *Abuela*'s ears. Apart from being famous for dropping the f-bomb, Chuck Mays was in the personal data-mining business, and he knew the dark side of social media better than any predator on the Internet. With Jack's legal guidance, Chuck had turned those skills against an online pedophile who had targeted the Mayses' teenage daughter. Jack had never asked for anything in return, but if ever there would be such a time, this was it.

In less than a minute Chuck returned Jack's call,

which Jack took on the Bluetooth speaker so that he could jot down notes, if needed.

"You want me to figure out a Facebook password?" said Chuck. "Are you fu—"

"Yes, I'm serious," said Jack. "And please mind your language. I have my grandmother in the car with me."

"Oh, sorry. My fucking bad."

"Chuck!"

"Terrible habit. But okay," he said, breathing deeply, "I got it under control."

Jack glanced at *Abuela*, who thankfully had missed the f-bomb. She could converse one-on-one in English, but typically a stray word from some conversation between Anglos didn't elicit a reaction from her, unless, of course, she thought it had something to do with Cuba or Castro. *NBC News confirms that Iranian dictator Ahmadinejad has declared death to infidels*—"Ay, *Jack! Qué dijo de Fidel?*"

"So let me get this straight," said Chuck. "Of all the things you could ask for, you're burning a favor on a Facebook problem?"

"It's my client's account," said Jack. "It's been hijacked."

"Hijack?" said Abuela. It was one of those buzz words. "The plane?"

"No, no," said Jack. "Chuck, excuse me a second. *Abuela*, the planes are fine, I promise. Really, *todo está bien con los* airplane-os."

"Airplane-os?" said Chuck.

It even made Theo wince. "Worst damn Spanish of any half-Cuban boy in Miami."

Abuela sighed in despair, muttering something that translated roughly as *"Thank God your mother isn't alive to hear this."*

"Can we just focus, please?" said Jack. "Chuck, I need you to access my client's account and delete all of today's postings. Can you do it?"

"Sure."

"This is an emergency. Don't tell me you can do it if you can't do it *right now.*"

"Piece of cake."

"Is that a yes?" asked Jack.

"What else would I mean by 'piece of cake'?" said Chuck.

"Allow me to translate," said Theo. "Jack, he said: Piece-o of cake-o. Easy as pie-o. Like falling off a bike-o and hijacking an airplane-o."

"Hijack?" said *Abuela*.

"Enough with the hijacks!" said Jack. "Chuck, I need to be able to count on you for this. Shut the thing down, and make sure it stays down."

"No fucking problem, dude."

"Ay!" *Abuela* shrieked, covering her ears.

Jack cringed and took him off speaker, escaping a second f-bomb by literally a half second. Jack thanked him, and as the call ended, Theo pulled up to curbside check-in. Jack got out, grabbed *Abuela*'s suitcase, and then helped her out of the car. Fridays were always busy at MIA, but even with the cars and buses streaming past them, baggage attendants at work, and hundreds of travelers coming and going, Jack felt alone with his grandmother outside the terminal. It was the tear hanging from the corner of her eye that got him.

He gave her a hug. "It's going to be okay."

"I see this before. Old people go away. They no come home."

"Is that what you think? I'm just sending you away?"

"Like my friend, Beatriz. 'Oh, Nana, here your plane ticket to Chicago—just a nice visit to see your niece.' Two week later the moving van come. Beatriz never be back."

"That's not what this is about. Don't ever think that I would do that."

"Never did think. Before today." She reached up, cupped her hand on his face. "Bye, *mi vida*."

She tried to lift her own bag, which tore Jack apart. "Okay, stop, *Abuelu*, this isn't permanent. This is—"

"Jack," said Theo.

Jack shot a look over his shoulder. "Not now."

"Jack, really." Theo was walking around the back of the car with his phone in his hand.

"What now?" said Jack.

"You need to take this."

"I can't."

"Yeah, you can," said Theo, handing him the phone. "It's Sydney Bennett."

30
.

At two P.M. Jack was in Courtroom 22-A at the Miami-Dade Courthouse. Ben Laramore was seated with him at the table near the empty jury box. Celeste's mother had refused to leave their daughter's side at the hospital, but Jack had wanted at least one of his clients to attend.

Civil cases in Miami were heard miles away from the criminal justice center. The eighty-five-year-old courthouse on Flagler Street was once the tallest building south of the Washington monument, and its limestone facade and classic Doric columns continued to raise architectural expectations for first-time visitors. Most were disappointed. Far from the grand old courtrooms of yesteryear, Judge Burrows' courtroom was badly renovated office space that had been converted into an extra courtroom out of pure necessity. The sagging ceiling was held up by two pillars in the center of the room, which forced Jack and his client to stand at opposite ends of the table so that each could have an unobstructed view of the judge entering the courtroom.

"Good afternoon," said Judge Burrows.

"Good afternoon," the lawyers replied—one from Jack's side, five from BNN's table. Ted Gaines' booming voice was most audible.

Burrows was an affable old judge with more hair on his face than on the top of his head and a long, long history on the bench. Jack hoped that experience would work to his client's advantage. The written motion that BNN had filed right before the hearing confirmed that Gaines did, in fact, plan to seek dismissal of the case as a sanction for the Facebook postings. Generally speaking, judges who had "seen it all" didn't throw litigants out of court lightly.

"Mr. Gaines, I've read your motion," the judge said. "Having served on this bench for over a quarter century, I have to say that it is the rare case in which dismissal of the entire action is an appropriate sanction for violation of a court order."

Good start, thought Jack.

Gaines rose, buttoning his coat. "This is such a case, Your Honor."

"Tell me why."

Gaines walked smoothly around the table, framing himself between the two pillars in the middle of the room. Oddly, the architectural flaws seemed to reinforce his strength. "Judge, this court entered an order that required the plaintiffs to file their complaint under seal, not part of the public record. That order further precluded the plaintiffs from discussing those allegations in public."

"Yes, yes," said the judge, "and for the record I would point out that the hearing has been closed to the public, consistent with that order. Proceed."

"Just yesterday we brought to this court's attention certain postings that appeared on the Internet. Specifically, on Celeste Laramore's Facebook page. These postings tracked verbatim and in detail each of the substantive allegations against BNN in this lawsuit."

"I'm aware of that. And I also understand they were removed."

"They were," said Gaines. "Until this morning. They were back up, along with further so-called evidence against BNN."

The judge had the defendant's motion before him, which he was skimming while listening. "Tell me more about this new evidence."

"I'll read it to you," said Gaines. He had the printed Web page in hand. "And just to put this in context, the previous postings on Celeste's Facebook page have already released onto the Internet the plaintiffs' detailed allegations that doctors could have saved Celeste Laramore if BNN's alleged interception of the data transmission from the ambulance had not shut down the flow of information to the ER. Now, according to this latest posting this morning, we get this additional detail." Gaines put on his reading glasses, then read aloud: "'A physician who works at Jackson Memorial Hospital has reviewed the intercepted data and has confirmed that if the vital information had not been illegally intercepted, the ER physicians would have recognized that Celeste had a heart condition known as long QT syndrome. Armed with that information, ER physicians would have directed appropriate remedial steps, which would have almost certainly brought about Celeste's full recovery.' "

Jack glanced at his client, and he could see how difficult it was for Mr. Laramore not to react to what he firmly believed was the truth: His daughter should have been saved.

"What is long QT syndrome?" the judge asked.

Jack rose. "I can answer that, Your Honor."

"Please do."

"Long QT syndrome is a heart rhythm disorder. Some people are born with it, but it can also have other causes. Mr. Laramore informs me that Celeste has had it all her life. The danger is that it can potentially cause fast, chaotic heartbeats, which in turn may trigger anything from a sudden fainting spell to a seizure or even sudden death."

"Or, in the case of Celeste, a coma," said the judge.

"That's correct," said Jack.

"Mr. Swyteck, how widely known was it that Celeste had this condition?"

Jack checked with his client, then answered to the court. "Basically her family. Her physician."

The judge nodded, as if that was the answer he'd expected. "Let me tell you why I ask the question. I anticipate that you are going to tell me that you have no idea how these postings landed on Celeste's Facebook page."

"That's correct," said Jack. "And that is the truth."

"But this latest information posted on the Facebook page is highly specific. It doesn't say 'heart trouble' or 'heart problem.' It says long QT syndrome. Given the small universe of people who knew she had this condition, I'm having trouble seeing how someone other than your clients could have been behind the posting."

"It wasn't *us*," said Laramore.

The judge gaveled him down. "Mr. Laramore, I understand there is often an urge to speak out in open court, but when the court is addressing the attorneys, the clients do not speak. Am I understood?"

"We apologize," said Jack.

"Apology accepted. Mr. Gaines, if you could wrap up, please."

"Yes, Judge. The court has already hit the nail on the head. It only stands to reason that these postings are the work of the plaintiffs in this case. Who else would do it? I'm sympathetic to their plight. Their daughter is in a coma. They need money to pay her medical bills. They have no health insurance. But posting this information online in violation of this court's order cannot be tolerated. These egregious tactics amount to nothing short of extortion: 'Pay us a big chunk of money, or we are going to smear your reputation all over the Internet.'"

Jack was on his feet. "Judge, there has been no settlement demand from the plaintiffs."

"As if that's not coming," said Gaines.

"Mr. Swyteck, let him finish, please."

"Thank you," said Gaines. "Judge, like I said, we wouldn't be human if we didn't feel sorry for this family. But corporations are people, too."

"Uh, yeah," the judge snorted, "I'll believe that when the state of Florida executes one."

Gaines kept his composure. "Legally, a corporation is a person with the legal right to protect its reputation."

"I understand your point, counselor. I'm just saying."

Gaines continued, "We are not talking about one technical violation. This is a huge violation followed almost immediately by a second violation in contempt of this court's order."

"I get your point," the judge said. "Mr. Swyteck, what's your response?"

Jack rose. "First of all, Judge, my clients didn't post this information. We don't know who did."

"I'm not buying it," the judge said, "and not just because of what I said before, about how the information is so specific. The bottom line is that this is your client's Facebook page. If you were unable to control what goes on it, then you should have shut it down after the first violation. You didn't."

"Well, there's an emotional factor here, Your Honor. Mrs. Laramore did not want to wipe out the last few posts that her daughter put up on Facebook before she went into a coma. So we changed the username and password, effectively freezing the account."

"You did that at your peril, Mr. Swyteck. If you chose to keep the page up, you're responsible for what goes on it."

"Well, I disagree with—"

"Disagree all you want, but not on my time. Next argument."

"All right, I'll move on. But before I do, I just want to make the general observation of how unusual this whole situation is. Millions of lawsuits are filed in this country as a matter of public record. A tiny fraction of those cases are filed under seal. And when a case is filed under seal, the media often intervene and fight tooth and nail to make it public information. In fact, I did a little computer research before the hearing, and BNN itself has filed no fewer than fifty lawsuits to remove gag orders imposed by courts in various jurisdictions arguing that such orders interfered with a free press."

"Stop right there," said the judge. "Mr. Swyteck, you are way late in the day to argue that there is something wrong with the order I entered in this case directing you to file your complaint under seal. If you had a problem with it, you should have filed a motion to dissolve it. I assure you, the appropriate response is not to *defy* it. That's strike two. You're starting to annoy me. What else you got?"

"My main point, Your Honor, is that we didn't do it."

"I said, What else you got?"

"In response to Mr. Gaines' concern about his client's reputation, all I can add is that everything that has been posted is true."

"That's not the point," the judge snapped. "I ordered you not to make your allegations public, and you ignored my order. Twice. I think that leaves just one question to be addressed: What is the appropriate punishment?"

Gaines spoke up. "Your Honor, BNN requests a complete dismissal of the case with prejudice."

"Of course you do," said the judge, "but I'm just not inclined to issue the death penalty if there is some merit to the claim."

"Judge, there is no merit," said Gaines.

"Hard to say," said the judge, "with no evidence before the court. So here's what we'll do. Mr. Swyteck, I'll give you half a day to put on sufficient evidence to demonstrate to the court that you have a colorable claim. If you fail to make that showing, I will dismiss this case with prejudice. How does Monday at nine A.M. work?"

"That's not good," said Jack.

Gaines was smirking. "That's Mr. Swyteck's opportunity to convince Judge Matthews that he didn't bribe a juror."

The judge shook his head. "Not your week, is it, Mr. Swyteck?"

"No, sir. Not so far."

"All right. Tuesday. Nine A.M. See you then."

The judge gathered his papers, stepped down from the bench, and exited to his chambers. Gaines walked over to the court reporter and thanked her, never missing an opportunity to suck up to anyone who might be in a position to put in a good word for him to the judge. Then he walked toward Jack and stopped at the table.

"Not your week, is it, Mr. Swyteck?" he said with a smile, doing a fair imitation of the judge's gravelly old voice. Then his expression turned deadly serious. "And next week will be even worse."

Jack wanted the perfect comeback, but the only one that came to mind—*Yeah, for you*—would have made him sound like Hannah on the way out of their New York settlement conference. He just let it go. There was far more at stake than ego.

"Is the judge going to dismiss our case?" asked

Laramore. Most of the color had drained from his face, his eyes clouded with concern.

"Not if I can help it," said Jack.

"But Tuesday is around the corner."

"Yes, it is."

"You have three days to find witnesses and prove our case."

"I realize that."

"And you have another hearing on Monday. How are you going to do all that between now and Tuesday?"

Jack's gaze drifted across the courtroom. Led by Gaines, the BNN lawyers were filing out as a team, all smiles, as if they'd already won.

"We'll save the celebration for when the case is actually over," said Jack. "That's how."

31

Jack met Andie for happy hour at Ra Sushi in South Miami. It wasn't so happy.

They had an outside table beneath a canvas umbrella that seemed about as big as a circus tent. The sidewalk was still damp from one of those reliable afternoon thunderstorms that cooled things down and made outdoor life possible in July. Andie was helping herself to the edamame with sea salt. Jack was studying the menu. Raw fish was not really his thing, but he was learning to love it since Andie lived on it. He ordered the "crispy shrimp tempura roll," which was essentially fried shrimp in batter with rice. Not really sushi.

"Kind of like going to Il Mulino and ordering pizza," said Andie.

Jack had never been to Il Mulino, but he'd heard that the only way to get a reservation was to have Bill Clinton make it for you, so he took her meaning. "I'm getting better," he said.

She smiled, leaned across the table, and kissed him. "Yes, you are."

Jack smiled back, but an obnoxious ringtone

ruined the moment. It was a rap song unlike anything Jack would have downloaded, unless for reasons unknown he were specially commissioned by
the Library of Congress to catalog the number of
words in the English language that could be forced
to rhyme with "suck" and "bitch."

"What the heck is that?" asked Andie.

Jack pulled Theo's phone from his pocket and silenced it. "Theo loaned me his phone."

"Why?"

Jack checked the incoming caller—somebody
named "Squeezeplay"—and let it go to Theo's voice
mail. "When we were at the airport today, Sydney
Bennett called me on his phone."

"You talked to her?"

"For about five seconds. Then she freaked and hung
up. Theo let me keep his phone in case she calls back."

"So she obviously thinks your phone lines aren't
secure."

"And she would be dead right about that."

"Our techies gave you a secure phone to call your
clients."

"Yeah, but I don't know how to reach Sydney. She
has to call me, and she seems to have made Theo's
cell her number of choice. So until she calls again,
I'm serenaded by Lil Wayne and Shorty Shitstain."

"Jack, that's gross."

"It's no joke. There's a rapper named Shorty Shitstain, and Theo has his ringtone."

"Why am I not surprised?"

The waitress brought Jack his beer. Two twenty-
two-ounce bottles of Kirin. "It's two for one," she said.

"You're not drinking that," said Andie.

Jack reflected on his day. "Wanna bet?"

He filled his glass. Andie watched him drink about half of it down. Before he could wipe the foam on his sleeve and say ahhh, she dropped the news.

"What would you do if you couldn't see or hear from me for five months?"

"Huh?"

"That's what I thought you'd say." She shifted in her chair, sat up a little straighter. "The new assignment I've been training for. The only way I can do it is if I go all-in. No visitation. No phone calls."

"Why?"

"There have been some concerns raised. All stemming from the fact that I fall into the category of 'someone you love.'"

Jack knew exactly what she meant. If Andie went undercover, Rene's killer was a potential threat to the entire operation.

"Have you thought about passing on this assignment?"

She looked away, then back at him. "Is that what you want me to do?"

Jack poured more beer. He was suddenly ten years younger, sitting across from the sandy blonde with steely blue eyes who looked absolutely nothing like Andie and would eventually be his ex-wife. Marriage-killing questions like this one had become Cindy's trademark. *Is that what you want me to do?* Was Jack supposed to say, "No, honey, I want what you want"? Or was the correct answer, "I can't live without you, please don't go"? With Cindy, the right answer was, by definition, whichever answer Jack didn't give.

"Is this a trick question?" asked Jack.

"Only if you make it one."

Definitely a trick question.

"Okay, let's say you go all-in. You're committed for five months."

"It might not be five months," said Andie. "That's the outside time range."

"Let's assume the worst, five months. What would happen if Rene's killer were caught before then?"

Andie considered it, then seemed to light up, liking where Jack's train of thought was leading. "That would mean the threat against me is eliminated."

"Right," said Jack. "And when the threat is gone, there would be no need for you to be all-in."

"That's true."

"So the five months of 'no contact' might turn out to be only two months."

"Or one month."

"Or none," said Jack, "if he was caught before your assignment even started."

Andie reached across the table and slid her hands into his. "We have to make that happen."

Jack thought about the coming week. "You think we can do it by Monday?" He was only half serious.

His phone rang. No rap music—really, *his* phone. Jack was so tired of hearing Gaines' voice that he didn't care who might be listening. He just took the call.

"A hundred thousand dollars," said Gaines.

"For what?" asked Jack.

"Your client drops the case and we sign a confidentiality agreement."

"Seriously, that's your offer?"

"That's my *client's* offer. I'd offer you ten cents."

"A hundred thousand dollars barely covers ten more days in the hospital."

"That's ten more days of hope than your clients have now. Who knows? Maybe ten days are just enough to get Celeste out of her coma and back on her feet. Maybe when you present this offer to her parents, you point out how a hundred thousand dollars could make all the difference in the world."

"You're all heart," said Jack.

"Ah, sarcasm. So tiresome. And so rude."

"Your offer is rude."

"The offer is generous. It's your ticket out of a very bad situation."

"Because that's just the kind of guy you are, Mr. Kill-'Em-with-Kindness."

"You don't know the first thing about me, Swyteck. Some people get angry at big corporations who refuse to write a big check to a family like the Laramores. I get angry at lawyers like you who try to force companies to write big checks when the company has done absolutely nothing wrong. So if this comes across as personal, I don't apologize."

"No, it actually doesn't come across as personal. It comes across as unprofessional. So while I will comply with the rules of ethics and present your offer to my clients, I can virtually assure you that both your offer and your non-apology will be rejected."

"The offer is open until five o'clock Sunday night. Tell your clients to take it, Swyteck. While there's still a way out."

32

W ell played, Mr. Gaines."

Sean Keating's workday was ending where it had begun—in a bulletproof limousine that shuttled him between BNN headquarters in Manhattan and his fifteen-thousand-square-foot mansion in New Jersey. Keating had purchased one of the first Audi A8 L Security vehicles to roll off the line at the top-secret plant in Neckarsulm, Germany. Hot-formed armored steel, aramide fabric, special alloyed aluminum flooring, and multilayer glass—those core features and a patented antiballistic design stood between his life and the "extremists," who Keating was absolutely certain were determined to silence him and the controversial voice of BNN. Just to throw off the enemy, Keating's driver was under strict orders to take a different route to and from work every day. Tonight's diversion had been wider than usual. They'd stopped at the airport to pick up BNN's lawyer after a highly productive day in Miami.

"The pleasure was all mine," Gaines said as he returned the car phone to its compartment.

"How soon can we wrap this up?"

Keating noted Gaines' hesitation, as well as the quick glance at the bodyguard seated across from them in another row of leather seats. Keating had never formally introduced his lawyer to the Shadow, and he fully understood that it was simply Gaines' nature to be careful about saying too much in front of people he didn't know.

"Sharp," Keating said, "are you hearing any of this?"

The Shadow was completely stone-faced, his lips barely moving. "Only if you tell me to, sir."

Keating glanced over at his lawyer. "There you have it," he said.

Gaines smiled uneasily, as if knowing that he was supposed to be satisfied.

Keating said, "So how soon can you make this go away?"

"He'll come back with ten million," said Gaines. "But we won't need to go anywhere near that high. He's an amateur."

"Nobody who's handled as many death cases as Swyteck has handled is an amateur. Somewhere beneath that self-deprecating veneer is a lawyer who will burn you, if you let him."

"By Sunday night he'll be pissing in his pants and begging me to offer him fifty thousand dollars payable in biannual installments over the next twenty-five years."

Keating was unimpressed. "There are no hero points for saving me a few bucks, Ted. The CEO of BNN doesn't take this kind of interest in a personal-injury case because it's a matter of nickels and dimes. These allegations go to the heart of this network's integrity as a news-gathering organization. If it takes the million dollars I've authorized to settle it, so be it. It may make sense to take a shot at dismissal on Tuesday, but by Wednesday at the latest I want Swyteck's signature on a confidentiality agreement, and I want this behind us."

"I hear you."

Keating adjusted his seat. A footrest motored into position, and the full-body massage feature vibrated. Luxury was a close second to security.

"I read the rough transcript from today's hearing before Judge Burrows," said Keating. His seat was reclined at his preprogrammed fifty-degree angle, his eyes closed. "I have a few thoughts on how Tuesday should unfold, if this doesn't settle before then."

Gaines helped himself to a sparkling water from the mini refrigerator. "Swyteck has to survive Monday before we get to Tuesday."

"He'll survive Monday," said Keating.

"I wouldn't be so sure."

Keating sat forward, opened his eyes, and shot a look at his lawyer that left no room for doubt. "He *will* survive Monday. Now let's talk about Tuesday."

Gaines' expression—an unsettled mix of fear and confusion—was exactly what Keating had expected. It was a natural response to a laserlike glare from an insanely rich and powerful man who worked in a corporate bunker and rode to work in a virtual tank. Keating had seen the same reaction many times before—from men with much bigger balls than Ted Gaines.

Gaines drank from his green bottle of sparkling water. "Okay, let's talk about Tuesday."

"This hearing cannot be about BNN reporters shutting down the flow of information from the ambulance to the emergency room."

"That's the core of Swyteck's case. He'll lead with that."

"Not if Judge Burrows doesn't let him."

"The judge ordered him to put on enough evidence to show that his case has merit. That's his best evidence."

"You need to make the judge understand that this hearing isn't about Swyteck's best evidence. It's about the weakest link in his case."

Gaines seemed to catch his drift. "Okay, I think I see where you're headed."

"Do you?"

"Yes. Judge Burrows made it clear that he'll dismiss the case unless Swyteck is able to make a credible showing that he has some chance of winning. Your point is that Swyteck can't win by proving simply that BNN interfered with a data transmission. He has to be able to show that BNN's actions actually caused his client to go into a coma."

"*That's* what I want the hearing to be about. Who caused Celeste Laramore to go into a coma? Who's the real villain? Now, *that's* great television."

His last remark made Gaines pause.

"Not that this is about TV ratings," said Keating.

"No," said Gaines, "of course not."

"So that's the game plan," said Keating. "You go into court on Tuesday, and you don't argue about whether or not BNN intercepted data trying to find out if Celeste was alive or dead. You get as sanctimonious as you possibly can, you look the camera in the eye and say, 'Judge, we want to keep this short and simple. So for purposes of today's hearing, let's all assume—contrary to fact—that BNN interfered with the transmission of data from the ambulance to the ER. Your Honor, even if you make that assumption, Mr. Swyteck's case is still frivolous. Here's why.' You with me, Ted?"

"Yes," said Gaines. "Except I think you meant to say 'look the judge in the eye.'"

"What?"

"You said 'look the camera in the eye.' I think you meant 'judge.'"

"Right. Of course. Look the judge in the eye."

"Because there are no cameras in this courtroom. The complaint was filed under seal at BNN's request. The hearing is closed to the public."

"I understand," said Keating. He glanced out the window, thinking. Daylight was in its final moments, and the tinted glass was like a fuzzy green shroud over the headlights of oncoming cars. "We need to fix that," said Keating.

"Fix what?"

He glanced back at Gaines. "If we are going to take this all the way to a hearing on Tuesday, I'm going all-in. I want Tuesday's hearing open to the public."

"Excuse me?"

"You heard me. Tell the judge to open it up."

"Hold on a second," said Gaines. "We're the ones who got the judge to enter an emergency order that required Swyteck to file his lawsuit under seal. We're the ones demanding that the case be kicked out of court because Swyteck violated that order.

After all that chest-thumping about the need for secrecy, now you want the hearing on this motion to be open to the public?"

"Exactly."

"Come on, Sean."

"Swyteck had one good point today," said Keating. "We *are* the media, the free press, the First Amendment. BNN can't be arguing for closed hearings."

"The judge won't like the flip-flop."

"That's why you get paid the big bucks, Ted."

Gaines shook his head slowly, as if taken by the size of the task. But he didn't shy away. "All right," he said. "We'll get it done. If you're sure this is what you want."

"Absolutely sure. Look, the bloggers have already picked up everything that was posted on that Facebook page. The genie's out of the bottle, and we have nothing to lose by making this hearing public. We're hammering Jack Swyteck, and as the Sydney Bennett trial proved night after night, that makes for excellent television. This is prime stuff for Faith Corso."

Gaines drank the last of his water and sank farther into his seat, allowing his gaze to come to rest on the television screen in the console. The sound was off, but it was tuned to BNN. "Not that this is about TV ratings," he said quietly.

"No," said Keating. He found the remote, smiling wryly as he turned up the volume. "Not in the least."

33

J ack took BNN's offer straight to Ben Laramore. The hospital's main-floor cafeteria was crowded, no privacy, so they met in the friends-and-relatives lounge on the ICU floor. It was a depressing room with one window, forest-green walls, and black pleather chairs. The darkness was by design, so that visitors on night watch for a loved one in the ICU could slip away every now and then and catch some sleep. Around midnight the couches and spare blankets would be in high demand, but for the moment, Jack and his client were alone.

"A hundred thousand dollars does us no good," said Laramore. He was seated on the edge of the couch, leaning forward, elbows on his knees.

"That's what I told Ted Gaines," said Jack.

Laramore was staring at the floor, silent. Jack watched him in the dim glow of a small lamp on the end table. He'd known Ben Laramore for less than a week. Jack had seen him tired. He'd seen him sad. He had not yet seen him this way. He looked beaten.

Jack spoke softly. "I wasn't suggesting you should

take it. But it's my obligation as an attorney to convey every settlement offer to my client."

He looked up sharply. "Then do it."

"I just did."

Laramore jumped up, energized with misdirected anger. "No. Go tell Celeste."

"What?"

He grabbed Jack by the arm, pulling him up. "Come on. Go convey the offer to your client."

"Ben, please."

"I'm serious. You're licensed to be part of this half-assed system. Go do your job as a lawyer. Go tell Celeste that after putting her in a coma, BNN has graciously put enough money on the table to keep her breathing all the way until Wednesday. Maybe even Thursday."

"Ben, calm down and have a seat. Please."

Laramore breathed out in disgust, muttering a brief apology as he returned to the couch.

"He's pretty cocky, this Gaines," said Laramore. "Is that because the judge is going to throw us out of court?"

"Clearly Mr. Gaines thinks so."

"What do you think?"

"I think if we prepare for this hearing the same way we would prepare for trial, then we'll be okay."

Laramore leaned back and sank deeper into the stuffed pleather couch. "Let me ask you something," he said. "What is Celeste's case worth if we get past the hearing on Tuesday?"

"There will be plenty of fighting about that," said Jack. "A lot of expert testimony."

"Ballpark it."

"A twenty-year-old woman who could require sixty years of care. Total care, if she stays in a coma. Some level of care seems likely even if she comes out of it."

"So you're giving her no chance of complete recovery?"

"I've ruled out nothing. That's why I don't want to put a number in your head. But if we can establish liability, and if there is no significant change in Celeste's condition, this is an eight-figure case."

"And they're offering us a hundred grand?"

"That's the first offer."

"The *only* offer," said Laramore. "And that's the problem. Celeste doesn't have six months or a year for these guys to come up with an acceptable number on the eve of trial. She's been in a coma for six days. That's already too late for some of the cutting-edge procedures that doctors are doing for patients in comas. Every day that we dance around with these jackasses, another opportunity passes."

"That's why Tuesday is so important," said Jack. "Right now, BNN has us back on our heels. But if we make a good showing on Tuesday, we'll have the upper hand."

"You believe that?"

"I do," said Jack. "That's the main reason I came all the way over here."

"What, to tell me to keep my chin up?"

"No. To convince your wife that we need her help."

"No, absolutely not," said Mrs. Laramore. "I won't leave Celeste to go sit in a courthouse all day."

Jack and the Laramores were inside the ICU, standing right outside Celeste's room. The hallway was as far away from Celeste as Mrs. Laramore would go. They kept their voices low, mindful of other patients with open doors.

"The plan is for you to be our first witness," said Jack. "You can head straight back to the hospital as soon as you finish. Two hours, tops, including travel time."

"And what if that two-hour window is when Celeste finally opens her eyes?" Her upper lip trembled, and Jack wasn't sure if she could finish her thought, but he gave her time. "What if Celeste looks out and doesn't see her mother, doesn't have anyone to calm her fears or hold her hand and give her strength to wake up?"

Jack had no answer, and she wasn't looking for one anyway.

"I can stay here," said Ben.

She glared at her husband, clearly unhappy with the solution. "Celeste needs her *mother.*"

Ben glanced at Jack, then took his wife's hand. "Honey, this is so important."

"I wouldn't ask," said Jack, "but you, more than anyone, can make this judge see what kind of person Celeste is."

Her eyes welled, and her lip began to tremble again. "You want to see what kind of person she is?"

Before Jack could answer, she pushed open the door, popped in and out of the room, and emerged with a photo album. She opened it and showed Jack. "I've been going through this all day with her, talking to her, pointing things out, trying to trigger her memories. This is her senior year of high school and graduation," she said, pointing. "This is when we took her to college. This is Celeste and her room-mate." She flipped the pages. "And this is her just a couple of months ago. Mother's Day."

Jack looked at each of the photos, casually at first, then more carefully. He was struck by a theme that ran through the time period represented by the photos, not sure it could even be called a theme. But he didn't want to discuss it then and there, especially as distraught as Mrs. Laramore was.

"May I borrow this album?" asked Jack.

"No!" said Mrs. Laramore, clutching it. "I don't mean to be rude. But we can't lose this."

"I can e-mail JPEGs to you, if you want them," said Ben.

"That would be great, thanks."

"I need to get back," said Mrs. Laramore, and she disappeared into Celeste's room. Ben led Jack down the hallway toward the secured entrance and pushed the button on the wall to open the doors.

"I'll talk this out with my wife. And I'll get you those photos."

"Thanks, please do that."

Jack exited the ICU, and the doors closed automatically behind him. He continued to the elevator, confident that Mrs. Laramore could be talked into testifying. His mind was more focused on those photographs. Flashes of brilliance sometimes didn't seem so brilliant upon second look, but he was beyond certain that his more careful review of the photos, once e-mailed to him, would confirm his initial impression:

With each photo since high school--with the gradual passage of time, starting roughly with the death of Sydney's daughter—Celeste Laramore looked more and more like Sydney Bennett.

34

The funeral home was open until ten o'clock. At 9:55 P.M., Jack pulled into the parking lot and killed the engine. That was as far as he could go. He was frozen behind the wheel, shrouded in darkness, unable to open the door.

It had been Jack's intention to stay away from any memorial service for Rene. After his meeting with the Laramores, however, he'd spotted the notice posted on the bulletin board in the hospital lobby: REMEMBERING RENE FENNING, MD, LINCOLN FUNERAL HOME, FRIDAY, 6 P.M. TO 10 P.M. The Jackson Memorial family had lost one of its own. Jack wasn't part of that family, and Rene's boyfriend had nearly broken every bone in his right fist trying to make Jack understand that he was most unwelcome. Jack couldn't blame him for feeling that way. The sight of Rene's body on a slab in the morgue had made Jack want to punch himself in the face. Twice. Once for Rene's having ended up as "someone you love." A second time for the hurt he'd caused everyone else who had ever loved her.

It was a typical humid summer night, and the

stale air inside the closed car changed from warm to stifling in a hurry. Rolling down the window to cool things down would have been pure procrastination. Jack had to do what he'd come to do—or he needed to leave. There was always a spare necktie in his console, and with the help of the rearview mirror he tied a quick double Windsor. A shave wouldn't have hurt, but the best he could do was run a comb through his hair. He drew a breath, clutched his keys, and stepped out of the car.

You can do this.

Jack's heels clicked on the asphalt as he crossed the parking lot. Several visitors passed him on their way out of the funeral home, then a few more. One older woman was sobbing and dabbing away tears. Others appeared numb, or at the very least at a loss for words. Jack looked away, only to catch sight of the black hearse parked beneath the porte cochere alongside the building. The thought of Rene heading to the cemetery in the morning was almost incomprehensible. A random memory came to him of the way Rene had surprised him one weekend and shown up at his front door direct from Abidjan—in her words, "a sex-starved expat willing to traverse the globe in search of quality horizontal time." It was a nice combination, someone who could crack you up and turn you on at the same time. It all left a knot in his stomach. He walked faster to the door, and on his way inside, a woman at the front step seemed to recognize him but said nothing. Jack tried not to make eye contact with her or anyone else, fearful that he might be asked to leave.

There was a small gathering of guests at the

sign-in register in the lobby. Jack decided that he wouldn't sign. Several other clusters of quiet conversation dotted the room. Bouquets of white roses and chrysanthemums adorned antique tables. It was all very subdued and traditional, except for the life-size photographs of Rene that flanked the entrance door to the parlor where she lay. On the left was a younger and dust-covered Rene, the volunteer pediatrician whom Jack had met in western Africa. Only a handful of people knew that period of her life. On the right was Dr. Fenning, a more current shot that was recognizable to all who had come to grieve.

"Swyteck?"

Jack turned. It was Rene's boyfriend.

"I asked you not to come," said Dr. Ross.

The perfect response was trapped somewhere between his brain and his tongue, but damned if Jack could get it out. "I didn't come to make a scene," said Jack, "and it wasn't my intention to go inside and see Rene without your blessing."

"Walk with me for a minute."

Dr. Ross started toward the main entrance, and Jack followed. He led Jack all the way outside and across the driveway, to a patch of grass that was just beyond a stand of bushy palm trees in front of the funeral home. There were crushed cigarettes on the ground, and the night air still hinted at a recent smoke.

"I can't say that I was going to invite you," said Dr. Ross, "but in a way I'm glad you came. There's something I need to tell you."

Jack braced himself.

"Don't worry," the doctor said. "I'm not going to hit you."

"That's a step forward."

It was too dark to tell if the doctor had cracked a semblance of a smile, but it would have been a sad one. "When we lost Rene, she was on her way to meet you."

"Yes, unfortunately, that's true."

"Do you have any idea what she was going to tell you?"

Jack wasn't sure how forthcoming he could be. "It was Rene who convinced me I should represent the Laramore family in their lawsuit against BNN. Thursday's meeting was a follow-up on that, but I don't know what it was about specifically."

Ross looked away, then back. "Well, I do know what she was going to tell you. *Specifically.*"

"How?"

"We talked the night before she died. She told me what she'd found."

"What did she tell you?"

He started to answer, then stopped. "Did you see the posting on Celeste Laramore's Facebook?"

It seemed like a change of subject, but Jack went along. "Yes, I saw. But I should tell you, those were posted in violation of a court order. I can't discuss what they say."

"That's fine. You have your orders. But the reality is that those postings were up long enough to leak all over the Internet. And they're all over the hospital, too. Surely you can appreciate the interest in a claim that the media interfered with the transmission of data from the ambulance to the ER."

"It was certainly of interest to Rene," said Jack.

"Which brings me back to my original point,"

said Dr. Ross. "One of those Facebook postings said something to the effect that a doctor at Jackson had reviewed the data and confirmed that if the transmission had gone through, doctors in the ER would have recognized that Celeste had a heart defect and started treatment that could have stopped her from slipping into a coma."

"I know what you're talking about," said Jack. "But like I said, I can't discuss that."

"I'm not asking you to discuss it. I just want you to hear what I'm saying. The unnamed doctor who reviewed the data: that was Rene."

Jack was surprised—but he wasn't. "Are you sure?"

"Yes, Rene reviewed that data. She drew that conclusion. As I said, she was on her way to tell you that when she was murdered."

"That couldn't have been an easy decision."

"It was quite courageous, if you ask me." Dr. Ross waited for a couple of visitors to pass on the way to their car, then continued. "Rene and I were up half the night before your meeting, talking about it. She wasn't sure if telling you was the right thing to do or not. We finally agreed she should."

It gave Jack even more respect for Rene, but he couldn't help wishing she'd come out the other way. "Did she talk to anyone else about it?"

"No way. She was agonizing over this and reluctant to get more involved than she already was. Her intention was to pass along the information to you and step aside."

Jack processed it. "So at the time of Rene's death—before this ended up on Facebook—there were only two people who knew what Rene was going to tell me."

"Right. One was Rene, and she was dead before things started popping up on Facebook. The other is me, and until this very moment, I haven't told anyone."

Jack said, "Which raises the question: Who posted that information on Celeste's Facebook page?"

"I haven't had time to think this through," said Dr. Ross, "but just talking it out with you makes it seem obvious, doesn't it? There's only one person it could be."

"The man who killed her," said Jack.

Dr. Ross looked back, stone-faced. "It makes sense, right? He got that information out of her before he killed her."

An uneasy silence came over them. The extraction of information before death only added to the heinous nature of the crime.

"You need to tell this to the police," said Jack.

"I know. I will." He buried his hands in his pockets and looked off toward the street. The extraction theory was weighing heavily on them both. "I need to get back inside," the doctor said.

"And I should probably be going. But thank you for this," Jack said, extending his hand.

Ross shook it, though he didn't look Jack in the eye. He stepped away, and Jack went in the opposite direction, toward his car.

"Swyteck," Dr. Ross said, stopping him.

Jack turned.

"Rene always said you were a decent guy."

Jack gave a nod of appreciation. The doctor continued toward the funeral home. Jack walked back to his car, alone.

35

.

At one fifteen A.M. Jack was in bed but still awake. He got up and made himself a cup of tea in the microwave, cleared away a place to sit on the couch, and watched about twenty minutes of a *Friends* rerun that he'd seen at least a half-dozen times before. Chamomile always worked for Andie when she had trouble sleeping. It just made Jack need to pee. When he came out of the bathroom, Max was waiting for him at the door.

"Sorry, boy. It's not time to run."

Max almost seemed relieved. He climbed up on the settee and went right back to doggy sleep. Jack looked at him with envy and crawled into bed. Then he reminded himself that he needed to follow up with the Kayal family about sending Max away for a while. One more thing to do.

Andie stirred on the other side of the mattress.

"What's wrong, Jack?"

Wow. What a question. Jack answered it the best he could. "Nothing."

She rolled toward him, draped her arm across his

chest and her leg atop his thigh. "It's going to get better," she said.

"I know."

"You have to believe that."

"Optimism is my middle name. Jack Optimism Sly-teck."

"You're better than Faith Corso. Don't let her keep you up at night."

"It's not her," said Jack. "I'm just having trouble understanding how the hell I got here."

Andie propped herself up on her elbow, looking him in the eye. "How do you think you got here?"

"Two years ago Neil Goderich called me, said he was sick, and asked me to do him and the Freedom Institute a favor. So I cover a hearing. Neil dies eight weeks before trial, and the judge says I'm the only living attorney of record, the case is going to trial, so I'm Sydney Bennett's lawyer. Now everybody wants to hang Sydney and her lawyer for buying off a juror, my old girlfriend is dead, and I have until Tuesday to figure out how to keep hope alive for two devastated parents whose daughter is in a coma."

Andie just looked at him, one of her patented expressions that said everything without saying a word.

"What?" said Jack.

"That's how you think you got here? Really?"

"Obviously that's the *Reader's Digest* version."

"No, that's the Jack Swyteck version."

"What do you mean by that?"

The left eyebrow arched, the telltale sign that she was about to unload exactly what was on her mind.

Then she said it. "You got here because you love it."

"I *what*?"

"Take Rene out of this. That's a horrible tragedy, and we'll catch the guy who did it. But the Sydney Bennett trial, where all this began. You got in it because you love this stuff."

"That's so not true."

"It makes you feel better about yourself to say you didn't want this case, that you did Neil a favor and got strong-armed by the judge into defending Sydney Bennett."

"And how would that make me feel good about myself?"

"Because this is exactly the kind of case you would want. But you didn't want to take it."

"This is starting to sound like analysis."

"In your mind, being ordered by the judge to defend Sydney Bennett makes it more acceptable to your fiancée. There, I pointed it out: the elephant in the room."

"No, I think it's Max. Those mangos are murder."

"Don't make jokes, damn it." She came closer "Look. Jack. I love you so much, but there's a reason we're engaged and still haven't set a wedding date. And it's not because we're too busy. It's because we're still . . . negotiating."

"Negotiating?"

"Yes. There's no other word for it. I'm being very honest. I don't want you to turn me into something I'm not, any more than I should turn you into something you're not."

Jack was silent, but he knew where the conversation was headed.

"I'm taking this undercover assignment," she said. "I could be away for five months. For me, that's not negotiable."

"That's fine. I want you to take it," he said.

"And I love you for that. That's not the problem. The problem is, I *don't* want you to represent people like Sydney Bennett."

"So for you, undercover work is nonnegotiable, but you want my selection of cases to be negotiable?"

"No, I want you to stop making yourself miserable, stop trying to be a pleaser. Stand up and say, This is me, this who I am, this is not negotiable. And I'm just going to have to find a way to get over that . . . if we're ever going to set a wedding date."

He brought her closer.

"Weird," said Jack.

"What is?"

"That actually made me feel better."

She kissed him gently.

"And confused," said Jack.

"Why?"

"Oh, I don't know. Could it be because what you just said is completely unlike anything you've ever said to me before?"

"I've evolved."

"More like transformed."

"Let's just say a little birdie sang in my ear."

"A birdie, huh?"

She let out a little laugh, but it was cut short by Shorty Shitstain. Theo's ringtone. Jack still had his friend's cell phone, and it was vibrating on the nightstand. He reached over and grabbed it. This time there was no SQUEEZEPLAY or COOCHIE MONSTER in the caller ID. It was just a random number—at two o'clock in the morning.

"I'm going to take this," he said, and he answered it: "This is Jack."

"Oh, thank God! Jack, you have to help me!"

She was in a panic, but he immediately recognized the voice. "Sydney, calm down."

"Calm down? I'm out here on my own, I can't even close my eyes to go to sleep, and now I saw on TV that Judge Matthews expects me to show up in court on Monday."

"He wants to know about the guy who met you at the airport."

"He's crazy, okay? Sick and crazy. He tried to choke me."

"What?"

"He came to me like he was my friend, gonna sell my movie rights, gonna make me a million dollars. Then the first night we were alone together he turns into this crazy man."

"You didn't tell me this before."

"I told you he was a creep, that I was going through hell. What is it about lawyers that they need to have everything spelled out from A to Z? Is that so you can give your client the big 'I told you so'? I didn't *fire* him, okay? I escaped! The guy is *sick*. I'm lucky to be alive!"

Jack sat up on the edge of the mattress. "Sydney, you have to listen to me. You're in a lot of danger."

"No shit!"

"What I'm trying to say is that you need more help than your lawyer can give you. Where are you now?"

"I can't tell you. I can't tell anyone!"

"We need to get you protection."

"Yeah, like the whole world wants to bend over backward to help me, Jack."

"Listen to me. My fiancée is an FBI agent. She's here with me. I can put her on the phone right now to talk if—"

"No! If you give her that phone, I'm hanging up."

"All right, don't hang up. But I want you to memorize her number," he said, and then he gave it to her.

"I'm not calling the FBI. You're my lawyer. You have to protect my not-guilty verdict. Please, please. I'm begging you. I can't come back for another trial."

"Maybe you can come back, if you call the FBI." He blurted out Andie's number again.

"I can't! You have to do whatever it takes to stop that judge from throwing out the verdict. No way can I put myself in a courtroom or any other box where he can find me."

"Who is this guy?"

"His name is Merselus."

"Merciless?"

"Might as well be." She spelled it.

"What's his last name?"

"That is his last name. Or maybe not. I don't know. He just goes by Merselus. He found me when I was in jail, said he was a Hollywood agent. When he actually followed through and got the money for the private airplane to my father, we figured he was legit. Or at least I thought my fucking dad would have checked him out to make sure he wasn't just another crazy son of a bitch with a hard-on for Shot Mom."

"Your father—"

"I gotta go. I gotta go *right now!*"

"Sydney, wait!"

"Just help me, okay? He tried to strangle me, Jack! Don't you get it?"

Jack started to reply, but she was gone. He put the phone on the nightstand and glanced at Andie. She'd heard only one side of the conversation, and Jack wasn't ready to share the other half. He was thinking of Celeste. And Rene. Then he touched his own neck, recalling his personal encounter with this Merselus.

Yeah, Sydney. I do get it.

36

·

Merselus entered his apartment and locked the door—two deadbolts and a chain. It was dark inside, save for the faint glow from the closet, and the room smelled of mildew from the afternoon rain. A forty-year-old roof was no match for Miami's summer cloudbursts. Merselus could have afforded a much nicer place, but he preferred the anonymity that came with a cheap apartment, no questions asked. He didn't need a team of Ritz-Carlton servants trying to memorize how he liked his eggs in the morning, what newspaper he preferred, or what time he wanted his bed turned down. The longer-lease apartments in his complex faced the river, but his week-to-week rental was on the street side, directly across from a nightclub. Even on the third floor, his boarded window was no barrier to the urban-jungle noise rising up from the sidewalk outside the club. Men growled like lions with an aching sack, the modern-day version of chest beating. Women laughed like hyenas in heat—some way too loud, giving away their eagerness. The pulsating music from a passing set of gangsta wheels was familiar to him, and Merselus fudged a lyric here and there until the song came clear in his head: "Not Afraid" by Eminem.

Definitely not afraid.

Merselus placed his phone on the nightstand and plugged in the charger. The glowing crystals said 2:32 A.M. He was tired, but he couldn't lie down and close his eyes. There was something he needed more than sleep. Much more.

How Sydney had slipped through his fingers—literally—was beyond him. Prior to her release, they'd spoken to each other only on the jailhouse telephone, and she'd totally bought the Hollywood-agent story he'd fed her. Selling the movie rights to her trial was only the beginning. Sydney wanted to be a star, and her first performance had proved her a natural—that passionate embrace on the runway, as if she were reuniting with a long-lost lover, exactly the way he'd choreographed it.

In your face, Swyteck.

After three years in jail, Shot Mom would have jumped on the casting couch with the first guy to throw money at her. It was their second night together when her pants had come off. He remembered how she loved his hands, his huge strong hands, and how he'd worked her so hot that she was tasting herself from his long, wet fingers. And then he'd made his move. One hand still working her loins into a frenzy, as he remembered it, and the other rising up from her breasts to her neck. Gently at first, his hand slipped into position. Then his fingers closed around her throat, but not too much pressure, nothing too alarming, just enough to bring about the enhanced sensation of genital stimulation and oxygen deprivation. Months of planning were on the verge of becoming reality, working Sydney with both hands. There was a fine line to maintain, and it wasn't between her wanting it and fearing it. Merselus knew from experience: They wanted it *because* they feared it. The line not to cross was fearing it *too much*. That line would be crossed only when he so chose, when it was no longer her moment, but his, for the taking. At least that had been the plan. Somehow, he'd pushed Sydney too far, too soon, and when she scratched him like a cat across the face, he instinctively let her have a taste of what he'd given Celeste Laramore. Not enough to send Sydney into a coma, but enough to put her out for at least an hour—at least as long as Swyteck had lain unconscious alongside Main Highway. Thirty minutes later, when he'd returned to check on her, he discovered how badly he'd miscalculated—how she'd fooled him. Sydney was gone.

It wasn't surprising, he supposed, the way he'd undershot on the application of pressure to Sydney's carotid sinus. Just two days before, he'd pushed it too far with Celeste Laramore, sending her into a coma. He'd overcorrected on Sydney and pulled back too much, allowing her to recover too fast. This was an art, not an exact science. It was all a matter of touch. He wondered if he was losing his.

No way.

Merselus got his laptop computer from the closet and carried it to the bed. He removed his shirt and opened his pants. With a click of the mouse, he entered the dark side of the Internet, the world of file swapping and peer-to-peer trading. Return to the virtual world was risky. If he weren't careful, he could exhaust himself and chill his drive to conquer the real thing. That very possibility made him all the more angry with Sydney. It was her fault. She had left him this way, left him with no choice but to go back to this place. It was easy to get caught up, to stay here night after night, till the rage subsided.

This time, just a quickie.

Merselus knew the exact file he was looking for, and he found some loser in Budapest offering it for swap. It was cumbersome for Merselus to put himself in the position of having to trade to get his own videos back. But releasing his work to a peer-to-peer network, where it would be traded thousands of times on computers around the globe, put a safe distance between Merselus the creator, and Merselus the consumer. No one in law enforcement could ever unravel the chain of custody and trace the obscene file back to its creator. It was the pornographic version of laundering money.

Merselus clicked DOWNLOAD, and the thumbnail came into focus. At first he could see the top of a woman's head, her chestnut hair. Then her face came into view, eyes wide with fright. Then her long, slender neck wrapped in a leather collar. She was on her knees, hands and feet bound, naked except for the collar and spiked harness that was strapped so tightly below her breasts that she was bruised and bleeding at the ribs. The image was a bit grainy, which was a good thing. It made her face a little fuzzy.

It enhanced her vague resemblance to Sydney.

Merselus scrolled to the bottom of the page, to a message that was superimposed on the image, written in bold red letters: CHOKE ON IT. And she would, too. Some pervs got off on the kiddie porn, turned on by underage girls having sex for the first time. Others—guys like Merselus—got off on women having sex for the very *last* time.

He moved closer to the bed, towering over the image on the screen, preparing himself for two minutes of insanity that would leave him and her—especially her—breathless. This one had shown such attitude at one time, real push back, just like Sydney. She'd even tried to talk him into reversing roles, to let her try erotic asphyxiation on him, but he was no fool. The hotel maid would have found him the next morning hanging in the closet with his dick in his hand. No one, however, would ever find little Miss Choke-on-It. These two minutes were all that remained. His self-made films didn't come close to capturing the excitement of the conquest, but they were better than raw memory. They were his movies, his moments.

With a click on the START arrow, there began another dark night down memory lane.

37

·

Jack and Andie did a Saturday-morning run through Crandon Park to the beach and back. It wasn't a race. Still, it bugged him that the only way to make his pace a workout was for Andie to run backward while pulling along a dog on a leash.

"I think Max wants to go again," she said.

They were in the driveway, Jack hunched over with his hands on his knees and trying to catch his breath. "We'll see how spry he is when he hits forty."

Andie took Max for another three miles. Jack recovered in a hot shower.

Jack's to-do list was chock-full. Sydney's remark about Merselus—"he found me in jail"—had put one more thing on it. Jack wasn't sure if that meant he called, wrote, or came to see her. He sent Theo to the women's detention center to get a log of every visitor, every caller who had contacted Sydney. By the time Theo returned, Jack had killed a pot of coffee and mapped out the strategy for the upcoming hearings.

"We'll have it this afternoon," said Theo.

On a weekend, that wasn't a bad job of cutting

through the red tape. "We can check on it after we see Mr. Bennett," said Jack.

A follow-up with Sydney's parents was at the top of Jack's task list. He'd called them immediately after his phone conversation with Sydney. Sydney wasn't a minor, but they were her only family, and Jack felt they should know that their daughter was apparently on the run and in danger. Her mother had seemed appreciative of the call—enough so that she'd promised Jack that both she and Mr. Bennett would meet with him in the morning. But that was before her husband had snatched the phone away from her and bid Jack good night. Jack decided to show up anyway.

Theo drove. They were in Miami Gardens before lunchtime. The garage door was open, and Geoffrey Bennett was inside, lifting weights on his bench press. He was dripping with sweat, his arms and chest pumped up from too many reps. He was actually in better physical shape than Jack would have expected—a reminder that even though the Bennetts were grandparents, they were just a few years older than Jack. Still, the nylon shorts were way too formfitting for a man his age, and the thick leather weight belt was a notch too tight, as if vanity refused to let him admit that his waist had expanded even an inch in the previous ten years.

"Is Ellen here?" asked Jack.

"What's this about?"

"I'd like to speak to your wife."

"She's not feeling well. What do you need?"

It was the same old story. No one got to Mrs. Bennett except through her husband.

"I need to know who Merselus is," said Jack.

"Who?"

"Sydney says that's the name of the man who met her at Opa-locka Airport on the night of her release."

"You mean Merselus," said Bennett. "I thought you said merciless."

"It's becoming a common mistake."

"I like that name," said Theo. "Merciless. Has a bad-ass rapper ring to it. Like Killa Sin or Gangster Starr or—"

"Shorty Shitstain?" said Jack.

"Whatta you know about Shorty?"

"More than I want to," said Jack.

Bennett glanced at Theo, then back at Jack, as if not sure what to make of them. "Why would I know who this Merselus is?"

"He tried to strangle your daughter after they left the airport."

Bennett paused before answering, staring at Jack. "That's disturbing, to say the least. But that doesn't mean I know him. To the contrary, do you think I would put my daughter in the hands of someone like that?"

"Sydney said they connected when she was in prison. More to the point, she thought you had checked him out before she trusted him to be her agent."

"Well, that would be just like her to blame someone else, wouldn't it?"

Theo grumbled. "Just cuz she's the one doin' the blamin' doesn't mean you ain't to blame."

"The big guy actually has a point," said Jack.

"Look, her mother and I did what Sydney asked us to do. She told us she had a big-shot agent who was going to take care of her, but they needed us to lease the plane in my name to keep the Hollywood connection out of the press. The money landed in our bank account, and I took care of the plane. That was my whole involvement. And her mother's. We never met the guy, never talked to him. That was the end of it."

"You didn't ask—"

"I didn't ask anybody anything," said Bennett. "I wanted Sydney out of jail and out of our hair."

Jack studied his expression, taking a read. "That's a good story."

"It's the truth."

"What do you think, Theo?"

"I'll tell you what I think," said Theo. "I think somebody in this house needs a good ass-kicking."

Bennett took a step back. "Is that a threat?"

"No, that was purely an expression of opinion. See, the man asked me what do I think. I told him what I think. That's an opinion, and if you want to get legal about it, the opinions expressed here are solely those of Theo Knight and do not necessarily reflect the policy or position of Jack Swyteck, P.A., the Florida Bar, or the pansy-ass association of nonviolent white guys who keep friends with former death row inmates just in case they might need to call up an ass-kicking. You got a problem with that?"

"I—I don't think so."

"Good. Cuz if I was threatening you, I would—"

Jack extended his arm, stopping Theo before he could take another step closer.

Bennett made his chest swell. "Y'all need to leave my property."

"You need to think about what I said," Theo said.

"Let's go," said Jack.

They walked back to the car, and Bennett returned to his bench press, the free weights clanging as Jack and Theo climbed inside and closed the doors.

"Pansy-ass association of *what*?"

"Sorry, dude. Was just makin' a point." Theo started the engine and pulled away from the curb.

"I'm almost afraid to ask for another opinion, but what do you think? Does Mr. Bennett know Merselus?"

Theo put on his shades, eyes on the road. "Just like his daughter. Liar, liar, pants on fire."

Jack glanced out the window as they passed the Bennett house. He noticed Mrs. Bennett watching from the front porch, her gaze following their car down the street. A bright yellow sundress made her perpetual tan look even darker than usual. Colorful sundresses were what she had worn almost every day for Sydney's trial.

"The key here is to talk to someone in this family who doesn't wear pants."

"Then let's do it," said Theo.

Jack thought of all the times he'd tried to have a one-on-one conversation with Sydney's mother. "It needs to be handled just right. Ellen literally hasn't left the house since the trial started. She doesn't even have a cell phone. We can discount a lot of what her husband says, but I don't doubt that she's battling depression."

"Just call her, Jack."

They stopped at the STOP sign. The Bennetts' street was in his passenger's-side mirror, and Jack could see down the block to their house in the reflection. Ellen Bennett was still standing on the porch, having watched their car all the way to the intersection.

"No," said Jack. "Once a seed is planted, the worst thing you can do is dig it up to see how it's growing. Give her a little more time. She'll come around."

38

A ndie finished her three-mile run with Max in record time. She showered and spent the rest of the morning on a chaise longue in the backyard, struggling her way through one of those recorded instructional CDs that promised complete fluency in a foreign language for ninety-eight percent of users faster than you can say, *I must be part of the two percent*. Max was in a perfect "sit/stay," head cocked, ears peaked, and a puzzled expression on his golden face. Apparently, he didn't speak Chinese.

"Max," she said, followed by her best attempt to say "Come" in a language she hadn't spoken since her days in the Seattle field office. It was part of her training for her undercover assignment, Operation Big Dredge. Counterfeit goods galore from China were expected to come through the widened Panama Canal and the expanded Port of Miami. A brushup on Mandarin Chinese would be useful.

"Max, please. A little encouragement."

He cocked his head the other way.

"I think we're hopeless, buddy."

Andie removed her earbuds, shut down her iPad, and went back inside the house. She was pouring a cup of green tea—that part of China she got, no problem—when her cell rang. She had a feeling about the unknown number on the caller ID.

"This is Agent Henning," she said.

There was a slight pause, then a voice that Andie recognized, even though they had never spoken to one another: "Swyteck told me to call you at this number."

Andie gripped the phone. "Sydney?"

"Yes."

"I'm glad you called. You're doing the right thing."

"He didn't give me much of a choice."

"Who didn't?"

"Jack," she said, and just the mention of his name seemed to bring an edge to her voice. "He thinks he can just pass me along to you, like I'm not his problem. I *am* his problem. He's part of this. He's as much a part of this as I am."

"Okay. I understand you're angry."

"I'm angry, I'm tired, I'm fed up with the whole fucking world treating me like I'm some kind of monster. Tell Jack he needs to help me."

"Jack can't help you. Work with me and the FBI will—"

"No, this isn't a call to the FBI. I'm talking to Jack's girlfriend. You tell Jack that if he wants to find out what happened to his *other* girlfriend, he needs to help me, okay?"

"What do you know about Rene Fenning?"

"I know I don't want to end up like her. And I'm

guessing you don't want to, either. So you take off your FBI hat, you have a nice talk with your fiancé, and you tell him that when Sydney Bennett calls him, he better listen. You got it?"

"Sydney—" she started to say, but Andie could tell she wasn't there.

Andie put her cell down. Max came to her and put his head on her leg, seeming to sense her stress.

"Yup," said Andie, rubbing his neck. "I think we got it, all right."

39

.

"W hoa," said Theo. "She is hot, hot, hot."

Jack was waiting with him outside the Patti & Alan Herbert Wellness Center on the University of Miami campus. A creek and rocky ravine circled the center like a castle moat, and the narrow footbridge over it was the only access to the main entrance—which made the bench at the end of the bridge a prime viewing spot for the endless stream of co-eds on the way to or from a workout. The clingy black spandex left little to the imagination.

"Down, boy," said Jack. "She's probably twenty years old."

"And your point is . . . ?"

Jack didn't even try to explain. For more years than he cared to admit, beautiful twenty-year-old women had been mere girls to him.

"I mean, dude, it's not like I said I want to buy her a bottle of vodka or go vote with her."

"Theo, I get it. And by the way, you don't have to be twenty-one to vote. It's eighteen."

"Since when?"

"Since before you were born."

"So she could vote to have sex with me."

Jack massaged that aching spot between his eyes. "You know, it's a good thing only half the things you say are serious, or we just couldn't be friends."

"It's not that half the things I say are serious. It's everything I say is *half* serious. There's a difference."

"Seriously?"

"Yeah. Well . . . half."

Jack kept an eye on the main door. It had taken several phone calls from Celeste Laramore's father, but Celeste's roommate had finally agreed to talk to Jack. The plan was to meet outside the wellness center.

"That's her," said Jack.

"Whoa. She is totally—"

"Quit," Jack told him.

Jenna Smith seemed to recognize Jack as she crossed the bridge. She was dressed like all the other young women on parade, though it was impossible not to notice that she spent a few more hours a week in the gym than most. Her hair was in a ponytail. De rigueur, a cell phone was in her hand.

"Hi, I'm Jenna."

She extended her free hand, and Jack shook it. "Nice to meet you, Jenna. This is—"

"Theo Knight," he said, "head of voter registration."

"What?"

"Ignore him," said Jack. "Thanks for meeting with us."

She nodded once, more acquiescence than enthusiasm. "Mr. Laramore said it was important."

"It is," said Jack. He led her to a picnic table beneath a stand of palm trees where they could talk. She laid her pink workout bag on the bench beside her and placed her cell phone on the table in front of her. Jack and Theo sat opposite her, the afternoon sun warm on their backs.

"How is Celeste doing?" asked Jenna.

Jack wasn't sure how to answer. "We're still hopeful."

"That's the same thing Mr. Laramore told me." Her phone chime sounded like a bicycle bell. She glanced at a new text from someone and quickly thumb-typed a response. "He also said you wanted to talk about the night Celeste got hurt."

"Right," said Jack. "I watched a recording of your interview on TV. You told Faith Corso that you and Celeste had just come from a Sydney Bennett look-alike contest. Of course, now we all know there was no such contest."

"And you want to know why I lied."

"That's about the size of it," said Jack.

She glanced at Theo. "Is he a cop?"

"Him? No. He's my investigator. You can talk freely."

Jenna drew a breath. "I lied because . . . well, because that was the story Celeste gave me."

"Say that again," said Jack.

"We went out that night, and she looked so much like Sydney Bennett it was freaky. She said we were going to a look-alike contest on South Beach. I say, 'Okay, cool.' Then she started driving and I say, 'Hey, aren't you going the wrong way?'"

"What did Celeste say?"

"She says, 'Jenna, can you keep a secret?' I say 'Of course.' And then she tells me that there's no contest. That we're going to the women's detention center."

"Did she say why?"

She shifted nervously. "She said she was getting paid a thousand bucks just to be in the crowd, act like Sydney, and get on television."

"Didn't she realize how dangerous that could be?"

"Well, we knew people were a little crazy about this trial, but most of them were, you know, women who like a good soap opera. We didn't think anyone would be crazy enough to hurt her. And this was a *thousand* dollars, for like an hour's work. Celeste really needed money. Her dad lost his job, so she was getting no help from home."

"I'm very aware of that," said Jack, thinking of the health insurance problem. "But back up a second. I'm still not sure why you lied to Faith Corso. Why did you tell her you had just come from a look-alike contest?"

"I was scared. I wasn't sure if what Celeste did was illegal. She lied to me, so I figured she was covering up something. It wasn't up to me to blow any whistles on her. We were BFFs. I went with her story. I mean, like I said, she asked if I could keep a secret."

"Do you know who paid her the thousand dollars?"

"No idea. She never told me."

"Do you know if she got the money? Or was she supposed to get paid afterward?"

"Honestly, I don't know." Jenna's phone chimed again, and she checked it. "My friend's getting tired of waiting. Is there anything else?"

"Actually, yes," said Jack. "Celeste's dad e-mailed

me some photographs of Celeste—about a half dozen or so from high school to the present." He pulled them up on his iPhone, showing them to her.

"So?"

"I'm struck by the transformation," said Jack. "She cut her hair. Changed the style. Darkened the color. The makeup got more noticeable. She seemed to favor tighter clothing. It seems like, over time, she was looking more and more like Sydney Bennett."

She scrolled through the pictures. "I can see your point. But what of it?"

"That's what I'm asking you," said Jack. "Did you ever have a conversation about that? Was it something she was consciously trying to do?"

"I don't know about that. I mean, she was definitely interested in the case. More than most people I know, anyway."

"When you say 'the case,' do you mean the trial? Or was she interested before the trial?"

"Before."

"Do you know why?"

"Not sure. She had a criminal-justice class she was taking. I figured it was that. She even went and talked to Sydney's lawyer, the guy before you."

Jack did a double take. "Neil Goderich?"

"I don't know his name. The guy who died."

"That's Neil," said Jack. "Celeste met with him? Do you know why?"

"Not really. Like I said, she had that class she was taking. Or maybe she wanted a job. Working for a lawyer is lot more interesting than flipping burgers."

"When did they talk?"

"Six months ago, maybe."

Jenna's phone chimed again. Another text from her workout buddy. "I really have to go," she said, rising.

Jack and Theo rose. "You've been helpful, thanks," said Jack.

"No problem," said Jenna.

Jack and Theo stayed at the table as she crossed the bridge to the main entrance and disappeared inside the wellness center.

"I take it you didn't know she met with Neil," said Theo.

"You got that right," said Jack.

"What do you make of that?"

He glanced at Theo, then back at the entrance doors. "I need to dig for some missing notes."

40

.

Jack spent the rest of the afternoon at the Freedom Institute. Hannah Goldsmith met them there.

"You gotta turn on the AC," said Jack. A growing V of sweat pasted his shirt to his back.

"Sorry, not on the weekends," said Hannah. "Not in the budget."

Jack knew that rule. Hannah's father had enforced it strictly up until the day he died.

In twenty-eight years, the old house on the Miami River that was the Freedom Institute had changed little. Four lawyers shared two small bedrooms that had been converted into offices. The foyer doubled as a storage room for old case files, boxes stacked one on top of the other. The bottom ones sagged beneath the weight of denied motions for stay of execution, the box tops warped into sad smiles. Harsh fluorescent lighting showed every stain on the indoor/outdoor carpeting. The furniture screamed "flea market"—chairs that didn't match, tables made stable with a deck of cards under one leg. The vintage sixties kitchen was not only where lawyers and staff ate their bagged lunches, but it also served as the conference room. Hanging on the wall over the coffeemaker was an old framed photograph of Bobby Kennedy. Hannah's father had often said that it was the former attorney general who had inspired him to move on from president of the *Harvard Law Review* to founder of the Freedom Institute.

"I honestly don't know where else to look," said Hannah.

They'd adopted a team approach, combing through box after box of archived attorney notes. Neil had never been a computer guy, so if any notes of his conversation with Celeste Laramore existed, they would have been in hard copy. After a dozen boxes, they were empty handed.

"I suppose it's possible he didn't keep any notes," said Jack.

"Dad always took notes," said Hannah. "The problem is that he used everything from legal pads to toilet paper, and only he knew where he put them."

"It's also possible that Celeste's friend is dead wrong about Celeste ever having met with Neil."

"Before you draw that conclusion, let me call my mom," said Hannah. "Could be some boxes at home we can check."

Hannah dialed. Jack went to the kitchen for a cold drink. The old refrigerator made a strange buzzing noise when he opened it. Jack silenced it with a quick kick to the side panel, the way Neil had taught him. He pulled up a chair at the table and checked in again with Andie.

"Anything more from Sydney?" asked Jack.

Andie had called several hours earlier and told him all about Sydney's lecture to Andie as Jack's fiancée, not to Andie the FBI agent.

"Jack, really. Don't you think I would call you if I'd heard from her again?"

"I suppose so."

"And the way she left it, the next call is to you, not me."

"Can't wait," said Jack.

"When are you coming home?"

"Not sure. Just so much to do between now and Monday morning. Maybe we can do a late dinner."

"Sounds good."

"Love you, 'bye."

Jack tucked away his phone and went back to the refrigerator. He wasn't thirsty, but the chilly air felt good. It made him smile to recall the first time Neil had caught him cooling off in front of the open refrigerator, thwarting the no-AC-on-weekends rule. "My opposition to capital punishment has only one exception," Neil had told him, "and you just committed it."

Jack walked to the living room where Hannah was giving a second look to one of her father's boxes. Jack turned his attention to the countless plaques, awards, and framed newspaper clippings on the wall. It had been years since he'd read some of the older articles. While the newsprint had yellowed with age, the clippings still told quite a story, from Neil's roots in civil rights litigation in the South— "Volunteer Lawyers Jailed in Mississippi"—to his role as gadfly in local politics: "Freedom Institute Lawsuit Against Miami Mayor Sparks Grand Jury

Indictment." All were impressive, but Jack's gaze locked onto the framed article by the window with the eye-catching headline: "Groundbreaking DNA Evidence Proves Death Row Inmate Innocent." Jack took a half step closer, reading a story he could have recited in his sleep:

> *After four years in Florida State Prison for a murder he did not commit, twenty-year-old Theo Knight—once the youngest inmate on Florida's death row—is coming home to Miami today . . .*

"Some legacy, huh?"

Jack turned. It wasn't Hannah. It was her mother—Neil's widow, Sarah. She was carrying a box of Neil's notes that she had brought from the house. Jack went to her, took the box, and gave her a warm embrace. He hadn't seen her since the funeral.

"How are you, Sarah?"

"I'm doing okay," she said.

Hannah took the box from Jack. "I can go through this."

"Actually, I'm curious to see if the notes are in—"

"Please," said Hannah, shooing him along. "You can barely read my father's handwriting anyway. Catch up with Mom. I can handle this. Really."

Jack thanked her and followed Sarah down the hallway.

"Hot as hell in here," said Sarah. "You been to the refrigerator yet, Jack?"

"How did you know?"

Sarah smiled as they entered the kitchen. She got a cold soda. Jack still had his.

"I spoke with your fiancée," said Sarah.

"You spoke to Andie?" he said.

"Do you have another fiancée?"

"No. I'm just—What did you talk about?"

Sarah took a seat at the table. Jack joined her. "You," she said.

"How did this come about?"

"We talked briefly at Neil's funeral. I got to know her a little. But seeing all that you're going through with the Sydney Bennett case made me want to follow up."

"With Andie?"

"Yes. Why does that surprise you?"

"For one, she didn't mention it to me."

Sarah smiled like an insider. "I gave her a lot to think about. She's probably still processing it."

"What do you mean by that?"

She drank from her soda bottle, then seemed to shift gears. But Jack could tell it was going to tie together somehow. "Do you know how Neil and I met?"

Jack tried to remember the eulogies. "A Grateful Dead concert?"

She laughed. "No. It was when I was living in Mississippi. I was married to a man I'd met at Columbia. College is a great equalizer, especially when you're young and in love. He was from Jackson, so after graduation we went there to live. We bought a little house. Got a dog. I joined the Junior League with all the other well-to-do ladies on the north side of town. The fact that I was Jewish was our little family secret. I never told anyone. Not even his parents— they knew, of course, but they could handle it so long as I was willing never to mention it. One night we were sitting in the living room watching TV. This was the summer of sixty-four. Freedom summer. President Johnson had just signed the Civil Rights Act. The SNCC—Student Nonviolent Coordinating Committee—was recruiting hundreds of college students to come to Mississippi and register Negro voters. I was sitting right next to my husband on the couch when that story came on the news, and he just lost it. Started railing against the effing Jew-boy lawyers coming down to change things."

"I presume Neil was one of them?"

"Actually, he was. But how we rode off into the sunset in his MG Midget is another story. My real point is this: I'd been pretending for so long that I was someone I wasn't that my own husband had forgotten who I was. Who I *am*. All for the sake of a relationship. Do you know what I'm saying, Jack?"

Jack thought back to how this conversation had started—with her remark that she'd given Andie "a lot to think about."

"Let me guess," said Jack. "You're about to tell me that I'm Sydney Bennett's lawyer not because a judge forced me to take the case. But because this is who I am."

"Wow," she said, "you're a quick study."

"No, I'm not. Andie and I had this same conversation yesterday. I asked her where it came from, and she said a little birdie sang in her ear. I don't know how you did it, but you two seem to be singing the same tune."

Sarah smiled thinly. "I didn't do anything, Jack. Andie's a smart cookie."

"That she is."

Sarah sat back in her chair, glanced around the room. "Thirty-two years ago this month, Neil and I started the Freedom Institute."

"That is impressive."

She looked at him from across the table, her expression very serious. "It's a shame it has to close."

"What?"

"We had to let Eve and Johnny go last week. That brings us down to two lawyers. I can't run this place. I haven't practiced law in over a decade. I've talked to Hannah about taking over, but that's asking a lot of a twenty-six-year-old lawyer fresh out of law school. And to be honest with you, I'm not sure she has the passion. With Neil gone, it's going to die."

"That would really be sad."

"Yes, it would. Because when it dies, a little corner of justice dies with it. That sounds pretty corny, doesn't it?"

"From anyone but you it would," he said.

She reached across the table and squeezed Jack's hand. "Go home to your fiancée."

He nodded, rose from his chair, and kissed her good night on the cheek. He was almost to the hallway when he stopped in the doorway and turned. "Thanks for having that talk with Andie."

"You're welcome," she said. "But watch out. Someday I could call in that favor. You never know what I might ask for in return."

Jack gave her a little smile. "Good night, Sarah."

"Good night, my friend."

41
·

Monday morning came quickly. Jack and Hannah were in Judge Matthews' courtroom at the criminal justice center. Sydney Bennett, of course, was a no-show.

Judge Matthews started promptly at nine A.M. "Mr. Swyteck, you may cross-examine the witness."

"Thank you," said Jack. The courtroom was exactly the way they'd left it upon Friday's adjournment. A packed gallery. Ted Gaines seated in the front row of public seating, directly behind the prosecutor. Melinda Crawford and her assistant at the table for the prosecution, near the empty jury box. Brian Hewitt sat alone in the witness chair, wringing his hands as Jack approached.

"Mr. Hewitt," said the judge, "I will remind you that you are still under oath."

Jack positioned himself in front of the witness, feet apart and shoulders squared, full eye contact. It was the "control posture," the body language of a trial lawyer that denied wiggle room during cross-examination. Jack said good morning, then went straight to work.

"Mr. Hewitt, you've never met Sydney Bennett, am I right?"

"No."

"Never talked to her?"

"No."

"Never got a hundred thousand dollars in cash from her."

"Well, no."

"You've never met me before."

"No, sir."

"Or my colleague, Hannah Goldsmith."

"No."

"Never even talked to us before."

"That's true."

"Never got a hundred thousand dollars in cash from us."

"No."

Jack walked back to the podium. No real need to. He just wanted to move, make sure all eyes were following him.

"Now, as I understand your testimony, you were offered fifty thousand dollars for a hung jury. And a hundred thousand dollars for a not-guilty verdict."

"That's correct."

"I can see how someone could buy a hung jury. All it takes is one juror. You simply refuse to vote guilty no matter what, even if the eleven other jurors are beating you on the head with a hammer to vote guilty."

"Is there a question?" asked the prosecutor.

"My question is this," said Jack, "Mr. Hewitt, you never stood up in the jury room and announced, 'Hey, folks, I don't care what you say, I am *never* going to vote to convict Sydney Bennett of murder.' You never said that, did you?"

"No, of course not."

"You would never have said that," said Jack, "because you didn't want to make them angry at you."

"I don't understand the question."

"Your goal wasn't to get a hung jury for fifty thousand dollars," said Jack. "You wanted the not-guilty verdict—the hundred-thousand-dollar prize."

Hewitt shifted uneasily, exposed for what he was. "Who wouldn't?"

"And you understood, did you not, that to return a verdict of 'not guilty,' the jury had to be unanimous. All twelve jurors had to vote 'not guilty.'"

"Yes, I knew that."

"So you needed to *convince* the other jurors."

Hewitt looked cautiously at Jack, as if sensing a trap. "I guess so."

"Well, Mr. Hewitt, you didn't go to juror number one and say 'I'll pay you ten thousand dollars to vote not guilty,' did you?"

"No."

"You didn't make that offer to juror number two, did you?"

"No."

"You didn't offer to share your hundred thousand dollars with any of the other jurors, am I right?"

"That would be correct."

"So if you were going to get the hundred-thousand-dollar not-guilty verdict, you had to *persuade* the other jurors."

"I suppose that's true."

The prosecutor rose. "Judge, I don't really see the point of this questioning."

"I'll give the defense some latitude," said the judge. "But let's move it along."

Jack stepped closer to the witness. "When it came time to persuade your fellow jurors to vote not guilty, you didn't bring any phony documents into the jury room, did you?"

"No."

"You didn't bring any phony pictures into the jury room?"

"No."

"You didn't fabricate a medical examiner's report, did you?"

"Not at all."

"You didn't use anything but the evidence that was introduced at trial, am I right?"

"Yeah, that's right."

Jack paused and glanced at Hannah. Her expression seemed to say, *So far, so good.*

"Mr. Hewitt, you're not a trial lawyer, are you?"

"Hardly."

"You haven't received any special training in the powers of persuasion, have you?"

"No."

"In your entire life, have you *ever* convinced eleven other people to change their minds about something as important as whether a twenty-four-year-old woman should be convicted of murdering her daughter?"

"I can't think of anything."

"Mr. Hewitt, you were able to *convince* the other jurors to vote 'not guilty' because they already believed my client was innocent. Isn't that right, sir?"

"Objection. The witness couldn't possibly know that."

"I don't know," said Hewitt, taking the prosecutor's cue.

The judge looked down from the bench. "Mr. Hewitt, please wait for me to rule on the objections before answering a question. The objection is sustained."

Jack waited a moment, setting up the next question. "Mr. Hewitt, convincing the eleven other jurors to vote 'not guilty' was the easiest hundred thousand dollars you ever made in your life, wasn't it."

"Objection."

"Sustained."

"I think the witness' opinion on that is relevant," said Jack.

"The objection was sustained," said the judge. "Move on."

The prosecutor rose. "Judge, I would move to strike this entire line of questioning. I don't see how any of it is relevant."

Jack shot her a look of incredulity, then addressed the court. "Your Honor, the simple point is that this alleged bribe had absolutely no impact on the outcome of the trial. The prosecution failed to prove its case beyond a reasonable doubt. Sydney Bennett was found not guilty. End of story."

The judge rocked back in his high leather chair,

thinking. "Well, I'm not sure that's the test, Mr. Swyteck. I'll take the prosecution's motion under advisement. Any further questions for this witness?"

"Yes, Your Honor," said Jack. He faced the witness. "Mr. Hewitt, let's talk about the day you were arrested."

Hewitt shifted nervously. Obviously not his favorite topic. "Okay."

"You went to the Bird Bowling Lanes, correct?"

"That's right."

"Now, you didn't choose that location, did you?"

"No. He did. The guy who paid me."

"You didn't pick the time, did you?"

"No. He said be there at seven o'clock."

"You didn't select the locker where he left the money."

"No. He did."

"You didn't tell him where to leave the key—tucked into the baseboard by the drinking fountain."

"No. He did that."

"So let me set the scene," said Jack. "You walked into the bowling alley just before seven, like he told you to."

"Right."

"And no one stopped you."

"No."

"You walked toward the drinking fountain and got the key from behind the rubber baseboard, like he told you to."

"Yes."

"No one stopped you."

"No."

"You went into the locker room and opened the locker, like he told you."

"Mmm-hmm."

"No one stopped you then, did they?"

"No."

"You got the money out of the locker, like he told you to."

"Right."

"You did everything just like he told you to."

"Yes."

"And all was going just fine until you stuffed the cash into your bowling bag and walked out of the locker room. *Boom!*" Jack shouted, stirring the audience in their seats. "Two FBI agents were all over you."

"Yeah, that's pretty much how it happened."

Jack went back to the podium and double-checked his copy of the written confession. "And the first thing the FBI agent said to you was, 'What you got in the bag?'"

"Something like that, right."

Jack stepped away from the lectern, a quizzical expression on his face. "Mr. Hewitt, how do you suppose that the FBI knew that you were going to be at that bowling alley, at that exact time, with all that money in your bowling bag?"

"Objection. Calls for speculation."

"Let me put it this way," said Jack. "Mr. Hewitt, did *you* call the FBI and tell them you were going to be there?"

He looked at Jack, as if the question were stupid. "No."

Jack glanced at Hannah, who cued up the recording. "Judge, at this time we'd like to play for the witness the audio recording of the anonymous tip that was phoned into the FBI's Miami Field Office at three forty-seven P.M. the day of Mr. Hewitt's arrest."

"No objection," said the prosecutor.

With the judge's approval, Hannah hit PLAY. The courtroom seemed to reach a deeper level of quiet. There was a moment of static hiss, and then the call replayed over the speakers.

"Bird Bowling Lanes. Tonight. Seven P.M. Hundred-thousand-dollar bribe to juror number five in the Sydney Bennett murder trial. Look for the guy who opens locker number nineteen."

The recording ended. Jack tightened his stare as he approached the witness. He had taken a chance by playing that tape, broken the cardinal rule of cross-examination, not a hundred percent sure that he was going to get the testimony from the witness that he needed. But it was a risk worth taking. And from the expression on the witness' face, Jack could see that the payoff was imminent.

"Do you recognize that voice?" asked Jack.

"It's the guy," said Hewitt. "The guy I met at Government Center who said he'd pay me the money."

"So, just to be clear: Your testimony is that the man who told you to go to the bowling alley at seven P.M. to collect your money is the same guy who told the FBI to be at the bowling alley at seven P.M. to arrest you."

"That's what I hear," said Hewitt. "That's his voice."

Jack changed his tone, as if prodding the witness to feel some resentment about the setup. "Whoever paid you this money . . . he *wanted* you to get caught."

"Objection."

"Yeah, that's exactly right," said Hewitt.

The judge stared down from the bench again. "Mr. Hewitt, I told you to please refrain from answering until I rule on an objection. Sustained."

"I'll rephrase it," said Jack. "Mr. Hewitt, are you aware of any reason why Sydney Bennett would have wanted you to get caught taking a bribe?"

He shook his head. "I really can't think of one."

"Thank you. No further questions." Jack stepped away.

The prosecutor rose. "May I have redirect, Your Honor?"

"No," said the judge. "I want to devote the remainder of the time I've set aside for this hearing to the defense. Mr. Swyteck, on Friday we briefly discussed the possibility of your client testifying. As I mentioned, someone needs to explain that video at Opa-locka Airport, which shows Ms. Bennett's obvious affection for the man who bribed Mr. Hewitt. Is she coming or not?"

"She's not here now, Your Honor."

"Well, it's now or never. Have you spoken to her?"

"Yes, I have, Your Honor."

That drew a response from the audience, the first public confirmation that Jack was in touch with the missing Sydney Bennett.

"And what's the problem?" asked the judge.

"Sydney Bennett can rebut this whole charade.

The problem is simply that she's afraid to come here."

"Afraid of what?" said the prosecutor. "Being found guilty of jury tampering on top of murdering her daughter?"

Nice line, Jack thought as a wave of snickers coursed through the gallery. *Did Faith Corso write it for you?*

The judge gaveled down the rumbling, restoring order.

"Judge, may I approach the bench?" Jack asked.

The judge waved him forward. The prosecutor followed.

"Judge, to demonstrate why my client is afraid to come into this courtroom would require me to reveal certain facts that could compromise the investigation into the murder of Dr. Rene Fenning. The two are *that* related."

"What?" said Crawford, incredulous.

Jack continued, "It would also require me to present the testimony of a certain FBI agent who can confirm Ms. Bennett's expressed fears. That agent is about to begin a five-month undercover assignment. Neither an undercover agent, who is by definition trying to keep a low profile, nor the details relating to a pending homicide investigation should be put on display for TV cameras in a packed courtroom if there is an alternative. I would request the opportunity to proffer my evidence in chambers and, if possible, avoid making it part of tonight's broadcast on BNN."

"This is a stall," said Crawford. "He doesn't have his client ready to testify, and Mr. Swyteck is just stalling."

"It's not a stall," said Jack. "If I can have thirty minutes of the court's time in chambers, I can convince the court of that."

The judge leaned back, considering it, then breathed a heavy sigh. "All right. You can have thirty minutes. I will see you at one o'clock in my chambers. And, Mr. Swyteck," the judge added.

"Yes, Your Honor?"

"Bring your FBI agent with you."

42

A chorus of jeers followed Jack and Hannah down the courthouse steps as they left the Justice Center. In two hours the defense had to be back in Judge Matthews' chambers. The Shot Mom haters had been playing to cameras outside the courthouse since eight thirty A.M., and they would be there when Jack returned at one P.M., braving ninety-five-degree heat and ninety-percent humidity. The jury-tampering allegations had given the mob a shot in the arm, and their sheer stamina was astounding.

Jack rode shotgun on the way back to the office and made a phone call while Hannah drove. It was the first time a judge had ordered him to "bring your FBI agent with you." Andie took the news better than Jack had expected.

"I'll talk to my ASAC," she said. "I'll need his approval."

"Remind him how cooperative I've been with law enforcement since Rene's murder. I even let the FBI monitor my cell phone."

"That will help."

"Andie," said Jack, using his I-need-this voice. "It's important."

"I get it," she said.

They were on Main Highway, less than a quarter mile from Jack's office. The sun glared on the windshield, flickering from light to dark as they cruised in the intermittent shadows of sprawling banyan limbs. They passed the gated entrance to Ransom Everglades Upper School, and Jack glanced uneasily at the stone wall along the jogging trail. Right behind that wall, near the large oak, he'd met a stranger he now knew as Merselus and received the threat against "someone you love."

"Are you selling your office?" asked Hannah.

"No, why?"

She slowed the car as they approached the driveway. "Then why is there a For Sale sign out front?"

"Stop here," he said as she turned into the driveway. Jack got out and checked the sign: JUSTICE FOR SALE, it read.

Jack looked farther down the jogging trail, a tree-lined stretch of rooted-up asphalt that ran from his driveway entrance to the T-shaped intersection at the end of Main Highway. There were more signs, one about every fifteen feet, each with the same message: JUSTICE FOR SALE. The anger rose up inside him. It was one of those watershed moments, a little thing that triggered much more of a reaction than it should have. Cumulatively, he'd had enough. Jack pulled the first one from the ground, yanked a second, then another. He gathered up about a dozen of them and walked back to the car, muttering under his breath.

"Jack, it's no big deal," said Hannah.

Jack opened the door, threw them into the backseat, and then slammed the door shut. Hannah parked the car and followed him up the steps and into the office. The screen door slapped shut behind them. Bonnie was at the reception desk, working the phone. She had the frazzled expression on her face that Jack was seeing far too much of lately. She slammed down the phone as he entered.

"I need that air horn," she said.

"Not again," he said.

"Nastier than ever," said Bonnie. "All this 'justice for sale' nonsense. They're picking that up from Faith Corso. That's the running subtitle of her show. And you don't even want to know what her fans are saying online about you."

"Bloggers are back?"

"Oh, my Lord," said Bonnie. "It's insane. It's ugly. It's—"

"It's thinkism," said Hannah.

"It's what?" said Jack.

"That's the name Dad gave it. Thinkism."

"And what exactly did Neil mean by that?"

"It's the new 'ism,'" said Hannah, "born of the Internet. Race and gender are less important in the virtual world. It's more about what you think. But the way Dad saw it, some people will always need a reason to hate. If they can't see you and hate you for how you look, all their hatred is aimed at what you say. Racists and sexists just aren't cool anymore. But they can all be thinkists, spread the same kind of emotional and irrational hatred, and not only will they get away with it, but people will actually follow their Tweets. Before you know it, there's a virtual lynch mob outside your door trying to hang you from a tree for thinking differently than they do. Thinkism."

"Neil came up with that?" asked Jack.

"Yup."

"One smart guy," said Jack.

"He was definitely no thinkist."

Hannah's cell phone rang. She stepped into the hallway to take it. Jack followed up with Bonnie on the Internet postings.

"Is there anything that you think I should be concerned about?"

"Yeah, all of it."

Hannah stepped back into the room, her face ashen.

"What's wrong?" said Jack.

"It was him," she said in a flat, serious tone. "The same voice I played in the courtroom today."

Bonnie said, "Now he's calling *you*?"

Jack said, "He probably figured out that my cell is monitored by the FBI. It's the same reason Sydney has been calling me on Theo's phone. What did he say?"

"It was short," said Hannah. "I didn't even have time to think. I should have recorded it."

"It's okay," said Jack. "What did he say?"

"He said, 'Tell your boss I watch BNN. Tell him I heard him say Sydney Bennett is afraid to come to court. Tell him if he mentions one word about me to the judge, it's someone he loves all over again.'"

She paused, and the reference to "someone you love" gave Jack chills.

"Did he say anything else?" asked Jack.

"Yeah," said Hannah. "He said to check the signs."

"The signs?" said Bonnie.

Jack knew immediately. "The For Sale signs."

Jack hurried out the door and down the steps, his footfalls crunching in the pea-gravel driveway as he raced to the car and yanked open the door. The signs were piled loosely in the backseat where he had left them. He grabbed the one on top and checked it more carefully, but there was nothing of note—just the message, JUSTICE FOR SALE. He did the same with the second, the third, and three more. Finally, he checked the backside of the seventh sign and froze.

There was simply an address: 1800 Davis Road, Apartment 406.

"What is it?" asked Hannah.

Jack showed her and said, "My great-uncle's address."

"Your great-uncle?"

Jack's throat tightened. "*Abuela*'s brother in Tampa. It's where I sent my grandmother."

43

At one P.M. Jack and Hannah were in chambers. Judge Matthews was seated in a tall leather chair behind his oversize desk. The American flag was draped on a pole behind him and to his right, and the flag of the state of Florida was to his left. A rectangular table extended forward from the front of his desk to create a T-shaped seating arrangement, the defense on one side of the table and the prosecution on the opposite side. At the narrow end of the table, directly facing the judge, was FBI Agent Andie Henning. With her was an assistant U.S. attorney, who looked to be at most three or four years senior to Hannah.

"Mr. Swyteck, the floor is yours," said the judge.

The AUSA spoke up. "Before we begin," she said, "I wanted to make sure the court is aware of the relationship between Mr. Swyteck and FBI Agent Henning."

"I'm aware. Mr. Swyteck, proceed."

Jack spoke while seated, as was customary in chambers. "Judge, I want to begin by saying that although this is an unusual way for me to oppose the government's motion to set aside the not-guilty verdict, the chain of evidence that I am about to proffer does, in fact, confirm that Sydney Bennett had nothing to do with the bribe paid to juror number five in her criminal trial."

"That's what we're here for," the judge said.

"First, we do not dispute the testimony of Mr. Hewitt that the man who offered him the bribe is the same man who met Sydney Bennett at Opa-locka Airport on the night of her release."

"Excuse me," said the prosecutor, "you mean the man who *embraced* Sydney Bennett at the airport."

"Ms. Crawford, you will have your say," said the judge. "Continue, Mr. Swyteck."

"We would also ask the court to accept Mr. Hewitt's testimony on cross-examination that the man who offered him the bribe is the same man who made the anonymous call to the FBI that led to Mr. Hewitt's arrest."

"We don't dispute that," said the prosecutor.

"Good," said Jack. "The evidence I would proffer is that this same man has done the following things. First, he attacked me about a block away from my office and demanded to know where Sydney Bennett was. We have a hospital record and a police report to substantiate that attack. Second, that same man murdered Dr. Rene Fenning."

"What?" said the prosecutor.

"Excuse me, Ms. Crawford. I'll ask the questions. But Mr. Swyteck, I think her question is a good one: *What?*"

"This is the sensitive part of the criminal investigation that I mentioned in the courtroom this morning. The killer's 'signature,' so to speak, has not been released to the public. That is to avoid the possibility of copycats or other compromising factors."

"What is the signature?"

Jack glanced at Andie, then addressed the judge. "My attacker told me that if I did not lead him to Sydney Bennett, he would hurt someone I love. Rene Fenning is someone I used to date. Years ago. She was on her way to meet me for coffee when she was murdered. Her body was found with the words 'someone you love' written on her abdomen."

All eyes—the judge's, the prosecutor's, the assistant U.S. attorney's—were suddenly aimed at Andie.

Andie shifted uncomfortably. "This, uh, isn't what it sounds like."

"No, not at all," said Jack.

"Well, isn't that special," the judge said. "If we could all step out of *Peyton Place* for a moment, let me ask you for this clarification, Mr. Swyteck. I see the link between the man who bribed Mr. Hewitt and the one who called the FBI. I see the link between the man who attacked you and the one who murdered Dr. Fenning. But I don't see the link between the two. What is it?"

Jack said, "The link is a conversation I had with Sydney Bennett on the telephone early Saturday morning. She called me. She was terrified. She told me that the man she met at the airport was named Merselus, that he tried to strangle her, and that she was now on her own, on the run, afraid for her life, and afraid to come into court."

The prosecutor raised both hands in the air like an umpire. "Hold on a second. Judge, I know this is just a proffer, but the court can't seriously allow this evidence into the record. For one thing, how does the defense intend to introduce this evidence? Is Mr. Swyteck going to be a witness?"

"That's where Agent Henning comes in," said Jack. "We live together. She overheard the conversation."

The judge looked straight at Andie, down the length of the long rectangular table. "Agent Henning, is it true that you heard Ms. Bennett say all those things to Mr. Swyteck?"

"Actually, I heard only one side of the conversation. I heard Jack talking to her. Then he told me what she said after they hung up."

The prosecutor groaned. "So we've got double hearsay," she said. "The defense proposes to have Agent Henning tell the court what Mr. Swyteck told her that Sydney Bennett said to him. I think maybe I'll object," she said, adding a dose of sarcasm.

"Ms. Crawford has a point," said the judge. "And you've got an attorney-client privilege problem on top of it. A lawyer can't just come into court and reveal the things his client said to him unless his client has agreed to waive the privilege."

"With all due respect, that seems a bit hypertechnical," said Jack. "I'm confident that Sydney Bennett would waive the privilege under the circumstances and allow me to tell you what she said."

"That's not for you to decide," the judge said. "The privilege belongs to the client. Only the client can waive it."

If the judge himself was mounting that kind of opposition, Jack could feel all momentum slipping away. The prosecutor seized on it.

"Plus," said Crawford, "we're left with the fact that this highly unreliable evidence proves nothing. The issue here is whether Sydney Bennett was involved in bribing a juror. This hearing isn't about who killed Dr. Fenning."

Jack responded, "Judge, it all comes down to one thing: This Merselus, whoever he may be, is obsessed with Sydney Bennett. It fits with our theory that he bribed the juror on his own in order to get Sydney acquitted. When things didn't go well between him and Sydney at the airport and Sydney ran away from him, he attacked me to find her. When that didn't work, he killed Dr. Fenning to show me that he fully intends to act on his threats. When that didn't work, he called the FBI to make sure they arrested Hewitt red-handed when he collected his bribe."

"I don't get that last part," said the judge.

"He knew that Hewitt's arrest would force Sydney to come out of hiding and return to this courtroom. The bottom line, Your Honor, is that if you force Sydney Bennett to come out of hiding to defend this motion, you are playing into this killer's hands."

"Oh, come on," said the prosecutor. "That's a sky-is-falling argument if I ever heard one. If anything, Merselus is an old boyfriend—some rich sugar daddy, I daresay—who bribed a juror to get her acquitted, and then once she got out of jail, she dumped him. She used him, just like she uses everybody else in her life. He got mad and made an anonymous call to the FBI to get Brian Hewitt caught collecting his bribe. That would put Sydney back in jail, where she belongs."

The judge considered it. "Ms. Crawford actually does have a way of making things fit."

The judge's leaning was no surprise to Jack. It had been clear throughout the trial that he was of the mind that Sydney Bennett had murdered her daughter. The prosecutor continued to hammer away.

"Judge, we are talking about a manipulative, conniving woman who murdered her two-year-old daughter and was caught embracing the man who bought off a juror."

"Okay, I have your argument," said the judge. "Let me tell you where I come out. Mr. Swyteck, as the record stands now, I believe the prosecution has demonstrated that Sydney Bennett is sufficiently connected to the jury tampering in this case to justify overturning the verdict of not guilty."

"Judge, but—"

"Don't interrupt," the judge said. "Since we do have the FBI here, I'm feeling charitable today. I'll give you seventy-two hours to bring in Sydney Bennett. I'm not forcing her to testify, but I am telling you that, even if I allowed you to go forward with the evidence you've proffered, it isn't enough to save your client's not-guilty verdict. If she isn't here in this courtroom within seventy-two hours, I will enter an order granting the prosecution's motion to set aside the verdict on the grounds of jury tampering. And I will issue a warrant for the arrest of Sydney Bennett. That's my ruling. Are we clear?"

"Yes, Your Honor."

"Very well," said the judge. "Mr. Swyteck, notify my assistant if and when you are ready to proceed."

44

.

"We should send her to New Jersey," said Theo.

Jack was back at his house on Key Biscayne with Theo and his grandmother. Immediately after finding the threat from Merselus on the back of the JUSTICE FOR SALE sign, Jack had put Theo on an airplane to bring *Abuela* back to Miami.

"New Jersey?" said Jack. He was standing in the kitchen, and Theo was seated on one of the barstools at the granite counter. *Abuela* was in the bathroom. "Why New Jersey?"

"It's where they film that show that's all over the Internet—*Shit Abuelas Say*. She'd be awesome."

"Theo, I can't begin to count the number of reasons why that would be a bad idea."

"Half serious, remember?"

"Got it."

The toilet flushed in the bathroom down the hall. It was *Abuela*'s fourth visit since the plane had landed. That happened when she was nervous.

"Where your mop?" she asked as she entered Jack's office.

"My map of what?"

"No *mapa*. Mop. *El baño. Ay! Dios mío.*"

"*Abuela*, we have a cleaning service."

"What they clean? Your wallet?"

"New Jersey," said Theo, his voice rising.

Jack ignored him. "Sit, please."

Theo helped her up onto the barstool beside him. Jack came closer to the counter, leaning toward her. "I know all this back and forth from Tampa to Miami must seem really crazy to you, but I don't want you to worry. You'll be safe here."

"I stay here with you?"

"Yeah. I talked it over with Andie, and that's the best thing."

She smiled. "*Bueno.*"

There was a knock at the door.

"I'll get it," said Theo, but when he got up, his foot caught on the stool. It sounded like a multicar pileup on I-95 as he and the stool hit the tile floor, but Theo was okay. He crossed the living room and opened the door. It was the neighbor's son, RJ.

"Hi, Max!" RJ shouted.

Max lifted his head. He'd slept through the multicar pileup in the kitchen, but he was suddenly wide awake and barking as if he had smelled RJ approaching a block away from the house.

"That's some watchdog you've got there," said Theo.

Max was all over RJ, and they went down for a wrestling match on the floor. RJ quickly had the upper hand. He was big for thirteen, a force on the middle school basketball court in his size-twelve shoes, and Jack regarded him as poster child for twenty-first-century Miami: Cuban on his mother's side, Lebanese on his father's, and his favorite food was sushi, which he'd learned to roll himself from his uncle, whose fiancée was Japanese. When Max was pinned, RJ looked at Jack and said, "We're leaving for Charleston tomorrow. I just wanted to see what time you wanted me to pick up my travel buddy."

Jack hesitated. The original thought had been to send *Abuela* to Tampa to stay with her brother and to send Max away for the rest of the summer with the Kayals, who rented a beach house in South Carolina every year. Jack knew RJ was going to be disappointed.

"Actually, there's been a change of plan," said Jack.

"Max can't go?" said RJ.

The sadness in the boy's voice was bad enough. The pathetic expression on Max's face made it even worse. It was as if Mighty Casey had just struck out and they were in the heart of Mudville. Jack glanced at *Abuela*, who shot him a reproving look that seemed to say, Have you no heart? Send the dog!

"You know what?" said Jack. "Let's just stick to the plan. I'll have him and all his stuff ready for you tonight."

The joy was back as RJ gave Max a bear hug, along with a quick rundown of how much fun they were going to have at the Kayal family reunion. *Abuela* seemed satisfied. Jack was going to miss his early-morning ritual with the cold black nose in his face, but it was only for a short time—until the threat against "someone you love" was lifted.

The phone rang, and Theo answered it. "It's Hannah," he said as he handed Jack the phone.

"What's up?" Jack said into the phone.

"I just left the women's detention center. They finally coughed up the visitation records that Theo asked for on Saturday. I'm going through them now."

"Anything of interest?"

"There are a couple names on here I don't recognize, so I'll need to follow up on them. But what made me call are the names I *do* recognize."

"What do you mean?"

"Well, there are the familiar names you would expect. Me. You. Geoffrey and Ellen Bennett. My dad. Those are all multiple visits. And then way down on the list, there's a name that jumped out at me. Just one visit."

"Who is it?"

"Celeste Laramore."

Jack's mouth opened, but no words came.

"Jack, you there?"

"Yeah, I'm here."

"I thought you should know right away, especially since you have that hearing before Judge Burrows tomorrow about the *Laramore* case. I thought it could be important."

Now, there's an understatement.

"Thanks, Hannah," said Jack. "Thanks for the heads-up."

45

Score one for us.

Jack wasn't keeping a blow-by-blow score in his head, but Tuesday morning's hearing in the civil case against BNN was definitely going his way. It began with the loss of credibility BNN suffered when Ted Gaines requested that television cameras be allowed at the hearing.

"Let me get this straight, Mr. Gaines," said Judge Burrows. "Before the plaintiffs even filed their case, you rushed into my courtroom and persuaded me to enter a gag order that prohibited them from discussing the case publicly, correct?"

"That's correct," said Gaines. "These scandalous allegations against the news-gathering practices of my client would cause irreparable harm to BNN's reputation and standing."

"I understand that argument," said the judge. "And I also understand that just a matter of hours after those allegations appeared on Celeste Laramore's Facebook page, you filed a motion to dismiss the case with prejudice as a sanction for violating that order. Also correct?"

"Yes, sir," said Gaines. "For twice violating that order."

"But you want today's hearing to be open to the public and broadcast on television. Do I have that right?"

"Yes, Judge," said Gaines. "The reality is that once these allegations appeared on the Internet, there was no way to undo the damage. You can't put the toothpaste back in the tube, as the saying goes."

Gaines continued with a forceful First Amendment speech about the public's right to know, but the judge was no fool, and BNN's flip-flop was no less galling. For the first time, Jack felt momentum on his side. It made Jack lead with an argument that he hadn't planned on making.

"I would ask the court to reconsider its earlier determination that my clients were responsible for the Facebook postings," said Jack.

"On what grounds?" the judge asked.

"Yesterday, in criminal court before Judge Matthews, I proffered evidence regarding an unidentified man who is obsessed with my client, Sydney Bennett. That man has threatened me and committed other criminal acts in his effort to force me to reveal Ms. Bennett's whereabouts to him. The proffer was made in chambers due to the sensitivity of the evidence as it relates to an active homicide investigation. I request the same opportunity in this case—to proffer evidence that this same man has tried to sabotage this case against BNN. We believe these Facebook postings are yet another way to bring harm to me, my clients, and my career in his ongoing effort to coerce me into revealing Sydney Bennett's whereabouts."

"Two objections," said Gaines. "First, we have the proverbial what-has-opposing-counsel-been-smoking objection."

The judge banged his gavel. "That's out of order, Mr. Gaines. Your second objection had better be a good one."

"Yes, Your Honor. This court has already ruled that the Laramores are responsible for the Facebook postings by virtue of the fact that they should have taken down the page if they couldn't control it. Some 'unidentified man' doesn't change that."

"Mr. Gaines' point is well taken," said the judge. "Your request for reconsideration is denied, Mr. Swyteck."

"But—"

"No 'buts,'" said the judge. "The purpose of today's hearing is to find an appropriate punishment for the violation of this court's gag order—specifically, to determine if the lawsuit against BNN has sufficient merit to make dismissal too harsh. I want to reiterate, however, that this hearing will not become a mini-trial of *Laramore v. BNN.* There is just one issue: Even if BNN interfered with the data transmission from the ambulance, was that the legal cause of Celeste Laramore's coma? Am I clear?"

"Yes," said Jack.

"Good. The court will recess for twenty minutes. When we resume, the hearing will be open to the public, including television media. Mr. Swyteck, be prepared to call your first witness."

"The plaintiff calls Virginia Laramore," said Jack.

Celeste's mother was actually the third witness. The first had been Jack's friend and computer expert, Chuck-my-name-rhymes-with-f*** Mays—he worked cheap—who had explained how a hacker had crashed the wireless communication between the ambulance and the emergency room. Witness number two had been a cardiologist—a friend of Rene's boyfriend, Dr. Ross. (Ross had done a one-eighty since busting Jack in the chops.) The cardiologist added an extra layer of expertise to the medical opinion that Rene had lost her life trying to share with Jack: that an uninterrupted data transmission from the ambulance would have revealed that Celeste had a heartbeat irregularity known as long QT syndrome, and doctors at the hospital could have prescribed treatment in-transit that could have prevented her from slipping into a coma.

The testimony had gone well. So well, in fact, that Jack decided to keep Mrs. Laramore's testimony short—just enough to put a face on the case.

The bailiff swore the witness, and after brief background, Jack moved to the substance of her testimony.

"Mrs. Laramore, has your daughter ever been diagnosed with a heart abnormality?"

She was a demure figure in the witness stand. Concealer and fresh courtroom attire couldn't hide the strain of the last nine days. Jack had told her to ignore the media, but her eyes cut across the court-room in the direction of the television camera every few seconds. She was beyond nervous, to the point of distraction.

"Yes," she said softly.

"Mrs. Laramore," the judge said, "you will have to speak a little louder."

"Yes," she said, though it wasn't much louder. "When Celeste was five, doctors told me she had something called long QT syndrome."

Jack remained behind the podium, leaving plenty of distance between himself and the witness, trying hard to make her feel less pressured. "I won't ask you for a medical explanation of the condition," he said. "We've already heard from a cardiologist. Is it your understanding that long QT syndrome is a kind of irregular heartbeat?"

"That's my understanding."

"And is this something that Celeste was treated for?"

"Yes. From time to time."

"What kind of treatment have doctors prescribed for her in the past?"

"There are medications you can take to control the irregularity."

"Did you give her those medications?"

"Yes. As prescribed."

"How did she respond to those medications?"

"She was fine. No problems."

"The medications controlled the irregular heart-beat?"

"Yes, very well."

She held a wadded tissue in her hand, which she

was squeezing into oblivion. Jack debated whether to stop right there, but he had just a couple more questions.

"Now, did Celeste's doctors ever tell you what could happen if she did not receive medication?"

She swallowed hard, then spoke. "It could be a lot of things. She could feel dizzy. She could faint. Or, you know, worse."

"She could go into cardiac arrest, correct?"

"Yes."

"Did any doctor ever mention the possibility of a coma?"

Her hands began to shake, and Jack regretted having put too fine a point on his question.

"Yes, I'm sure," she said. "It's a whole litany of things. At the time I thought they were just trying to scare me into making sure that I was vigilant about giving her the medicine. I never thought . . . I never thought it would actually happen."

She was at the point of breaking down. Jack had gone far enough. "No further questions, Your Honor."

The witness rose quickly, eager to leave.

"Mr. Gaines?" said the judge. "Cross-examination?"

Mrs. Laramore stopped, and the dread on her face as she settled back into the hot seat was apparent even from where Jack was seated.

Great television, I'm sure.

"I have a few questions," said Gaines as he approached the witness. He buttoned his coat, squared his shoulders, and stood tall. Mrs. Laramore seemed to shrink bit by bit with each tick of the clock.

"Good morning, Mrs. Laramore. Let me start by saying how sorry I am about what happened to your daughter. But I'm sure Mr. Swyteck has explained to you that it is our position that BNN did nothing to cause these tragic circumstances."

She didn't answer.

"Mrs. Laramore, can you tell me what long QT syndrome is?"

"It's a heartbeat irregularity."

"Oh, come now, you can do better than that, can't you?"

Jack rose. "Objection. Your Honor, we've had medical testimony."

Gaines said, "Mr. Swyteck asked for her understanding, Your Honor. It's my right to explore the extent of her understanding."

"Overruled. But let's keep this focused."

"Yes, Judge. Mrs. Laramore, do the best you possibly can. What is long QT syndrome?"

She took a breath, let it out, then began. "An electrocardiogram measures electrical impulses as five distinct waves. Doctors label the waves using the letters P, Q, R, S, and T. The waves labeled Q through T show electrical activity in your heart's lower chambers. The space between the start of the Q wave and the end of the T wave—the Q-T interval—is the amount of time it takes for your heart to contract and then refill with blood before beginning the next contraction."

Gaines nodded. "That's pretty impressive."

"She's my daughter."

"But that was probably better than most doctors could describe it."

"She's had it all her life. I've learned a lot about it."

"You take a great deal of interest in your daughter's medical condition, don't you?"

"What mother doesn't?"

"Has anyone ever told you that you take an abnormally high level of interest in your daughter's health?"

"No."

"Really?"

"Objection."

"Sustained. 'Really' is not a question in my courtroom, Mr. Gaines."

"Sorry, Judge. Now, Mrs. Laramore, your daughter was taken to Jackson Memorial Hospital early Sunday morning, nine days ago. When did you get there?"

"Later that same day."

"And how much time have you spent at the hospital since then?"

"Today is the first time I've set foot outside the hospital."

"Is that so? You sleep at the hospital?"

"Yes. There's a guest lounge right outside the ICU. I sleep on the couch."

"And when you're not sleeping?"

"I'm at my daughter's side."

"When you say you've never set foot outside the hospital, do you mean that literally?"

"Yes."

"So you've never so much as walked out the door for some fresh air, taken a walk?"

"No. If my daughter opens her eyes or even twitches a finger, I want to be there."

"So it's not enough if your husband sees it. *You* have to see it."

"I'm not sure I understand."

Jack rose. "Judge, I don't understand the relevance of this, either. I object."

The judge leaned back, thinking. "I assume Mr. Gaines has a point."

"I do," said Gaines.

"Then make it. We're getting dangerously close to lunchtime."

"Yes, Your Honor. Mrs. Laramore, let's go back in time a bit. When Celeste was a child, is it fair to say you were equally attentive, always at her side when she was sick?"

"I tried to be."

"Celeste was a sick child, wasn't she?"

"That depends on what you mean by 'sick child.'"

Gaines walked back to the podium and picked up a file folder. "Twenty-two visits to five different emergency rooms before the age of two. I would consider that 'sick.' How about you?"

This kind of information would never have taken Jack by surprise if the case had proceeded to trial in the normal course. As it was, Jack was hearing it for the first time.

"May I see that, counsel?" asked the judge.

Gaines nodded. He handed a copy up to the judge and seemed more than happy to share as he gave another copy to Jack.

Gaines continued, "Judge, we obtained these medical records from the Florida Department of Children and Family Services. The name of the child has been redacted to comply with privacy laws. I would ask the witness to review them and confirm that these are, in fact, medical records for her daughter."

The judge inspected the stack of records in his file, then looked up. "You may approach the witness, Mr. Gaines."

Gaines took firm, deliberate steps toward the witness stand. Terror was the only word to describe the expression on Mrs. Laramore's face as he handed her the medical file. "Take your time," Gaines told her, "and remember you are under oath when you tell Judge Burrows whether these are your daughter's medical records."

Jack considered an objection, and upon seeing the papers shake violently in his client's hand, his internal debate ended. "Judge, I object."

"On what grounds?"

"This has nothing to do with the issue of whether BNN caused Celeste Laramore to go into a coma."

"To the contrary," said Gaines, "it has everything to do with it. If I could just have a few follow-up questions."

"Objection is overruled," said the judge. Then he leaned over the bench, looked the witness in the eye, and asked, "Mrs. Laramore, are these your daughter's medical records?"

If she had any inclination to lie, the judge's stare had scared her out of it. "Yes," she said. "They are."

"Thank you."

It may have been Jack's imagination, but Gaines seemed to reposition himself for a better camera angle. "Let's walk through some of them, shall we?" said Gaines. "Start with the one right on top. How old was your daughter at that time?"

"Eight weeks."

"She was suffering from what?"

"Severe dehydration and low blood pressure."

"Next chart. How old?"

"Ten weeks."

"Chief medical complaint was what?"

"Fever. Diarrhea. Vomiting."

"If you go down to the middle of the page to the line that is highlighted, the ER nurse reported that the temperature was normal, correct? No fever?"

"That's right."

"Next page. Your daughter was twelve weeks old. Chief medical complaint was what?"

"Some kind of rash."

"Some kind of rash, huh?"

"And sleep apnea."

"Was there any verification of the apnea?"

"I don't know."

"Look at the next highlighted line. Could you read that aloud, please?"

Her hand was shaking. It took her a moment to steady the paper and read it. "It says 'Apnea—as reported by mother.'"

The judge interrupted. "Counsel, do you intend to go through each and every one of these records? It's quite a stack."

"My point is almost made," Gaines said. "Let me get straight to the bottom line. Mrs. Laramore, turn to the page that is flagged by the yellow Post-it, about two-thirds of the way down your stack of records there."

Jack followed along with copies.

"Can you tell the court what this is?" asked Gaines.

"It's a blood test report."

"Blood test for your daughter, correct?"

"Yes."

"Would you read the highlighted portion of the box at the bottom of the report, please?"

Jack glanced at his own page. He saw the answer that Mrs. Laramore finally uttered: "High concentration of diuretic," said Mrs. Laramore.

"The blood test confirmed that someone was giving your daughter a high dose of a diuretic, isn't that right?"

"Yes."

"Had any doctor prescribed a diuretic?"

"Not to my knowledge."

"In fact, that would have been a really stupid thing to prescribe, wouldn't it, for a child who had presented to the emergency room for dehydration"—he paused to check his notes—"eleven times?"

"That wouldn't be smart, no."

"And yet *someone*," he said, his voice taking on an edge, "was giving your daughter diuretics."

"According to the blood test, yes."

He moved closer, tightening his figurative grip on the witness. "Mrs. Laramore, you're aware, are you not, that excessive use of diuretics can cause long QT syndrome?"

"Objection," Jack shouted.

"Sustained."

"That's fine," said Gaines. "If the court wishes, we can bring in a dozen doctors who will testify to that fact."

"The court wishes you to ask your next question."

"Yes, Judge. Mrs. Laramore, doctors have told you, have they not, that your daughter's heart condition was caused by excessive use of diuretics?"

"Objection."

"No, I'm going to allow that one," said the judge. "It's a different question."

The witness shifted uneasily. "Yes. Doctors have told me that."

There was a murmur across the courtroom, as if the observers sensed that Gaines had truly scored.

Gaines took another step closer, his voice rising. "Mrs. Laramore, *you* gave your daughter those diuretics, didn't you?"

"No."

"*You* caused her long QT syndrome."

"No!"

"Objection!" Jack shouted. "This is pure harassment."

Gaines repositioned himself yet again, as if someone had pointed out the perfect spot in the courtroom for TV coverage. "Judge, we intend to show that the QT syndrome was caused by the victim's own mother, who presents a classic case of Munchausen syndrome by proxy."

"What?" said Jack.

"Her daughter presented to the ER nearly every two weeks before her second birthday. Mrs. Laramore shows a high level of understanding of her daughter's medical condition. She has never left her daughter's side since she's been hospitalized. This is a psychology that thrives on the illness of children. The diuretics given to her daughter caused symptoms that fed the mother's illness, but they also caused long-term heart problems for Celeste."

"Judge," said Jack, "it doesn't matter *how* Celeste got long QT syndrome. The point is that it's treatable and would not have resulted in a coma if BNN had not interfered with the transmission of vital information from the ambulance."

"I'll sustain the objection. Counsel, please approach the bench."

Jack came forward, and Gaines stood with him at the judge's bench.

"Mr. Swyteck, your objection is well founded because, yes, in a strict legal sense, you are right: It doesn't matter how Celeste got long QT syndrome. The law says that a wrongdoer takes the victim as he finds her. I'm sure Mr. Gaines is well aware of that rule of law. But if these allegations of Munchausen syndrome by proxy are true, Mr. Swyteck, you need to settle this case. To be blunt about it, the sympathy value of your case has been neutralized. These are smart lawyers you're up against. They are going to find a way to get this information before the jury if and when this case goes to trial. If not in the courtroom, it will definitely be in the media. And as much as I tell jurors not to read newspapers or watch TV, they do. This is the sort of thing they will hold against your case and your client."

"I guess that's why BNN wanted today's hearing on television," Jack said, unable to resist a swipe.

"That's an outrageous accusation," said Gaines.

"I won't ascribe any motives to anyone," said the judge. "I'm denying BNN's motion to dismiss the case. But take my warning to heart, Mr. Swyteck. You've got serious problems."

Jack turned away and glanced at Mrs. Laramore in the witness chair.

Don't I know it.

"The witness may step down," the judge announced. "We're adjourned."

46

I don't want to talk about it."

That was all Virginia Laramore said to Jack after the hearing before Judge Burrows. Jack was fine with it, at least until the handful of inquisitive reporters stopped trailing them out of the courthouse, down the granite steps, and to the parking lot. The media coverage wasn't nearly as extensive as it had been for the Sydney Bennett hearing, but one reporter followed them all the way to the car, asking over and over, "Mrs. Laramore, did you abuse your daughter?" The question was met with silence, punctuated by Jack slamming the driver's-side door.

Jack was behind the wheel and turning onto Flagler Street when his client finally opened up.

"Celeste was adopted."

Jack hit the brake, then looked straight at her. "What?"

"All those medical records are from the time she was with her birth mother. Ben and I adopted her after IRS took her away and she was put in foster care."

Jack pulled the car over to the curb and put it in PARK. It wasn't easy to get tough with a woman whose daughter was in a coma, but Jack was losing patience. "Why didn't you tell me that? And, for God's sake, why didn't you shove it in Ted Gaines' face when he attacked you like that?"

"Because Ben and I have never told anyone outside the family that Celeste is adopted. And I've never even told Celeste that her birth mother was abusive. I wasn't about to make that blowhard Ted Gaines the first person to hear it. Especially not on television. Celeste has already made enough headlines for his disgraceful client."

Jack couldn't disagree. "I'm sorry you had to go through that today," he said.

"It's the second worst thing I've ever had to deal with."

Jack knew the first.

"Can we get back to the hospital, please? I want to be with Celeste."

Jack put the car in gear and drove. Instinct told him that Mrs. Laramore would have preferred to ride in silence, but questions remained, and Jack was running out of time. He'd spoken to Ben Laramore about the visitation records from the women's detention center and gotten no explanation. He needed to ask again.

"Why did Celeste visit Sydney Bennett in jail?"

Mrs. Laramore was looking out the side window. "I'm no more help than Ben on that one. We don't know."

"Why do you think she went? Your best guess."

"No idea."

"Celeste's roommate told me that Celeste also visited Neil Goderich, Sydney's first lawyer. We've searched through all Neil's notes and can't find a single record of their meeting."

"Maybe it never happened."

"Can you think of any reason why Celeste would have met with him?"

"A formality, maybe? She wanted to visit Sydney and needed to clear it with her lawyer. But that's just a guess."

It seemed like a reasonable guess. "But that still doesn't tell us why she wanted to visit Sydney."

"No," Mrs. Laramore said as she massaged the bridge of her nose. "This is giving me a headache."

"I'm sorry, but I have to press. This adoption news may be leading me down the wrong path, but it may be the answer to some of the questions I've been asking myself. Questions that started with those photographs of Celeste that Ben sent me."

"What about them?"

Jack cut across traffic to take the expressway on-ramp. "There's a definite transformation in Celeste's appearance."

"She grew up."

"No, it's not just the difference between being seventeen and being twenty. Sydney Bennett was arrested three years ago. That's when her face first appeared on the news. There's a vague resemblance between Celeste at age seventeen and Sydney when she was arrested. Over the next three years—as Sydney's face was more and more on television—the resemblance gets stronger. Mostly due to the way Celeste started wearing her hair, how she wore her makeup."

"Are you saying she was *trying* to look like Sydney?"

"Maybe I am."

"That's ridiculous."

"Is it? I don't mean to pry," said Jack, "but if you've never told Celeste that her mother was abusive, you probably haven't told her much at all about her. Is it possible that Celeste started to wonder?"

"She never asked me about her."

"Did she ask Ben?"

"Not that he ever told me. But I honestly don't see where you're going with this. And could you please drive faster? I really want to get back to the hospital."

Jack's focus on the conversation had dropped his speed well below the limit. He took it up to sixty, which still left him in the slow lane on the busy westbound Dolphin Expressway. They were coming up on the exit for Jackson Memorial Hospital when the real question finally popped out of Jack's mouth.

"Virginia, do you know who Celeste's birth mother was?"

"No. Ben and I were never foster parents. We came into the picture after the birth mother's rights were terminated and Celeste's foster parents decided they couldn't afford to adopt another child. I got medical information and such, and I think under Florida law I could have gotten the mother's first name, if I'd wanted it. But the birth mother's identity was just something I never really wanted to pursue."

Jack turned at the Twelfth Street exit, and they stopped at the red light at the end of the ramp. The hospital where Celeste lay in a coma was in sight. Jack glanced at her adoptive mother.

"I'm thinking it may be time to find out," he said.

47

•

Ted Gaines' flight landed at LaGuardia Airport a few minutes before nine P.M., just in time to see the Tuesday-evening edition of the *Faith Corso Show*. He didn't like what he was seeing.

"Friends," said Corso in a somber tone, "it was a dark day for this network in a Miami courtroom today."

Dark day?

Confused, Gaines stepped closer to the flat-screen television that hung by a bracket from the ceiling. He was in Figaro's, a bar directly across from the gate where his flight from Miami had deplaned.

Corso continued, "As her twenty-year-old daughter lay in a coma, Virginia Laramore was viciously attacked on the witness stand by prominent attorney Ted Gaines. The issue in the case was simply this: Who caused Celeste Laramore to go into a coma? Of course, we here at BNN deny any responsibility for that tragic course of events. But Mr. Gaines simply went too far. In the worst case of overzealous lawyering I have ever witnessed, he proceeded to accuse Mrs. Laramore of abusing her own child and causing the heart condition that resulted in her slipping into a coma. In support of his attack, he introduced into evidence a series of medical records showing that, before the age of two, Celeste Laramore had visited the emergency room more than two dozen times. Mr. Gaines should be ashamed of himself, and he should have done his homework. My own reporters have investigated this matter, and we have this exclusive story for you, and this important message for Mr. Gaines: Celeste Laramore was adopted, you moron!"

Gaines shuddered. It was suddenly hard to breathe.

"Yes," said Corso, "adopted. Those medical records showing physical abuse were all before Celeste was adopted—'rescued' may be a better word for it—by the Laramore family. Now, friends, as I mentioned, Mr. Gaines is the attorney for this network. I'm risking my own job by saying this, but I pray for the sake of the Laramore family and for the sake of Lady Justice that Mr. Gaines will no longer be the lawyer for the network I am proud to call home, the network that prides itself on getting the story right and on doing the right thing—your Breaking News Network."

Gaines ground his teeth together, clenched his fists tight, and tried to breathe. The anger inside was more than he could contain. He stepped out of the bar and found a quiet place by the kiosk for a "lids" vendor that sold baseball caps. His hand trembled with anger as he dialed Keating's private line. The CEO answered as if he were expecting the call.

"How goes it, Ted?"

"You son of a bitch, you set me up."

"Well, hold on there, counselor."

"Hold on, my ass. It wasn't my idea to go after Virginia Laramore as an abusive parent. You wanted it. You gave me the records. You said your investigator checked it out. That was all a lie. You knew all along that Celeste was adopted, didn't you?"

"Now, why would I do that to you, Ted?"

"Why? What better reason to ruin a trial lawyer's hard-earned reputation than to manufacture ten minutes of self-righteous glory for Faith Corso on national television?"

"That was awfully brave of Faith, wasn't it?" Keating said smugly. "To risk her job and call on her own network to fire its high-priced lawyer?"

"It was *staged*."

"It's *all* staged," Keating fired back. "You know that better than anyone."

"I don't know what kind of sick game you're playing. But I'm done with it. I quit."

"Too late," said Keating. "Check your e-mail. A letter went out from my office two minutes ago dismissing you from the case."

Gaines moved away from the kiosk and the businessman who was checking out a Yankees cap. "You are as low as they come," Gaines said, hissing into the phone. "Is there anyone you won't destroy in the name of entertainment?"

"My mother died six years ago. So the answer is no. Good luck to you, Mr. Gaines."

The call ended.

Gaines shoved the phone into the pocket of his

blazer and turned around to check the TV inside Figaro's. He was standing too far away to hear, but it took little imagination to figure out what Faith Corso was saying. His photograph—not a flattering one—was on the screen directly above the BREAK-ING NEWS banner. Bold red letters ran diagonally across his face.

FIRED, it read.

He closed his eyes in disbelief. *You fool, Gaines. You complete fool.*

48

.

Sydney Bennett's pulse pounded, her heart racing at better than two beats per second, her chest heaving as she struggled to catch her breath. Darkness was her friend, really. It made her harder to find. But each night her mind played tricks on her, the slightest noise setting her off in a fit of panic.

She crouched low behind the overgrown bushes, her back to a wall of rough stucco, her knees to her chin, all too aware of the sound of her own breathing.

Quiet!

She was soaking wet, shoeless, and wearing only a T-shirt and underwear. She'd sprinted all the way from the swimming pool, across a parking lot, and down the sidewalk a good two hundred yards before ducking into the bushes. Voices on the other side of the wood fence around the pool area had freaked her out in the middle of an improvised bath. For the past two days she'd been hiding in a vacant town-house at Whispering Pines, one of those gated communities where all the units looked exactly alike. It was a brand-new development, but not a single one of the three dozen townhomes had ever been occupied. South Florida was littered with empty developments like this one, residential ghost towns, the remnants of a reckless build, build, build spree that had swept developers into bankruptcy, buyers into foreclosure, and big banks into bailouts. Much of Whispering Pines had fallen into disrepair, overrun by weeds and mold. Some units were at least minimally maintained, the owners apparently clinging to the hope that the market might someday rebound, but even after seven broken windows Sydney couldn't find a single one that had running water. The developer or the bank or whoever owned the property was keeping up the clubhouse, however, so the slightly green pool was her bathtub.

What was that?

She heard the voice again, the one that had scared her off from the pool. A man's voice.

Merselus?

She couldn't tell if it was him, but she knew he was after her, that he'd never stop until he found her. The man was relentless. Obsessed. Maybe even crazy. Though he could also be convincing, even charming. He'd certainly fooled Sydney. He had a business card, a résumé, and enough money to rent a private airplane. He also had a plan. He'd led her to believe that the plan was to sell her book, make a movie, and make Sydney Bennett a star. It was all a ruse. If she'd had Internet access in the detention center she could have probably figured out that his talent agency was nonexistent, that he'd never actually sold the books and movies he'd claimed to have sold, that his plan for Sydney was something else entirely.

There it is again!

Sydney held her breath, willing herself into silence. No movement. No sound. Completely still. She knew she could do it. She'd controlled her fears enough to fool him once before.

It had been just their second night together. After a short flight to Palm Beach County, Merselus had taken her to a beach house in Manalapan that, he said, belonged to "a wealthy client" who was discreet enough never to tell the media where Sydney was hiding. It was paradise: her own room, a king-size bed, a view of the ocean, and a private bathroom that was bigger than the cell she'd lived in for the past three years. Merselus stocked the refrigerator with all her favorite food and whatever she wanted to drink. He was a perfect gentleman—until he woke her at three A.M. It was as if he'd written a script and somehow expected her to know it. He'd started with controlled aggression, but pure anger took over as she flubbed her next line, didn't do what he'd scripted, didn't go wild with excitement, didn't play the part of the sex-starved jailbird who craved the way he ripped off her panties, grabbed her crotch, and rubbed her raw. The way he squeezed and pulled at the base of her breasts, as if he were trying to rip them from her body. The way he'd tried to force his whole hand deep inside her, as if she were yearning for more than any one woman could possibly handle. And when his other hand slipped up around her throat, she'd managed to strike back with what little nails she had, short prison nails, carving a deep red line across his face. It only made him crazier, angrier, more brutal. Suddenly, both of his hands were tight around her neck, there was no way to breathe, and Sydney was certain that she was going to die as the intense pounding inside her head and unbearable pressure behind her eyes gave way to blackness.

I hear it.

Footsteps on the abandoned sidewalks of Whispering Pines—they were getting louder. Someone was approaching.

Don't move, don't run.

It was the same strategy she'd employed in that bedroom in the beach house after she'd regained consciousness—lie there on the bed, completely still, pretending that she'd yet to recover from Merselus and his attack. And then when she was certain that he'd left the bedroom and gone to sleep . . .

Run!

Sydney leaped from her hiding spot behind the bushes and started to sprint down the sidewalk. A scream cut through the darkness, and Sydney ran even faster. There were footsteps behind her, but they were fading, not following. She stopped and turned.

What the hell?

She narrowed her eyes, struggling to see in the moonlight. It was kids—some punks on summer vacation looking for a secluded place to share a bottle of vodka and have a party.

Sydney hunched over, hands on her knees. She was exhausted, tired of running, tired of living in fear of Merselus, tired of taking baths in a fucking green swimming pool.

She caught her breath, stood up, and headed back to the pool area to collect her dirty clothes.

Girl, you gotta find a pay phone.

Jack stared at the television screen, speechless. The *Faith Corso Show* had reached a new low, if that was possible. Still, Jack had to dig very deep inside himself even to begin to feel sorry for Ted Gaines.

"He deserves it," said Andie.

They were watching together on the couch, Andie leaning against his shoulder. *Abuela* was in the kitchen cooking enough *ropa vieja* to last him six months.

"I need to call the Laramores," said Jack. "They need to know the adoption is public."

"Try to make Mrs. Laramore see it as a positive," said Andie. "I know this is something they didn't want blasted all over the television. But it needed to come out, after the accusations Ted Gaines made against her."

"That's the way to spin it, I guess."

"Don't think of it as spin. You're just doing the best you can."

"Thanks."

Jack reached for the phone, then paused. Andie herself had been adopted, and even though they'd talked about it before, Jack had been reluctant to mix the Laramore situation with hers. But any insights into shortcuts on finding a birth mother would be useful at this point.

"I have this long-shot theory about Celeste," he started to say, but it was interrupted again by what was becoming a familiar string of profanities with rhythm—Theo's ringtone. Jack still had his phone. He picked it up and checked the number.

UNKNOWN, the screen said, which gave Jack even more reason to answer.

"This is Jack."

"It's me," she said, and he knew immediately it was Sydney.

"Are you on a cell?" he asked.

"No. Pay phone." Jack could hear the traffic noise in the background.

"Do you have a cell?" he asked.

"Yeah. Merselus gave me an iPhone when he met me at the airport, but I'm sure that's just so he could listen to every call I make."

"That's perfect."

"No, it's not perfect," she said, her voice trembling. "I don't even turn the damn thing on because I know he can track me with GPS."

"Listen to me, Sydney. I'm going to put Andie on in a minute. She can tell you how to disarm the GPS tracking. And then you're going to turn that phone on."

"What? No! He is going to find me, and he is going to kill me!"

"Merselus is not going to find you. We are going to find *him*."

"How?"

"You need to do exactly what I tell you to do," said Jack.

49
.

At eleven P.M. Jack was pacing across the rug in his family room, ready to leave the house, waiting for the cell phone to ring.

"You don't have to do this," said Andie.

If it were about Sydney, Jack would have agreed with her. But it was about putting a stop to the guy who had left Celeste in a coma, strangled Rene, and threatened his grandmother. The plan wasn't to get Sydney her life back. It was to catch a killer.

"Yeah, I do," said Jack.

Sydney's iPhone from Merselus was the key. All of her calls to Jack over the next ninety minutes would be from that phone to Theo's cell. Using Jack's cell wasn't an option, as suddenly having a conversation with Sydney on a line that Jack had essentially abandoned after Rene's murder would have surely raised suspicions in Merselus' mind. It was enough that Sydney's iPhone was infected with spyware, and the FBI had the technology in place to confirm that someone was actively monitoring the call in real time. And then they would know that Merselus was taking the bait.

At five minutes past the hour, Theo's cell rang. The intent was for the ensuing conversation to be for effect only, tied loosely to the script that Jack and Andie had worked out in advance. The less Sydney said the better, and Jack crossed his fingers in hopes that she didn't screw it up. He put the phone on speaker so that Andie could hear.

"Did you make a decision?" said Jack.

"Yes."

"When can we meet?"

"Slow down," said Sydney. "Just so we're clear, I'm not saying for sure that I'll testify in court. I'm not promising I'll even go to court."

Jack stopped pacing and bit back his anger. Just ten seconds into the implementation of the plan and Sydney was already ad-libbing. *She really does think she's a freakin' movie star.*

"That's fine, Sydney. I just want us to get together and talk. When can we meet?"

"Tonight."

"Okay. Let's meet at—"

"At eleven thirty, Bayfront Park, in front of the central fountain."

That wasn't Jack and Andie's plan, but Sydney hung up before Jack could respond. Jack put the cell phone away, looked at Andie, and said, "She's following her own script."

"She obviously doesn't trust you," said Andie.

"Or anyone else, I would imagine."

Andie's cell rang. It was her tech agent. The call

lasted less than a minute, and then she shared the news with Jack.

"Sydney's call to you was monitored," she said.

"At least something went as expected," he said, alluding to the curve Sydney had thrown them about the meeting place.

"The FBI can work with her ad-libbing," said Andie. "But that doesn't mean you have to, Jack."

Jack thought about it. "If Merselus wanted me dead, I'd already be dead."

"That's one way to look at it. But this is not without risk. Merselus could figure out that you're trying to set him up and retaliate. He could come around to the view that you're the only thing standing between him and Sydney and decide it's time to take you out. Any number of things could go wrong."

"Are you trying to talk me out of this?"

"I want you to go in with your eyes open."

Jack weighed it another minute, his gaze drifting down the hallway and coming to rest on the door to the guest bedroom, where *Abuela* lay sleeping. "What am I supposed to do, wait for my grandmother to end up like Rene?"

Andie didn't answer.

"And while I'm at it, maybe I should tell the Laramore family that I have to drop their case against BNN because it could be dangerous to find out who grabbed their daughter by the throat. And I can just keep using Theo's cell for the next six months while the FBI monitors my private phone lines, I can send Max to go live permanently with the Kayal family, and I can just forget about ever taking another walk from my office to Theo's bar unless I want to get choked by some psycho jumping out of the bushes."

"It's maddening, I know."

"Way beyond maddening," said Jack.

"So, it's a go?"

Jack started toward the front door. "Yeah," he said as he grabbed his car keys from the hook on the wall. "Let's do this."

50

.

Jack reached the park about ten minutes early, not quite eleven twenty.

As the name implies, Bayfront Park abuts Biscayne Bay in downtown Miami. Biscayne Boulevard, the city's widest thoroughfare, borders on the west, separating thirty-two acres of greenery, walkways, and serenity from the sheer face of the towering Miami skyline. To the south is the high-rise hotel from which the big glowing orange drops every New Year's Eve—which Jack and Andie had learned the hard way was the perfect place for folks who hate cold weather but love that Times Square feeling of ringing in the new year while drowning in a sea of loud, drunken strangers.

"I see you," said Andie, her voice somewhat mechanical sounding in his earpiece. Jack did not reply; he had no microphone, as moving his lips could have tipped off Merselus that he was wired for communication.

"Walk a little slower if you can hear me," said Andie. She was confirming his reception.

Jack slowed as he approached the Flagler Street entrance to the park's main east-west axis. The central fountain was in sight and due east, halfway between him and the shoreline. The Miami Dade Courthouse was a short ride away on the elevated Metromover. Over the years, in many a trial, Jack had strolled past the park's central fountain on his way to the beach chairs on the shoreline, where he would consult with passing dolphins and manatees on what verdict his jury might return.

"Okay, we're good," said Andie. "Keep moving."

Jack resumed walking at his normal pace. Each step took him deeper into the canopy of tall trees and farther away from the urban glow of the office towers behind him. Soon he was entirely dependent on the moon and the streetlamps that lined the walkway to break the darkness. The amphitheater was up and over the embankment to his left, as was the Feng Shui Garden. Jack stayed on course, walking directly toward the fountain. It was quiet at this hour, essentially an oversize concrete bowl of motionless water on an enormous circle of coral-stone pavers in the dead center of the park.

"Stop," said Andie.

He did. Jack was standing on the outermost ring of stone pavers that encircled the fountain. A string of park benches ran along the outer perimeter. Jack counted five homeless people asleep on the benches.

He wondered if one of them was Merselus.

Jack's phone rang. The tech agents had rigged it so that Andie could hear.

"Answer it," said Andie.

Jack took the call, expecting it to be Merselus. It wasn't.

"Meet me on the platform at the Bayfront Station," said Sydney.

Jack turned around. Miami's Metromover was an elevated tram system that wound through downtown and the financial district. Jack could see the Bayfront Station from where he was standing, but this wasn't part of the plan at all.

"What?" he said.

"You heard me."

"Sydney, what are you doing?"

"Bayfront Station. Eleven forty-five."

The call ended. Jack checked the time. He had fifteen minutes—enough time, but none to waste. He walked while waiting for Andie's instructions.

Andie moved into reactive mode. She and her tech agent were inside an FBI special communications van, which was parked at ground level inside the garage at One Biscayne Tower, directly across the boulevard from the park. Two tech agents in the field were feeding her live-streaming video from surveillance cameras. She radioed position one on the rooftop.

"Novak, can you get Bayfront Station from your current location?"

"That's affirmative," he said.

She knew position two—one of the "homeless" on a park bench near the central fountain—would be useless in his current location. She radioed him with instructions: "Hernandez, relocate to the top of the embankment at the amphitheater. You will be eye level with the Bayfront Station platform."

"Roger that."

She checked the map on the computer screen. No changes to perimeter control were required— the same streets and alleys were implicated. The ground team, however, required adjustment. Andie started with the undercover agent who was dressed, wigged, and made up to resemble Sydney Bennett— the bait to draw out Merselus.

"Pederson to Bayfront Station. Eleven forty-five arrival."

"Roger," came the reply.

The rest of the ground team also needed adjustment if they were going to be in position to move in when Merselus showed his face. There were two more homeless guys, a touristy couple strolling in the park, a guitarist with a plate of coins sitting outside the entrance to the Metromover station.

"Position three, to south entrance of Bayfront Park; position four, to bus stop at Flagler; position five, to corner of Southeast Second Street; position six"—the guitarist—"stay exactly where you are."

Andie checked the computer screen one more time. The final relocation was critical, and it took her tech agent a minute to compute the angles and come up with a clear line of fire for her sniper.

"Haywood," she said into her radio. "Rooftop, Edison Hotel. Friedman will meet you at the service elevator at the back of the building."

"Roger."

Andie switched to another frequency for the final instruction.

"New destination is covered, Jack. Proceed to Bayfront Station."

51

·

Andie's instruction ended with a crackle in Jack's earpiece. *New destination is covered.* He wondered what that meant, exactly. A SWAT team in position? A sniper ready to take out Merselus? *Paramedics standing by in case it all goes wrong?*

Jack was already at Biscayne Boulevard, the western border of the park. Traffic was light on the four northbound lanes between him and the elevated people-mover station, which rose up like an oil rig from the urban sea of concrete and asphalt.

Jack stepped to the curb, then looked up at the platform across the street. A rubber-tired tram entered the station, and its doors slid open. One passenger got on. Two people stepped off and took the escalator down to the turnstile. The tram pulled away, leaving the platform unoccupied. Jack drew a breath, taking in the warm night air, and then started across the street.

Andie's voice was in his ear again. "No rush, Jack. Decoy to arrive exactly at eleven forty-five."

Decoy. He knew what Andie meant—the female

agent disguised as Sydney Bennett, the bait who would lure Merselus into the trap. Jack's head was already filled with worry, but Andie's last communication had triggered yet another one, as he couldn't help but wonder how many times Andie herself had been the decoy in one of her undercover operations.

Jack jogged across the fourth lane to avoid being flattened by a Porsche coming around the corner. Bayfront Station was at the fulcrum of what had once been a famous hairpin turn in the first and only Grand Prix race to actually run in the streets of downtown Miami. Some drivers thought the race was still running.

"Guitarist is one of ours," said Andie as Jack approached the street-level entrance to the station. The tune sounded like something from the Gypsy Kings. The guy actually wasn't bad.

"You're early," said Andie. "Don't want you trapped on the platform with nowhere to go. Stand where you are and listen to the musician."

Jack stopped. The guitarist transitioned into Cat Stevens' "Moonshadow." Really damn good.

"Okay," said Andie, "take the escalator up to the platform. Decoy will arrive in ninety seconds."

Jack fished a couple bucks from his wallet and bought a Metromover token from the machine. He dropped the change in the musician's open guitar case, which drew a string of "Thank you, thank you, thank you." Nerves had a way of triggering funny thoughts, and special agent Cat Stevens had Jack thinking that it wasn't just lawyers who yearned for another career.

"You're welcome," said Jack. He pushed through

the turnstile and started up the escalator. It seemed painfully slow, but Jack knew it was just the circumstances. Halfway up he spotted the Sydney decoy on the sidewalk across the street. She was walking toward the station.

He wondered if Merselus saw her as well.

Jack stepped onto the platform. It was cooler up there, a salty breeze blowing across the park from the bay. His gaze fixed on the FBI decoy as she crossed Biscayne Boulevard. She didn't look all that much like Sydney Bennett. The blond wig, the scarf, the sunglasses at night—the entire getup was more like what Sydney might look like if she were trying not to be recognized in public.

Jack moved to the thick yellow warning line in front of the track, right at the edge of the elevated platform. No trams were in sight. He looked up and down Biscayne Boulevard. To the north he could see all the way to the arena, home of the Miami Heat. He spotted a few pedestrians along the sidewalk, not knowing which ones were FBI agents, no way of knowing whether one of them was Merselus. If someone didn't make a move on the decoy quickly, the whole mission would be a failure.

Jack's phone rang. He checked the number. It was from Sydney's phone.

Andie's voice was in his earpiece. "Answer it."

Jack put the phone to his other ear. "This is Jack."

Silence.

He glanced toward the escalator. The Sydney decoy was on her way up.

"This is Jack," he said into the phone.

No response.

Anger rose up inside him. Sydney's entire role in the operation had been simply to call on her iPhone and tell Jack to meet her at the central fountain at eleven thirty. If Sydney was on a mission to take over and screw things up, she was playing a dangerous game. Jack put his phone away, but it chimed immediately with a text message.

Check the bench, it read.

He turned around to face the wood bench in front of the billboard in the center of the platform. The bench was vacant. He was completely alone on the platform until the Sydney decoy reached the top of the escalator. Jack glanced at her, then back at the bench, and something caught his eye. He stepped closer, closer. Then he saw it clearly, a polished copper hoop hanging from the armrest on the bench.

It was Rene's necklace.

"Don't touch anything," the undercover agent told him.

Jack stepped away from the bench, sickened by the symbolism of the swap.

"He's got Sydney," Jack said.

The agent said something into her hidden microphone about "abort," which took it from obvious to official that the mission had failed.

Jack's gaze drifted back to the necklace on the bench, and he wondered if Sydney was still alive— and how much time they had.

52
·

Andie's surveillance and apprehension team quickly shifted gears to abduction and recovery mode. The FBI communications van was at the exit to the parking garage, poised to speed down Biscayne Boulevard. Andie was buckled into the passenger seat with tech support on the line.

"I need a location," she said, her patience waning.

"No GPS reading," her tech agent said.

"Damn." Andie was certain that Merselus had found Sydney because she had screwed up the FBI's directions on how to disarm GPS tracking on her iPhone.

"We're triangulating now," tech said.

Andie crossed her fingers. The electronic pulse that every cell phone in the power-on mode transmitted to cell towers every eight seconds was distinct from GPS tracking, but the process of triangulating between a cell phone and towers took more time.

"Got it," he said, and he gave her an approximate address, give or take a hundred-yard radius. Triangulation was less precise than GPS. "That's the best we can do."

"That's on the river."

"North of the Brickell Avenue Bridge," he said. "I'm sending you the coordinates now."

"Send them team-wide," said Andie. "And thanks."

The driver hit the gas, and the tires squealed as the van raced out of the parking garage. They were headed south on Biscayne Boulevard as Andie confirmed backup and got on the line with Special Agent Crenshaw, whose team was already on the move in a black FBI SWAT van.

Crenshaw asked, "How current are the coordinates?"

"About four minutes ago."

"Four minutes? They could be five miles from there by now."

"It's all we've got to go on for now."

"How about an update?"

"Not likely. Our guess is that he texted rather than called to try to keep the phone on for less than eight seconds. He barely missed it. We got one reading when he sent the text, which by itself may not have been enough for us to triangulate. Got a second pulse just before the phone was powered off, which gave us a little more data to work with. I wouldn't expect him to turn on the phone again and send another pulse."

"Did you issue a BOLO?"

Andie understood the point of his question. A be-on-the-lookout alert could draw everyone into the conflict—from local police to the neighborhood crime watch. Or even the media.

"BOLO went out three minutes ago," said Andie.

"Shit," said Crenshaw.

"Had to do it," said Andie. "If they're speeding down I-95, I need highway patrol in the loop."

"Be on the lookout for what, though? Do you honestly think Sydney Bennett looks anything like what she looked like in trial?"

"Probably not. But we have a decent image of Merselus that we lifted from a snippet of enhanced video taken by a Coast Guard officer of him and Sydney on the runway at Opa-locka Airport. He may not even know we have it, so it may be helpful."

"Send me that now," said Crenshaw. "And while you're at it, why don't you supplement the BOLO with the usual multijurisdictional caveat."

"And that would be . . . what?"

"Tell the locals to stay out of my way," said Crenshaw.

She knew he was only half-serious—maybe a little more than half. "Roger that," said Andie.

53

·

Midnight came. Jack was driving across the Rickenbacker Causeway to Key Biscayne, halfway home and flanked on both sides by the dark waters of Biscayne Bay. With a slight turn of his head to the left, he could admire downtown Miami and the sparkling skyline that stretched along the shore of the mainland. The view was beautiful—deceptively so, as the city seemed oblivious to Merselus and his plans for the night. Rene, her necklace, and Sydney were heavy on Jack's mind when the phone call came from Andie.

"Are you okay?" asked Andie.

"Yeah. Where are you?"

"You won't see me tonight."

He got that answer a lot in response to "Where are you?"

"Do you want me to notify Sydney's parents?" Jack asked.

"It's covered."

"Good. Not exactly two of my favorite people."

"Which reminds me. Don't lie awake tonight

mulling over your long-shot theory about Celeste Laramore's biological parents. It went nowhere. DNA tests showed no possible biological connection between Celeste and anyone in the Bennett family—Sydney, her parents, Emma. No one."

Andie had told him from the get-go that he was getting carried away with the physical resemblance between Celeste and Sydney. "Still don't understand why she visited Sydney, why she started looking more and more like her."

"My bet is that Celeste thought she could be related to Sydney, or maybe even wanted it to be true. I hate to speak badly of a young woman in a coma, but frankly I think it was some kind of weird celebrity worship. Granted, Sydney was the worst kind of celebrity, but she was still a celebrity."

"Maybe," said Jack.

"I gotta go. I'll call you."

"Stay safe," he said, and the call ended. Jack checked his speed. He was on the downward slope of Miami's highest bridge, the end of the causeway and the beginning of the island of Key Biscayne and its notorious speed traps. He brought it down to thirty-five m.p.h. and dialed Theo at his bar. Music and crowd noise were in the background.

"How's *Abuela*?" Jack asked. Jack hadn't told his grandmother what he and Andie were up to, but she had still felt uncomfortable staying at the house alone, so Theo told her it was national Take an *Abuela* to Work Night.

"She's awesome," said Theo. "She's sharing a booth with Uncle Cy and on her third Cosmo-Not."

Cosmo-Not was Theo's version of a nonalcoholic

Cosmopolitan. Uncle Cy was Theo's great-uncle, an eighty-year-old relic of Miami's Overtown and its jazz heyday of the mid-twentieth century. Cy was still quite the saxophone player, with emphasis on *player*.

"Tell Cy to keep his hands to himself," said Jack.

"Will do. How did it go tonight?"

"Don't really want to talk about it."

"Got it."

"I'm almost home, and I'm embarrassed to say that I forgot all about picking up *Abuela*. Too damn much on my mind."

"No problem. I'll drop her off."

"Thanks."

"Unless she hooks up with Cy."

"Don't push it," said Jack.

Jack ended the call, tucked his cell away, and just drove. The monotonous hum of tires on asphalt was the backdrop for his thoughts. He passed the Seaquarium, home to Flipper the dolphin and Lolita the killer whale. He wondered if they were asleep; and if they were asleep, he wondered if they were dreaming; and if they were dreaming, he wondered if these highly intelligent legless mammals ever dreamed about walking like the trainers who fed them. Then he shook off the silliness and accepted the fact that the old games he played to trick himself were futile. Never in his life—not even as a high-school boy obsessed with the hair and lips of Julia Roberts—had he managed to conjure up a successful diversion from worries and concerns that were certain to keep him wide awake and staring at the ceiling till dawn.

Jack steered into the driveway and killed the engine. The headlights remained on for a few moments, then blinked off. The house was dark, and the porch light was off. The narrow driveway was the only opening in a thick ficus hedge that extended like a castle wall across the front and along both sides of his smallish yard. It was great for privacy, but at ten feet it had grown way too tall, and it made the night seem even darker. He was glad *Abuela* had decided not to stay behind by herself.

Jack opened the car door, stepped out, and then froze. A man was sitting on his front doorstep. He rose slowly—not a threatening motion, but Jack proceeded with caution as he walked around the front of his car and started up the sidewalk. The man waited, and Jack soon recognized the face.

"Mr. Bennett?"

Sydney's father answered in a low voice, his tone and body language conveying not so much reluctance, but resignation. "We should talk," he said.

54
.

Merselus killed the lights. His one-room apartment on the Miami River went dark, save for the glow from the LCD of his laptop on the dresser. He closed the laptop and, in the darkness, slid it into his backpack. It fit nicely in the slim and padded pocket—safely separated from the fully loaded Glock 9-millimeter pistol, four extra clips of duty ammunition, and a nine-inch diving knife with a serrated blade. He took the knife, slipped on the backpack, and pressed the serrated blade to Sydney's throat.

"Come on, come on, come on," he said in rapid-fire delivery.

Sydney's wrists were bound behind her waist with plastic handcuffs. A gray strip of duct tape covered her mouth. Her legs were free, which allowed her to walk, but she wasn't moving fast enough. Merselus grabbed her by the hair and pushed her toward the door.

"I said *come on*."

Sydney fell to the floor. Merselus unlocked the

door, pulled Sydney to her feet, and spoke right into her face, eye to eye.

"Do what I tell you to do, and nothing else," he said. He put the knife back to her throat, pressing hard enough this time to draw a drop of blood. "It's that simple. Nod if you understand."

It was a shaky nod, but she managed.

"Good girl," he said. "Now I'm going to take the tape off your mouth, and when we walk out of this apartment, I want you to lean into me. If we pass anyone on the way to the car, you're just a little drunk and I'm holding you up. You got it?"

She nodded again.

He pulled off the tape, which drew a whimper of pain but not another sound from her. Then she breathed deep, mouth open, as if gobbling up air. He grabbed a windbreaker from the closet, draped it over his hand with the knife, and put his arm around her waist. The windbreaker hid the plastic cuffs on her wrists as well as the knife at her spine. Then he pulled her closer and opened the door.

"Here we go," he said.

The three-story complex was a converted motel, thirty years overdue for a makeover and a developer's whim away from being razed for a new high-rise. Each apartment had just one door, which opened to the outdoors, and a single window with a noisy air-conditioning unit that faced the parking lot. Residents rented month to month, or in Merselus' case, week to week. His apartment was on the second floor, and he guided Sydney toward the external stairwell. They were halfway down the stairs when Merselus spotted a Miami-Dade Police squad car cruising slowly through the parking lot. Just the sight of it confirmed his fears. Somehow he'd taken longer than eight seconds to send the *Check the bench* text to Swyteck. The cell had emitted not one but two electronic pulses, double the information he had been willing to release to cell towers in the area, just enough data for law enforcement to work with. Some tech agent had done the computations and triangulated Sydney's iPhone. They had a bead on his location. A degree from MIT, six years in Silicon Valley, twenty-seven patented algorithms for M-rated video games that had allowed him to retire at age thirty-one and never think twice about a hundred-thousand-dollar bribe to one of Sydney's jurors—and he slipped on triangulation.

Son of a bitch!

He pulled Sydney behind the wall of yellow-painted cinder block at the stairwell's midlevel landing. The pungent odor of a homeless guy's fresh urine hung in the air, but they stayed put, out of sight from the passing patrol car. Merselus gave the police a minute to go by. When the squad car reached the far end of the parking lot, he forced Sydney down the stairs toward apartment 102 on the ground floor. Merselus wasn't friendly with any of his neighbors, but he'd made a point of studying the makeup of the entire complex. He knew that apartment 102 was occupied by a seventy-year-old man who lived alone.

The patrol car rounded the turn at the end of the parking lot and headed toward a block-long stretch of identical apartments in the west complex. Merselus knocked on the hollow metal door to apartment

102 and positioned Sydney so that anyone who peered out through the peephole would see only the face of a frightened young woman. There was no answer, but a light inside set the closed draperies aglow in the window. Merselus banged harder on the door, and he kept pounding until a sleepy and shirtless old man wearing only pajama bottoms opened it.

"Girl, what the hell are you—"

The old man choked on the rest of his words as Merselus whipped himself around the door frame. In a blur of motion, the knife pierced his skin, and the serrated blade tore a two-inch opening between his ribs. His mouth was agape in a futile effort to cry out in pain as the blade twisted and ripped an even bigger hole in his punctured heart.

Merselus pulled out the knife and let his victim drop to the floor—first to his knees, then onto his side. He lay motionless, the gray hairs on his chest awash in so much crimson. Sydney stood frozen and wide-eyed with fear. Merselus shoved her through the open doorway, dragged the old man farther inside the apartment, and shut the door. The blood-soaked carpeting squished beneath Merselus' feet as he stepped around the lifeless body.

"Tough luck, old man," said Merselus. "Already got all the hostages I need."

55

The SWAT leader's voice was in Andie's ear, and he wasn't happy.

"Henning," he said via microphone, "tell Miami-Dade to stop patrolling the parking lot before they get my men killed!"

Andie was standing outside the communications van in a dimly lit parking lot behind a vacant warehouse. The black FBI SWAT van was parked beside the van. The chosen location was strategic: two buildings downriver from the apartment complex. The way the Miami River bent to the north, Andie actually had an unobstructed view from the parking lot behind the warehouse to the waterfront apartment units. It was the FBI's makeshift command post—close, but not too close, to Merselus' apartment. Andie was in constant communication with the SWAT leader in the field, in position and ready to begin negotiations if a hostage situation developed.

"Are the officers on foot or in vehicles?" asked Andie.

"I've seen two squad cars. Don't know if there's a foot patrol. But I've got four team members in stealth on a yellow-light site sweep. If MDPD officers in uniform start knocking on doors, it'll be a disaster."

A yellow-light sweep meant no busting down doors, no gunfire—just a pass through the area to collect information and assess the situation.

"I'll shut it down right now," said Andie.

Merselus switched on the TV. The television media's obsession with breaking news could be his friend in a situation like this. Nothing quite like the local *Action News* chopper to reveal police positions and give the bad guy a bird's-eye view of law enforcement strategy. As yet, none of the stations had jumped on the story. He kept the television on but muted the sound, just to stay alert to any noises in the parking lot.

"I can't breathe," said Sydney.

She was sitting on the floor with her back to the wall, her wrists still fastened behind her. The problem was the double pillowcase Merselus had put over her head. He wasn't trying to suffocate her—not yet, anyway. He just couldn't take it anymore, the way she cried and carried on every time she caught an eyeful of the dead old man on the floor. He'd known women to find a way to peek out from behind blindfolds before. A couple of pillowcases, one on top of the other, were infallible. And he'd found it amazing how long a young woman in good health could go that way without actually suffocating.

"Just be still," he said.

Merselus looked for a place to sit, but there was none. He'd turned the room into a makeshift fortress. Anyone trying to force his way into the apartment would have to pass through a mountain of furniture. The entire room had been cleaned out, except for the television. There was a crack of light at the edge of the wall and along the top of the window. The drapes were so old and worn that, in spots, the lining had lost its blackout quality. Merselus considered that a positive, since the room would brighten with the swirl of police lights in the parking lot—if and when they came.

"Quiet," he said. He could have sworn he'd heard something. He had to move the mini-refrigerator to get to the door and put his ear to the hollow metal. He heard nothing, but he waited. Then he heard it again.

Pounding.

What the hell?

No, it was knocking. Distant knocking. They were knocking on apartment doors. From the sound of it, they were still several doors away. But no doubt about it: The police were actually going door to door.

Idiots!

Merselus switched off the television, and the room went black. Then he positioned himself at the doorjamb, held his pistol at the ready, and waited.

56

Jack listened, trying not to interrupt, as Geoffrey Bennett talked. They were alone in Jack's living room, Bennett seated on the couch and Jack in an armchair. Bennett would occasionally look Jack in the eye, but for the most part, his gaze was cast downward at the coffee table.

"There's another side to Ellen," he said of his wife. "A dark side."

The pause seemed to invite inquiry from Jack. "How dark?" he asked.

"Dark enough to get mixed up with a monster like this guy Merselus."

Jack caught his breath. "When you say mixed up . . ."

"I mean," he started to say, then stopped, as if it were unspeakable.

"They were lovers?" asked Jack.

"Love had nothing to do with it."

Jack moved to the edge of his seat, leaning forward. "Look, if you know something, you need to just come right out and say it. The FBI is working right now, trying to find Merselus and stop him from hurting your daughter."

Bennett breathed in and out, then continued. "Ellen and this guy linked up on the Internet. I'm not exactly sure when, but it was definitely before Sydney got arrested."

"Before or after Emma's death?"

"Before," Bennett said, swallowing hard. "Definitely before."

"You say 'definitely' before. Why do you say that?"

He looked Jack in the eye and said, "Because he killed her."

It was hard to comprehend, as many times as Jack had heard the world say his client was guilty. But something in Bennett's voice almost made Jack believe it. "How?" Jack asked.

"Threw her in the swimming pool. Emma could swim as well as any two-year-old. You teach the little ones to go right to the side of the pool, grab onto the ledge, and do the hand-over-hand choo-choo train to the shallow end, where they can climb out. But every time she grabbed the ledge," he said, his voice quaking, "Merselus would pry her fingers loose. She kept swimming back, and he'd pry her loose again. After a while, she got too tired to swim back."

It was making Jack ill just to hear it, the thought of a two-year-old girl fighting to hang on, no match for an adult who knew she couldn't fight forever. He thought of Emma's little legs churning, too, and her feet scraping the bottom of the pool——exactly the way Jack's forensic expert had described it.

"Why would he do that to Emma?"

"Because he's one very sick bastard."

"Yeah, he is," said Jack. "But that doesn't answer my question. There are lots of ways for sick bastards to get their thrills. Why Emma?"

"I don't know."

Jack could tell that he was holding back. "I think you do," he said, his gaze tightening.

Bennett looked away, then back. "About a month before Emma died, Ellen hired a babysitter so the two of us could go out. When we came home, the babysitter was all upset. She said that Emma asked her to touch her privates. So, like I say, I don't know for a fact. But I think Merselus killed Emma because she was getting old enough to, you know . . ."

"To talk about who was abusing her?" said Jack.

Bennett nodded.

The sick feeling inside Jack was getting worse. But there was anger, too. "Why in the hell did you wait all this time to say something?"

"Ellen said they could pin it on me. You heard those rumors of me being an abuser, some people even saying I was the father of Sydney's child. Where do you think that shit got started? Ellen and her sick son-of-a-bitch boyfriend could have sunk me."

"So you let them pin it on your daughter instead?"

"I knew that would never stick."

"I'm not sure how you could have known that. I was her lawyer, and until I heard Judge Matthews' clerk say 'not guilty,' I thought we were looking at the death penalty."

"Trust me. I knew Sydney was not going to be convicted."

"Are you saying it was you who bought off juror number five?"

"No, no. They did. Ellen and Merselus. They let me in on it so I wouldn't feel the need to save Sydney from the death penalty. The fix was in, so to speak. So I just . . . went along. Kept my mouth shut. I shouldn't have, I know. What Sydney went through is beyond horrible."

He slumped back into the couch, as if drained, bringing a hand to his face. Then his shoulders heaved, two quick jerks, but he quickly brought the sobbing under control. Jack was certain that if Geoffrey Bennett had been of a constitution any less rich in testosterone, he would have seen a grown man cry. That, or Sydney wasn't the only member of the Bennett family who longed to be an actor.

"We need to get this information to Agent Henning right now," Jack said. "I can try to reach her by phone, but I know I won't get through. She'll have to call us back. Meantime, you and I are going to take a ride right now to the FBI field office."

Bennett nodded slowly, signaling acquiescence as much as agreement, and rose from the couch. Jack led him to the door, showed him out, and locked the door behind them. They stepped down from the landing and onto the sidewalk. Jack was a half step ahead of Bennett when the bushes rustled and a woman's voice pierced the darkness.

"Stop right there."

The men stopped, and Jack saw the gun.

"Ellen, no!" shouted Bennett.

"Don't make a move," said Mrs. Bennett, "neither one of you."

·

57

M erselus stood at the door, listening.

He'd turned off the noisy air conditioner to hear better, and the dark room was becoming an oven. He was too focused to care or even notice. He knew that there were twelve units on each floor in this wing of the complex, all facing the parking lot. An old motor lodge was anything but sound-proof and, judging from the direction the sound had traveled, he determined that the police officers had started with apartment 112 at the other end of the wing and were working their way down in order. He'd counted three distinct rounds of knocking so far. By his estimation, they were still at least six units away from apartment 102.

"I need to breathe," said Sydney.

She was still sitting on the floor near the closet, toward the back of the room, hands bound behind her back and double pillowcases over her head. She sounded so weak and frightened. It was the kind of pleading that would have been a sexual turn-on for Merselus in another setting. Under this kind of pressure, it made him angry beyond control. Merselus hurried across the room, yanked the pillowcases off her head, and dropped to one knee. He grabbed her by the throat so hard that the back of her head slammed against the wall.

"Do you want to end up like Celeste?" he said in a voice that hissed.

Beads of sweat rolled down her face, and wet wisps of hair were matted to her red cheeks and forehead. Her breathing was quick, shallow, and shaky.

"*Do you?*" he repeated. His tone was even harsher, and his grip tightened, silencing her breathing. Sydney's eyes bulged with that telltale struggle for air. She shook her head in reply, and Merselus released her throat. She rolled her head back and gasped for more air as Merselus rose from his knee.

"Why," she started to say, and paused. Then she somehow managed to get out the rest. "Why did you hurt Celeste?"

He dropped to his knee again and grabbed her by the jaw, forcing her to look him in the eye. "Because I thought she was you."

She stared back at him, frightened and confused. He released her jaw, curious to hear her response.

"You wanted to kill me right there?" she said. "Right outside the jail?"

"Yeah, because you snubbed me."

"What?"

"You were supposed to throw yourself in my arms when you saw me, remember?"

"I did. By the airplane on the runway."

"But you *didn't* when I found you in the parking lot."

"That wasn't me."

"I was watching Faith Corso on my mobile, and she said you had been released into the crowd. Things were getting dangerous. I went to you. I told you my name. I said let's go, I'll take you to the plane."

"But—"

He grabbed her arm, silencing her. "You looked at me exactly the way you're looking at me now— like I'm a creep, and like you never heard of anyone by the name Merselus. The second I took your arm," he said, squeezing tightly to make his point, "you tried to run."

"But—that wasn't *me*."

"Celeste sure looked like you. And after all I went through to get your cute little ass out of jail, I was *not* going to be snubbed by some bitch who turns and runs."

Merselus heard another round of knocking. It sounded like the police were right next door. He quickly tore off a strip of duct tape and covered Sydney's mouth. Then he went back to his position at the door and listened.

"Sorry to bother you, ma'am," he heard one of the cops say to the neighbor in apartment 103. Then he heard the door close, followed by a pair of approaching footfalls on the sidewalk. Then they stopped.

"Check that out," the same cop said.

"Looks like blood," the other cop replied.

The old man's blood. Merselus hadn't noticed any on the other side of the threshold, but splatter was always a risk.

Three booming knocks rattled the door. "Miami-Dade Police Department. Open up."

Andie was on the phone with MDPD Sergeant Jake Malloy. In her other ear she had her SWAT team leader, who was awaiting her confirmation that local police had ceased the door-to-door sweep. Andie was making no headway with Malloy. His response was to share an update that, in his mind, confirmed that MDPD's plan was working.

"Two of my patrol officers just reported blood outside the door to apartment 102."

"We know that already," said Andie. "Our SWAT unit spotted it in the first sweep. But the plan isn't to walk up and knock on the door. Pull your officers back!"

The crack of four quick gunshots ripped through the night. Andie heard it three ways—her radio communication with SWAT, her cell connection with MDPD, and the echo that reverberated down the black Miami River to the parking lot behind the vacant warehouse where Andie was standing. The next thing she heard came over her cell, a man shouting to MDPD Sergeant Malloy.

"Officer down!"

58

Jack kept an eye on the pistol in Ellen Bennett's hands. She seemed to read his mind.

"Yes, I know how to use it," she said.

After three years of Shot Mom and threats against the whole Bennett family, Jack didn't question it. "This isn't smart," he said. "Just put the gun—"

"Shut up!" she said.

A breeze rustled through the ten-foot ficus hedge around Jack's yard, as if to remind him of the downside to landscaped privacy. Ellen Bennett was standing just off the stone path to the driveway, between Jack and his car, about five steps away from Jack and her husband. She held the gun with both hands, arms extended. She was aiming at her husband, but it would have taken only a split second to target Jack. If not point-blank range, it was darn close to it.

"I know why Geoffrey came to see you," she said, speaking to Jack.

Bennett said, "You don't know anything, Ellen."

"Quiet!" she said, pointing her gun for emphasis, her voice quaking. "I'm talking to Mr. Swyteck."

There was just enough moonlight for Jack to see the range of emotion on her face—anger, frustration, fear. Jack tried his most soothing tone. "Would love to talk to you. Let's do it without the gun."

She pushed on. "I bet Geoffrey didn't tell you that he's the one who met Merselus online."

"Stop, Ellen," said Bennett.

"I bet he didn't tell you about all the other strangers he's brought into our marriage. If you can call it a marriage. Twenty-five years of strange men who do unspeakable things to the wives of other men while their husbands watch and enjoy."

"That's enough," said Bennett. He took a half step toward her, but she stopped him with a menacing thrust of the gun in his direction. She continued in an angry but unsteady voice.

"I bet Geoffrey didn't tell you what he did when his wife started to look middle-aged. When the videos he made of me were no longer the lure on the Internet that they once were. Did he tell you about that, Mr. Swyteck?"

"Please," said Jack. "Let's put the gun away, all right?"

"Ellen, I'm warning you," said Bennett.

"Hah!" she said, but it wasn't a laugh. She was on the verge of tears. "*You're* warning *me*? Who's in control now, Geoffrey? I should have done this so long ago, before you could use your own daughter as bait for perverts like Merselus."

Bennett shot a sideways glance at Jack. "She doesn't know what she's talking about."

"I'm speaking the *truth*!" she said, her voice cracking. Her eyes darted back and forth from her husband to Jack, as if she were pleading with Jack to believe her. "Geoffrey didn't tell you why I did nothing, did he?"

"What?" said Jack.

"Damn it, Ellen! I told him Merselus did it!"

Did nothing. Her words were like a light switch for Jack, a confirmation of that gut feeling he'd carried with him since the start of Sydney's trial, continuing through his visits to the Bennett house after her release.

"Merselus didn't kill your granddaughter, did he?" said Jack.

She shook her head, glowering at her husband.

"It wasn't Sydney," said Jack.

"No, of course not."

"Thirty seconds ago I would have said it was Geoffrey. But now I know it wasn't him, either. Right, Ellen?"

She didn't answer.

Jack pressed on, his theory still gelling in his head. "I know what you meant, Ellen. But I want to hear it from you. What did you mean when you said you 'did nothing'?"

Her voice shook, and it seemed to take every bit of her strength just to steady the gun. "I'll bet Geoffrey didn't tell you how it killed me that my own daughter was living the same life I'd lived. How much it killed me to know that Geoffrey was already working on Emma, making her so sexually aware that she even talked to the babysitter about it. Geoffrey didn't tell you that, did he? That's why I did nothing. She was next. I *knew* she was next."

Did nothing. Jack needed to square that with what

his forensic expert had told him about the cause of Emma's death. There had to be more to what Ellen was saying, and suddenly it all made sense. "Tell me," said Jack. "Tell me what happened when Emma fell in the pool."

She didn't answer right away, but the expression on her face told Jack that he had nailed it.

"Maybe I would have made a better decision," she said through tears. "Maybe I would have been thinking more clearly if I hadn't been drinking the way I do to get through every day of my life. But at that very moment, when I heard that splash in the swimming pool, I truly believed that this innocent little angel was better off dead!"

"You did nothing," said Jack.

"I . . . I did nothing," she said, her voice shaking.

"That's not true," said Bennett. "Damn it, Ellen! It was Merselus!"

His continued defense of his wife made no sense to Jack, until Bennett's words from the other day came back to him. In his own twisted way, Bennett was beating back adversity to "protect what was left of his family."

This time, Ellen Bennett was having none of it.

"That's just another lie, Geoffrey! Lies, lies, and more lies! Twenty-five years of living your lies!"

"Ellen, stop—"

The crack of a gunshot dropped Bennett where he stood. As Jack dived to the ground for cover, another shot rang out, then another, and another. Each shot hit its mark—three to Bennett's chest, one to his belly, and the last two directly to the head. She kept squeezing the trigger even after the chamber was emptied. Crying and on the verge of hysterics, she threw the gun at Geoffrey. It hit him in the face, but he didn't flinch. There was no reaction of any sort. She dropped to her knees, fell forward, and buried her face in her hands, sobbing.

Jack rose slowly, but he didn't move toward her. Ellen Bennett remained on the ground, wailing. Jack let her be, her husband's lifeless body just a few feet away from her in the grass. He pulled his cell phone from his pocket and dialed 911.

59

G o!" shouted Merselus as he yanked open the apartment door.

Three clean-through bullet holes in the chest-high door panels marked his response to the police officer's knock. He was certain that at least one of those shots had hit the mark. The fact that there was no body to step over told him that the downed officer had been dragged to safety by his partner. Merselus kept Sydney directly in front of him, his human shield, as they exploded through the open doorway and into the night.

"Run, run, run!" He was pushing her from behind, almost faster than she could move her feet, and with each word he squeezed off another round in the direction of the patrol car for cover. There was no return fire, surely for fear of hitting the hostage. As they approached the car, Sydney tripped at the curb and fell hard onto the asphalt. Merselus fired two more rounds at the squad car as he flung open the car door. Then he lifted Sydney from the ground, using the bindings behind her back like a handle as he shoved her across the driver's side and over to the passenger seat. Sydney crouched low, her head below the dashboard.

"Stay up!" he shouted, pulling her toward him on the seat. A hostage in the line of fire was his best shot at getting the police to hold their fire.

The car started quickly, and the engine revved as Merselus backed out of the parking spot so fast that Sydney lunged forward and banged her head on the radio. Merselus pulled her up, back into her shield position. The tires screeched and the car raced across the parking lot toward the main exit. He was almost to Miami Avenue when a lone police officer jumped into the path of his vehicle and assumed the marksman's pose. Merselus jerked the wheel from left to right, putting the car in serpentine mode to prevent the cop from getting a clear shot at the driver. He accelerated enough to send a message that vehicular homicide wasn't just a bluff. Sydney screamed as the speeding car bore down on the officer, but at the final moment the cop dived behind a parked car without firing a shot. The car fishtailed as they squealed out of the parking lot and turned onto Miami Avenue.

An ambulance raced toward them as they sped away. If it was for the old man in apartment 102, they were too late. If it was for Officer Knock-Knock, they might arrive in time.

"Just let me go, please," said Sydney.

Merselus almost chuckled. "Yeah. Like that's gonna happen."

60

The white sedan was a blur as it sped past the vacant warehouse on South Miami Avenue. The nearest law enforcement vehicle in the area was the FBI communications van, just two buildings downriver.

"Let's go!" shouted Andie as she jumped into the passenger seat. She activated the siren and the blue police beacon on the dash. Her partner was behind the wheel. The van roared out of the parking lot, and the not-yet-buckled tech agent in the back of the van slammed into his wall of equipment as the van squealed around the corner.

"Shit, guys!" he said as he climbed up from the floor and into his seat.

Andie got on the radio, no time to apologize.

"In pursuit of late-model white Chevrolet sedan headed north on South Miami Avenue toward Flagler," Andie said into the microphone. "Subject is armed and dangerous. Appears to have at least one adult female hostage with him. Identity unconfirmed, but possibly Sydney Bennett. Request perimeter control to block all arteries and expressway on-ramps east of I-95 between Northwest Eighth Street and Southwest Third Street. Raise all drawbridges between Northwest Fifth Street and Brickell Avenue."

"Copy that," came the reply.

Andie hung the mic in its cradle and then unbuckled her seat belt long enough to put on a Kevlar vest—just in case.

City blocks are short in downtown Miami, and the van raced through one intersection after another, the siren blaring. The western edge of downtown was definitely not a pedestrian area after midnight, especially on weekdays. Storefronts were dark, many of them barricaded with roll-down shutters of corrugated metal. Streets and sidewalks were empty, scarcely a parked or moving car in sight. North-south traffic signals were programmed for long green lights—not that a red light or anything else would have stopped Merselus.

Four blocks ahead of them, the Chevy made a sudden turn east on Flagler Street.

"I think we got him," Andie's partner said.

Unless Merselus planned to jump the curb and drive through Bayfront Park straight into the bay, he would have to go left or right at the T-shaped intersection at the east end of Flagler Street, taking Biscayne Boulevard either north or south. Just as Andie radioed for additional backup, the Chevy made a hard left turn into an empty parking lot, cutting north toward the Miami-Dade College campus. The FBI van did the same, maintaining pursuit due north, weaving around the concrete parking bumpers in the empty lot.

"He's headed straight for a fence."

Just as the words crossed Andie's lips, the Chevy crashed through a chain-link fence at the end of the parking lot and careened to the right. Broken metal fence posts and an entire section of chain link lay strewn across the asphalt, and the van bumped and rolled over it as they drove through the hole in the fence. They were suddenly on brick pavers, not asphalt, speeding down an empty pedestrian-only walkway in the heart of the urban campus. The FBI van was quickly gaining ground.

"I think he's got a flat," said Andie.

They'd closed the gap to less than a half block when the Chevy stopped so short that the orange taillights rose another foot from the ground. Merselus had reached a dead end: the three-foot-high, in-ground security posts that normally stopped vehicles from coming the other way, from the street to the pedestrian walkway. The driver's-side door flew open, and Merselus fired at the van as he ran from his vehicle. There was a loud pop and starburst crack in the windshield as a bullet whizzed through the space between Andie and her driver, and the van screeched to a halt.

"Are you hit?" Andie shouted to the tech agent in the back.

"No."

"Check on the hostage!" Andie shouted to her partner as they hopped out of the van.

With weapon drawn Andie ran past the school auditorium, past the half-block-long lecture hall, and down a narrow side street, pursuing Merselus on foot. She was closing in on him and had him in sight as he ran across the street. He stopped to try the door to the McDonald's, and for a brief instant Andie feared a hostage situation, but the restaurant was closed and the doors were locked. He turned and ran up the block, then disappeared into an alley across from the campus. Andie's legs were pumping at full speed, but she came to a quick stop at the alley's entrance. It was a narrow opening, barely wide enough for a single vehicle to pass between the five-story buildings on either side. She stood to one side, her back to the wall. Winded from the all-out sprint, Andie had no choice but to breathe in the stench of an overloaded Dumpster that filled the warm night air. She was still wired for communication with the van, and as she caught her breath, she whispered an update on Merselus.

"Subject entered alley east side of First Avenue, twenty yards south of McDonald's restaurant."

With her back still pressed to the wall, she turned her head just enough to peer cautiously into the dark alley. It stretched less than fifty yards from end to end, with only two street openings—the entrance Merselus had taken, and the exit at the opposite end, which fed into a Metromover station. Andie spotted just one streetlight about halfway down, but it was burned out. The moonlight did little more than create confusing shadows in what seemed like a black tunnel. Slowly, Andie's eyes adjusted, and the alley's transformation from mere shadows to recognizable objects began. Keeping close to the wall and her gun at the ready, Andie entered with caution. She was ten feet into the darkness when she stopped and listened.

A siren wailed in the distance. Multiple sirens.

Backup was on the way. But by the time they arrived, Merselus might be long gone.

Leading with her gun, crouched in the marksman pose, she stepped deeper into the darkness, one tentative step at a time. Bars covered the windows and doors that faced the alley, blocking off escape routes, telling her that Merselus was still somewhere in the alley. She heard a noise from behind the Dumpster. Quickly, without making a sound, she moved to the wall, took cover behind a telephone pole, and waited. Her heart pounded. The sirens in the distance grew louder. Suddenly, a squad car pulled up and blocked the opposite end of the alley. Flashes of amber from the police beacon bathed the dark alley, and Andie could hear the MDPD officer key the loudspeaker.

"Police! Put your hands up and—"

A barrage of gunfire echoed in the alley—Merselus' response to the police command. With his intended escape route blocked by a squad car, his only way out was to turn around and exit the way both he and Andie had entered. Merselus continued firing at the police as he pivoted and ran down the alley—away from the squad car and toward Andie.

"FBI, freeze!" Andie shouted.

Merselus was squarely in her sights until, suddenly, he couldn't see anything—not for the darkness, but for the burst of brightness from a police spotlight. It was from the same squad car that had sealed off the end of the alley and had sent Merselus running toward her. He was still coming at her, and the blinding beam of white light stretched like a laser all the way down the alley from the squad car, hitting him in the back and Andie squarely in the face. On the run, Merselus turned his fire in Andie's direction. Andie had some protection behind the telephone pole, but the spotlight robbed her of any serious ability to hide. Chunks of the wood pole splintered off as Merselus fired without pause at the only law enforcement officer between him and his escape.

Andie wanted to return fire, but she couldn't see well enough to take a shot at a moving target. Staring into the spotlight, she was more likely to miss Merselus and hit the police at the other end of the alley with a stray bullet.

Merselus was approaching hard and fast, so close now that Andie could hear the pounding of his footfalls on the pavement. The alley was ablaze with the high-powered spotlight, and Andie was within twenty feet of an armed serial killer, unable to see her target. In another moment he'd be on her, and if Andie didn't act fast she knew she'd be his hostage or dead. Two more of his bullets grazed the wooden pole she was hiding behind. When a third round cracked the brick wall beside her, Andie dived from behind her cover and logrolled to the center of the alley, coming to a stop on her stomach. In one continuous motion, she raised her Sig Sauer and took aim from a worm's-eye view—a completely different angle that took the blinding spotlight out of her line of sight—and squeezed off a single round. She heard one last gunshot, followed by an unmistakable thud on the pavement.

She was eye to eye with Merselus as the alley went eerily silent.

61

Jack's front lawn was aglow with the flash and swirl of blue and amber beacons. An MDPD squad car was behind Jack's car in the driveway. An assistant deputy sheriff opened the rear door, and Ellen Bennett climbed into the backseat without resistance, her head down and her hands cuffed behind her back.

Parked on the street in front of Jack's house was an ambulance, though it wasn't needed. This was a job for the medical examiner's office, and the ME's team was already on the scene. A white sheet covered Geoffrey Bennett's body on the lawn, and the ME's gurney was on the walkway, ready to receive the so-called victim.

Jack avoided using that word—*victim*—in his witness statement to the police. He was standing on his front porch with the first officer on the scene, recounting the worst night of his life. Or at least one of them.

"Just to be clear," said the officer, "you're not Mrs. Bennett's attorney, are you?"

"No. Definitely not."

Jack's cell rang. It was from Sydney's iPhone—the same number that had started his run from Bayfront Park to the Metromover, and that had transmitted that final text message: *Check the bench.* Jack stepped away from the officer and took the call, bracing himself to hear Merselus' voice. It was Sydney.

"Jack, where are you?" she asked, her voice filled with urgency.

"At home. Are you okay?"

"Yeah, pretty much. I'm with the FBI."

"Is Andie with you?"

"No. She went—"

Sydney stopped in midsentence, which alarmed Jack. "Sydney, answer me. She went *where*?"

"She went chasing after Merselus," said Sydney.

Jack's heart sank. That wasn't what he wanted to hear.

"But I think I see her coming now," said Sydney. "Yeah, that's her. She's—"

"See if she can come to the phone," said Jack.

There was silence in Jack's ear, but Jack could tell that the line was still active. A moment later he heard Andie's voice.

"Jack?"

"Hey, are you okay?"

"Yes."

"Thank God. Anyone hurt?"

"One officer from Miami-Dade was shot, but I'm told he'll make it. A poor old man who lived in the same apartment complex as Merselus was not so lucky."

Jack took a moment to absorb the bad news. "What about Merselus?"

"One bullet to the heart. Dead."

"Sniper?"

"Uh-uh," said Andie, "no sniper."

Jack could hear it in her voice, so he didn't need to ask the follow-up. But after a deep breath that crackled over the line, she told him anyway.

"It was someone you love."

62

BNN and the *Faith Corso Show* crammed a month's worth of sensationalism into the next two days. The most surprising thing to Jack was how much of it they managed to get right. The least surprising—and most troubling—was what BNN refused to acknowledge: that the demise of Merselus and his Internet buddy Geoffrey Bennett was of no help to Celeste Laramore and her family.

Jack flew to New York to do something about that. Hannah went with him. The trip was in some ways déjà vu, reminiscent of Jack's disastrous settlement conference with BNN's lawyers on the eve of filing Celeste's lawsuit against BNN. This time, however, Jack brought Sydney Bennett along.

For five days, the media had been hounding Sydney and her lawyer. They all wanted the same thing: the exclusive interview that would finally reveal the truth about Emma's death, and even better, expose the darkest secrets of the Bennett family. On Jack's advice, Sydney refused to speak to any of the TV talk-show hosts, with one exception: Faith Corso.

"Thank you so much for coming," said Corso.

They were in the main conference room on the thirty-third floor, just like Jack and Hannah's previous meeting with BNN. This time, however, there were far fewer lawyers in the room—most notably, no Ted Gaines. Corso sat with hands folded atop the polished walnut conference table, her back to a floor-to-ceiling window and the panoramic view of Midtown. To her left was Kay Dollinger, the energetic producer of the *Faith Corso Show*. To Corso's right was the gray-haired Stanley Mills, BNN's general counsel and vice president of legal affairs. Jack sat directly across the table from Corso, flanked by Hannah and Sydney.

"What a pleasure it is to finally meet you," said Jack. Hannah shot a quick glance in his direction, as if to see if his nose was growing.

"Let me tell you what we have in mind," said Corso, quickly shifting from *we* to *me*. "I see this as a two-part interview. Part one will be live in the BNN studio, just Sydney and me. We'll talk about her arrest, the trial, her release from prison, her short stay with Merselus, her escape from him and recapture, and then her rescue by the FBI. The live segment will end with her telling us where she was when her daughter drowned, how long she knew the truth about Mrs. Bennett's role in Emma's death, and why Sydney kept silent about it. We may bring in a psychiatrist at this point—an objective professional to talk about how common it is for children who are the victims of sexual abuse to refuse to name their abusers, how victims are silenced by their own sense of guilt and shame even after they reach adulthood, how this is especially true when the abuser is a parent, and doubly so when the mother is compliant in the abuse of a daughter."

"No psychiatrists," said Sydney.

Jack touched her arm, reminding her not to talk.

"The psychiatrist is optional," said Corso. "Part two will be taped. We'll visit the Bennett house, where Sydney can walk me through her life under the same roof with a monster like Geoffrey Bennett. We'll go to the runway at Opa-locka Airport where Sydney met Merselus, the hotel where he attacked her, and the places where she went into hiding before he caught up with her at Bayfront Park. The final segment will be shot outdoors at the Bennett swimming pool."

"No pool," said Sydney.

Jack tugged her elbow, another reminder.

"The pool is not optional," said Corso. "It's the centerpiece of the story."

"Here's a possible solution," said Jack. "No pool. Instead, we visit the exact spot outside the women's detention center where Celeste Laramore was attacked."

Corso made a face. "How is that a solution?"

"It gets us focused on the real story."

The general counsel spoke up. "Excuse me, Mr. Swyteck. But we are not going to turn this television interview or this meeting into a showcase for your *other* client's lawsuit against BNN."

"I don't see the two as separate," said Jack.

"I don't see the connection," said Corso.

"The most basic connection is the cost."

Corso narrowed her eyes. "The cost of what?"

"Of Sydney's interview," said Jack.

"We agreed to pay her a hundred thousand dollars," said Corso.

"You *offered* a hundred thousand," said Jack. "The cost is five million."

"That's ridiculous."

"Payable to Celeste Laramore."

The general counsel rose. "I don't see much point in continuing this discussion."

"You're about to," Jack said in his most serious tone.

"Faith, let's go," said the general counsel.

"Have a seat," said Jack, "unless you have absolutely no interest in a two-minute explanation of why five million dollars is letting you off cheap. And by 'you' I mean your boss, Mr. Keating."

Slowly, the general counsel lowered himself back into the chair. "Two minutes," he said.

Jack focused his gaze mainly on Corso as he spoke. "Celeste Laramore was paid a thousand dollars to show up outside the women's detention center looking like Sydney Bennett on the night of Sydney's release."

"That's not news," said Corso. "We were the ones who broke that story."

"And you reported that it was Sydney's defense team who paid her—to be a decoy for Sydney."

"We stand by that story. We had a source."

"A source? Really?" said Jack. "What's interesting to me is that, so far, the only person to confirm that Celeste got paid to be outside the jail on the night of Sydney's release was Celeste's roommate. And I know she's not your source, because I've talked to her."

"I'm not required to divulge our source."

"Agreed. But here's my theory. Your 'source' is the person who paid Celeste the thousand dollars."

"Like I said, I don't reveal sources."

"I guess that's especially true when your source works for BNN," said Jack.

"Excuse me?"

"Let me be more direct: Celeste was paid by BNN."

The general counsel scoffed. "I'm losing patience for this."

"Forget patience," said Corso, shaking her head. "I'm insulted. But let's put that aside for a second. Why on earth would BNN pay Celeste to be a Sydney Bennett look-alike?"

"Because the entire media world knew that Sydney's release would be anticlimactic. The expectation was that Sydney would be whisked away in the dark, and a parking lot full of Shot Mom haters would be left with no one to spit on. Not very exciting television. That's why no other network planned to cover her release the way yours did. But BNN had an angle. For a measly thousand bucks, you were able to give the crowd what it wanted, give the TV audience something to watch, and give the BNN reporters on the ground something to talk about besides an eighteen-year-old redneck in a John Deere cap who wanted to ask Sydney to marry him."

Corso put on her TV face, her most sanctimonious expression. "We would never stage anything for the sake of television entertainment."

"Ted Gaines might have something to say about that."

"What is that supposed to mean?" said Corso.

"Nothing. I digress."

The general counsel shook his head. "Mr. Swyteck, are you suggesting that BNN somehow planned for Celeste to be attacked and end up in a coma?"

"No. The attack that put Celeste in a coma wasn't your plan—but it was your fault, and it was your problem. So two days later, you shifted all responsibility from yourself by blaming someone else: me. Before anyone said one word about Celeste getting paid, BNN had the exclusive report that the defense team had hired a college student to be a decoy on the night of the release. You manufactured yet another reason for the American public to hate Sydney Bennett and her lawyer. And you had the whole world blaming someone other than BNN for what happened to Celeste."

"That's quite a theory," said Corso. "But not much evidence."

Jack glanced down his side of the table. "Hannah, show them."

Hannah powered on her iPad and handed it to Jack, who then laid it flat on the table between himself and Corso. The image was right side up for the BNN team's viewing.

"What's this?" asked Corso.

"Celeste Laramore and three other contestants in a Sydney Bennett look-alike contest."

"That contest was canceled, I was told," said Corso.

"The one on the night of Sydney's release was canceled. But for that whole week before Sydney's release these contests were quite the rage. This one was at a bar called Pendleton's in the Design District, five days before Sydney's release. Celeste won."

"Good for her," said Corso.

"Good for BNN," Jack said. With a touch of the screen, he brought up the next image. "This one is from the same night. It was taken by the security camera at Pendleton's."

"Some guy leaving a club," said Corso. "So what?"

Jack touched the screen again, this time working it with his fingers the way Hannah had taught him. The zoom got tighter and tighter, until finally the only image on the screen was a man's face.

The general counsel leaned into the table for a closer look. There was enough surprise in his expression to make Jack wonder if he was part of the bigger plan. "That's Mr. Keating's bodyguard," he said.

"Roland Sharp," said Jack. "I believe he's affectionately known as the Shadow."

Corso quickly dismissed the whole thing, which in Jack's mind only confirmed her involvement.

"So the guy likes to go clubbing," she said. "What does that prove?"

Jack ignored the question, staying on the offensive. "We found the money," he said. "A thousand dollars in cash. Celeste hid it in her closet."

Corso didn't flinch. "That doesn't even begin to prove that it came from BNN."

Jack's stare tightened. "It was inside one of those plastic dossiers you can buy at any office supply store. I'm told by an extremely knowledgeable FBI agent that plastic is an ideal surface when it comes to lifting fingerprints. That same FBI agent also told me that a certain bodyguard's fingerprints were found on this particular dossier."

Corso and the BNN general counsel exchanged uneasy glances, but they said nothing.

"Whoops," said Hannah.

Jack rose, as did Sydney and Hannah.

"You think about our offer," Jack said, standing behind his chair. "Five million. Payable to Celeste Laramore. The whole matter can be resolved with or without your interview of Sydney Bennett. Your choice. But Mr. Keating and his thousand-dollar blunder will be part of any interview that Sydney grants. That you can count on."

Jack and his team headed for the door. Jack opened it, and Sydney stepped out first. Hannah was right behind her, and she was almost out the door when she stopped and did a quick about-face. The four-foot-eleven pit bull was apparently feeling another déjà vu moment.

"I *told* you we were gonna kick your—"

"Hannah," said Jack, giving her the same down-girl expression that he'd given her at the conclusion of their ill-fated settlement conference.

"Sorry, boss," she said.

Jack watched her all the way out into the hallway, but he didn't follow. He stood in the open doorway for a moment, his hand on the brass door handle. It wasn't that he was searching for something to say. It was simply a message that there was nothing more to be said.

Finally, he stepped out of the conference room, closing the door quietly on Corso, her producer, and one unhappy lawyer.

One month and eleven days after Celeste Laramore slipped into a coma, Jack received a phone call from her father.

"Celeste opened her eyes!"

It was the best news Jack had heard since the check from BNN had cleared. The prognosis was still uncertain, but it was a first step toward a recovery that many doctors had predicted she would never take. It would be a long road, though Jack wondered whose might be longer—Celeste's or Sydney's.

Although Jack's demand on BNN had been for five million dollars "payable to Celeste Laramore," it would never be in Sydney's blood to do anything for free, and the Laramore family agreed to cut a check for a hundred thousand dollars to her on the condition that it go toward the cost of the mental health treatment she needed. Jack's last conversation with Sydney had been her call from Miami International Airport, two hours before her flight to Utah. She was entering a sixty-day program at a wellness facility for victims of sexual, physical, and emotional abuse. Sydney had sounded determined to succeed, but Jack doubted that she would ever return to Florida—unless, as part of the healing process, she felt compelled to get some kind of explanation from her mother in Florida State Prison.

Jack, too, got a share of the BNN settlement. He had his own idea of "recovery."

"Dude, you sure you want to do this?" asked Theo.

They were in Theo's car at the Twelfth Avenue exit from the Dolphin Expressway. Downriver, in the distance, stretched one of the most picturesque vistas of the Miami skyline, but Jack's near focus was on a seedier stretch of riverfront along the expressway, where so much had happened the month before.

"I'm sure," said Jack.

"It's a lotta dough."

Fifteen percent of anything over a million dollars was the discounted fee arrangement that Jack had given the Laramore family. It was less than half of what most lawyers would have charged, but Theo was still right: a lot of money, especially for a few weeks of work.

"I told Andie to think of this as my way of becoming debt-free," Jack said.

"That's cool."

They crossed the drawbridge and continued on North River Drive toward an old neighborhood along the river. Once exclusively residential, the area had evolved into a haven for small business. Many historic houses remained, preserving some feel of the old neighborhood, but they were now home to Pilates studios, computer-repair shops, and everything in between. The Criminal Justice Center was less than a mile away—which was precisely the reason Neil Goderich had chosen this location for the Freedom Institute. Jack smiled as they turned onto Northwest Ninth Court.

Court. Jack suspected that Neal had felt a little karma when, as a young and idealistic lawyer, he'd made that same turn off North River Drive and fallen in love with the perfect place that wasn't located on a street, avenue, boulevard, terrace, lane, or road.

"What the hell?" said Theo as they pulled up at the curb in front of the house.

Jack climbed out of the car, stepped onto a sidewalk that had been ravaged by the roots of a century-old oak, and walked straight to the Gomez Brothers moving van that was parked in the driveway. The rear cargo doors were open, and Jack recognized the oak filing cabinet that one of the men was wheeling up the ramp on a dolly. The move-out was under way.

"Unload the truck," Jack told the mover.

"Who are you?" he replied.

"Al Haig. I'm in charge."

"Huh?"

It was another old Neil expression, but there was no time for a history lesson on who was running the White House after President Reagan was shot.

Sarah emerged from the house and stepped onto the front porch. She spotted Jack in the driveway and waved, but there was sadness in her every motion, right down to the way she moved her hand.

"Excuse me a second," Jack told the mover. "Don't put another thing on that truck."

Jack walked up the gravel driveway and climbed the old wooden steps to the porch. Theo followed.

"Thanks for coming," said Sarah. "We can use the help."

"You can't leave this place," said Jack.

She breathed a heavy sigh. Just those few words from Jack were enough to make her eyes well. "Jack, we don't have any choice."

Jack removed an envelope from his back pocket and handed it to her. "You're *not* moving," he said.

She opened the envelope, peeked inside, and froze.

"Oh, my. This is . . ."

"Two hundred and fifty thousand dollars," said Jack. "From the BNN settlement. Hannah had a hand in that victory. I kicked in a chunk of my share, too."

Her mouth opened, but the words were on a few-second delay. "Jack, I can't take this."

"I can," said Theo as he snatched it from her hand.

"Knucklehead," Jack muttered. He grabbed it and gave it back to Sarah, who took another deep breath.

"I don't know what to say. This is just . . . amazing," she said, her voice cracking with sheer joy and gratitude. Then her face lit up, her whole body seemed to respond, and she suddenly looked younger to Jack than on the day they'd met. She pulled him close and gave him an embrace from the heart that Jack would never forget.

"Thank you," she whispered into his ear. "Thank you so much."

"No hug for me?" said Theo.

"What did you do?" asked Jack.

"I'm the schmuck who has to haul all that shit off the truck after Mr. Gomez looks at you like you're *loco*."

Sarah laughed. "Come on, we'll all do it."

"Gladly," said Jack.

Together, each with an arm around the other's waists, they walked down the steps and slowly crossed the lawn.

"You know," said Sarah, "this doesn't change what we talked about before. Hannah still isn't my first choice to run the institute. No more than you would have been fifteen years ago."

Jack smiled as their walk continued across the grass. "One step at a time, Sarah. One step at a time."